PRAISE FOR JACK LIVINGSTON AND HIS JOE BINNEY MYSTERY NOVELS

"FORCEFUL, VIVID DETECTIVE-FICTION with memorable characters . . . Firm action, and Joe's somber yet flavorsome delivery."

—*Kirkus Reviews*

"Joe Binney, who . . . drinks like a fish, smokes like a chimney, lives grubbily . . . and readily succumbs to any attractive woman's advances . . . tells his story in a distinctive voice, and Jack Livingston has given him a story worth telling."

—*The New Yorker*

"Joe Binney keeps you amused, engrossed and puzzled . . . a good series."

—*United Press International*

"The best writers write the best sentences: it's as simple as that to admire Jack Livingston. If he were a drink, he'd be a Jack Daniels."

—S.F.X. Dean

Jack Livingston's books have been twice nominated for the Best Private Eye Novel of the Year by the Private Eye Writers of America, and for the British Crime Writers Association Annual Award for Best Mystery.

HELL-BENT FOR HOMICIDE

formerly HELL-BENT FOR ELECTION

JACK LIVINGSTON

A SIGNET BOOK

To Dick Bane
Whether he likes it or not

Signet
Published by the Penguin Group
Penguin Books USA Inc., 375 Hudson Street,
New York, New York 10014, U.S.A.
Penguin Books Ltd, 27 Wrights Lane,
London W8 5TZ, England
Penguin Books Australia Ltd, Ringwood,
Victoria, Australia
Penguin Books Canada Ltd, 2801 John Street,
Markham, Ontario, Canada L3R 1B4
Penguin Books (N.Z.) Ltd, 182-190 Wairau Road,
Auckland 10, New Zealand

Penguin Books Ltd, Registered Offices:
Harmondsworth, Middlesex, England

Published by Signet, an imprint of New American Library, a division of Penguin Books USA Inc. This is an authorized reprint of a hardcover edition published by St. Martin's Press.

First Signet Printing, January, 1991
10 9 8 7 6 5 4 3 2 1

1

"Now Charlie Welland is dead," David Carlson told me with a sober expression on his well-tended face. I had just fixed my own countenance in a reflexive spasm of sympathy when he added, "The son-of-a-bitch."

It wasn't the first time I'd been caught out by my inability to hear a tone of voice or, indeed, any voice at all. I really must go by the facial expression linked with the words. I lip-read. Sometimes this is very effective, sometimes an embarrassing fumble.

On the other hand, David Carlson, CEO and majority stockholder of Carlson House, was known to be a difficult man to read under any circumstances. He had inherited the publishing house from his father, Amos Carlson, who had been a business buccaneer long after buccaneers had gone out of style. The old man had had one of those fabled careers that put me in mind of Lawrence of Arabia or Glubb Pasha. He had once been treasurer of an emirate and had lost an eye in a dispute with a hot-headed spendthrift Arabian princeling. The eye had been replaced with a glass orb and it was said that one could always distinguish the glass from the McCoy because the glass eye was the one with the friendly expression.

Both of David Carlson's eyes were organic, and a friendly expression could not be discerned in either one of them. Although he had come up through the standard Hotchkiss prep and Princeton eating club zone of ascendancy, he had none of the preppy manner about him nor even much of Princeton's gentility. His clothes were not Ivy League; they were London bespoke. The sole gesture he made toward his collegiate history was the Phi Beta Kappa key suspended from a gold chain on his vest. A gold watch his father had given him along with the company anchored the chain in his vest pocket. As his father had been, he was a big, raw-boned fellow. His hair, touched with gray, belied the youthful, lineless appearance of his skin and his sharp, vigorous air of command. His mouth was deeply carved and sensual looking.

He had caught me off base because the preamble to all this had been a rather leisurely description of Charlie Welland, and a regional salesman in the textbook division of Carlson House. Carlson had described him as an industrious, sober, family man who had for twenty years successfully sold Carlson textbooks to the various public education departments in the middle southeastern territory. Welland's performance on Carlson's behalf had been called reasonably satisfactory by the owner and CEO. Only reasonably, however; in Carlson's opinion nobody, but *nobody*, really put in a full day's work except himself.

Welland had a wife and two kids who lived in a "decent little house" in Dobbs Ferry—within easy commuting distance of Manhattan. Welland was not known to drink beyond the call of business sociability nor to play around sexually in any way to excite attention. If he gambled at all it was certainly not in Atlantic City, Las Vegas, or Reno. No gambling tabs were outstanding (and Carlson had checked this himself, Carlson being a high roller who had knowledgeable people eager to return his phone calls and proffer any information within reason).

Yet, given his exemplary behavior, it was undeniable that Charlie Welland had seemed to disappear from the face of the earth some three weeks before my meeting with Mr. Carlson. The first sign of his disappearance had been a phone call to Ed Riskin, the sales manager, from Welland's wife, Aggie, alone and worried in Dobbs Ferry. Charlie had been in the uxorious habit of calling home every other night while he was on the road (which was frequent) and now he had missed two calls successively. Had there been a sudden change in schedule? Aggie wanted to know. Ed Riskin wisely kept his mouth shut except to say that these things were unpredictable and that he would check into it. Wisely, again, he did nothing, not wanting to upset any domestic apple carts. However, Charlie's weekly sales report did not land on Riskin's desk at the appointed hour nor for three days afterward. Riskin called Charlie's motel. There was no answer from his room. Riskin talked to the manager. Had Mr. Welland checked out? No. Riskin left a message. The message went unanswered. Three days later Riskin checked with Aggie, who now was very worried. There had been no domestic phone calls. Three days later, with great reluctance, Riskin called the sheriff of Caunotaucarius County and reported Charles Welland as missing.

During this recital of events I had been flipping through the files in my memory for the many cases in which I had located an errant husband in mid-life crisis and dragged him kicking and screaming back to reality—unlovely as it is. I have never been particularly happy with these cases, but they are part of my livelihood; there is no avoiding them, and they provide a good fee for relatively little work. While I fingered my mental filing cards I also reflected on the deep, deep, deep pockets of Mr. Carlson.

But that pleasant reverie was interrupted by the announcement that Mr. Welland was dead, followed by the harsh characterization of his ancestry. Now I had a different case. I closed the file and began to search elsewhere.

"The sheriff did the smart thing," said Carlson. "Instead of sending out all-point bulletins and all that crap, he got in his car and started driving around the country roads, and the country roads down there, you know, are as hairy as hell. He guessed that Welland, like a lot of other salesmen, had got bored, got loaded, and went out looking for a little fun. There's also the fact—" Carlson took out an illegal cigar, cut the end with a small gold tool and lit it—"that the sheriff knew every existing wreck in the area, and I guess there are plenty of them." Carlson contemplated a cloud of blue smoke. "So while he was driving back and forth in the hills he didn't have to waste time looking at wrecks he already knew about. Sure enough, he spotted a new one in some weeds at the bottom of a ravine. And that was Charlie. His car had gone off the road and down the hill. They're not quite sure how long he'd been down there, but they guessed it was quite a while."

"So you've found Charlie Welland," I ventured, wondering again what kind of case was being set up before me.

"Yes, we've found Welland, all right, but there's something else missing." Carlson got up from his rich leather chair behind the massive mahogany desk and went to the window. He puffed deeply on his cigar as if reordering the facts in his elegant head. He stood staring out the window under the gold-brocaded draperies. When he turned to speak to me, his expression left no doubt that what else was missing was more important than the disappearance—death in fact—of Charlie Welland. "There's a hundred and fifty thousand dollars worth of textbooks missing," said Carlson. "That is to say a hundred and fifty thousand dollars worth of textbooks plus the hundred and fifty thousand dollars we should have received for them. Both the books and the money are missing."

He waved the cigar to cut me off. "We could absorb the loss," he said, his hard blue eyes reflecting how little he liked the idea. "Hell, the insurance company would probably cover it, although they'd boost our premium next time around. That's not the real problem. The problem is that I don't know how this happened, which means that it could have happened before, and which also means that Charlie Welland may not have been the only salesman running this kind of swindle. So I want to know where the money went and where the books went.''

Am I truly self-defeating? Self-destructive? Against all rationality of self-interest I asked Carlson, ''Wouldn't your sales manager be the one to . . .''

But he chopped me down impatiently. ''Of course he would,'' said Carlson, ''providing that he wasn't part of the swindle. The next step would be the insurance investigators but insurance companies can be got to, and further, when they've solved the immediate problem and made the deal, that's the end of it. They wouldn't go looking for hidden losses that I might never have known about and never made a claim for.

''Ed Riskin,'' he continued, ''doesn't even know why you're seeing me. The story is that you're a relative of a friend and looking for a job—as yet unspecified.''

He returned to his chair and stared at me across the half acre of mahogany. ''I'm putting you on a retainer at the rates your secretary quoted to me over the phone.'' (Oh, my God, I thought. What did Edna tell him? Edna was convinced that I should operate as a public service. The deep pockets I had foreseen began to shrink.) ''I want you to stick with this until the whole thing is cleared up.'' This was more an order than a suggestion. The cigar jutted up at an angle. ''The books in question are high-school texts. There has been a lot of trouble with them and we had to bring them back for more and more editing—censoring in fact. We spent a fortune grinding up the goddamned things so that finally they don't really teach anything at all. Everything was pending the decision by the County Board of Education, and while they're only a county, their decision is usually accepted by the entire state. So the sale was important. Did it go through? Was it turned down again? I don't know. I don't want to put the question blankly to anyone down there because that invites a solid answer which could just as well be negative. So I want somebody to feel around, dance around, as Charlie Welland should have been doing, goddamn him.''

The old self-defeating impulse took over again. ''Mr. Carlson,'' I told him, ''what I know about textbooks you could stick in the corner of your eye and never feel it.''

''You don't have to know anything about textbooks,'' Carlson assured me. ''What you do have to know about is people and swindles. And also you have to be clean. I've checked around, and you seem to fill the bill. Also,'' he smiled, and it was not a pretty sight, ''you seem to have a sort of disarming, obsequious look that ought to go down pretty well.''

''Thank you kindly,'' I said.

''So I'm using you as an emissary,'' Carlson announced. ''You have an appointment for dinner tomorrow at the Thornwood with the Superintendent of Education, whose name is Dana Martingale.''

''What am I supposed to do with this guy?''

The blue eyes snapped with impatience. ''As I told you, dance around. Feel him out. Find out what the hell is going on.''

''The Thornwood,'' I mused. ''Is that one of those boutique restaurants on Columbus Avenue?''

His eyes bored into my face. ''The Thornwood,'' he instructed me, ''is one of the most famous resorts in the country. It is a national institution. It's located in the heart of Caunotaucarius County.''

''The heart of . . .''

''You can be there, can't you?''

''Sure. I guess so,'' I faltered. ''I'll have to check the airlines. I don't know . . .''

''The Thornwood has its own railway station. A lot of bigwigs go up there from Washington. You'll be met at the station and taken to your room, which I've also booked. Forget airplanes. I've got your train ticket here.'' He reached into an orderly pile of documents on his desk and extracted an Amtrak ticket, which he shoved at me.

"The train leaves Penn Station at five o'clock this afternoon. Be on it.''

2

"A train! No kidding!'' Edna's lovely green eyes gleamed at the thought. "I've never been on a train.''

There was a pause in the conversation as a chilled air blew through the space of years between our generations. Even in my adult lifetime passenger trains had been a dying animal, or rather more precisely, a dying snake whose writhings had become feebler and feebler as the country rolled toward sunset. Edna's pretty face was wreathed in an expectant smile. The smile was doomed to vanish.

"I'm afraid this isn't going to be your first chance,'' I said, clearing my throat. As I had sadly predicted, the smile disappeared and her lips formed a down-turned, disappointed line.

"Why not?''

"Somebody's got to watch the store,'' I said reasonably. "And there's a lot that needs doing in this case right from your desk.''

Edna chose to deliver a low mean blow. "So who's going to handle the telephone for you down there?'' she demanded.

"I may have to work by message or telegram,'' I admitted. "But I hear this Thornwood is a very classy place with all kinds of government poohbahs running around. They probably have some kind of arrangement for the deaf.''

Her face would not let go of its sullen disappointment. "This work you want me to do here, it's mostly telephoning, isn't it?" she asked.

"Yeah, pretty much."

"So why can't I do it from down there at this fancy resort you say has probably got all kinds of modern equipment?"

I sighed and settled back in my chair. Edna had remained standing during this colloquy. Her posture accentuated the magnetically attractive figure that constituted one of my main reasons for not taking her along. "Would you get me a cup of coffee," I asked her piteously, "and then let me try to explain and get out of here? I have to got home and pack and be at Penn Station by five."

She was back at my desk at the speed of light, and plunked the coffee down in front of me. She sat in the golden oak clients' chair and stared at me with her face clenched in disappointment and anger. There is an imperishable nine-year-old kid at the core of Edna, and it is this kid I love and will love forever. The moment had come, however, to change the field of combat. I saw that this whole thing would become a lot easier if I put her on the defensive. I sipped at my coffee and held up my hand. "First thing of all," I said, scowling, "what kind of rates did you quote to Mr. Carlson over the phone?"

"Your regular rates," she answered, her eyebrows climbing.

"Which are?"

"On the printed schedule we mail out to inquiries."

"Aha," I pounced. "My regular rates are on the new schedule we haven't got back from the printer yet."

"Those rates don't go into effect until . . ." Her speech faltered and stopped.

"Until the first of this month, which is already in its fourth day. You have done us out of the nine and one-half percent increase that you and I so laboriously worked out so that we should not be working for nothing."

She sat back in the chair, dismayed. I fixed her with my special snake-to-rabbit look. "See that you don't quote those old rates any more," I told her, "or we'll both wind up in the poorhouse if, indeed, the developers have left a poorhouse standing."

"Joe," she said, the rabbit shaking off the trance. "Why can't I come along with you?"

This was a much better attitude to work with. "First of all," I said, "I was very serious about your having a lot of work to do up here." I pulled a sheet of paper out of my breast pocket. "Starting with the name at the top, Charles Welland, who is deceased, I want you to check out the finances of every one of these guys. As far as Welland is concerned, I want you to find out if his widow has been making any unusual or extravagant purchases. She'd be a little bit nuts to start throwing away money this early, but you never can tell what people will do. So if there's a new Jaguar in the driveway, I'd like to know about it.

"The next guy on the list," I pointed to Ed Riskin's name and address, "is the sales manager of the textbook division. Carlson has a reasonable suspicion, well founded in my estimation, that no salesman could run a scam for very long without the sales manager knowing about it. We're not talking about nickels and dimes on the expense account here. We're talking about shipments of books, big blocks of finance that make up the foundation of the company. If a lot of those blocks are being pulled out without Carlson knowing about it, then the company is going to fall on its ass. You'll notice," I pointed out to her, underlining the figures with a pencil, "that Riskin's income—salary and commissions—comes to six figures, but only just to six figures. If you subtract income taxes and so forth, you've got to figure how much discretionary income he's got. When you reach that figure you start comparing it with what he's spending and see if maybe he isn't slopping over the edges. Six figures doesn't mean as much as it used to mean.

"And so the following names on the list are the

other regional salesmen, like Charlie Welland, who may be part of the action. Their income doesn't go to six figures, but, like Welland's, it is substantial. I want you to work down the list, regionally, starting with the names that are closest to Welland's territorially and work outward from there.''

''All this,'' said Edna—her face had achieved a sort of glazed look—''will be done mostly by telephone, right?''

''Well,'' I began.

''So why can't it be done from Thornwood?''

I pulled out the ticket Carlson had given me, dumped the envelope on the desk, and with my forefinger pushed out an American Express card made out to Joseph F. Binney (the F. is for Francis) but billed to Carlson House Publishing, Inc. ''I am going down there as a representative of Carlson House,'' I said. ''That is the beard.

''You'll notice that this card is billed to Carlson House, which means that they will be watching every dime that rolls off the expense account. Mr. Carlson is very wealthy, but he is not noted for generosity. I'm already going to take a beating on the rates you quoted him and I'm going to take a beating on the expense account because, as you very well know, there are a thousand incidental expenses that go into just simply walking around, killing time and so forth. I doubt that I'll get a dime of it back. Also, as you can see,'' I pointed to the figure on the ticket, ''railroad transportation, while ancient and honorable, is not free. No way will Carlson pay for your passage. Rooms at the Thornwood, I am given to understand, are not cheap. Mine will be billed directly, but who is going to pay for yours? Meals,'' I added inexorably, ''I am going to be staying on the American plan, where my meals are served in the dining room. But you, you with your endless munching, who will be willing, nay, able to pay for yours?''

She was licked and she knew it. She tried to retreat gracefully. ''This train you're taking,'' she said. ''It just runs back and forth from Penn Station to this resort?''

"By no means," I assured her. "In fact, it is two trains. The first one goes from Penn Station to Washington, D.C." I opened the schedule that had been thoughtfully provided. "And you see here," I said, pointing, "I board the *James Whitcomb Riley,* which leaves Washington at nine thirty-five this evening and arrives at Thornwood at—*my God?*" Edna jumped. I hadn't really looked at the schedule before. Ice formed on my forehead. "Three-oh-five A.M. Jesus Christ! The middle of the night? What half-wit put this schedule together?"

Edna sat back, happy at last.

"Christ almighty," I complained. "I'll be stumbling around there in the dark with my bag still asleep."

"The *James Whitcomb Riley,*" Edna observed smugly, "is a pretty funny name for a train."

I stared at her. "Funny? Why funny?"

"Well, I mean, who was James Whitcomb Riley? Some railroad engineer?"

I decided to confound her. "It's called the *James Whitcomb Riley,*" I said portentously, "because after it passes through Thornwood it goes all the way to Peru."

"Peru! Let me see that schedule!" She ran her finger down the list of stations. "Oh," she said, relieved, "Peru, Indiana."

"Yes. Indiana. James Whitcomb Riley, as your English teacher should have told you, was the Hoosier Poet, a very famous American poet who came from Indiana."

"Never heard of him."

I was gratified that she at least had heard of Indiana. I said, "You never heard of Little Orphan Annie?"

"Oh, sure. The musical. *'Tomorrow, tomorrow.'* The song."

"Alas," I said.

"He wrote that?"

"Not the musical, no, although he once performed as a minstrel. No. He wrote the poem, upon which the comic strip was based, upon which the musical was based, upon which the motion picture was based."

"Wow," said Edna with a genuine flash of admiration. "How do you know all these things?"

"I know all these things because I have not spent the greater portion of my life following the plot outline of 'General Hospital.' "

She smiled a sad little smile at me. She reached over and touched my arm. "Joe," she said, "be realistic. You really need me on this trip. Don't pretend that I wouldn't be worth the expense. That isn't true or even fair. In the first place, and please don't be hurt, but how are you even going to know when you're getting in to this place Thornwood? It's going to be the middle of the night. You're going to be asleep. They're going to call the station, you know? You could sleep right through it and wind up in Peru."

"I've thought of all that," I answered gruffly. "The conductor's going to have to shake me and stand me on my feet, that's all."

The grim line of the disappointed nine-year-old reappeared.

"Look," I said. "I'm going to level with you. If I were some kind of big shot from Washington or New York, or even pretending to be one, you could come along and there wouldn't be any kind of problem. That kind of thing is expected and taken care of. But I'm only supposed to be a sales rep from a publishing company. Pretty much of a nonentity. If I show up in this joint with you on my arm it is going to excite a lot of attention—attention that I don't want and can't use." I raised my arms helplessly. "Look, Edna," I told her—not without fear—"You're just too goddamned pretty for me to take you to a place like this."

There have been very few moments in my life when I was grateful to be deaf, but this was one of them. The green eyes bulged with rage and astonishment. The sweet mouth opened wider than I had ever seen before. I am sure it emitted a shriek. *"Do you mean to sit there and tell me that you're not taking me along because I'm too pretty?"*

"God help me," I said. "That seems to be the case."

She was stunned. I collected my tickets and papers and left her sitting there, woebegone, looking very much indeed like Little Orphan Annie.

3

I had dug out the old thousand-miler, which I hadn't worn in years—the traditional dark blue shirt of the old-time drummers that was alleged to not show the coal dust (nor the sweat stains) for a thousand miles of train travel. I had set it off with a yellow tie, which I then discarded since it seemed to resemble a headlight, and put on a light blue summer tie. I got on my gray summer suit, put the blue one in my bag along with slacks and a sports jacket, and, with other necessary accoutrements, I was ready to go.

But when I had looked in the mirror just before departing I recognized with despair that I was back at the same old stand—a private detective cunningly disguised as a private detective.

That was all put behind me as I sat in the lounge car of the *James Whitcomb Riley* plunging toward Peru and points beyond. I nursed along my vodka and tonic, having decided that it wouldn't do—no matter what hour—to show up with bourbon on my breath. I tried to keep my attention fixed on the soft cover book I'd picked up in the station—Stephen Jay Gould's *The Mismeasure of Man*. But while the book was absorbing, even entrancing, my attention strayed to the window where the shadows of the countryside, ghostly images revealed by fits and starts of moonlight, rolled past me. Small towns, crossroads, and hamlets that would remain forever nameless to me flickered through the window in yellow dots of electricity.

We pulled into Manassas and history went thundering through my head. It's the echo you pick up in trains, whether you can hear or not, the echo of history as the train grinds over the same ground, perhaps even the same roadbed that had been soaked in blood and churned by bombardment. The old cannons boom, the desperate yells ring out, the bugle calls, the horses screaming in the dark, the rallying cries, the wavering flags revealed through battle smoke, the shot and shell. The generals' names gallop up out of the darkness— Scott, McDowell, Patterson, P.G.T. Beauregard, and Jackson, whose men were said to stand like a stone wall not far from where I was sitting with my hand curled round a tall cool drink.

We pulled out of Manassas. I got up and bought myself another drink and then returned to Professor Gould. At Charlottesville it became clear that the bar would close, it being midnight. I got myself one last kicker before closing and sank back into the book for another hour. But by one o'clock my eyes had begun to droop. I started back to my coach seat, paused by the conductor, who was shuffling through his papers at the far end of the lounge, and asked him to wake me with a shove at my seat number when Thornwood came round the bend. Why didn't I simply go to sleep when I got on the train? I could have acquired a good five hours. A shy confession: I was too excited by the trip. Like Edna, I too have a nine-year-old kid kicking around inside me.

It was a stunned and reluctant nine-year-old who responded to the conductor's determined shake. I staggered out of my seat and only when the conductor pointed urgently to my bag in the rack did I remember it. I got cautiously down on to the station platform, where I wandered in a helpless circle with my bag in my hand, for all practical purposes still sound asleep. At last I stopped and dropped the bag. I looked around in the darkness that was illuminated only by a single lamp set so high on the pole that the yellow light nearly failed before it hit the ground. I noticed that two other passengers had disembarked with me, a man and a woman. My sleepy senses grappled with them. The man was short and fat and very well dressed; the woman was tall, slender and beautiful and was also very well dressed. They stared at me with what I suspect was distaste. While I was staring back at them I saw them stiffen with expectancy. Well, then—someone was coming. We would not be left alone to perish on this isolated platform. A weak smile stole across my features. Someone touched my elbow, and I turned to see a tall, well-set-up black man in a chauffeur's uniform. I could barely read his lips in the gloomy yellow light, but he had said, "Mr. Binney?" and that was good enough for me. He picked up my bag and led me to a long black Cadillac. The bag went in the trunk and I went into the commodious rear compartment. The chauffeur was about to enter the front when something interrupted him. The short fat man had raced up to him and a brief excited conversation ensued. The chauffeur came around to the back again and opened the door. By the light of the dome I saw him say to me, "The lady and gentleman would like to know if you would mind sharing the ride with them back to Thornwood."

"Not at all," I replied. There was enough room in the back for a card game.

After their luggage had been stowed they got in the other door (the man first) where they huddled at the opposite end of the seat and glowered at me. Apparently their appointed transportation had not worked out so smoothly as mine. They were down several points. When we got to Thornwood they disappeared into its maw and I never saw them again. I remember them only because they seem to have been unpleasant fragments of a dream.

Thornwood itself rose very like a dream in the early predawn hour. The immense white portico, supported by a regiment of pillars, stretched endless arms in greeting as the car rolled up the graveled drive. This first image of the place also remained in my memory as part of a disconnected dream because I never saw it quite like that again.

There was no nonsense about registering at this early hour. My bag and I were taken quickly to my room, where I undressed and collapsed into a welcome sleep.

I awoke to an unfamiliar odor, so unfamiliar that it was almost scary. Fresh air! Truly fresh air that blew gently through the screen of the open window of my room, fresh air laden with the scent of pine blowing down from the mountain and the innumerable plantings—none of which I could name—that surrounded the building. I felt marvelously rested, marvelously awake and alive. Through the open window I could see the beautifully tended grounds that stretched for acre after acre, and beyond them the wall of deep lustrous green where the mountains raised their gentle convolutions. The room itself was immaculate with ivory woodwork and old solid furniture that expressed a subdued cheerfulness. It spoke of courtesy, gentle demeanor, and a blithe disregard for the ravages of time. Time? It was ten o'clock. I cleaned up and went down for breakfast.

Before entering the dining room, however, I stopped off at the desk and registered properly. After I had signed in the clerk discovered a message in my mailbox. The note was handwritten on the back of a business card. It said: *Mr. Binney: Please ask for Mr. Martingale's table at six.* Engraved on the front with the information: *Dana C. Martingale, Superintendent of Education.* The lower right-hand corner backed up this display with a phone number.

It would be nice and businesslike to say that I spent the day grappling with my problems, which were many, but the truth is that I simply relaxed and drank in the easy charm of the place. It was quite a bit for a city boy like me. I wandered all over the old well-manicured grounds, comfortable in slacks, sports shirt, and loafers. The huge building itself seemed to remain cool all day without noticeable intrusion of air conditioning. The public rooms repeated the impression of my private room upstairs; they were immaculate and well furnished with old solid furniture. Historical paintings, some of them life-size, decorated the walls, and each and every one of them was satisfactorily dreadful. Most of them, it seemed, were copies of copies of copies. I grinned at them. They were totally inoffensive and had a sort of sweet faded smile behind them like the offerings of a maiden aunt.

Remembering the rigorous faces of public educators from my school days, I was careful to change out of my casual clothes and put on my good blue suit, a white shirt and sober tie before going down to the dining room. I was shown to Martingale's table, but no one was there. Should I order a drink while I waited? I wanted one badly but decided against it. I sat quietly and stared ahead as I had been taught to do in school. I barely restrained myself from folding my hands and putting them on the table as I once had on the school desk in front of me. I stared through the little knots of people entering for dinner. What I had in mind was some bald-headed old beagle in a gray sack suit and gold-rimmed glasses.

What was coming toward me, however, had absolutely no resemblance to it. A young man in wraparound sunglasses that set off blindingly white teeth was beaming down on me. He was clad in a black silk suit of Italian cut and had on him enough accoutrements from Gucci's as to constitute a walking billboard for that firm. The thin briefcase he carried was shining black crocodile with unmistakably gold clasps securing it. The platinum band on his watch was thick, but the watch itself was no thicker. After introducing himself and shaking my hand he did, thank God, take off the sunglasses when he sat down across from me.

"Are you having a drink?" he asked me. I gratefully answered, "Yes. Bourbon and soda, please." A waiter glided up quickly and the splendiferous young man ordered drinks—or at least one drink, mine, since what he ordered for himself, a Virgin Mary (a Bloody Mary without the vodka) does not qualify as a drink in my bright lexicon.

Even before the drinks were served he turned his klieg light smile on me, shining it out of a well-tanned youthful face, and said, "Now, Mr. Binney, just what exactly can I do for you?"

I had opened my mouth to reply, but he had already turned away as the waiter served the drinks. Behind the waiter stood a well-wisher in a business suit, who pumped Mr. Martingale's hand and engaged him in what looked like a very hard sell to me. Martingale took a crocodile wallet from his breast pocket, removed one of his elegant cards, wrote something on the back with a slim gold pen and handed it to the well-wisher. A series of smiles flashed between them, and the well-wisher strode away—a happy man.

Martingale turned back to me and the selfsame practiced smile split his face again. "Well, of course, I'm down here because of Charlie Welland's accident," I began. While I was speaking—faltering, I think is a better word—I was watching his eyes. They were a deep expressive brown, but in fact they were expressing so many things that interpreting them got in the way of my language. Certainly they expressed a sharp, no-nonsense attendance to business. Yet behind that facade there lurked two other attitudes: one was a wary alertness seeking out any hidden agenda in this meeting and the other was a rather cool, withdrawn, sympathetic amusement at the mere fact of my existence. I agree that this is an awful lot to read into an eyeball, but reading eyeballs is my business.

I was still stumbling into my routine with, "Y'know Charlie was very important to us and he's certainly going to be missed," when the complicated brown eyes skirted upward to glance over my shoulder. Behind me stood yet another businessman, much better dressed than the first one. He was wearing the regulation blue blazer with gold buttons (innumerable gold buttons, it seemed), gray flannel slacks, and highly polished moccasins. I don't really remember his face because the glory of his clothing erased the character of the man. A lively conversation developed between them, which I was not privy to because the visitor had come over to squat down by Martingale's chair and Martingale's face was turned away from me. This meeting climaxed with the businessman giving Martingale *his* card, which Martingale secreted in another compartment of his crocodile wallet.

When they were finished, Martingale looked up to me and said, "Why don't you go ahead and order for yourself. I'm having dinner later this evening."

The next few minutes were taken up by my flagging the waiter and ordering dinner for myself along with another bourbon and soda. During this brief intermission Martingale talked to two more suppliants and I was hard put to get his attention back to me.

"So I'm down here to kind of pick up the threads of where Charlie left off," I began again. "Not that I feel I can step right into Charlie's shoes, but I have to start somewhere, and I want to find out where he stood with some of his negotiations . . ." This all seemed banal enough to me as I played it back in my head, but Martingale said sharply to me, "Negotiations such as what?"

I was trying to assemble a reasonable sounding answer when Martingale was joined by *two* men who launched into a vociferous duet addressed to him, which he shortly turned into a trio. By the time this libretto subsided my dinner was served (steak, rare, baked potato, salad—*you* know). So I was forced to launch into my spiel over forkfuls of perfectly broiled steak and truly baked, not steamed, potato. "Well, whatever negotiations he was working on," I mumbled through the delicious steak that was warming my gullet. "For instance . . ." But Martingale was interrupted yet again, and I was left alone to finish my meal.

"Dance around. Dance around," Carlson had in-

structed me. He hadn't told me that I was to be part-
nered with Fred Astaire. I tried vainly to comprehend
what these tableside conferences were all about but
could come up with only very foggy conjectures. Certainly numbers were frequently mentioned, but to what
these numbers applied I had no real idea. They spoke
in a rapid shorthand with what I suppose was a good
deal of business argot. Measurements were also thick
in the conversations—grosses, tons, barrels, units (an
all purpose word there) but of what materials I had no
idea. Percentages and points also tumbled from their
lips, but percentages of what and points of what I
couldn't figure out. Neither were visible numbers
scrawled on a tablecloth as they used to be. It seemed
that each and every conversant had a little hand-held
calculator (Martingale's was a thin gold one) and when
the final numbers were reached on a calculator they
were shown around—but not to me. All this was followed by the exchange of business cards around, frequently with names and numbers scribbled on the back.

By the time we were left alone I had finished my
coffee. Martingale switched his attention back to me.
"The negotiations I had in mind," I plunged in hur-
riedly, desperately, "were where we stood with *Forging of a Nation,* the history text for high school . . ."

The deep amusement of the brown eyes came to the
fore. I thought I saw almost the hint of smile on his
lips. "High-school history text, yeah," said Mr. Martingale.

"We'd sort of like to know if it's satisfactory now
or if they need some more work on it. I mean Charlie
never sent in his last report. We don't know whether
to go ahead—"

"I have nothing to do with that," said Martingale
abruptly, the amusement freezing into a kind of icy
contempt. "Milly Rutledge is the one you have to see
about that."

"Milly Rutledge," I repeated. I took out a notebook
and laboriously wrote down the name. "And who is
she?"

He stared at me. "Charlie never mentioned Milly Rutledge to you?"

"Look," I pleaded, "I've just been thrown into the breach here. I'm sure Charlie must have mentioned her to Ed Riskin, but everything's being done in a rush. Charlie's accident, you know . . ."

"Milly's the one who runs the Board of Education," said Martingale. "She's Secretary of Education. She's a fixture there. She's been there for almost forty years. You want to talk about textbooks, you talk to Milly."

"She down here at Thornwood with you?"

This time he was genuinely amused. This time the smile was even attractive. "I don't think that Milly's been more than three miles from her office in thirty years," he said. "You'll have to come on down to Caunotaucarius if you want to see Milly."

I thought this over. "Well, I guess I can catch the next train down," I began.

"You can ride in with me in the morning if you want to," he said graciously. "My car's picking me up at nine. I'm stopping off at the board office anyway, so I can introduce you to Milly."

"That would be wonderful." I brightened.

"Meet me at the desk tomorrow morning and we'll fix you up in Caunotaucarius." He glanced at the platinum jewelry on his wrist (time indeed is money). "I have to rush away now," he said. "See you in the morning."

I watched him as he walked away from the table. He was self-consciously sprightly, very much of a presence. There are ties printed in New York with the legend: DAMN I'M GOOD! Martingale exuded this notion of self-esteem. The tail of his black silk jacket twitched in rhythm to his energetic walk. DAMN I'M GOOD! Twitch, twitch, twitch.

Hootchy-Gucci.

And what had I accomplished? I wondered as I flagged the waiter for another drink. Young Martingale's character seemed to be one of those impregna-

ble types, as if made of fire-hardened glass. He did
not drink; he did not eat; and he certainly did not
smoke. Was he married? Somehow I doubted it. No
man ever departed a domestic household looking quite
like that. He struck me as more of a momma's boy,
but with a much harder edge to him than most of those
lads reveal. He was intimidatingly healthy. He was
shrewd. On top of his shrewdness there seemed to be
a genuine intelligence, which is quite a different thing.
On the other hand, he was very much a manufactured
man, a facade. I thought that perhaps in the car, where
no one could interrupt us, I'd get a chance to peek
behind the facade.

Back up in my room I dug into my kit for the fine
leather drinking case that had been a gift from a grateful client. I fixed a bourbon and branch water and
stared out my window into the twilight that was ac-
quiring silver from the high riding moon. I became
lonely. I missed Edna, goddamn it. The whole view
from my window, the hills shading into the dusk and
the treetops being slowly lighted by silver caused me
to well up with a nostalgia that had no roots at all in
my history. It was a nostalgia for times and places I
had never really known, a vanished America that I felt
I was looking at here from my window in this huge
old building tucked in the western skirts of the Al-
leghenies. I could not see the moon from my window,
but its light spread westward out toward the Cumberland and the Gap through which Daniel Boone had
traveled, not so differently from the bears that surrounded him in the woods. And the woods themselves,
will we ever see anything like them, the great virgin
trees that struggled with the vines, Virginia creepers,
thicker than a man's arm, on which Daniel Boone had
swung? And out through the Cumberland Gap, the
neck of the bottle, we had spread on to the Cumberland Plateau, and then on to Peru, the midwest and the
plains of Illinois, Missouri, were Boone had died at
last, and Kansas where his family had come at last to
rest.

It bothered me that Edna had never heard of James Whitcomb Riley. Sure as hell, Riley would never have been a candidate for the Nobel Prize in Literature, but he was among the very first voices in the Midwest, and there was something about the title of his last volume of verse that chimed in my bones—*An Old Sweetheart of Mine*—something that spoke softly of mandolins being strummed on the banks of the Wabash.

And if Edna had never heard of Riley, sure as hell she had never heard of Vachel Lindsay, let alone John Peter Altgeld, of whom Lindsay had written. *Sleep Eagle forgotten . . . under the stone.* No, she would have missed that quickening of conscience rising from the Great Plains. Had she heard of Sandburg? Not the establishment figure, but the crazy young poet haunting the newspaper offices in Chicago, the Sandburg who had written the working stiff's lament to his wife: *I wish to God I never saw you Mag.* Edgar Lee Masters: had she ever heard the tinkling echo of:

Where are Ella, Kate, Mag, Lizzie and Edith,
the tender heart, the simple soul, the loud, the proud,
*   the happy one?*
All, all, are sleeping on the hill.

No, nor of Robinson Jeffers out there in California, where the dream had rolled to its sunset—*Shine perishing republic!* Was that a poem or a curse?

Goddamn it, I thought angrily. Why don't they teach kids how to read? Are they afraid it's too dangerous?

4

The limousine that carried us away was different from
the one that had picked me up at the station, although the
driver was the same. Sober, competent, gentle, he
stowed my bag in the trunk and opened the back door
to the ballroom-sized tonneau. Martingale was already
in place, and it was here that I noticed we had a different car. This one had a telephone, a telephone that
Martingale was already using. The black crocodile
briefcase was propped open on a folding table and a
carefully opened edition of the *Wall Street Journal* was
laid lengthwise next to it. I had only *The New York
Times*, which I'd picked up at the desk, to offer as a
badge of respectability. Stocks and bonds are not my
bag, murder and mayhem, both national and international being more in my interest.

Except for a bright-eyed nod in my direction over
the telephone, Martingale had no apparent interest in
me this morning. As the big car swung down the graveled drive he began to extract from his briefcase innumerable folders, brochures, and financial prayer
books that had PLAN THIS and PLAN THAT stamped on
the covers. He worked away at comparing figures and
making notes with his slim gold pen. He was more
conventionally dressed this morning with a businesslike good blue suit and a bright red tie, all the trinkets
were still in place. He lathered away at his numbers,
making the occasional phone call when he appeared to
strike mother lode. He was busy and alert, all right,
but I couldn't convince myself that what he was working at had anything to do with the running of a school
system. The facade was still there, impermeable and
glassy, and I didn't think that I was going to be able
to peek behind it here in the car, interruptions or no

interruptions. I retreated to the front page of the *Times* and buried myself in the glories of world leadership as demonstrated in Beirut.

The trip down to Caunotaucarius took two uneventful hours under the guidance of a superbly expert driver. We could have kept a brimful glass of water on one of the polished tables without spilling a drop. The lush greenery of the late spring countryside interspersed with dusty little towns and crossroads rolled past the window. The outskirts of Caunotaucarius did not differ much from these settlements, but then the view suddenly thickened with competing gas stations, fast-food joints, used car lots, and rather generously extended saloons (DANCING TONITE! LIVE BAND!).

There were only a few blocks of small banks, pawn shops, and linoleum stores, all encased in buildings erected around the turn of the century, before we pulled up in front of the county courthouse and its small cohort of other official buildings. We proceeded around to the back, where the driver pulled into a reserved parking space. When he opened the door for me I stood up and told him: "I just want to let you know that that was one of the best pieces of driving I've ever enjoyed."

He said, "Thank you, sir," his face grave and immobile. He reached in his coat pocket and handed me a card: GENTRY LIMOUSINE SERVICE—JACKSON DASHWOOD—306-9125.

"Would you be Mr. Dashwood by any chance?" The barest hint of a smile at the corner of his lips and the slightest of nods indicated that this was so.

Martingale was standing off on the other side of the car, staring with full incomprehension at us. It may never have occurred to him that you could actually speak to a driver without giving him an order. And yet I obviously had no orders to give. He attracted my attention and said, "Come on. I'll take you up to Milly." We headed for a red brick building off to one side while Dashwood extracted Martingale's gleaming

one suiter from the trunk and carried it toward the
courthouse.

After we'd entered he asked me to wait while he
went to see Milly. I was left alone on the spacious first
floor of the building, a large clear area at the bottom
of a light well. The sides of the rectangle were punctuated with old-time office doors of the frosted glass
variety. Martingale headed for one at the opposite end
of the building.

Standing alone I was struck with a memory I'd never
thought of recalling. The building was a school. It was
the smell that got me, the smell of sweeping com-
pound that had been ground for a century into the
smooth worn floorboards, which had, like their human
counterparts, turned gray with age. The place was also
haunted with the smell of furniture polish that had been
rubbed into the oak railings of the stairs that marched
from floor to floor up to the fourth at the top. That
gave way to the skylight filtering sunshine down to the
bottom floor where I stood. This was the *assembly
area* I smilingly recalled, where kids from all those
early grades would gather round to sing ''Oh Christ-
mas Tree,'' at the appropriate season.

I was still smiling in my reverie when Martingale
appeared at my side to say, ''Milly's busy. She's in a
conference, and they say she can't see anybody till two
o'clock.'' He stared at me then, as if I had somehow
arranged this hitch in the smooth flow of progression.

I had begun with an uncertain, ''Well . . .'' but he
jumped in impatiently, saying, ''You might as well get
your room and have lunch.'' He had already moved
toward the door, and I followed him. We were standing in the parking lot before he spoke again. ''Dash
can take you over,'' he said. ''After that, you're on
your own, although I told them to expect you at two.''

From where I was standing I could see the red brick
structure of an old hotel that had the legend HOTEL
CAPTHORNE in gold letters on a black vertical sign.
What I wanted most in the world right then was to
march over to Hotel Capthorne, sign myself in to the

fly-specked register, go up to the room, and fix myself
a drink, even though it was early for a drink. I have a
deep, abiding love of old hotels, and the Capthorne
appeared to me as a rare jewel. I brought myself back
to reality with a quick glance at Martingale. *"Dash
can take you over"* meant that the rooms Martingale
had in mind were not within walking distance. "That
would be very nice," I said.

"See you around," said Martingale. He turned and
headed for the back door of the courthouse. *Twitch,
twitch, twitch.* Mr. Dashwood came around to me. I
asked him, "Do you happen to know where Mr. Welland, Mr. Charles Welland, was staying here in
town?"

"I'm sorry, sir, but I don't know the gentleman,"
said Mr. Dashwood.

"He was a salesman, a textbook salesman," I urged
him. "Can you give me any idea of where he probably
would have stayed?"

"Did he have a car?"

"Yes. A rented one I think."

"Then he probably stayed at the Motor Lodge."

"Can you take me over there?"

"Will you be wanting to rent a car?"

It hadn't occurred to me before but I answered almost automatically. "Yes. Yes, I think I'd better."

"What we'll do then," said Mr. Dashwood, "is I'll
take you to the Motor Lodge, where you can register,
and then I'll drop you off at the Hertz, which is on my
way back to Thornwood. You shouldn't have any trouble getting back to the motel."

Since I didn't want to take up any more of Dashwood's time than was necessary, I left my bag at the
desk of the Motor Lodge after I'd signed in. I was
dropped off at the Hertz agency as he'd promised, and
he waited only long enough to make sure that a car
was available for me before the long black limousine
swept out toward the highway.

Back at the Motor Lodge I asked the clerk, "Isn't

this where Mr. Welland was staying when he had his accident?''

The clerk was a portly, middle-aged man with hair that was just going gray. He was wearing a green blazer adorned with the company insignia. There was a sympathetic look on his face as he asked, ''Did you know Mr. Welland?''

''Only by reputation,'' I answered. ''I'm down here sort of trying to take over where he left off.''

''He was in room four-oh-six,'' said the clerk, whose name, I now discerned in the badge below the insignia was Ed Logan. ''It's a corner room with a nice view. Mr. Welland always took room four-oh-six. Would you like to have that room? It's a little more expensive, but if you're staying a while . . .''

''Gee,'' I said. ''I think that would be wonderful.''

Ed Logan was also very accommodating in the matter of my sending a telegram to Edna explaining my change of address. I filled out the blank and he phoned it in for me.

He gave me the key along with instructions on how to get to the corner of the fourth floor, which was the top floor in this building. Unlike the structures in Manhattan, buildings here tended to move sideways rather than upward. The room itself echoed the spendthrift attitude toward space. It was standard motel, all right, with two big double beds, plastic furniture and hideous lamps. However, it was generously supplied with windows on both sides of the corner, and frosted glass doors led out to the balcony, which looked into a green range of foothills. I unpacked and did indeed fix myself a drink despite the early hour. I took it out to the balcony. My watch was just closing on twelve noon.

Before leaving I checked out every nook and cranny of the room. There was not the barest scintilla of a suggestion that a man named Charlie Welland had ever stayed here—or any one else, for that matter.

I was five minutes early at the Board of Education, but as I came in and looked across the assembly area I could see that the conference had already broken up.

There were a number of people milling around in front of the office door at the other end of the building. Four of the people were men and two were women. As I drew closer I paid more attention to the women. One was small and skinny with a vindictive look about her, in her face and in her demeanor. She wore a dark blue go-to-meeting dress and a blue straw hat. She was in the process of collecting her umbrella and checking her purse. The other woman, I guessed, was the Milly Rutledge I had come to see. She wore an ample print dress with a floral pattern in green that wasn't terribly far removed from wallpaper and a pair of Red Cross shoes. A pair of black-rimmed spectacles hung from a cord around her neck. She looked to be in her seventies. A band of white hair framed the upper part of her face, which was pink and broad and punctuated by sharp blue eyes. The heavy cheeks descended into a bulldog jaw. As I watched her conversing with a tall, beefy, white-haired bloke in a pearl-colored quasi-western outfit, I could see that she was being *very, very nice!* The strain showed.

I arrived and stood at the edges of the group. The sharp blue eyes fastened on me as an escaping convict's might have focused on a ladder leaned against the wall. "You must be Mr. Binney," she said commandingly. "I've been expecting you."

My God! I was back in the fifth grade. Everyone turned and looked at me. "Mr. Binney represents Carlson House Publishers," she told the group. The collective expressions turned vinegary. She might have announced that I had just emerged smoking from hell. "He and I must discuss many of the subjects you've brought up in the meeting. The changes you've suggested are not easy to make, you know, and there isn't much time left to make them."

The overfed Roy Rogers type stepped back to take a good look at me. He jerked his head back a little to settle his mane. "You're from New York, are you?" he asked with a rather grim, pitying smile.

"That's right, sir."

"Never could understand why anybody'd want to live there."

"God's will, I guess."

He had one of the big stupid faces in which a dangerous shrewdness dwells. It clouded over and the old schoolma'am stepped between us. She smiled up at him and said, "Reverend Barlow, you really must excuse us now because Mr. Binney will have to call in the changes all the way to New York after we've gone over them." The other members of the group stirred about, impressed and pleased with themselves.

Barlow raised his palm in benediction. "I bring God's blessing on your meeting together," he said. "And I'm sure you'll remember that God will be listening to every word you speak in there." He nodded toward the appointed place of our unholy seclusion. Milly Rutledge clenched her bulldog jaw and grinned at him. I stood there like an idiot with my hands hanging at my sides.

"It's been a great pleasure and a wonderful experience, Reverend," she said to him. "I'm grateful to you all. And now you must excuse us." She grabbed me by one of my limp arms and pulled me through the doorway.

Inside the office she closed the door with no lack of determination, strode behind her desk and collapsed into a big leather chair. She ripped open the top right hand drawer, jerked out a pack of Tareytons and lighted a cigarette with a book match before I could get my Zippo out. She exhaled a huge cloud of smoke and glared at me. "I hope you don't mind if I smoke," she said, her blue eyes piercing the haze.

I burst out laughing.

She continued to glare at me, and then the big smooth cheeks began to quiver. The bulldog jaw trembled and she too began to laugh. The printed flowers on her bosom jumped and jiggled. She settled back in her chair and took a long luxurious drag. Finally she spoke.

"I usually try to schedule these meetings outside my

office," she said, "somewhere where I can be called to the phone. But this time they gathered in here and I've been more or less trapped for three hours. Well . . ." philosophically she waved the cloud of smoke away, "that's why I'm here. It's what they pay me for." She took her first good look at me and a very faint expression of dubiety crossed her features. "You're here to replace Charlie Welland?" she asked me.

"Sort of," I answered cautiously. "I'm here to tie up the loose ends anyway. After that, I guess, they'll see if I'm good enough to hang in here."

She visited me with a long shrewd look. "You're quite a change from Charlie Welland," she observed.

"I didn't really know him," I said nervously. "Never met him, in fact. I was in a different territory, and somehow we never connected.

"For instance," I added, trying to move away from *that* subject, "I have to confess that I don't really know how to approach what you folks were talking about out there in the hall. You found something wrong with *The Forging of a Nation?* Some mistakes somewhere?"

Again I got the long, level look. "Mr. Binney," she said, and I could tell by the way she framed the words that she was getting used to the idea that I read lips, "have you read the book?"

"Well, gee," I stammered. "You know I only just got this assignment and I rushed down here, so I really haven't had a chance . . ."

"The Forging of a Nation would be an excellent title," said Millicent Rutledge, "if by forging you mean counterfeiting."

I was nonplussed. "Well, I'm awful sorry to hear you say anything like that," I began, hoping that I sounded like your average shitkicking salesman. "I thought it had been all wrapped up."

"Have you even looked at the book?" I shook my head shamefacedly. "Have you cracked it open?" I pursed my lips. "It's gorgeously illustrated," she went

on, "which will be a great help to those students in
our high schools who are totally illiterate. Also," she
continued remorselessly, "there is enough white space
on those expensive pages to snowblind an Eskimo.
This is a great relief to students who are assigned to
read pages one-thirty-seven through one-forty-seven.
They nervously flip through it and find out that ten
pages contain about twelve paragraphs of baby talk."

I wanted to say forcefully, *"Goddamn it, I didn't
write the goddamned book!"* Instead, I ventured timidly, "Miss Rutledge . . ."

"Call me Milly," she commanded. "Everyone
does," she smiled grimly, "not excluding the janitor."

"Well, then, Milly—and by the way, please call me
Joe—I got the idea that those people you were confer-
ring with, uh, they want a little more information in
the book?" I searched wildly for some phrase that
would be closer to the vocabulary. "More textual
bulk?"

The big flowered shoulders began to shake. The
laugh had started deep in her chest and then irrepres-
sibly broke out on her face. *"Textual bulk!"* She continued to laugh and reached for a Kleenex to dab her
eyes. "That's a beaut. Where did you pick that one
up?

"No, no," she wiped her eyes and waved her hand
as if dismissing a class. "That's not what they're looking for. Textual bulk." She suppressed the wreathing
of another burst of laughter. "No," her face drooped
into something more of a careworn expression. "What
they're trying to do is chase out the liberal bias in the
book."

"Is there a liberal bias in the book?"

"Oh, certainly."

"Then you agree with them?" I nodded at the door
through which they had departed. I was mildly surprised.

"It's not my business, Mr. Bin—Joe—to agree with

anybody or disagree. My business is to try to educate the children around here as best I can.''

''But the best education would certainly be—''

''Would be what?'' she demanded. ''Do you have the answer? Do you think you know?''

Dumbly I shook my head.

''Well, thank God for that,'' she said. She too nodded toward the door. ''Those people there,'' she indicated, ''they think they know. They don't realize it but they want to raise the children up to be the leadeneyed.''

A vague memory of something passed like a cloud behind my eyes. I couldn't place it. It was a reference of some kind that I couldn't identify. I held my peace.

''Ah,'' she said. She took another cigarette from the pack, lighted it slowly and puffed out a reflective cloud. ''It's my problem, really, not theirs. I was trained in history and I have to bite my tongue every time I read a glossy paragraph in one of our secondary texts or listen to those good people tell me what history ought to represent. I don't have the same trouble discussing science texts, although that's much more volatile these days. I simply don't have any emotional involvement in it.'' She paused, leaned back and stared at the ceiling. ''The reason I get emotional about history is that I was trained in the old school. When the new method came in in the forties, it hit me just about midstride. I've been straddling the two systems ever since, even,'' she nodded toward a pile of manila folders at the edge of her desk, ''in the little study I've been doing about Caunotaucarius.

''The old method,'' she said, talking not so much to me as a point over her shoulder, ''was based on a humanistic, empathic understanding of human character. It didn't pretend to absolutes. The new system wanted history to be a science, to set up structures as firm as Newton's physics, so it could be as reproducible as a scientific explanation. It never really worked, of course, because each historical event is unique. And yet it is alluring.'' She sat up suddenly and propped her elbows on the desk. "The possibilities are haunting because if the new system is right we can predict large political events as surely as they can predict the return of Halley's comet."

"And if we predict them, avoid them?"

"Now that is the fascinating question," she answered. "That is *the* fascinating question, is it not? So fascinating," she said, stubbing out her cigarette and rising, "that I'm going to invite you to have lunch with me—" she put up her hand—"but absolutely Dutch, you understand. My name does not appear on anyone's expense account."

"You name wouldn't—" I began, but she cut me off with a gesture.

"My terms or nothing."

I acquiesced gracefully. She took a dark cloth coat off the coatrack near the door. I helped her on with it—it was little more than a duster. Then she took a big floppy hat off the top of a filing case and fastened it to her white hair with a hatpin the likes of which I hadn't seen since I was a kid. She was about to leave, but then bethought herself and returned to the desk, where she scooped up the pile of manila folders and put them in the bottom file drawer of her desk. She locked the drawer, looked up at me and said, "Predictability. If there's one thing I'm tempted to predict it's that this building and all its contents, including myself, is going to get blown up sky high one of these days."

5

"My favorite definition of history," said Milly, "isn't from a historian at all. It's from James Joyce: 'History is a nightmare from which I am trying to awaken.'"

We were sitting in the back booth of a restaurant

that obviously was the long standing resort for her lunchtime. The booth had been reserved and I felt that, somehow, it would always be open for her. A gleaming martini had been set in front of her (this suggested to me why the booth was in the back and why she sat facing away from the crowd) without her having mentioned a thing. When it was served, I gratefully ordered a bourbon and soda.

"The question of how to teach history in the primary and secondary grades is an idle one," she continued. "Teaching factual history would send all those poor little children screaming home to hide under their beds." She took a very tiny sip from the rim of the glass, barely breaking the surface tension of the cocktail. It was impossible not to recognize that this martini, like the restaurant, was a long standing tradition.

"So we have to look at the other side of the coin," she told me. "And that was expressed by some German whose name I forget but who I remember, of course, was very definitely German. He said, 'It is the duty of the old to lie to the young.' " She smiled grimly. "I try to stand the coin on edge," she said.

I maintained a respectful silence although my head was full of questions—not only about history and history textbooks but about the leisurely conversation in her office and the five-minute walk we'd had across the courthouse common.

We had sailed out the back door of the Education Building with me feeling very much like a tugboat escorting the stately liner, S.S. *Millicent Rutledge*. In her big straw hat and the lightweight coat blowing out behind her she had steamed along the pathway cutting through the well-tended grass, very, very much a personage. Wisely, because of my deafness, she did not try to talk to me during the walk and I was content to take in the atmosphere of the county seat—the courthouse crowd idling on the cast-iron benches, some of whom nodded to her, and others who were sunk in consultation with their attorneys or despair. Lunchtime was over for most people so there were no brown-

baggers in sight, but neither was there any trash discarded from a lunch bag on the lawn. I noticed two
war memorials: a cast-iron doughboy with the rakishly
tilted tin hat and the rifle held loosely in both hands.
He was staring from some distance at a cenotaph that
had been raised for the local dead from the Second
World War—a long list of names. There was no visible
memorial for the Civil War, nor, for that matter, for
the Korean War or the Vietnam War.

As we approached the edge of the common I noticed
that a knot of about a dozen people were listening to
an orator. As we drew closer I was startled. I had
thought that the orator was standing on a box or a
bench. He was standing on his own two feet. Even
more striking than his height was the crown of blond
curly hair, bleached and sun-streaked nearly white, that
was flung to his shoulders. His face was tanned and
weather beaten. He was wearing a tattered blue shirt,
little more than a rag, unbuttoned and flapping in the
breeze as he waved his arms. The old brown pants he
wore were shredded from the knees down. When we
arrived at the edge of the common to cross the street,
Milly paused and looked at me to speak. "Honey
Lewis," she said, nodding at the orator. "The white-
haired boy. Sim Lewis's boy. A shame. A terrible
shame." We marched across the street and into the
restaurant.

"Children think they are inured to violence because
they watch car chases on television or silly chain-saw
movies," Milly went on to me over her cocktail.
"Worse than that, adults believe that children are inured to it. But children know that all that two-
dimensional nonsense is a game. They are carefully
screened from the true facts of violence, just as they
are from true adult sexuality. Of course they're not
prepared for it. Even we, as adults, are not prepared
for it."

The luncheon special was served. Neither of us had
put in an order, but apparently Milly's lunches ran on
well-worn tracks. It was lamb stew, something I am

usually quite cautious about in strange restaurants. I tasted it gingerly. It was delicious.

"Let us take, for instance, the Spanish Civil War, a watershed of modern history. It gets scarcely more than a glance in any secondary text. But suppose we did give it the full treatment, as one finds it in a full-scale history. Suppose we were to describe the strike in Asturias where a policeman was seized by a mob. His eyes were torn out and he was held prostrate while a young woman squatted and urinated into the empty sockets.''

I stared at my lamb stew.

"It was a celebrated case,'' she continued blithely as she dug into her plate, "made more so by the fact that the mob was fired upon by policemen who were ignorant of what had happened, and the only person killed in that random firing was the young woman who had desecrated the lynched assault guard.''

She chewed thoughtfully on her stew. "Should we describe that to the children? How should we explain it? Should we describe the actions of the opposing side? The Moors of Franco's army who calmly went through the hospitals slaughtering the wounded who put their helpless hands up to ward off the sabers?'' She chewed away and stared over my shoulder.

"Go back to the sixteenth century,'' she urged me. "In our history books the children see the Holbein treatment of Henry the Eighth, something of a jolly old soul if you don't look too carefully at the eyes. Should they be told that given the ratio of population Henry the Eighth was responsible for the execution of about the same number of people that Hitler was? That some of these victims were infants so young that as Sir Walter Raleigh described it, they could scarcely crawl to the block?

"When children read the romantic nonsense about Mary, Queen of Scots, and the Earl of Bothwell, should we tell them that Bothwell's major contribution to Mary's life was syphilis? And that when Bothwell was captured by the Danes he was chained to a rock in a dungeon so that he could neither sit nor stand? He finally went mad there, you know.'' She chewed away and glanced at the ceiling. ''I don't think it's ever been settled whether he went mad from the syphilis or the torment. It's an interesting question.''

I had been staring at her so intently that I was startled by the shadow that fell across the table. When I looked up a sunburned man in a broad campaign hat wearing a gold star on his short, gray whipcord jacket was speaking to Milly. Her face was turned in profile to me so that I could not see what her response was, although she was smiling hospitably. She gestured toward me, her face still slightly turned away. Apparently she was making introductions. She turned to me then, and said, ''Joe, this is John McCleod, Sheriff of Caunotaucarius County.''

Well, then. This was the man who had located Charlie Welland's wrecked car. Carlson had praised him for his intelligence, but the brown tight face that stared down at me seemed to hold more toughness than smarts. He had one of those seamed leathery faces that bespeak a long history of ''handling'' people. There was a kind of indomitableness about it, not challenging, but filled with the absolute certainty that whatever kind of trouble you brought he would handle very quickly, most probably with a supple leather sap. He was not a very big man, not as tall as I am and certainly not as heavily muscled. On the other hand there was a wiriness and a certain easy slouch in his attitude that suggested whatever muscles he did have were very tough and could be brought instantaneously into play. ''So, Mr. Binney,'' he favored me with the hint of a smile, ''you're in the book business, are you?''

''Yes,'' I answered, trying to look alert and amiable. ''I'm down here filling in for Charlie Welland until we get things sorted out.''

''Mr. Welland a friend of yours was he?''

''No,'' I said quickly. ''I'm from a different territory, New England, really. I hardly ever saw him.''

''Going to be with us here for very long?''

"I don't really know," I responded honestly. "As long as it takes to get things straightened out, anyway." I decided to change the direction of the conversation. "They told me up at the office that you're the one that found Charlie's car. That right?"

"That's right," answered McCleod. "Year-old Ford Victoria. Black. Down off the old Mine Five road."

"I suppose they've hauled the car away by now," I said. "The insurance people."

"Naw," said McCleod. "It was totaled. A terrible mess. Nothing worth the trouble of hauling it up that ravine. They'll let her lay. Adjuster come down to take a look, but it didn't take him two minutes to write it off."

"Well," I said, summing up, "I'm just temporary down here, a stopgap until they find somebody to put in Charlie's place."

"See you around." McCleod touched the brim of his hat. Then he turned and said, "Nice seeing you again, Miss Milly. Anything you ever want just holler."

Milly bade him farewell with a friendly smile and a nod. I watched him go. There weren't very many people left in the restaurant at this post-lunch hour, but he stopped briefly to speak with the few who were.

"So we have to give the children a mild gloss of history, and the main effort goes into keeping it harmless." She had picked up the conversation where it had dropped, and I had to pull my wits together to follow her. My eye was still on the sheriff. "And that can be a little more difficult than you might think." She polished off the last of her stew and sat back in her chair. "Reverend Barlow and his Christian Parents Association want a certain strict interpretation of historical events that doesn't fit any rational system of historical explanation. I can't give it to them because to do so would be unconstitutional—illegal. Reverend Barlow believes in the inerrancy of the Bible. This makes serious problems for a public school system."

The waitress had brought dessert and coffee. The

dessert was tangy lemon pie with a creamy chiffon topping. The coffee was fresh, hot, black, and powerful. Milly attacked her pie and I followed suit.

"At that it could be worse," said Milly. "Barlow believes in the inerrancy of the Bible, but Honey Lewis out there," she nodded toward the street, "believes that the Bible is the *only* book that should be taught." She emphasized this with a forefinger jabbed at the table top. "He wants to burn down all the schoolhouses, burn all the books except the Bible, trash all the TV sets, tear down the movie houses, and generally turn us back to the pastures of the year One A.D.

"Chris Barlow doesn't much like Honey Lewis," she told me, dabbing away a bit of topping from the corner of her mouth, "because he's at least smart enough to see that Honey is a kind of reductio ad absurdum of all the right thinking that Chris is trying to push over on us. There is also the fact that he's jealous."

"Jealous?" I was surprised. It didn't seem possible that anyone could be jealous of a man in rags.

Milly said, "You'll notice that while there weren't too many people standing there listening to Honey, they really were listening. They weren't shuffling around or yelling back. Now Chris Barlow is on the radio a lot and even on local television, and he tends to get people all gowed up on country music and some good old hymns before he starts to preach. But when he does preach it's kind of cow-like, you know? *Moo—Moo—Moo. 'All you good people out there. All you God-fearing Christians'—Moo—Moo—Moo.* But now you take Honey. When you listen to him—and you're never going to hear him on radio or television because he thinks those are instruments of the devil—but Honey when he preaches he is musical and his voice is beautiful. It goes way, way up and then down, down, down, and there is a kind of rhythm and Old Testament poetry to his language, although there's not a single soul in Caunotaucarius who really understands what he's talking about, or perhaps I should say is willing to understand what he is talking about.'' She took a sip of the strong coffee and stared at the ceiling. Her pie was gone, every single bit of it. Demolished.

''He preaches about the Ragged Stranger. Infinite, infinite variations on the Ragged Stranger. Most people, I believe, think he is talking about Jesus, but I don't believe that. I believe that he is talking about Death. I believe that he is saying that Death is the Ragged Stranger and we should be prepared to meet him. It gives people around here the willies, but the boy has never done a lick of harm. What's more, nobody in these parts is ever going to stop anybody from preaching gospel, whether they do it with snake handling or do it in speaking with tongues or do it rolling on the ground. It's an old, old tradition here, borne out of poverty, isolation, illiteracy, and ignorance. It was absolutely necessary for a long, long time. It was the only spiritual sustenance these people ever got. People can laugh about the tent shows, the revival meetings that always seemed to be just about nine months removed from a flood of birthdays, the circuit preachers and the Bible pounders hollering off a stump, but this was all these people had. Medicine men, even tinkers coming down the road were the only opening out for an awful lot of these folks.

''Of course it's all city now.'' She gestured to the rear of her where gentlemen in pretty good suits were conversing earnestly. ''Hardly anybody knows why this place is called Caunotaucarius. That was the name the Indians gave to George Washington. Actually, they gave it first to his great-grandfather, John Washington, and then they landed it on George. It means 'Taker of Cities.' George Washington did a lot of surveying around here. He had great plans for this part of the country. He loved the big river that runs through the town. But as you might have noticed,'' she jerked her head backward, ''it's become pretty much of an open sewer.

''Still and all,'' she continued, ''with all the city doings, there's still a lot of country or small-town folks coming up even if they're only passing through to look for work. Nobody would stand for a sheriff or a policeman hauling off somebody like Honey Lewis. So they have to let him alone, vagrancy or no vagrancy, riot act or no riot act.''

"Riot act?'' I was a bit surprised. "He's inciting to riot?''

"If you stand up there and say you want to blow up every single building in town, and smash up every single automobile, and burn up every single book, and drive all the folks in town out to the mountains and pastures to live like God's innocent creatures, I suppose that could be called inciting to riot, yes.''

She pursed her lips in thought. "I think Chris Barlow, although he snickers at the boy, I think he's a little bit afraid of him. I don't think the Chamber of Commerce or Jack McCleod would be too unhappy if Honey decided to stay up there in the hills and go preach to the birds and animals. I don't think they'd mind that at all.''

She began to make those swimming motions common to all women, young or old, who are preparing to depart. I became alarmed. I said, "Milly, before we leave, if you don't mind, we sort of got away from the main reason I came down here. What is the status of *The Forging of a Nation?* I mean, what am I supposed to tell Mr. Carlson?''

She sat back in her chair. "Why I thought you understood that, Joe,'' she said with a look of troubled surprise. "There's no chance we can use your book. Even Charlie Welland should have understood that, and I'm pretty sure that he did.''

"But,'' I protested, "you were saying to the Reverend Barlow and those people that we were going to call in changes—''

"Changes in a book already bound?'' She waved it aside. "You shouldn't listen to things like that,'' she said. "I have to stall them until I get something else in place.'' She stared at me. "Joe,'' she said, "would you be insulted if I told you I think you look like an honest man?''

Again I burst out laughing. I couldn't help it. I took out a Lucky and lighted it. "Shoot," I said.

"There is no hope for your book at all," said Milly. "I have another one that will probably fill the bill if I wave my fingers in front of them and promise them the moon. But I have to go with the other book, not yours.''

My smile faded. I was disturbed by something beyond the fortunes of Carlson House. "You really let those people dictate what you're going to teach the kids?'' I asked her.

"No," said Milly. "Not that way." She gave up the idea of leaving. She took out a cigarette again and lighted it so swiftly I had no chance with my lighter. "It is a problem of balance," she said, exhaling a cloud of smoke. "What I am trying to do is preserve rationality. We cannot dare to tell the children the truth about almost anything, but we can preserve a certain sense of rational progression so that the intelligent ones can go on to pursue an education or at least a rational pursuit of their personal lives. The others, of course, will become what I mentioned before—the leaden-eyed.''

The cloud passed again behind my eyes, but this time a tiny fork of lightning sparked out of it. I snapped my fingers. Milly looked startled. "Vachel Lindsay," I said. "I was thinking about him just last night down at Thornwood.''

There was an appreciable difference in the way she looked at me. "Do you know it then?" she asked me.

"My brain is certifiably second rate," I told her. "I remember first lines and tags but what goes between them often falls through the cracks. I always have to go back and look it up." I stared at her. "Do you know it?'' I asked her.

Milly leaned back in her chair and closed her eyes. The cigarette was forgotten in her hand. I watched her lips very closely because it is hard to read recitation, and even harder when the speaker's eyes are closed. She said:

> *"Let not young souls be smothered out before*
> *They do quaint deeds and fully flaunt their pride.*
> *It is the world's one crime its babes grow dull,*
> *Its poor are ox-like, limp, and leaden-eyed.*
>
> *Not that they starve, but starve so dreamlessly;*
> *Not that they sow, but that they seldom reap;*
> *Not that they serve, but have no gods to serve;*
> *Not that they die, but that they die like sheep."*

She opened her eyes. "I've taught too many little boys," she said, "who went on only to fill up graves."

I remained very quiet, very still.

Milly said, "I try to draw a reasonable compromise. You can't laugh off people like Barlow, at least not down here. What you try to do is keep them from corrupting intelligence. Barlow," she said, drawing on her cigarette, "doesn't even begin to understand the forces pushing behind him."

"Forces?" I asked her. "The Chamber of Commerce? The big church councils?"

"Oh, much larger and grander than that. There is a diplomatic, political, and academic effort underway to reassess the Enlightenment—the philosophical underpinnings of the Constitution. This isn't a conspiracy of any kind," she hastened to assure me. "It's a scholarly and honest reassessment. The feeling is that we can no longer afford the value-free tenets of the Constitution. Their point is that it was all very well for the eighteenth century, but now we are living in the twentieth. In aid of this, apparently, they want to go back to the sixteenth and sweep the *philosophes* aside. I don't agree with their point of view, honorable as it is. I think they forget that George Washington was born less than fifty years after the nineteen witches were hanged in Salem. The founders had a very lively appreciation of how systems based on religious conviction had torn up the world, which is why they wrote it out of their constitution. If they were alive today they would see what it is doing to the Middle East and may well do to the West, what with our new letch for Armageddon.

"The fact is," she added, stubbing out her cigarette, "hardly anyone really likes the Constitution. It throws us too much on our own resources. It . . ." but here she saw me looking up at someone who was approaching us. She turned around to see who it was and said, "Why, Maria, dear, what is it?"

The young woman had apparently seen me before, although I had not seen her. She nodded in my direction and then bent down to say something to Milly. Something I couldn't see. When she straightened up, Milly was already gathering her things to leave.

"A slight emergency." She grinned at me. "Nothing so earthshaking as our discussion, but requiring my indispensable presence." She laid a few bills and some change on the table cloth, knowing, it seemed, to the penny how much her bill would be. While she was counting it out I took a good look at the young woman she had called Maria. She was in her late twenties, a dark-complected brunette with deep expressive brown eyes. She was dressed simply in a green blouse and brown skirt. When Milly looked up she introduced us. "This is Maria Thorndyke, my administrative assistant," she told me. I got my chance to nod and smile. It didn't seem to provoke any wild response in Miss Thorndyke. "I have to run," said Milly. "But be sure to come in and see me soon. Set up an appointment with Maria here." I was pondering how I would work that out without a telephone when they bustled out of the place.

I had one more drink before I paid the bill and strolled back to the courthouse parking lot. Honey Lewis had apparently gone back to the hills. There was no crowd, but neither was there any litter where there had been a crowd. I got in my car and headed back to the motel.

When I opened the door to my room the strong Western sun was burning through the frosted glass doors that gave on to the balcony. I could see the outline of the wrought-iron table and chairs that were set out there. I could also see that someone was sitting there with elbows propped on the table.

6

Was it a burglar? If so it was a very leisurely burglar. Still, one never knows what those nutty bastards are up to. Was it the maid? Had she decided to take a shot out of my traveling bottle, fix herself a drink and enjoy the afternoon sun? The easy slouch of the shadow at the table didn't look female to me. The hell with it, fearless Joe Binney said to himself. I crossed the room and slid back the door.

"Well, Sheriff McCleod," I said in greeting. "Do you mind if I join you?"

"Plunk yourself down," he invited me, nodding amiably at the other chair.

"Mind if I fix myself a drink first? You gave me a start. As a matter of fact, will you join me? Bourbon's all I've got, but it's good bourbon. Or would you have known that already?"

He smiled a tight little smile. "Old Fitzgerald's fine by me," he said.

"Branch water all right?"

"Fine by me," said Sheriff McCleod.

The Motor Lodge still had enough self-respect to provide real glass drinking glasses. They were the timeless standard hotel glass that lends itself to formidable volume in a drink. I fixed us a couple of dandies, noting the regrettable retreat in the level of my bottle, and took them out on the balcony. There wasn't any ice in the room and I didn't feel like making the long trip down to the ice machine. I put the drinks on the table, sat down and raised my glass in salute. We both took the obligatory sip. McCleod pursed his lips appreciatively.

"What brings you to my room, Sheriff?" I asked him. "Not to mention my briefcase, my suitcase, my medicine chest, and my clothes closet?"

"Just curious."

"Curious about what?"

"Curious about who you are and why you're here."

"Well, as I told you at the restaurant, I'm a sales rep for Carlson House—"

"Salesman my ass," said Jack McCleod. "Where'd you get that hole in your face? That ain't a bullet wound and it sure ain't a cutting."

"This?" I instinctively put my fingers up to the circular depression high on my right cheek. In time it had shrunk to about the size of a quarter. "Well, if you must know, it's a rat bite."

"A salesman with a rat bite." He hoisted his glass for another sip and stared at me over the rim of it.

"A rat-bitten salesman," I agreed. "The fact is I got mugged in New York and the folks threw me down an elevator shaft in a warehouse. I was out for a quite a while and some rats joined me for lunch."

"That could be," he nodded. "I've seen what rats do. That could be." He stared at me. "What were you doing when you got mugged?" he asked me.

"Well, I was on my way to a sales meeting—"

He put his hand up to halt me. "Mr. Binney," he said, "if that happens to be your real name, I'm enjoying your whiskey, and it's very pleasant out here, but I haven't got all day. One look at you in that restaurant there and I knew you were never no salesman. When I come up here I went through your things, like you said, and there ain't one single solitary thing that makes you look like any kind of a salesman at all. Now I'm sittin' here nice and easy and just waiting for you to tell me what you're doing down here and particularly why you're bothering Miss Milly."

I was surprised, hurt in fact. "Miss Rutledge has complained about me?"

"Miss Milly doesn't have to complain for me to keep an eye out for her. I just want to know what your game is. And just between you and me, I think I'm being real nice."

"Well, whether you believe it or not, I am down here on Carlson's business. If you don't believe that you can tell Mr. Carlson himself in New York. I'll give you his direct number."

"The insurance company send you down here?" he demanded.

"No." I denied it absolutely and honestly.

"The car insurance? The life insurance?"

"I haven't got a thing to do with any insurance company."

McCleod sighed. "I guess we'll have to do this by the numbers," he said. "Would you mind showing me some identification, just so I know what your name is real?"

I took out my wallet and extracted my driver's license. I laid the license before him and was about to return the wallet to my pocket when he said, "Supposin' you just leave the wallet out here where I can take a peek at it, all right?"

This was my moment to decide. Either I could stand on my rights and tell Sheriff McCleod to go fuck himself, an idea that was growing strongly in its appeal, or I could play ball. I looked at him very carefully. If I were going to pursue any kind of investigation down here having McCleod in my way would be tantamount to swimming the English Channel with an anvil around my neck. And yet, of course, I did not trust the good sheriff. I'd watched him in the restaurant and he was very much part of the county courthouse crowd. I think that I can be forgiven for observing that county courthouse people are not widely regarded as an extremely trustworthy group. Indeed, they might be said to fit into Ali Baba's cave with nothing more than a change of costume. Nonetheless, Sheriff McCleod for the moment had me on the hook. I let the wallet lie.

He took a pretty luxurious look at the driver's license with its hideous color photo of me, rat bite and all. "I guess this says you're Joe Binney all right." He nodded somewhat regretfully. He opened the wallet then and dipped into the card compartment on the left. From this he took my library card, my Social Security card, some business cards, and finally my own business card. He put this last to one side, looked up and stared impassively at me. From the other compartment in the wallet he produced the folded photostat of my private investigator's license and my pistol permit. He put these next to my business card. His expression had changed from impassivity to absolute stoniness. "You carrying anything down here?" he asked me. "There a gun in the room someplace I missed?"

"Nossir," I answered him.

"You gonna tell me a lot more lies now about no insurance company hiring you?"

"That wasn't a lie," I answered. "As a matter of fact I haven't told you any lies at all. I am down here to represent David Carlson of Carlson House Publishers. The first and most important thing you ought to know is that my business with Milly Rutledge is perfectly legitimate. I'd never even heard of her until Dana Martingale, the Superintendent of Education, suggested that I talk to her. The reason I'm seeing her is that one of Carlson's history textbooks is getting tangled up in sales complications. Charlie Welland didn't explain this very clearly in his sales report, and Carlson wants to know what's going on."

"You're trying to tell me they'd hire a private detective to find out about a botched-up sale? Mr. Binney, I've only been served just one drink here, and that's my first of the day and I ain't drunk half of it yet."

"All right," I said. "I agree there's more."

"There'd better be."

"There are certain numbers on Charlie Welland's account that don't add up right at Carlson House. Mr.

Carlson has got a suspicion that Welland was stealing and he wants to find out how it was done.'' I put up my hand. ''This isn't because he's trying to get money back from a corpse or the corpse's family. He thinks that if Welland was doing it, maybe everybody's doing it, and he'd better get it stopped.'' I raised my drink. ''That's the truth, and that's the whole truth.''

He pushed the photostat toward me as if it were a dead mouse. ''This here piece of paper,'' he said, ''doesn't give you the right to go poking around in people's affairs down here you know.''

''No,'' I admitted. ''But it doesn't prevent me from looking into the internal affairs of a New York company either. That's all I intend to do. I'm not looking for any privileges.''

Sheriff McCleod took a long sip of his drink and ruminated. ''You were asking about Welland's car,'' he said. ''That was one of the things that put me on to you. Why would you be interested in the car?''

''Well, first thing of all,'' I answered, ''you said it was totaled. Does that mean it burned?''

''Naw. It didn't burn. Just tumbled down there and smashed the hell out of everything.''

''I might just take a run out there and have a look at it.''

''We already went over it pretty good,'' the sheriff objected mildly. ''I don't think there's a hell of a lot for you to look at.''

''Was it a rental car or his personal car?''

''Oh, it was his own car all right. New York license plates and all. Matched up with the registration in his wallet.''

''I think I'll definitely have a look then,'' I told him. ''I'd be looking for something different than you were.''

''Anything you find,'' said Sheriff McCleod, ''I want to know about.''

I nodded a rather reluctant agreement. ''This Mine Five road,'' I said, ''can I pick it out on one of the road maps?''

"Well, it ain't nothing but a dotted line."

"Could you tell me how to pick it up?"

"I'll draw you a map," said the sheriff. We went inside then to get a sheet of Motor Lodge stationery. He spread it on top of the dresser and drew a large road, the highway, and a smaller road curling off it to the left. He drew in a box at the junction. "You take Ninety-Five here," he said nodding toward the highway outside the window, "and follow it west for about five miles. Keep your eyes open to the left of you, and when you see a big Shell station you'll know you're getting close. About half a mile past the Shell station you'll see a clapboard restaurant with two gas pumps out in front, and there's usually some big rigs parked out in the back. That's Dooley's truck stop. You get in the left-hand lane there, cross over the highway at the next turnoff and make a U turn to come back to Dooley's. The Mine Five road picks up right behind Dooley's." He followed the curve of the Mine Five road with his pencil and made an X that intersected the curve. "There's sheer cliff on one side where this road cuts through and a sheer drop on the other, so you be careful. Now, where I put this X here you'll be at the top of the hill and you'll see one of those signs for trucks to gear down. There's a wide place in the road right after that sign and you can park your car there. You walk downhill from there about a hundred yards and look down into the ravine and you'll see Welland's car. If you're going to climb down there, and I wouldn't advise it, you better not wear your good Sunday-go-to-meeting clothes."

He handed me the map. "That suit you?"

"That's fine," I answered. "Thank you." I thought for a bit. "This Mine Five road," I asked him, "where does it go?"

He stared at me. "Why over to Mine Five, of course," he said. "The big strip mine over by Blue-stone."

"Bluestone?"

"It's a mining town. Been there forever. The road

snakes around the strip mine and then goes into the main drag of Bluestone.''

''Ah,'' I said wisely. ''I see.''

He looked at me again, closely. ''When do you figure on making this trip?''

''Tomorrow if I can.''

''About what time did you have in mind?''

''That's something I really can't say,'' I answered honestly. ''I'm expecting some information from the office, and I don't know what time that will arrive or whether it will have something else for me to do. So I can't really tell you anything except that I'll be making the trip in daylight, of course.''

The sheriff evaluated this and pursed his lips. He picked his hat up and set it carefully on his head. ''Well, all right. But you let me know what you find,'' he said. He gave me a farewell nod that was filled with scrutiny and let himself out the door.

Well, I thought grimly, as I watched the door close, Joe Binney, Ace Private Detective, didn't handle that one too well, did he? Sheriff McCleod had just strolled away with all the marbles. He had walked off with all the information one could possibly have about me save a dental X-ray. I went back to the balcony to reclaim my violated wallet and put the forlorn contents back in their compartments. I stared back into my room. The uninvited presence of Sheriff McCleod had robbed my quarters of even the tiny bit of personal familiarity anyone is able to impose on the stamped out character of a motel interior. I pondered the idea of fixing another drink out on my balcony where I could watch the green hills gather shade as the sun moved west. It seemed too desolate, too depressing. I glanced at my watch; five o'clock was in the offing. No doubt there was a happy hour in full sway downstairs, a bar I had as yet to visit.

By God, it *was* happy hour and drinks were half price. A big sign said so. The big sign notwithstanding, there were only two other people in the bar. They were middle-aged men in polyester summer suits of a particularly virulent shade of blue running to lavender. Apparently they had bought the suits at the same sale. They were deep in conversation and did not even notice me come in.

I sighed and sat at the bar and ordered my standard. I took a sip and cast a despairing look around the room. When I looked back, however, prospects had brightened immeasurably. A young woman had slipped through the doorway and seated herself at the other end of the bar. It was a graceful figure that adorned the stool, and though her back was turned to me, I tried to catch a glimpse of her face in the mirror behind the bar. The face was framed by a dark glossy coiffeur. When her face turned a little more toward the mirror my pulse quickened. She was very attractive and beautifully made up. The eye shadow gave her face a depth of mystery. My pulse quickened even more as the mystery became familiar and burgeoned into recognition. It was Maria Thorndyke, Milly's administrative assistant, but it was a Maria Thorndyke that had nothing to do with boards of education. I picked up my drink and moved in.

"Miss Thorndyke," I said, trying to regulate my voice so that it wouldn't scare her out of her wits, an unfortunate effect my greetings sometimes have on unprepared people. "How nice to see you here." I noticed that she had nothing in front of her on the bar. "Will you join me in a drink?"

She *had* been startled, damn it. She stared at me, her eyes widening. "You're Mr. Binney," she said slowly, identifying me at last. I smiled an acknowledgment. "Well," she said uncertainly, "I'm not going to be here long but . . . a white wine?" I flagged the bartender, who poured the insipid mess from a gallon jug. She took a tiny sip and said, "Thank you." I raised my glass.

"You know Dana Martingale, don't you?" she asked me.

"I had dinner with him last night," I told her. That seemed eons ago.

"Have you seen him here in the bar?"

"No."

"How long have you been here?"

"Since five o'clock. Made the happy hour right on the button."

"I was supposed to meet him here at five o'clock, but I'm five minutes late," she said, troubled. "I hope he didn't just pop in and leave."

My heart sank at seeing a pleasant evening being jerked out from under me and also at the prospect that behavior as churlish as the possibility she imputed to Martingale should be more or less expected. "He didn't come in," I told her. "I would have seen him." Privately, I was hoping he had just had a car accident.

Now that I looked at her more carefully it became obvious that she had fixed herself up for a "do." She was wearing a very good dark blue cocktail dress and expensive pumps that went with the "outfit." A beaded evening bag lay beside her on the bar. Her make-up had that flawlessness that bespeaks an hour or so at the mirror. The perfume was *Joy*. Behind the entire facade there lurked a fugitive sense of vulnerability. It was clear that the evening was very important to her, more important, I thought, than any evening should be to a girl as pretty as Maria Thorndyke.

"Is there going to be some kind of party here?" I hazarded.

"No." She seemed shocked at the idea. "Dana Martingale's fraternity is having a reunion down at Thornwood. He's just picking me up here."

Instead of at the rooming house, I thought. That would account for the tentative air, the nervous glances toward the door.

"He'll be here any minute," I reassured her. "Nobody'd be very late for a girl as pretty as you are."

It wasn't a pass. It wasn't even the imitation of a pass. But the startled glance she threw me suggested that men didn't say things like that to girls any more, at least not to Maria Thorndyke. I decided to get her mind off her problems and at the same time help myself out a little. "While we've got a few minutes," I said, "there's something you can help me with—my being a stranger and all." I pulled McCleod's rudimentary map out of my jacket pocket.

"I thought I might go for a little drive tomorrow," I told her. "Get to see the country a little. Somebody told me there was a pretty drive up over the mountain on a road that goes to Bluestone. You ever hear of it?"

It did get her mind off her problems. "Bluestone?" she asked me astounded. "They told you to drive to Bluestone?"

"Well, just for the drive, the scenery."

She thought this over. "I suppose there's scenery," she said dubiously. "It does go over a mountain." Her fingernail traced the curve that McCleod had drawn. "But you're not going to find much in Bluestone."

"Really?" It was my turn to be surprised. "I got the idea it was a pretty lively place where you could have a little fun."

"Fun? In Bluestone? It's about the most depressed, depressing place I can think of. The mine's only operating at about twenty-five percent. Most of the men down there have been laid off. I can't see where you'd have much fun."

"Well," I said, looking into my glass, "I like to gamble a little. I got the idea there might be a card game or something down there."

"What would they gamble with?" asked Maria, "bottle caps?"

"I'll be darned," I said ingenuously. "Maybe I got it wrong. You sure this map the guy drew goes into Bluestone?"

"Looks like it," she said, absorbed now in someone else's problem. "If that's the Mine Five road with the X on it, it goes into Bluestone all right." I handed her a pen from my shirt pocket. She began to continue the curve. "It comes down off the mountain, like this, and then it snakes around the strip mine, and then it comes all the way around to cross the highway again—" she drew in another section of the highway—"and goes into Bluestone." She drew a circle and printed BLUE-STONE over it.

Neither of us was aware that he had come up behind us and was peering over our shoulders. It was only when I raised my eyes from the map and caught the flash of white in the mirror that I realized that Dana Martingale was standing, smiling, behind us. He was done up in a tropical dinner jacket with a maroon bow tie and matching cummerbund. It was the first time I'd seen him looking what I considered to be tacky. It wasn't that the outfit was rented, it fit him too well for that, but there was a provincial, institutional air about the getup suggesting that he'd had it around for quite a while. I began to wonder what fraternity it was that he belonged to.

"So, you've met," he said. He smiled his perfectly adorable smile.

Maria, I glumly observed, responded with the appropriate adoration.

"Sorry, I'm late," he said to her. "Got tied up. But we really have to make some time to get there by seven." He took her arm. She grabbed her clutch from the bar with the other hand. "See you," he said to me, nodding pleasantly. I nodded back. They headed for the door, and this time the twitch I was watching wasn't his.

7

I had felt the road tremble beneath me.

That is why I was draped over a sapling, slowly regaining consciousness, aware of a pain like fire on my whole right side, and staring down into the depths of a ravine. It had been that odd trembling, a vibration from the soles of my feet, that had caused me to look

around and leap. I had been grazed and knocked to
one side in mid-air. So I was caught in a sapling growing from the side of the ravine rather than spread out
as a long and ugly grease spot in the road.

My only visual memory was of an enormous onrushing vehicle the size of a freight car brushing past
me.

I was very reluctant to leave the security of the sapling. My right side burned, but I experimented with
moving my right arm and then the leg and foot. Nothing was broken, it seemed, although the foot felt a bit
funny. My left side seemed to be okay.

I looked up and saw that I hadn't fallen very far
down. A few bushes offered me handholds to get back
on top. I reached for them and tested them gingerly
before I pulled myself up. I was almost to the top
before I put weight on my right foot and felt the pain
shoot through my leg. There was a little click in my
brain, however, that told me *not serious*. What I had
here was a twisted ankle, a strain at the most. When I
stood up at the top on the shoulder of the road I tested
it some more. It would walk, and in fact it would *have*
to walk. I was still clearing my head as I put a hand
up alongside it. That is when I felt the sticky ooze of
blood. I had been knocked unconscious by the side-
swipe. I looked fearfully up and down the road to see
if any more thunderous behemoths were bearing down.
The road was empty. No vibrations—nothing. This did
not mean, my throbbing head told me, that the road
would stay empty. Nonetheless, I would have to leg it
down to the junction.

The road had been just as empty when I started out,
cursing, on my way back. I had driven up to Sheriff
McCleod's X marks the spot, parked my car at the
designated widened shoulder, and began to walk toward where the wreck was alleged to be. I realized
that Welland's car would have had to be going at some
speed if it had crashed to the bottom. The slope of the
drop was not precipitous. The car would have had to
sail out over the edge.

Then I spotted it—a flash of twisted chromium. From where I stood I could pretty much see the path it had taken—out over the edge and then crashing through some trees, snapping them off, to land at the bottom, half covered with foliage. I began to ease myself down along the same pathway. The distance, negotiated by handholds in the undergrowth, was about three hundred feet. This isn't much when it's strolled along a sidewalk, but it is one hell of a drop for a flying car.

And the car itself at the bottom told the whole sad story. It had landed pretty much nose down and the splintering branch of a cottonwood had gone through the windshield. That had been the end of Charlie Welland. The plastic covered dashboard was painted with dried blood. It must have been a hell of a job getting the body out of there.

The glove compartment had burst open at the impact as had, I suspected, the opened doors of the car that hung uselessly like broken wings. I felt around inside the glove compartment and discovered what I had expected—nothing. The seats had been dislodged, first by the impact and then most probably by the sheriff's crew. I crawled into the jumbled body of the car and began searching the floor. I was looking for scraps of paper—anything. There was nothing, neither front nor back. The trunk lid had sprung open. The trunk was empty and when I lifted the carpeting there was nothing to be seen but bare metal. When I straightened up I looked at the lid itself. The interior bracing of the lid was intact. I looked around for a tool to pry the bracing loose. The people who removed the body had also removed the spare tire and the jack from the trunk compartment. I found a splintered green branch and used that as a pry bar to wrench the bracing loose. When I had torn it out, a piece of yellow paper, folded over, dropped to the deck of the trunk. It was a bill of lading headed COMPUTRIX. Listed in it were a series of items, apparently put down in a kind of shorthand that meant absolutely nothing to me. I put it in a plastic sandwich bag and shoved it in my jacket pocket.

I got pretty filthy searching under the car, running my hands through the black oil that had soaked the ground. Then I began a slow laborious search around the perimeter of the wreck, extending each time into ever widening concentric circles. I had hoped that something else might have flown out the ruptured doors at the final crash. If anything had it was no longer to be found—at least by me.

At the bottom of the ravine I was shaded from the noonday sun, but even at that the heat of impending summer was beginning to bore into me. I had gone about as far afield as anything could be flung, I thought. I came back close to the wreck and stared at it. It had been a terrible death for Charlie Welland if he had been conscious when it hit. There was no question that he was alive when the car smashed finally to the ground. The spray of blood attested to that. The car, a crushed beetle, gathered itself in secretiveness. Already the ground cover was taking over, creeping up the sides and snaking through the rents and spaces of the metal. In a little while the vines would wander through those openings; young trees would start from whatever patch of sunlight journeyed through. The car along with Welland's fate would become part of the countryside. The metal would rust and crumple. The foliage would take over and devour it. I stared at it and thought of Sandburg again: *I am the grass./Let me work.*

I felt the heat of the day a great deal more as I worked my way up the side of the ravine. It was not really a difficult climb—no mountaineering was called for. But as I worked my way up branch by branch and bush by bush, slipping and sliding in my city shoes, I thought of how difficult it must have been for the sheriff's crew to lug the body up. It wasn't the kind of straight drop where you could hoist up the wire stretcher hand over hand. It had to be laboriously snaked up inch by inch and foot by foot as I was doing here.

I clambered to the top at last and sat by the edge of

the road to smoke a cigarette. Whatever thinking I was doing at those moments was purely unconscious, absorbing and sifting what I had seen through the filter of my instincts and my unconscious memory. I flicked my cigarette into the ravine as a farewell gesture and started up toward the plateau where my car had been parked. I wasn't aware of what I wasn't seeing. I kept expecting my car to heave into view. But when I arrived at the plateau, the wide shoulder of the road that looks out over the ravine and the mountains in the distance, I realized with a shock that brought out even more sweat on my body that my car simply wasn't there.

I kept walking back and forth over the ground where my car had been, dazed, unbelieving, as if I were expecting the car to spring up out of the ground and pat me on the shoulder—a practical joke. Could it have rolled away? It didn't seem possible. The road was level here, and I had set the parking brake. I walked back in the direction I had originally come from and peered down the mountain road, half hoping to see the car. The road there was a long straightaway but no car was to be seen. The road was empty. I suppose my mouth hung open as I came to the slow astonished realization that my car had been stolen. *Stolen!* Out here in the middle of nowhere! My curses must have shocked the pure mountain air. Birds took flight. I thanked God that at least my hike back into town would be downhill. The grade was very steep.

It is very lucky for me that I had noticed the vibration. My mind was paralyzed with rage, and instead of trying to figure things out it was occupied with the invention of fresh curses vented into the ravine. The vibration began as a tingling, and then suddenly the road shook, trembled. I cast a sudden look over my shoulder in time to see the gleaming flat radiator of a truck cab that towered over me. I leaped in the only direction I could go—toward the ravine—and some part of the truck hit my right side. That was all I knew until I regained consciousness in the sapling's crutch.

I was too occupied with reassembling my body and testing my right ankle for several hundred yards to think clearly. I had hiked down the long straightaway and was beginning to round the first curve when the realization hit me. *The truck had been driving on the wrong side of the road!* The truck, a monster if I ever saw one, had been careening down a not very stable mountain road in the left-hand lane. I suddenly felt weak—aftershock. I sat on the ledge of the ravine and smoked a cigarette. It hadn't been any kind of an accident. Somebody in a truck the size of a locomotive had tried to squash me like a bug. Somebody had stolen my car and then tried to kill me. I shook a little—aftershock and shock itself.

The rest of the trip downhill consisted of my walking and revolving like a lighthouse lamp, grimacing as I accidentally put weight on the injured ankle. When I grimaced the side of my face hurt. I would now have something to show Sheriff McCleod to go along with the rat bite.

As I hiked in my revolving way around the final curve, Dooley's truck stop came into view below me. Two big rigs were parked side by side in the parking area behind it. The sight of them gave me pause. I had been concentrating on Dooley's as a goal to my halting descent from the mountain, but now I wasn't at all sure that this was a safe haven. Could one of those trucks have been the one that brushed me? Was some big murderous bastard sitting on a stool in there chuckling to himself? I thought about this as I slowly finished the descent down the side of the road and negotiated the last few hundred yards on the level straightaway that formed the beginning to the Mine Five road.

I limped into the parking area up behind the big trucks. I wasn't sure whether I could be seen from the building, nor, of course, even if anyone was watching. I got into the space between the rigs from the rear. The big open gondola trailers were empty as far as I could make out, although I couldn't see over the top of them. I walked up between the two cabs towering over my head and reached up to lay a hand on one of the massive hoods over the engine. It was cold—or at least no more than sun-warmed. I felt the other one: identical. It didn't seem likely that it had been either of these monsters that had clipped me. I headed for the building up in front.

Dooley's was a low rambling structure that in my estimation had been painted exactly once, when it was built, which would have been, it seemed to me, about fifty years ago. I limped around to the front of the building, where there were two pickup trucks parked near the door. The interior was divided into two rooms. The screen door opened on the lunchroom, which had all its cooking equipment in sight behind the counter. The lunchroom gave on to another room behind it that operated as a general store. Two men in tee shirts and jeans, both wearing Caterpillar caps, were sitting at the far end of the counter. I was happy to notice that they both had a bottle of Falstaff in front of them. Beer was available, and I was an eager customer. The man behind the bar apparently worked as a fry cook as well as bartender and counterman. He had a stained white apron on over his tee shirt and jeans. He too wore a cap with CATERPILLAR stamped across it.

All of them looked up when they heard the screen door slam, and all of them continued to stare at me as I approached the counter. I asked for a beer, and the unmusical sound of my voice gave them further cause for wonder. The counterman set a bottle of Falstaff in front of me—no glass—glasses were not de rigueur in this humble establishment. The counterman did not take his eyes off me as I took my first, long, desperate swallow of beer. I put the bottle down. "Had a little accident," I told him. "Where's the can?" He jerked his head toward the store section.

When I got a look at myself in the mirror I didn't blame them for staring. There was a lot more blood than I had supposed and some of it had leaked down on to my collar. I cleaned it all up with a soaked paper towel and saw that the damage was superficial. I would have a fairly ugly bruise over the cut but that was all. It was up near my temple—not far from the rat bite.

I went back and finished my beer and waved the counterman over for another. He had joined the young men at the other end of the bar. When he handed me my second bottle I told him, ''I wonder if you could do me a favor. I'm deaf and can't use the phone. I wonder if you would call Sheriff McCleod for me and ask him to come out here. I'll pay for the call. Tell him it's Joe Binney who asked you to call.''

It took him a few seconds to put the significance of all this together. I suppose he was wondering why the sheriff should recognize the name of a stranger. It is pretty certain that whatever accent my speech takes these days it is nothing like the way of speaking these people have down here. I was very much a stranger, a very strange stranger. On the other hand, I knew the sheriff's name, and, it would seem, he knew mine. The counterman went to make the call.

I was finishing my third beer before he arrived. The two fellows down at the end had hung around out of curiosity for as long as they could. They kept checking the Budweiser clock behind the bar, and finally got up and left. I felt the vibrating thunder of the big diesels starting up in the yard. The building trembled as they moved away. Another couple of men came in. They were a little older and somehow different from the drivers. They were wearing workshirts, although they had the regulation Caterpillar caps on them. When they sat at the counter their attitude was not that of the other two. There was no expectancy to them. They were served with Falstaff, but I noticed that they took very small sips from the bottles. They were making it last. They began some kind of earnest philosophical discussion between them. I discerned that they were unemployed.

McCleod came in and sat next to me. He was already seated before I knew he was there. I saw him shake his head to the counterman to signify that he didn't want a beer. "So," he said to me, "you got another hole in your face, huh?"

"Funny things are happening," I told him.

"Accidents are funny?"

"There wasn't any accident."

"How'd you get hurt then? Johnny said there was a lot of blood up on your head."

"Two things happened," I said. "Somebody stole my car and then somebody tried to run me down."

A very sour expression occupied McCleod's face. He looked at me. He said, "Fellas like you come down here and right away you start in with all kinds of stories. If you had an accident, say so. Don't always try to blame the other fella."

"I don't know who the other fella is," I answered. "But when I find out I'm going to have a little talk with him."

McCleod sighed. "All right," he said. "Stolen car. You know how many of those I get? You know where they're stole from? From rollin' down a hill. From drunks leavin' 'em where they can't remember. From plain ordinary borrowing. One out of ten complaints is actually stole." He fixed me with an impatient stare. "Now, just where was you car stole from?"

"Right where X marks the spot," I said. "Right where you put that X on the map you drew for me."

"On top of the hill?" I nodded. "There ain't anybody would steal a car out of there," said Sheriff McCleod. "You must have got yourself mixed up."

"I didn't get mixed up."

He sighed again. "All right. Let's hear it."

"I parked where you told me to. I went down to where I could look at the wreck. I went through it. When I came back up my car was gone."

"You find anything?" he interrupted me.

"Not a thing. Picked clean."

He nodded, satisfied.

"There's more," I told him. "When I got back to the top and saw my car was gone, I started walking back—in the left-hand lane so I could see any traffic coming on. It isn't much of a road." He nodded. "One of those big trucks came up behind me. Of course I couldn't hear it, but I could feel it—the vibration." He stared at me, half unbelieving. "I jumped just in the nick of time. It sideswiped me." I touched my bruise. "If I hadn't jumped it would have wiped me out. It was driving full speed downhill in the left-hand lane."

"It's a narrow road," the sheriff observed. "Those trucks take up a lot of it."

"They pass each other, don't they?"

"Coming around a curve they're going to cheat a little on the other side."

"This was a straightaway. There's no way he couldn't see me."

"All right," said the sheriff. "We'll go back up there, and I'll tell you what you're going to see. Either we're going to see your car just where you left it because you took the wrong path back up the ravine, or we're going to find your car in the bush somewhere where it rolled down the slope. C'mon with me."

We got into the sheriff's red-and-white car with its star on the side. The back seat was screened off with a heavy wire grill. A riot gun separated the two front seats. Gas-loaded billy clubs were nestled in each front door. It was a very official, very authoritative car. The sheriff picked up the mike to his radio and called in. He listened intently while I stared out the windshield. He had a few more things to say into the mike, and then we started up Mine Five road.

We didn't try to talk on the way up. He was a good driver and he paid attention to what he was doing. Apparently the radio squawked a few times because he tilted his head and picked up the mike to answer. We rounded the curve near the summit and drove up the straightaway where the truck had grazed me. When we got to the top I clenched my jaw. The sheriff looked at me. He was not smiling.

The blue Nova was sitting exactly where I had parked it.

8

The remainder of my Old Fitzgerald got a workout when I settled back in my room. This time I took the trouble to get some ice.

Sheriff McCleod had turned down the offer of a drink, saying it was still too early. He had followed me back to the Motor Lodge and seen me up to my room. I think he just wanted to make sure that I had calmed down and wasn't about to go rushing off to settle scores. He needn't have worried.

It was McCleod's construction of events that I had become confused down there at the bottom of the ravine. "City fellas get into the bush and they just completely get turned around," he said. "I've seen it happen a thousand times." He was convinced that I had come up the wrong pathway in the ravine, reached another level spot in the road, thought that my car was missing and had panicked. "Now when a man panics," said Sheriff McCleod, "he's apt to do anything, and yet he won't remember exactly what it was he was doing." He felt that I had probably wandered away from the edge of the road and had been nicked by the big trailer truck that had been "cheatin' a little."

That was the sheriff's reading of the situation, and he was welcome to it. Needless to say, it was not mine. However, I nodded to him in a kind of grudging agreement so that he could leave satisfied. I saw him out.

I sat on the balcony, sipped my drink, and decided what I was going to do. When I finished the drink I went down to see Ed Logan at the desk. He hadn't seen me come in with the sheriff, so that the bruise on my cheek was news to him. He seemed a bit startled by it, but wisely kept his own counsel.

"I'd like to ask a favor of you," I told him. "I'm going back up to my room, where I'll leave the door open. Now, I want to make a private phone call, but I can't do it the regular way because I'm deaf and I can't hear the other end." He nodded. "I'd like you to send up one of the chambermaids to dial the number for me, make sure my party's on the line, and then hand the phone over to me. Can you arrange that?"

Logan said, "I can do that right here at the desk, Mr. Binney."

"No," I said. "Thank you just the same, but I have to make the call from my room, where I have all the papers and notes. I'd like to do it the way I said, if it's all right with you."

"Certainly. I'll send somebody up right away."

I went back to my room, fixed another drink, and waited.

A young black woman in a chambermaid's outfit appeared at the open door to my room. "Come in," I invited her. I stood up and held out a five-dollar bill. She regarded it with suspicion. "What I want you to do," I told her, "is dial a long-distance number on the telephone for me. I'm deaf so that I can't hear whether or not the other party answers on a regular telephone. I want you to dial this number and ask for Edna Purvis. When you're sure she's on the line, tell her that Joe Binney wants to speak with her and to hold on. Then hand the phone over to me and close the door behind you. Got that?"

She nodded, but there was still suspicion in her eyes. I got the feeling that this was a young woman on whom a lot of tricks had been played. "Back home," I explained, "I have a special telephone for deaf people that I can use. But it's special equipment and they don't have it here." I smiled encouragingly, forgetting the cut bruise on my cheek and my no-doubt fearsome voice.

She picked up the phone and looked at it as if it might suddenly spray acid in her face. Then she picked up the note with the number I had written on it and decided to dial. Was this going to be a dirty phone call? No. Whoever answered was legit. Her face relaxed. She spoke into the mouthpiece and then handed the phone to me. She went out holding my five-dollar bill and closed the door.

"Edna," I said into the mouthpiece, "I hate doing this but I've got some things to tell you and some things I want you to do.

"Now, keep cool, but somebody tried to rub me out today." I paused to let her calm down. "I'm perfectly all right. I wasn't really hurt. It wasn't a rumble. I didn't get into a fight or anything. Somebody stole my car when I wasn't looking and then tried to run me over in the road—the same road that Charlie Welland was killed on. It was all very slick, very tricky. But the whole thing makes me think that maybe Charlie Welland didn't just have an accident. Or if he did, the accident was caused on purpose."

I would have given anything at that moment to hear Edna's voice, something I have never heard nor never will hear. The telephone felt like an ice cube in my hand.

"Now what I want you to do is this. There's a thirty-eight in my bottom right-hand drawer with the holster. There's also a box of cartridges in there. I want you to take the whole thing out of my desk, pack it very carefully with a lot of newspaper so it doesn't slide around, and send it down here to the Motor Lodge. You got my change of address?" Stupid question to which I couldn't hear the answer. I gave her the address, repeating the telegram I'd sent. "It can't come through the mail, of course, but maybe UPS—wait." I paused. "I've got a better idea. Take the box down to the Port Authority Terminal and send it by Trailways Bus Freight. I saw a Trailways sign coming through here, and I'll go down and pick it up at the bus terminal here.

"Now, look, kid, there's nothing very terrible going on down here so don't get any wild ideas. I just think it would be a good idea if I had a little heat in case of an emergency. I thought this was all going to be checking out sales slips, you know? But it's got a little more complicated.

"Oh, and by the way, Edna, I don't know what you've turned up on that list I gave you, but I found a packing slip in Welland's car from a company called Computrix." I spelled it out for her, and gave her the address and the phone number on the slip. "See if you can get them to tell you if Welland was a customer, and if he was, how much he spent and what he bought. I can't make head nor tail out of what's written on the packing slip. You can start checking right away, and I'll mail you the slip in the morning."

I thought for a minute. "In case you're wondering, Edna, yes, I'm sorry I didn't bring you along with me. But it's too late for all that now. Just do as I ask, and I'll probably have this thing wrapped up in a few days and we can stick Carlson for a sizable bill. Take it easy, kid, and don't forget to check out that Computrix. I'm going to hang up now." And, reluctantly, hang up I did.

The ice in my drink had pretty much dissolved. I put another cube in it and went out on the balcony. I sat there sipping my drink and staring at the green hills in the distance. I confess, now, that I didn't really know what to do with myself. It was late in the afternoon, nearing the happy hour, and even if it had been a bright brand new morning I still wouldn't have known what to do with myself. Everything needed thinking through. Unfortunately, my garish room was not a place where I wanted to sit and think things through. There were interesting stories on the wallpaper—Mississippi river boats, what have you. I did not want to be told stories by wallpaper, particularly stories that recur over and over at every seam. I did not want to sit at a tiny desk and study logic diagrams by the light of one of those hideous, oversized crockery lamps (are they oversized so they can't be stolen?). Back at the office, I would have been able to bounce my apprehensions off Edna, bless her. In my apartment, I would have had all the comforts of home, including my walls full of books and my big dining room table where I do most of my serious work. In this room, as in all motel rooms, I felt like a fly stuck on a pin. This is what doesn't go into expense accounts, the dead space, the dead time, the period when the soul has succumbed to the smothering enclosure of vinyl and paintings of sad-eyed clowns.

I decided that I would join the happy hour. I cleaned up and changed my clothes.

The bar was just as barren as it had been at the opening of the last happy hour I'd attended there. In fact, it was worse. I was the only customer. Nonetheless, there was the bartender, a human face, not a sad-eyed clown, to look at. I ordered my drink and reflected that since most work stops at five o'clock, it was probably still a bit early for the clientele. The bartender served me, noticed the bruise on my cheek, and said nothing. Sure enough, five minutes later a pair of young men with a clerkish air about them came steaming in. They wore the cheap sports jackets and slacks of low-grade office workers, but they talked animatedly—they were on the way up. They were full of smiles—happy—happy. I got the feeling that the half-priced drinks were the only ones that they could afford, and they were making the most of it. More serious and sober types began to filter through the doorway. They were better dressed, but not a hell of a lot better. They wore suits, white shirts and sober ties. Most of them had glasses, pudge, and thinning hair. They too laughed and joked, but it did not look animated. There was something guarded about everything they said or did. I supposed that these people came from one of the monster chemical plants that now formed the economic base of the town. They were very, very different from the men I had seen down at Dooley's. This was an utterly different race of people. Their complexions seemed to have absorbed some of the fluorescence that lights their offices.

I was astounded to see her come in. This time there

was no delay in recognition. I saw her face as she came through the door. This time it was not carefully made-up. It was the workaday face. Her clothes, too, were her working clothes—another blouse, another skirt.

She sat at the bar and ordered something. It wasn't white wine because I saw the bartender reach for a bottle of vodka. She waited with an expression that was weary and forlorn as he fixed her a Bloody Mary, complete with oversized celery stalk. I let her take a hearty sip of it and even munch on the celery before I picked up my drink and moved down the bar.

"Hello," I said. "I didn't realize you were a regular here."

She regarded me with weary scorn. "I'm not a regular here," she said.

"Are you meeting someone here?" I asked her in all innocence.

She smiled a close-lipped rather desperate smile. "Well," she said, "I've met you, haven't I?" She took another belt of the Bloody Mary and crunched the celery with a savage bite.

"Do you mind if I sit down?" I suggested mildly, nodding toward the stool.

She shrugged and made the sort of gesture that implies, "I can't stop you." I eased my frame on to the stool next to her and put my elbows on the bar. "Doctor Binney has made a diagnosis," I told her.

"A diagnosis?"

"You have a hangover and you are sick of men."

"Doctor Binney has hit it right on the nose." She took another swig of the cocktail and pushed the remains of the celery stalk disgustedly away from her.

"Would you have dinner with Dr. Binney if he promises to speak soothingly and absolutely promises not to come on like the Rover Boys?"

She turned to look at me and there was an almost pleading look in her eyes. "I really am awfully tired," said Maria Thorndyke. "I wouldn't be much company."

"You have to eat something somewhere," I urged her. "Particularly if you have a hangover. One or two of those," I nodded toward her drink, "will set you up for a while, but unless you get some solid food in you, you'll feel even worse tomorrow. Dr. Binney knows all about it."

"I only got about four hours sleep last night," she protested sadly.

"It must have been a hell of a ball down at Thornwood," I observed.

"Yes, yes," she said wearily. "It was a hell of a ball, all right." She finished her drink. I finished mine in sympathy and semaphored for another pair.

When the fresh drinks were set in front of us and the bartender had moved away I asked her, "Are you all this beat up just from having fun, or was there something else?"

She fastened her eyes on mine. She took a sip of the cocktail and said, "You're a real mind reader, Dr. Binney." She put the glass down. "I may not have a job tomorrow."

"Poor performance on the job today?"

"Poor performance on things I thought had nothing to do with the job last night."

"Ah," I thought it over. "Mr. Martingale wanted his hundred and fifteen pounds of flesh, did he?"

Genuine laughter rearranged her face into something much prettier. "You guessed my weight," she said.

"I'm very good at that." Then I said cautiously, "Mr. Martingale seemed to me the kind of fellow who usually gets what he wants."

"Not from me he didn't," said Maria Thorndyke. She took a defiant sip of her cocktail.

"Actually, I don't know very much about him," I offered reflectively. "I had dinner with him. It was supposed to be a business dinner, but my business didn't seem to interest him much. I don't think we exchanged a hundred words, all told."

"Not enough money," said Maria. I had a little trouble reading her because her face was turned away.

"Did you say not enough money?" I asked her. She turned to me and nodded that this was so.

"That seems strange." I was genuinely puzzled. "Carlson House is a pretty big outfit. We sell textbooks all over the country."

"I don't think textbooks are high on Dana's list of priorities," said Maria.

This seemed even more mysterious to me. "What the hell," I said. "He's Superintendent of Education, isn't he? What could be more important?"

She turned to face me completely. "Building contracts for new schools," she said. "Demolition contracts for old schools. Repair contracts for other schools. Roofing contracts, equipment contracts, supplies, desks, furniture. Heating contracts, blacktop paving contracts. Building maintenance contracts. Textbooks are really a very small part of it."

"So he lets Milly—Miss Rutledge handle all the textbooks?"

"Oh, no. I didn't mean that. She passes judgment on the books, all right, but then the final purchase agreement goes through Dana. Everything goes through Dana. And it would seem," she added with a wry smile, "Dana goes through everything."

"I had a hard time figuring him as Superintendent of Education," I admitted. "I mean, he seems awfully young to have worked his way up to something like that."

She nearly choked on her Bloody Mary. "Worked his way up? Dana?" She put her glass down carefully. "Dana's a political appointee. The superintendent's job was bought and paid for by his family by a political contribution that would curl your hair."

"Is he qualified? I mean, does he have a degree in education and all?"

"He's got a degree, but it's in administration."

"MBA?"

"AA. An associate's degree from one of the local two-bit outfits."

I thought about this carefully. "Degree or no de-

gree,'' I said, ''he didn't strike me as being a
dummy.''

''I didn't say he was a dummy,'' she objected. ''Not
going away to school might have been a very smart
move on Dana's part.'' She shrugged and looked into
her drink. ''The MBA, after all, is there in order to
get you a good job, to give you entrée. Dana knew he
was going to get a good job. He already had entrée.
His power base is here. Why should he leave it? Besides,'' she added with a grim little smile, ''I also
think he just wanted to hang around and raise hell.''

''Who can blame him?'' I smiled back. ''But you
said last night it was a fraternity reunion. What kind
of fraternity is at . . .''

''That little dump on the edge of town? None. It
wasn't really a fraternity thing at all. It's some quasi-
military thing that's historically connected to the
county. I hear it was a big deal that they let Dana in.
That's why he was so eager to get there on time and
all that.''

''This all gets curiouser and curiouser. First you
suggest that the guy comes out of pots of money, and
then you tell me he's pleased as punch to be let into
some kind of local grungy outfit . . .''

''The Martingale money is new money,'' said Maria. ''And it's not real money, if you know what I
mean. It doesn't come out of the ground, the land. It
comes out of a chemical plant that they don't even
own. I mean they're just very high up in the corporate
structure, and they've invested wisely, and they've got
a lot of money. But it's not real money. I think the
family's only been here for about thirty years. Dana's
the great white hope who's going to establish them.''
She took a sip of her cocktail and set it down. ''I don't
think it's going to work. I think he's too eager—way,
way too eager.''

Something in her expression made me say, ''I hope
that your frolic last night didn't include a lot of walking.''

''Oh, no.'' She tilted her head up. ''He drove me

home all right. But he had a great parting shot when he reached over to open the door of the car for me. He said, 'As far as any future in education in this county is concerned, Missy—' I love that term, Missy—'you can forget it.' That's why I might not have a job tomorrow.''

"Aw," I began, trying to reassure her. "I don't think Milly—Miss Rutledge would let anything like that happen, would she?"

"Not if she could help it," Maria agreed, troubled. "But it's very hard to know where her authority begins and ends."

"From what I've seen," I said warmly, "it looks to be considerable. She looks to me as if she was the whole outfit."

"Well, she is and she isn't. She's where she is now exactly because she's always known when to take her losses."

"But I don't see how they could get along . . . I mean, who could replace her?"

"That's not really the question," said Maria. "The question is, who cares? Milly cares very much about educating the kids around here. She feels responsible, literally, for their education. She is—that dreaded word—serious. Nobody would want to let Milly go because she does all the work. But if push came to shove, if it came to demonstrating clout—yes, they'd let her go. She knows that. She's past retirement anyway, way past. It wouldn't be hard for them to make her take retirement."

"Why is she hanging on?"

"As I said—responsibility." Maria paused and took another sip. "But there's another thing, too. She's hard at work on that history of Caunotaucarius County, and it seems to mean a great deal to her. She's really a professional historian, you know. She was trained at Oberlin. That's where I met her, at a meeting of the Historical Association."

"You went to Oberlin?"

"No. Case Western Reserve. I got an MA in history

and I went to the meeting looking for a job, like most of the other people. I heard Milly give a talk on the value of local history, and I thought she was marvelous. I met her at an after hours cocktail party and said so. And she offered me this job down here. I jumped at it. It's not so awfully far from home, you know. I'm from Akron.''

''Where the tires come from.''

''Used to, anyway.''

I stepped back a few words. ''If she's so serious about writing history, why would she keep the job? I mean, if she retired she could devote full time . . .''

Maria giggled. ''Milly is embezzling,'' she said. I was thunderstruck.

''She uses me to go over to the county courthouse and dig out records, old records. I bring them back and she reads them, copies out what she wants, and I take them back. Nobody questions me because I work for Miss Milly. Nobody questions Milly. But she uses about ten percent of the salary the county pays me to go and fetch records. The typing I do for her I do after hours, on my own time. And I'd be happy to do it for nothing, but she insists on paying me out of her own money. It's a pretty small embezzlement.'' Maria laughed, twirling her glass, ''She's going to donate the history and all the proceeds from it to the Board of Education.

''I've learned so much from Milly . . . So much of the actual nuts and bolts of scholarship that I . . .'' Her head jerked up suddenly. ''You're being paged,'' she said. ''They're calling Mr. Joe Binney, please come to the front desk.''

I muttered, ''I wonder who's nuts enough to page a deaf man,'' and got off my stool. As I headed toward the door, however, I saw a tall, blond, middle-aged man in a gray business suit coming unmistakably toward me. I waited where I was. He stopped and stared at me suspiciously. Finally he asked, ''Are you Mr. Joe Binney?''

I admitted that I was—not without some trepidation,

however. The man's expression, the whole carriage of his body, imparted an attitude of threat mixed with impatience and poorly concealed interior rage. He stared at me for an uncomfortable length of time and then gathered himself to speak. He said, "Mr. Danford requests the pleasure of your company at seven." The sentence was gritted out as if it cost him a thousand dollars a word.

I was totally at sea. I began, "Well, Jeez, that's very nice but I . . ." when I felt a sharp dig below my left floating rib. Maria had got off the stool and come between us. She looked up at the big man in the expensive suit and said something to him I couldn't catch, but he nodded a shrugging assent. She turned to me then and said, "Joe, this is Mr. Kenneth Parnell, who is general manager of the Pendragon Coal Company."

I extended my hand. "Nice to meet you, Mr. Parnell." He seemed to regard my extended hand almost as an insult. Finally, however, he forced himself to touch it. I looked inquiringly at Maria. She seemed to have stars in her eyes. She said to Parnell, "Mr. Danford is inviting Mr. Binney to dinner? At the mansion?"

"That's right," said Mr. Parnell, and in his eyes behind the other emotions there entered the doubt of what he was saying. It was clear that he couldn't really believe it.

I said to Parnell, "This is unexpected but I've already invited this young lady to dinner, and I'm afraid I can't . . ." but there was a repeat of the sharp dig in my ribs.

Parnell said, "I'm sure that she is welcome." His face now had closed up completely.

"Thank you very much," said Maria Thorndyke. She was radiant.

"You'll be expected then at seven," said Parnell. For the first time his face expressed something other than threat. He was happy to have discharged his mis-

sion. He turned on his heel and left. I got the feeling
that he wasn't crazy about being a messenger boy.

I asked Maria, "What the hell is going on?"

She said, "Everything!" She paused. "My God,"
she said, her eyes jumping with horror. "I can't go
like this. Wait for me here. I'll be back in twenty
minutes." She ran out of the bar.

9

Mansion was a euphemism. The place was a castle. It
rose up in front of our windshield on an eminence that
surveyed the broad avenue below it. Towers, peaks,
and crenellations, punctuated by tall lightning rods and
chimneys, capped an enormous pile of rough brown
granite that curved into round towers at the corners
and offered up bays, dormers, and setbacks that broke
up the sheer mass of the building's front. The eye
jumped from peak to tower to facade, looking for a
rhyme or reason to the architecture, some hint of period, of style, of logic. There was none that I could
see. Was there an effect? I tried to sort it out as we
drove up toward the porte cochere—brute power and
defiance.

It wasn't really fair to get tossed up against a place
like this without preparation, although I don't know
what could have prepared me for it. We had decided
to come in Maria's automobile, a beat-up dusty little
Toyota. After all, she knew the way, and something
whispered in the back of my mind that enough tricks
had been played with my blue Nova for one day. It
had taken Maria a little more than a half hour to dash
over to her rooming house, get dressed in a good rose-
colored business suit (I got the idea then that her ward-
robe was not extensive). She filled me in as much as
she could over one quick final drink at the bar. Con-

versation in the Toyota had been almost impossible as she sped across town to a side unknown to me. We swept up a broad avenue past setback houses that were in themselves impressive establishments.

The mansion (or castle) was the home of the Danford family, and the Danford family were founders of Pendragon Coal, now expanded into Pendragon Industries. Pendragon owned most of the coal in this tier of the state. Where there was no coal it merely owned the land. Pendragon, Maria gave me to understand, was what she had meant in speaking of Martingale's coming from new money. Pendragon was not new money. Its history was ancient for these parts, fabulous. Gideon Danford and his wife, Dorothy, who herself came from extreme wealth, lived alone except for servants in this massive pile. They had produced one son, Elliot, who lived in New York City and ran the trading aspects of Pendragon from his offices there. The Danfords, Maria reckoned, must be in their late sixties or early seventies. The old man had not quite retired, but it was clear that he was handing over the reins little by little to his scion. It had been tacitly assumed that Elliot, in time, would give up the New York office and bring his family back to live in the Danford fortress.

This tacit assumption was not shared, Maria told me, by the forbidding Mr. Parnell, whom I had just met. Gossip was rife that a power struggle was going on between Parnell and Elliot Danford. It was also understood that the old man took neither side in the strangled little war but watched the conflict benignly from on high.

Maria put her money on Elliot. The Danfords, she emphasized, her eyes glowing, *were* Caunotaucarius County. They owned it.

That was the thumbnail portfolio I carried with me up to the gates of the mansion, but in fact it explained very little. What in the name of God did one of the giants of American industry want with my presence at his dinner table? Whatever the reason might be it did not seem to engage Maria's attention. For her it was enough that we were going. She had driven like a demon (demoness?) to get us across the sleepy town in ample time. There was more than mere curiosity or social advancement at work here, I reasoned. For one thing, the simple fact of her having dined at the Danfords' might be proof against any machinations inspired by young Martingale. Something would click, I was certain, in that little chromium brain of his.

We left the car looking like an abused plaything under the great arch of the porte cochere and went up to the huge double doors together. The doorbell almost made me laugh. It was a simple, tiny, round old-fashioned doorbell sporting a button of the kind that had been pushed by millions of vacuum cleaner salesmen. It didn't seem at all adequate to gain entry to something as wild and powerful as this. However, it did the job. Half of the portal swung inward and we were greeted by a handsome gray-haired black man who was wearing a white starched porter's coat. I sighed in relief that at least the servants were not in livery.

"Joe Binney and Miss Maria Thorndyke to see Mr. Danford," I said. I had the feeling that I should have presented a card—engraved.

"Mr. Danford will see you in the library," said the porter-butler (actually, he was the majordomo as it later turned out). He led us through an extensive foyer and into what I supposed can only be called the great hall. It was a ballroom of gigantic proportions. The parquet floor was decorated with huge Oriental rugs and surrounded by statuary of a distinctly Victorian cast. The hall was lighted by three chandeliers suspended from a white plaster ceiling that bore a grand design of foliage spreading outward from each center. At the far end of the hall a grand staircase swept upward in a curve. What took the eye, however, was not the broad curve of the staircase with its gleaming marble steps, but the gigantic stained glass window on the western wall that shed a glowing pattern of multicol-

ored light across the staircase and the floor beyond.
The window took up two stories in height, from the
bottom of the stairs to the ceiling of the second floor.
It portrayed a knight in shining armor leaning on his
sword in prayer. The knight was unmistakably Galahad.
The style was unmistakably derived from Burne-
Jones. It didn't have Burne-Jones's clarity of line—
that had got lost in translation—but the attitude, the
purity, humility, and sanctity were all there in the
curved bow of the shoulders and the meek aspect of
the enormous handsome head with its fall of yellow
hair. Around Galahad there grew a thousand vines and
blossoms, almost *milles fleurs*. The colors, driven by
the powerful evening western sun, radiated shards of
green, blue, ruby, gold, and a kind of crystalline white
that shone like snowy silver on the surfaces below.

Both Maria and I stopped in our tracks to look at it.
The butler, missing our footfall, also stopped and
turned back to us. He smiled, "Quite a spectacle, isn't
it?" he said. He waited patiently until we had gathered
ourselves, and then we followed him to a room off to
the right of the staircase.

When he opened the door to the library he paused
briefly and must have announced us, although I
couldn't see his face. The man behind the massive
carved mahogany desk stood up immediately and came
around to greet us. The room was not terribly large,
given the scale of the house, but in terms of size it
dwarfed the man coming toward us. This was in terms
of size only, however. There was a magnetism, a dy-
namism to this small gray-suited white-haired man with
his pink cheeks and guileless blue eyes that had the
effect of electrifying me. The whole immense pile of
a house was subjugated to him. It simply vanished. He
crossed the room and shook my hand, touching my
shoulder with his left. "Mr. Binney," he said. "Delighted that you could come this evening." He took
Maria's proffered hand. "Miss Thorndyke," he said.
"Delighted to meet you." He indicated two Hepple-
white chairs drawn up around a small glowing mahog-

any table. "Please sit down," he said. When we were seated he relaxed in a leather wing chair opposite us.

Mr. Danford beamed at us from his chair while I tried to take him in. The suit he was wearing was of the old-style Ivy League of the three-button jacket variety. There was not a spare inch of material or thread in its tailoring; it was absolutely unrelenting in its narrow shoulders and straight sober sides. A modern Chinese politician could have worn it without giving it a thought. The shirt was white and old. The tie was a sober blue with a pattern that had long since sunk back into its fundament.

Mr. Danford let us get as comfortable as we could—actually we were both sitting on the down edge of the Hepplewhites—and said, "I suppose you're wondering why I offered this rather presumptuous invitation."

Maria and I both sat at attention.

"You see," said the old man smiling, "I learned today that you had an accident on the Mine Five road."

Maria stiffened. I was astonished. "I'm sorry that Sheriff McCleod bothered you . . ." I began.

"Oh, it wasn't Sheriff McCleod who told me." He waved it away. "I got a call from my son Elliot in New York."

Things were moving far too rapidly for my taste.

"It so happens that David Carlson and Elliot are old friends from their days at Princeton together. Now, when you called your secretary—a Miss Purvis I believe?—she immediately got in touch with David and demanded that something should be done. It seems that she has become quite good friends with David."

This was certainly news to me. "I—I didn't know that," I faltered. Some detective! Maria was staring at me.

"David then called Elliot and explained the situation—particularly the location of the accident. This was enough to alarm Elliot, and so he called me and asked me to have you over."

"But why should the location—"

Mr. Danford held up a small white hand. "Mine Five Road really has no purpose other than to serve the Pendragon strip mine. It is a public road, of course. We deeded it over to the county long ago. But almost never does any truck use that road except Pendragon trucks or supply trucks on Pendragon business. Even then," he continued, "the supply trucks usually come up to the pit from Bluestone.

"So," he heaved a little sigh accompanied by a wan smile, "if you had an accident involving a truck on Mine Five Road, it must almost certainly have involved one of the Pendragon trucks. And if we're involved, I want to know about it."

"Actually," I said, "I didn't see the truck, and I certainly haven't been thinking about a lawsuit or anything like that. Sheriff McCleod seems to think it might have all been my fault. And in fact—"

He cut me off. "Elliot was rather emphatic," he said. "He told me David had complained that one of his associates had already been killed on that road, and he certainly didn't want to see a repetition of it."

Associate! That isn't how Carlson had described Charie Welland to me. I also found it rather heady to be elevated to the rank of an associate of David Carlson.

"So what we decided was this," said Mr. Danford, "and I must add that a good deal of it came from the very strong suggestions of Miss Purvis—Edna is her first name?—that you stay here in the Danford house until this is cleared up." He waved his hand and smiled, again rather wanly. "There is quite enough room," he said, "for us to put you up without any trouble."

"Well gee," I broke in, "I don't know . . ."

"Miss Purvis also very strongly suggested that some means of communication between you and her be set up here—special equipment, that is, because of your disability." He gave me a look then that told me more about him than anything else I'd seen. It was not a look of sympathy or contempt, but a look of deep, penetrating interest. The look signified that he wondered why I should have been singled out to sustain this kind of handicap. I had noticed this kind of look before as a brief flash in the big face of Reverend Barlow.

"I've tried to order one of those teletype machines they have for the deaf," he said, "but they don't seem to be readily available down here. However, the local telephone office does have something called a Code-Com, which they've agreed to install tomorrow morning." He raised his eyebrows in the tacit inquiry as to whether this was satisfactory.

"Code-Com," I assured him, "is just fine. It's what we use back in New York. It operates more or less like a telegraph key, but it's a flashing light instead of clickety click."

"Then you will be able to communicate with Miss Purvis?"

"Oh, yes. Thank you." I did not add that what I was going to communicate to Miss Purvis might very well melt the wires between here and New York. However, I did rouse myself to say, "You know, Mr. Danford, we came over here in Maria's automobile because she knew the way. I didn't know that I would be asked to stay the night. So I'm afraid I'll have to leave with Maria this evening, pick up my car and things, and come back tomorrow morning."

"I'd rather you didn't do that," said Mr. Danford. His expression had not changed, and of course I could not hear his voice, but there was something in the whole set of his body that absolutely floored any idea of contradicting him. "If you will give Johnson the keys to your car he can pick it up for you tomorrow morning when he goes in with Irma for the shopping. He can also pack the things in your room and bring them here."

"Well," I said. "This is all pretty drastic. I'm sorry Edna got everybody so stirred up about this . . ."

"I'm having Ken Parnell check into just who exactly was on the road this afternoon in any of our trucks. It really shouldn't be too difficult to get to the bottom of this. But until we do, I'd like you to stay here as my guest. As I mentioned before, Mine Five Road was once our personal property. To this day, however, we feel gravely responsible for anything that happens there."

He turned to Maria. "Miss Thorndyke, do you feel that you can drive home safely by yourself this evening?"

Aside from the greeting, these were the first words he'd offered directly to Maria. They appeared to startle her. "Oh, yes," she answered. "Certainly." But I could see a certain disappointment in her face. I think she had been planning on staying the night herself.

I saw Mr. Danford look up toward the doorway then and I turned to see the majordomo at the door. "Dinner is served," he announced.

"Would you like to take the elevator up?" Mr. Danford asked me, "or shall we take the stairs? I usually climb it to keep my figure." There was a twinkling smile behind the words.

"The stairs by all means," I answered. We swept up past the rapt image of Galahad and went to the dining room.

10

Even though the table was twelve feet long and almost half that in breadth it took up only a small part of the dining room. From the area surrounding it and number of chairs ranged against the wall I divined that it extended infinitely for state occasions. It was covered with a white linen tablecloth beneath which massive oak legs planted themselves firmly on the floor. Dinner was to be served from the huge oak sideboard, where the majordomo (I guessed that this was the Johnson that Danford had mentioned) was arranging things. At his side observing the procedure was a tall thin woman with gray hair in a beautifully cut light green summer dress. She had one of those finely modeled equine faces that requires the light of sharp intelligence to animate. Her expression was not animated. Danford introduced us and Mrs. Danford responded dutifully. Johnson held the chair at one end of the table for Mrs. Danford. Danford seated himself at the other end and Maria and I sat at opposing sides of the broad, thick table.

The room was paneled and the ceiling coffered. What held the eye, however, with almost mesmerizing force was the profusion of carving on the thick pilasters separating the panels and on the door frames and window frames. It was repeated in the mantelpiece of the huge fireplace at the end of the room. The wood was alive with foliage. Leaves and vines wound their desperate way in all directions as if attempting to escape the wood itself. Half hidden in the undergrowth were faces and figures of animals—not really identifiable by species—but brute ferocious faces of mythical beasts, some of which seemed half-human in the intensity of their glaring eyes. In the capitals of the pilasters and the corners of the door and window frames the complexity of the design became absolutely impenetrable. Leaves, vines, faces, and carved letters seemed to form and disappear under my staring.

My stare was interrupted by a flash of white. Johnson was serving. I turned to Danford at the head of the table to apologize for my absence. ''The carving,'' I said, ''is really fascinating. I've never seen anything like it.''

He smiled gently. ''Very old-fashioned these days, I'm afraid. More of a curiosity than anything else.'' He shrugged apologetically. Then, suddenly, he clasped his hands and bowed his white head. Grace was about to be said. I meekly followed suit, although

I had to roll my eyes up a bit to see when he would come to an end. It was lengthily said.

When it was finished I turned my attention to the table. Fruit cup was placed in front of me. The table-cloth was very old, yellowing slightly, and in the hem near my lap I could see a few stitches where it had been mended. The dinnerware was quite ordinary, of no identifiable brand or pattern, except for one thing. There was a plate or dish or bowl for absolutely everything, including the butter shell to hold the individual pat of butter, and everything matched. The silverware was ordinary silver plate—I forbore to look at the brand stamped on the back—but again, there was service for everything and it all matched.

We finished the fruit cup quickly. It had almost certainly come from a can and had been doled out with a careful spoon, perhaps even to the counting of the Queen Anne cherries. Soup was served with wafers, and although I could not see the pattern in the bottom of the bowl, it was very thin soup indeed of an indistinguishable flavor. The wafer I crumbled into it had more sustenance than the soup. Salad was served—a few limp leaves of lettuce, a slice of tomato, and a couple of capers. The light coating of oil and vinegar gave it whatever strength it had. The fish course was an utter mystery to me. It was a *piece* of fish, boiled into anonymity and disguised with a thick white sauce that tasted mostly of Pillsbury's all-purpose flour. It lacked the verve of library paste. I got it down and tasted the contents of my tumbler—water, not very cold water. Adam's ale.

I must say that I admired Johnson. I don't think I had ever seen anyone serve so expertly. He had enormous distances to cover in speeding around the table and yet he did it all with dispatch and without any show of haste. He might have been on roller skates.

The preliminaries had daunted, but also whetted my appetite. I looked forward to the entrée, which I saw Johnson preparing on the sideboard. When it was served, however, my cheeks caved inward. On my plate was a small slice of beef—roasted or boiled, it did not matter—with a streak of gravy artfully drawn down the center of it. Completing the circle of the plate were a small boiled potato with a sprig of parsley, one half of a boiled carrot and a tiny mound of string beans that had been cooked to grayness.

The beasts behind the foliage in the woodwork looked on with the vitreous stare of famine.

Dessert was rice pudding dotted with a few raisins. The coffee was a light mahogany, both in color and flavor.

My eyes had been searching the sideboard so eagerly that I hadn't been paying strict attention to the conversation going on among the Danfords and Maria. In fact, I never registered anything that Mrs. Danford had said at all. It was impossible not to notice the change in Maria. From the exhausted young woman I had met at the bar that evening she had changed to a brilliant-eyed, highly energized socialite. Maybe Henry Kissinger was right. Maybe power is the greatest aphrodisiac. At any rate, Maria glowed under Danford's attention.

What I picked up from the conversation was that Danford had known, apparently from Parnell, that Maria worked for the Board of Education. He asked her what she did there. When she told him that she was administrative assistant to Milly Rutledge he became quite mellow. "Milly Rutledge," he exclaimed. "What a good old soul she is. Really the backbone of the Board of Education. Has been for years. The whole town is very proud of her, although it wasn't unexpected. I remember that my father had an eye on her career. He was quite surprised when she went north to Oberlin instead of to the State University."

"Well," Maria said brightly, "they offered her a scholarship, didn't they?"

"Yes, I believe they did," the old man agreed. "Of course we always had a fund set aside at Pendragon for likely youngsters, but I believe Milly just leapfrogged it and went up north."

We were into the fish by then. I could see that a tiny cloud had shadowed his features at the thought of Milly's leapfrogging. It was whisked away with a kindly smile, however, as he asked Maria, "And you, do you come from Oberlin too?"

"Oh, no," she answered. "Case Western Reserve."

"Western Reserve!" He beamed. "Then you must have gone to Flora Stone Mather College."

Maria was puzzled. "Well—I did take some of my courses there . . ." Then she caught on. "Of course it's all co-educational now," she said. "Like Radcliffe or Barnard."

Again, the faintest shadow of a cloud passed over his face. Then he shrugged it off and said as much to me as to Maria, "You know, the family that endowed that college are the very same Mathers of the Massachusetts Bay Colony—Increase Mather and Cotton Mather and so on. My great-grandfather knew the family quite well when they were in Cleveland and my grandfather remembered being taken back up to Cleveland in the wintertime and seeing the great sleigh races they had along millionaire's row on Euclid Avenue."

Over the entrée he continued, "The Mathers had a great house on Euclid Avenue, along with the Rockefellers, the Hannas, and the Otises. It was the thing to do. My great-grandfather thought seriously of building one there. The Mathers, you know, were in iron ore. My great-grandfather, of course, went in for coal. Something made him decide to build the house down here instead of on Euclid Avenue, but I assure you the character and spirit of the house are purely Euclid Avenue—rather an anomaly down here, as you can see. A strange old monster. A relic, really. Most of the grand old houses in Cleveland have been torn down. It's all changed. And, in fact, they didn't last long. How strange that seems. But things change—they change—and keep on changing." He cast a regretful glance at the woodwork.

The vague air of regret lasted through the entrée.

Conversation was more desultory with Maria asking rather bright questions about architecture (the name Schweinfurth was mentioned, but I forget in what context), the number of rooms in the house (Danford thought around sixty-five or seventy—more than the Mather Mansion, which had forty-five), and whether the stone was native (it was not; it was imported from God knows where).

After coffee I was somewhat panic stricken. I had been starving when called to dinner, and now, having finished a seven-course meal (if you include the coffee) I was still hungry. There was not another grain of food in sight. It had all been whisked off the sideboard and sent back down in the dumbwaiter. Since there was no food, I desperately wanted a cigarette—at least to numb the nerve ends in my stomach. There was, however, no ashtray in sight. I was almost hysterically grateful when Danford rose and said, "Shall we go into the parlor?"

Johnson threw back the sliding doors to the parlor and when we entered that cavernous room, in which a honey-colored grand piano, a Bechstein, was almost lost, my eyes darted desperately from point to point in search of a smoking stand or an ashtray of any kind. They did not exist. We had all gathered around a settee and a few chairs in the center of the room, which more and more resembled a vintage hotel lobby to me, when I said to Mrs. Danford, "Would anyone mind if I had a cigarette?"

Mrs. Danford did not exactly recoil, but she did become immensely still. Mr. Danford's face swam up before me with the arched eyebrows of innocent inquiry. He said, "You smoke, do you?"

"Yes," I answered firmly. "I do."

"Let's move over here, then," said Danford. He gestured to Johnson, who had followed us in, and all of us went to an arrangement of chairs near the window. Danford indicated a chair for me at the window, and Johnson stepped over to raise it so that the evening air from the outside washed over me. He then went to a small cabinet nearby and extracted a tiny tin ashtray, which he handed to me. On it was stamped ST. LOUIS WORLD'S FAIR. I accepted it gratefully and lighted up. The others sat in a kind of semicircle, Mrs. Danford the furthest away, almost lost in the shadows. The three of them watched me with a kind of fascination as I lit my cigarette, inhaled, and blew a cloud of smoke into the out of doors.

When they had finished gaping at me—Maria's eyes were wide and radiant—Danford turned to her and said, "Speaking of Milly Rutledge, you know, I'm amazed that she hasn't retired by now. It's been years and years, hasn't it?"

"I'm sure she's planning to," said Maria. "But I guess she wants to finish up her work first."

"She has some plan for the Board of Education?"

"I didn't mean that," said Maria. "She's writing a history of Caunotaucarius County and she has all her materials and everything in her office there. I think she just doesn't want to move all her files out of the old B of E."

"My goodness." Danford shifted in his chair. "I had no idea. I'll have to look at the foundation rolls again. I can't imagine how I missed Milly's name."

"Oh, she's not on the foundation rolls," said Maria leaning forward. "I'm sure of it."

Danford appeared to be astounded. His pink narrow face under the white hair was shadowed with indignation. "Why, that's absolutely criminal," he said. "That sort of thing is exactly what the foundation is for. If there has been any trouble with her application I can assure you that I'll look into it very strongly tomorrow."

It was then that I saw it happening in Maria's face. The excitement had carried her over the edge. My hand with the cigarette rested on the window sill where the smoke curled outward into the night. For a moment the cigarette was forgotten. I knew that Maria was going to begin to say things that she shouldn't say, things that she *knew* she shouldn't say. Her eyes glittered from the pools of blue shadow she had so hastily put on. "I don't think Milly ever applied," said Maria.

Both Mr. and Mrs. Danford sank back in their chairs with surprise. "Why on earth not?" inquired Danford. "I can't remember how many times Milly herself has been given as a reference for people who did apply. After all, Milly knows everything about the Pendragon Grant. We could arrange for her to retire tomorrow to carry on her work. We—"

Maria's face took on a remoteness as she interrupted. "Milly has contradicted just about everything I learned at school," said Maria. "At school the department head hands out list after list of foundations, grants, what have you, to finance a study. The attitude is that studying on one's own is unthinkable, that working without the support of the government, a university, a corporation, a foundation—somebody somewhere back there who is big and powerful—simply is not done. Milly rejects all that. She doesn't think it's necessary or even good. She has even quoted to me the letter that Samuel Johnson sent to Lord Chesterfield that sort of put paid to patronage. She doesn't want to be patronized. She thinks it leaches a lot of the integral authority out of scholarship."

Danford smiled grimly. "I know the letter," he said. "But Doctor Johnson, whose doctorate was honorary as you probably know, had only to worry about money to support himself. Modern scholars—as well I know from the grants we have given out—need incredibly expensive equipment . . ."

"You mean computers," said Maria complacently. "Well, sure. That's what I was given to understand when I was doing my graduate work. Unless you could do a computer search of just about everything then everything was hopeless. Don't try to do any work. Drive a cab—and a lot of them *are* driving cabs. But Milly has another quote for that from the historian LeRoy Ladurie: that the computer is, quote, a huge supplementary brain within reach of the first imbecile, unquote, that ends up multiplying idiocies.

"She doesn't use a computer. Doesn't want one, not even a word processor. She writes her stuff in long-hand on yellow legal pads and I type it up in the evening and bring it back in the morning. And believe me, it's not easy."

Danford laughed. His eyes twinkled under the white eyebrows. "Good old Milly," he said. Then in mock seriousness he said, "I can't believe her handwriting is that bad. I mean so bad you have trouble reading it. That isn't the penmanship we were taught down here."

"Oh, it's not the handwriting," said Maria brightly. "It's the marginalia."

All three of us were puzzled by this and all of us sat forward a little.

"Milly seems to have a million second thoughts while she's writing this stuff," said Maria. "And she makes notes to herself constantly on the margins of the yellow sheets. A lot of times it seems to run into the body of the text and I very often simply type it right in. And now, to solve that particular problem, she's taken to using symbols and abbreviations that mean something to her but I suppose are meaningless to anyone else. They're certainly meaningless to me. They're not editorial signs and symbols, they're sort of personal symbols. Anyway, they don't get lost in the body copy."

Maria could not stop talking. The electricity generated by the sheer power of the mansion and the people who owned it had flowed into her. She was not conversing so much as she was chattering, almost wildly. "For instance," said Maria, "we're in the late part of the last century now and a new symbol has cropped up. It's a capital *G*—" she held up her left hand to illustrate a *G*—with a capital *D* hooked on and hanging from it. She completed the figure with her other hand. "I can't figure out what it means, but since there's usually an exclamation mark after it, I think it just possibly might mean *goddamn!*"

Both the Danfords stiffened in their chairs. The movement was almost convulsive. It stopped Maria with her mouth slightly open. Mr. Danford leaned slowly forward and stretched out his hand toward Maria. He said, "Young lady, I don't mean to upbraid you, but we do not permit the taking of the name of the Lord in vain in this house." He sank back in his chair then and stared at her. Mrs. Danford seemed to exhale very slowly. It all had the effect of paralyzing Maria mid-speech.

She managed to get out, "I'm—I'm terribly sorry. I didn't mean to . . ." and we all sat perfectly still, as if waiting for a lightning bolt to cleave the roof.

Little by little the tableau melted. The ceiling brooded over the injury done to the house by that careless curse while we attempted to resume conversation. "Come to think of it," I said smiling, trying to extricate Maria, "it could also stand for Gideon Danford."

Danford favored me with a wintry smile. "A little before my time, I'm afraid," he said. But the remark had caused Mrs. Danford to draw back once again. I had done her some deep interior injury. I gave up.

Conversation did resume, although it was made up of stuttering, stammering commonplaces. I had lit another cigarette and was watching Mr. Danford say to Maria, "You'll be sure to remind Milly of the meeting here this weekend, won't you?" Maria answered helplessly, "What meeting?" and Danford gave her a piercing stare.

"The Christian Parents' Association," he said, and his expression carried the weight of announcing a disarmament conference in Geneva.

Maria's face was a fluttering mask of uncertainty. "I'll be sure to remind her," said Maria, "but I can't honestly say she'll be here. I mean she does the bulk of her work on the history over the weekends, and the weekends are pretty much sacrosanct to Milly."

"More important than her work at the Board of Education?" Mr. Danford asked, his eyebrows arching.

This seemed to torch off Maria. Now *she* stiffened up, and for the instant looked quite regal. "Mr. Danford," she said. "For the work Milly Rutledge does for the Board of Education, which seems to be just about everything, she is paid exactly twelve-thousand five-hundred dollars a year. It's no secret. It's there for anyone to see on the county public payroll. I think Milly feels—I think anyone would feel—that at that salary she deserves her weekends to herself.''

Danford leaned forward. ''Someone from the Board of Education should be here,'' he insisted. He had been deeply wounded. Mrs. Danford was saying something but I couldn't see quite what it was since she was half in the shadows beyond the lamplight. What I saw in her resembled Francis Bacon's painting of the Cardinal whose mouth is moving as if in multiple exposures.

Maria looked at each of them. ''I'll see what I can do,'' she said.

It was all fairly gracious and graceful at the end, although my chucking the cigarette butt out the window on to their well-tended grounds seemed to cause some pain to Mrs. Danford. We saw Maria out and into her shabby little car. Johnson showed me to my room, which, surprisingly, was not very different from the one I'd had at Thornwood, except for the carving, of course, which seemed now to twine through the entire house. I gave him the keys to my car and told him where to find it at the Motor Lodge. I thanked God that the Old Fitzgerald was safely ensconced in my leather kit and would be packed automatically.

I sat on the edge of the soft bed and surveyed the room as Johnson stood above me. He reached into the side pocket of his white jacket and drew forth the tin ashtray stamped ST. LOUIS WORLD'S FAIR. ''You may smoke if you wish,'' said Johnson. His face was impassive, grave, but there was a riot of laughter behind his black intelligent eyes.

11

Breakfast was a poached egg on a limp piece of toast accompanied by a thimbleful of unidentifiable fruit juice and a cup of coffee that just might have been held over from the previous evening.

Nevertheless, I was content. I was alone at the great table in the same chair I'd had the night before. The table cloth had been removed and a place mat put before me. The deep oak surface of the table gleamed and reflected the silver bowl of wax fruit in the center. Mr. Danford had already been taken to his office, Mrs. Danford was gone to officiate at a flower exhibit. True enough, I was still hungry, but I was learning to live with it.

Earlier, Johnson had gone off with Irma and had returned with my automobile and my mail from the Motor Lodge. The mail and the keys to my car lay beside my plate. My bag with its liquor case intact and a nearly full carton of Luckies was safely resting in my room. My ankle announced only the barest twinge of memory from yesterday's excursion.

There were two letters from Edna, one thick letter by regular post that had been mailed Wednesday, the twelfth, and a Mailogram that had been sent overnight. I took them downstairs and out the back door to the garden where I could sit on a cast-iron bench and smoke without defiling the temple.

The thick regular letter from Edna began with an account of her pursuit of the Welland finances. So far as she could make out at this time no unusual purchases had been made in the last few weeks. Using various subterfuges she had called a number of car agencies surrounding Dobbs Ferry and in New York City (Jaguar, Mercedes, BMW, Cadillac, Lincoln,

Volvo) and a few local agencies that handle the really exotic numbers (Maserati, Ferrari, Lotus). No cigar. She had called Tiffany's, Cartier's, Van Cleef and Arpel's, and Harry Winston's. Nix, kid, nothing doing. (There are many other jewelers who might sell items just as expensive, but newly flushed money tends to go for the big, big names for the thrill of the thing.) She had called up numerous purveyors of expensive furnishings and interior decorators. Having the "decent little house" redone is one more vent through which recently acquired money might blow. She checked some of the more likely real estate offices— no inquiries on the purchase of a home had been forthcoming from anyone named Welland. Posing as a nervous temporary secretary, she had telephoned a number of the better known stockbrokers to check on Mr. Welland's account. She drew zero response.

Trying to find his bank she hit a stump, and this is what led to the guts of the letter. She had wanted to know at what bank Welland had deposited his paychecks, something that would be plain in the clearance of the check stamped on the back. When she called the accounting department of Carlson House to ask for this information they made trouble. She went over there to talk to them and they still made trouble. At a loss, she called the office of David Carlson, and he, himself, descended from his Olympian height to see what the trouble was in the accounting office. In the accounting office he saw Edna . . .

We had lunch at a place called Elaine's. Have you ever heard of it? It is full of writers and people like that—movie stars even. Everybody seemed to know David. [It was David already.] And everybody was very nice to him, coming over to the table and all. David said that some of the writers were very important. One of the important writers, a woman, who came over was beautifully dressed. I never saw anything like it.

Which reminds me. David is taking me to din-

*ner and I really need a new dress if he's going
to take me to places like Elaine's. Could I have
an advance on next week's salary so I can buy a
new dress? I really need it. I look like one of the
Most Needy they put in* The N.Y. Times *at
Christmastime. I mean I really need it. Can I?
He says we're going to someplace called the Four
Seasons. Please answer post haste.*

The rest of her letter was taken up with her struggle
with the bank. There really seemed to be no unusual
deposits or withdrawals. Everything, so far, had been
totally without reward. But this is what legwork is all
about (and it is rather lascivious to refer to Edna's efforts
as legwork). What she had done was invaluable. It had
cleared away the underbrush. It was like the work of those
fellows who had lugged Welland's body up the side of the
ravine—exhausting, but unrewarding.

She closed with:

*I don't know why you had all those mean things
to say about David. He is a perfectly wonderful
man. He is very well-read, witty and intelligent.
Everybody seems to think the world of him. He
seems to be very popular. Have you ever gone to
a restaurant called Lutéce? David is taking me
there to lunch tomorrow. I need clothes! Clothes!*

The letter fairly howled.

The Mailogram might as well have been a telegram.
It was hastily scribbled.

*Shoebox sent via Trailways. Should be there Fri-
day. Call me as soon as Code-Com is installed
at Danford's. Stay put at Danford's until we have
more information. Am chasing Computrix. Results should reach you Saturday morning. What
about the advance?*

> Love,
> Edna

I threw my second cigarette away and went back into the house, located Johnson in the pantry on the first floor. I asked him, "Do you think you could call in a telegram for me? I can't use the phone myself. It's very short."

"Certainly, sir," said Johnson.

I gave him my office telephone number and told him to charge the telegram to that number. Then I pulled out my notebook and wrote out the name and address and finally the message: BUY DRESS STOP CONSIDER IT BONUS STOP WATCH YOUR STEP STOP.

I watched while Johnson made the call. It wasn't much of a telegram, nothing like Robert Benchley's great message when he woke up one morning in Venice and wired his travel agent: STREETS FILLED WITH WATER PLEASE ADVISE.

"Watch your step" wasn't much of a warning, but what could I tell her? Elaine's, then Lutéce, then probably 21. These were perilous pathways for a girl like Edna. She didn't know who James Whitcomb Riley was. She didn't know the first line, *"Little Orphant Annie's come to our house to stay,"* and so she sure as hell didn't know the last lines of the poem—

"Er the Gobble-uns'll git you
    Ef you
        Don't
            Watch
                Out!"

It was not something I could squeeze into a telegram.

The day, like the huge house, yawned before me. I had slept late and now it was pushing on to eleven o'clock. The only sign of activity in the house were Johnson and Irma going about their appointed tasks and two cleaning women who came in daily for the endless round of dusting, sweeping, and scrubbing.

There was no sign of the telephone people who had been asked to install the Code-Com.

I began to explore the house. The kitchen and other functional rooms were tucked away on the first floor, which also contained the library and a sitting room on opposing sides of the staircase. Galahad continued to brood as I ascended the broad marble steps. The parlor off the dining room, where I had smoked my guilty cigarettes the previous evening, was balanced on the other side of the dining room by another parlor, apparently one to which the ladies withdrew when the men abandoned them for cigars and brandy. These were both ''withdrawing'' rooms or ''drawing'' rooms. I wondered if any witty sophisticated real life comedies had been played out in them. Somehow, I doubted it.

Going back through the first drawing room I discovered that it gave on to a billiard room that featured a really magnificent billiard table with legs on it the diameter of washtubs. The top of the table was protected with a fitted gray oilcloth cover, and while it was dust free, I got the idea that it hadn't been removed in many years. The billiard cues, some of them exquisitely worked in ivory, stood at attention in a long rack against the wall. They too, it seemed, had been standing a long, long time. The furnishings of the huge room were deep horsehair leather club chairs and settees. There was a big oak cabinet that apparently held liquor, since there was a heavy lock on it. I did not approach it.

A long shelf with a railing extended along one wall at just about eye height and on it were placed a long series of framed photographs. The frames varied—some silver, some gold, so I got the idea that these were presentations rather than family souvenirs. All the photographs except the groups were signed, and some of the names were legendary, names that rang with the chink of gold coins being dropped into a bag. One of the group photographs had obviously been taken in a railway car. The men gathered round in it had evidently completed a satisfactory if not historic deal. They were all very contented men, although their faces were as hard as flint. The poses in all the photographs were relatively informal and showed the larger part of the man—at least the upper story. Their bodies were all quite stout and well packed with hard, marbleized flesh. Many of them held cigars in their hands. Many of them, seated at a table, had glasses in front of them that almost surely held some kind of liquor. These were hard living, hard playing men. They were long since turned to dust. I couldn't see one of them that I would have placed later than World War I. Some of them, I thought, went back to the eighteen eighties.

Beyond the billiard room there was still another sitting room, smaller and again unmistakably masculine. There was a desk in it with writing equipment in an ornate cut-glass set on its top. No ink was in the inkwell, but it was sparkling clean. I got the feeling that this room had seen a lot of deals cut in its time—the men drifting quietly away from the hubbub of the billiard game.

I crossed back through the dining room to the ladies' drawing room and through there to the room beyond. This room, apparently, was the music room. A huge grand piano, a Bosendorfer, stood on a platform at one end of the room and the center space of the room was left clear for chairs to be arranged for the musicales. Down-stuffed settees covered with brocade were ranged along the wall. Beyond the music room there was a delicately appointed room to which ladies could retire if overcome by the passion of the Bosendorfer or overwhelmed by vapors.

My own room, like all the other guest rooms, was on the third floor. The grand staircase diminished somewhat leading to the upper story, but not so terribly much. Trunks, after all, had to be hauled up those stairs and so they were broad and sturdy enough to bear the load easily. On the third floor I looked into only those rooms on which the door had been left open.

Some of the rooms were much grander and ornate than mine, and I supposed that they were set aside for married couples. Others were much meaner than my room was, sparsely furnished with nondescript furniture. Were they for the unwanted guests? Maybe. On the other hand, they might have been set aside for children.

I was a little surprised at the scarcity of bathrooms, but of course with servants readily available to rush back and forth with chamber pots, hot water, and so forth, who needed bathrooms? The stairway narrowed sharply going to the fourth floor—the servants' quarters. After all, they had no trunks to carry up. The effect on the fourth floor was that of a cheap hotel. The ceilings of the rooms were quite low and in some rooms slanted down to cut off much needed space. No bed in any of the rooms seemed to be much more than a cot with the rigorous kind of bedstead you might have found in an aging orphanage. There was not a scrap of carpet to be found anywhere. The floors were either plain bare wood or cracked linoleum.

I eased my way back to the third floor and found my room. It was early for a drink, but I wanted one. There was something out of kilter about the whole house. There was this enormous opulence filled with vitality and arrogance and even a kind of terrifying gaiety. Where on earth had it all gone to? The eyes of the beasts behind the foliage in the woodwork had searched the room in amazement as if wondering where everyone had gone. All the rooms were unexceptionably clean, and most of them smelled of wood polish—but they were mummified. The photographs in the billiard room had informed me that the men who had come here had puffed heavily on thick Havanas and had swilled down oceans of wine, brandy, whiskey and gin. Their well-packed frames spoke of plate after plate of oysters on the half shell, lobsters thick with sauce, giant barons of beef, roast suckling pig, huge pies, and great cheeses. The heart of the house at that time might have been making itself sclerotic, but now it was dead. The thin little white-haired man and the angular woman who drifted through these rooms were ghosts compared to what I had seen. Where had it stopped? What on earth had happened? What had seized its heart and stopped it?

Lunch was a tuna fish sandwich on white bread cunningly cut into four quarters. It was served solemnly by Johnson along with a cup of something that must be described as coffee. I ate in lonely splendor.

After lunch there was still no sign of the telephone people, and yet I didn't want to leave the place until I had put in the phone call to Edna. I rescued my copy of Gould's *The Mismeasure of Man* and returned to the cast-iron bench overlooking the garden.

Professor Gould led me by the hand into a fascinatingly complex formula that had been used for classifying various degrees of human intelligence. He was careful and patient in trying to show me how it worked, but it took a long, long time for me to get to the point where I thought I understood the essentials of the formula. Then he showed that the people who had been using this formula to grade human intelligence and thereby change the lives of unsuspecting youngsters had been using it incorrectly. I rejoiced to see him put a blot on the escutcheon of the deep, not to say self-righteous thinkers who decided they were qualified to order man's fate. But then Professor Gould pulled an entirely unsuspected rabbit out of his beautiful hat. He showed that even had the formula been used correctly it would not have been sufficient to order the complexity of human intelligence, that the elegant and elaborate system I'd worked so hard at to grasp simply was not adequate to the task—nor was any other that Professor Gould could mention. What he had done made me smile. He had showed me how learned folks, even deeply committed folks, could be perfectly right and absolutely wrong.

I put the open book down over my knee and stared out at the garden. I am not much in the way of a nature lover and hardly know one bloom from another. But the garden now, in its infinite variety, looked far more beautiful to me.

I had been so absorbed in the problems that Professor Gould presented that the iron sinews of the bench had strangled my blood supply. I got up, staggering slightly, and decided to walk around the house to restore my circulation. When I got to the side of the house, however, I saw that the telephone truck had pulled up to the service entrance. I went back to retrieve my book from the bench—I didn't want an accidental shower spoiling it—and went back inside to see what was going on.

I had hoped that they would install the phone in my room, but I suppose that was asking too much. What I found was that they were installing the Code-Com right next to the central house phone that Johnson used in the foyer. I suppose it was the quickest, easiest, and cheapest way, but it also meant that any conversations I had with Edna would be public property. However, I could hardly pretend that the house was overcrowded, and I supposed that a quick glare at Johnson would give me the momentary privacy I wanted. I couldn't imagine that Mr. and Mrs. Danford would hang around to listen.

It took them about a half hour to get the thing set up. I thanked them and then thanked Johnson, who stood nearby curious to see how the thing worked. I supposed that if I satisfied his curiosity now, I'd have less of it to deal with later on.

I dialed Edna at the office number. The light flashed to show that the connection had been made. I said, "Hello, Edna? This is Joe."

The little light flashed out the well-worn magical letters in its series of dots and dashes: R U O K.

"Yes, Edna. I'm fine. I'm being treated like royalty here." I saw a flicker of satisfaction cross Johnson's face.

The ruby light flashed the letters: STAY THERE.

"Well, I can't go into seclusion, Edna. That's not

what I'm here for. By the way, what time is that package supposed to arrive?''

"3 PM."

"It's almost that now," I told her. "I'll go down and pick it up after I hang up. By the way, have you made any progress with that packing list?''

'' Y '' (Y stands for yes, N for no).

"When will I be able to see it?"

"SAT AM."

"Tomorrow morning? Wonderful. Anything interesting?''

'' Y VER ''

"Good. Was it mailed to the Motor Lodge or the Danford House?''

'' D H ''

"Okay. Did you get my telegram?''

'' Y THX ''

"You're perfectly welcome, kid. You've done a great job. I hope you have a ball. But as I said in the telegram, be careful. Don't bother to answer. Look, I'm going to hang up now, but with the Code-Com here I'll be in touch, and if anything breaks you can reach me through this phone. Okay? Have a good weekend, and I'll call you on Monday. Goodbye.''

'' BY ''

I hung up feeling, as I always did, a vague dissatisfaction with these one-sided conversations. It's true that I have never heard Edna's voice, but her pretty face is so expressive when she talks that almost any conversation with her is an occasion for cheer. The cold winking of the red light on the phone with its Phillips code, or rather our personal corruption of the Phillips code, is a sorry substitute. I looked up to where Johnson had been standing, but he was gone. I got the feeling that he had left just as I was hanging up the phone. I doubted that he was any the wiser for having listened and watched.

I sought him out in the labyrinthine ways of the kitchen and pantry complex. "I'm driving into town to pick up a package," I told him.

"I'd be happy to run the errand for you, sir."

"No, thanks. It'll give me a chance to stretch out and look around a little. I'm still a stranger in these parts, you know."

"Very well, sir." He offered me the barest flicker of a smile, but I could read the unspoken message in his face. It was the same advice I'd given Edna. *"Watch your step."*

The Trailways Bus Depot was a fairly important establishment in this town. Like most bus stations it was located in the low-rent district and like most bus stations it had a number of saloons as satellites. I picked up my shoebox without any trouble and locked it in the trunk of the car, which I had parked in a pay-and-lock garage. I ambled down to one of the less villainous looking saloons, enjoying every step of freedom from the big repressive house. I swung on to a barstool, feeling home at last, and had two vigorous drinks before asking the bartender, "Where do I go to get the best steak in town?"

He looked me over carefully before answering. "You gamble?" he asked me.

"Not really. I'm just looking for a steak. I'm starving."

He pursed his lips. "Well," he said, "the best place really ain't in town. It's just over the county line, the Dome Club. Most people go there to gamble—in the back, you know, but you can get a good steak there if you want it. I guess you don't have to gamble."

"I know what you mean." I smiled. "Thanks."

He gave me the unsurprising instructions on how to get there—out Route 95 past Dooley's and onward for another five miles. I left him a sizable tip.

The Dome Club was pretty much what I expected it to be—Mafia owned and operated without a doubt. The headwaiter was a bit startled; it was rather early for serious eating. He looked me over carefully and then relaxed in his tuxedo. Although none of the tables was occupied he led me to the one near the kitchen door. I didn't mind. Even the stench of the kitchen made me drool. Only one thing happened that I thought was out of character. A portly, elderly gent wearing an old suit and no tie was ushered to a very good table. The head-waiter treated the old fellow like a cut-glass bowl. The waiters hovered. The old man was utterly relaxed and at home. His eyes roved the room and flicked over me very briefly. There was nothing of the organization about him, and yet he obviously commanded respect. The table he had was quite large, so, I assumed, there would be guests. He was given a drink and then let alone, although I noticed that the waiters standing near me always managed to keep a careful eye on him.

My steak was served and I sent a silent message of gratitude to the bartender near the bus station. It was thick and ripe and perfectly broiled. The whole dinner was superb. I finished it off with cheesecake and perfect coffee. I belched out my thanks to heaven, paid with my special credit card and left. When I left I noticed that the old gent had a number of guests at his table. They were all dressed much better than he was.

When I got back to the mansion I found that I was just in time for dinner. A place had been set for me. The dinner was pretty much of a repetition of the previous evening's except that ham had been substituted for roast beef. The ham might have been a very good one for all I know, but the slice I had was so thin that I could hardly taste it. No matter. I laughed and told very mild jokes all through the meal. I'm sure they wondered what on earth could have caused my good humor.

12

My good humor lasted all the way through breakfast, which I shared with the Danfords next morning. It evaporated when Mr. Danford took a watch from his vest pocket, looked at it and said to me, "Well, Mr. Binney. This breakfast has run rather late. I see we've only got fifteen minutes left to prepare for the meeting."

"Prepare?" I asked stupidly. "Meeting?"

He said with an expression that had a certain amount of disappointment in it, "I assumed that you would have some sort of presentation for them, at least some notes with some sort of suggestions . . ."

"Them?"

"Reverend Barlow's group, The Christian Parents. We're meeting with them here at ten. It is now nine-forty-seven." He had taken out the thin gold watch again.

"Oh," I said. "Sure. Certainly." I had been wondering why the man was wearing a three-piece suit on a Saturday morning—but you never can tell. "I'll have to pop up to my room," I said. I rose and very nearly ran from the dining room.

Climbing the stairs I had to remind myself that they, unlike me, were not deaf, and that my curses would have to be kept silent, although the curses boiled up inside me with every step I ascended. In my room I pulled the bigger notebook I sometimes use out of my briefcase. As I flipped through it and ripped out a few pages of notes (I didn't want anyone looking over my shoulder) I reflected that there was one sunny side to this affair. Unless Mr. Danford was playing a very veiled cat-and-mouse game with me he still thought I was legit. I opened the window and lighted a cigarette. I puffed on it as I might have in front of a firing squad.

I was about to flick the butt out the window (Johnson had retrieved the ashtray) when I saw the van pull up. It was a big blue van with CHRISTIAN PARENTS' ASSOCIATION lettered on the side. Reverend Barlow, who had been driving, got out the front and then opened the sliding doors at the side. There emerged five of them, four ladies and one man—no, six, by God, and the last one to step down from the van not all that gracefully was Maria Thorndyke. She had the dazed, sullen look of someone who has been shanghaied. Gratitude bubbled up in my soul. I flicked out the butt, closed the window, and went downstairs.

They had huddled in a little knot at the center of the great hall except for Maria, who stood a little apart from them. Storm warnings were flying from every rebellious angle of her body. She was wearing lime green slacks and a white gauzy blouse. She had applied her make-up none too carefully. It was garish, and implied full battle dress. I went directly over to her. "Maria," I said, "how nice to see you." But I was asking many questions with my eyes.

Maria's smile of greeting acquired a bitter tinge. "My car broke down," she told me, "and Reverend Barlow was kind enough to let me ride in the van." I beamed a smile at Reverend Barlow, who smiled pinkly back at me. "As I told Mr. Danford," said Maria, "there was simply no possibility of Milly attending. She's up to her eyebrows in work. So Milly asked me if I'd show the flag." She heaved an enormous sigh. "So here I am."

Mr. Danford appeared from the region of the big staircase. Evidently he had come down in the elevator. The little group looked reassured at his appearance. I got the idea that this was the first time they'd been in the place and they were not only overwhelmed by the grandeur but a little frightened. Reverend Barlow made the introductions and Mr. Danford graciously shook hands all around. Then he led us to a room behind the staircase that extended between the library and the sitting room. This was an old-fashioned conference room with a long heavy table illuminated by green shaded bankers' lamps. Danford indicated that Reverend Barlow should sit at the head of the table, which he did with some trepidation, and Danford, himself, sat between the ladies on Barlow's left. The others disposed themselves on Barlow's right, and Maria and I sat facing one another at the tail end of the group. Altogether we took up only a very small part of the table, and I got the feeling that the furniture was mocking us.

Reverend Barlow offered the convocation, which I couldn't follow because his head was bowed, as was everyone else's. He then turned to Mr. Danford and asked him to address the meeting. Danford in his saintly way expressed great happiness at the opportunity to meet with these splendid people under his own roof. He pointed out that the Danfords had always had a deep and abiding interest in the education of the young citizens of this community and that the Pendragon Foundation had helped many of them in obtaining a higher education. He now welcomed the opportunity to hear what this wonderful group of Christian believers suggested toward the improvement of education in our community. He added that he was especially fortunate that the views of the Board of Education (Maria) would be represented as well as those of the publishing industry (me). Both Maria and I shrank back a little as the group peered down the table toward us. If the sound of Danford's voice matched his expression it must have sounded like the peal of golden chimes.

Barlow then turned to the woman on his right—a Miss Julia Tomkins it turned out to be—whom I recognized from the time I had seen the group talking to Milly. Miss Tomkins was fearful, determined, and agitated. She had obviously worked up a good deal of nerve to speak out plainly in the company of Mr. Danford. Although she began by addressing him, her gaze kept shifting down toward Maria and me. Miss Tomkins was a woman who needed enemies. I opened my big notebook, prepared to take notes.

Education in the United States, stated Miss Tomkins, had drifted away from its original purpose and from the Christian God who inspired it. Dangerous and atheistic tools were being put in the hands of innocent children by the Board of Education who bought them from non-Christian unbelievers (a good glare here at Maria and then me). The aim of the Christian Parents' Association was to drive these instruments of the devil from the schoolroom and to return to the original God-fearing principles of America.

Mr. Danford beamed at her. "I don't think that any decent person could quarrel with those aims, Miss Tomkins." The beam was returned by Reverend Barlow and his cohorts. Maria looked dubious, and I suppose that I did too. "The difficulty we have with this problem," Mr. Danford continued, "is that the whole world is changing very rapidly while we try our best to maintain our Christian principles. My understanding of the function of an education is that it should not only build a harmonious society but also enable these youngsters to go into the world to earn a living.

"Today we live in an era of very sophisticated technology," he said. "No one knows that better than I do, since I must grapple with these problems each and every day. In order for our children to go forth and take useful, meaningful jobs in today's industry their education must prepare them for it. In other words, a modern education is required for a youngster to support himself in a modern society."

"The Lord will provide!" said the woman to his right very sharply. My head jerked back at the rigidity and violence of her expression. The other members of the group were apparently assenting; they had all bowed their heads slightly to mutter an Amen.

Mr. Danford smiled sweetly at the lady to his right. "Yes, of course," he agreed. "The Lord works in wonderful and quite mysterious ways. But He also demands that we earn our bread by the sweat of our face, and in order to do this today our youngsters really must have an understanding of modern tools."

Reverend Barlow spoke up then. He said, "Mr. Danford, I don't think anybody here objects to our children learning how to read a tractor manual. What we object to is the strange and godless ideas being put into our children's heads. These textbooks talk as if there weren't any God at all, as if He didn't have anything to do with anything. They give our children very strange thoughts to think. These books, these lessons, are absolutely stuffed with secular humanism. They are putting the aims of mankind ahead of the aims of God.''

Danford looked over at me. I had been scribbling in my notebook. ''Do you see any remedy for this situation, Mr. Binney?'' he asked me kindly.

''Well,'' I said, ''I've been sitting here wondering how we're going to fit the aims of God into a tractor manual. What do we say? God made this tractor so you can earn a living? God ordained that the gear shift in this tractor is on the steering post?''

This was regarded as levity and was not well received. All of them stiffened slightly. Reverend Barlow said, ''I don't think the name of God has to be brought into a tractor manual, Mr. Binney.''

''I don't know about that,'' I argued. ''As Mr. Danford suggested, we may want to turn out students who can design a tractor, not just drive one. If he's going to do that he's going to have to learn some engineering. If he's going to do that, he's going to have to have some physics. If he's going to study modern physics, believe me, certain fundamental questions about God are going to be raised. Modern physics shades into metaphysics—we can't get away from that. What I'm trying to say is that if you fit out a kid with a straight-eight old-fashioned high-school education down here he just isn't going to cut the mustard up at MIT.''

Reverend Barlow looked at Danford and smiled triumphantly. ''Do you see what I mean now, sir?'' he asked him. ''Isn't that proof enough? This man cannot open his mouth without the devil flying out of it. I am not surprised that God cursed him by taking away his ears.''

I looked at Danford whose pinkish cheeks had gone absolutely paper white. Danford looked quickly at me and under his white eyebrows the blue eyes seemed to beg *''Don't say anything. Please don't say anything.''* I returned his tacit appeal with a tight little smile and glanced away to give him a chance to recover. His small hands had gripped each other on the table in front of him. I was not about to make a scene. Barlow seemed completely unaware that his remark had caused any discomfort. There was a grin of triumph on his big stupid slab of a face. Danford took a deep breath and peered down toward Maria. "Miss Thorndyke," he said. "Do you have any comments that might reflect the attitude of the Board of Education toward these problems?"

Maria's face was flushed, a darkening of her complexion. She too had her hands tightly clasped on the table. She took a deep breath and said, "First of all, everybody here has got to understand that I was sent here only as an observer. Any comments that I have to make are from my personal point of view and they shouldn't be interpreted as the views of Milly Rutledge. If I am asked to speak my mind, however, I will.

"I believe," said Maria, "that what the Christian Parents' Association requires of us is illegal and unconstitutional. We are supported by local taxes, state taxes, and federal grants. With support this widespread we cannot devote our attention solely to one particular religious view. We are forbidden to do this by the Constitution of the United States."

Danford leaned over and looked down at Maria with what seemed to be a kindly twinkle in his eyes. I think he felt that putting the argument on legal grounds gave everybody a chance to move away from emotional territory. He said, "But Miss Thorndyke, the Constitution is not the only groundwork we have for this country. There are earlier, I daresay more authentic plans for the fate of this country . . ."

"The Constitution of the United States," said Maria firmly, "is the oldest continuously working government document in the world. It can be said to have withstood the test of time. The plans you refer to such as those drawn up by Governor Winthrop of the Massachusetts Bay Colony were discarded by his own constituents. As far as I am concerned, the whole Puritan ethos came to an end in Boston at the Brattle Street Church when the wealthy members of the congregation announced that they would no longer confess their sins publicly to the congregation because it brought discredit upon them as wealthy and fortunate persons—which is to say visible saints—in whom God had demonstrated his powers. That was the end of Governor Winthrop's pious articulation for the future of this country. We must not forget that Governor Winthrop was already deeply troubled by the number of young men in his colony who had been convicted of interfering sexually with the livestock.''

Faces around the table became masks, impenetrable.

''With the schism between the sins of the wealthy and the sins of the poor creating an ever widening chasm,'' Maria continued determinedly, ''the Puritan ethos collapsed. Meanwhile, a community that had been founded on purely commercial enterprises in the south—North Carolina and Virginia—seemed to find an equable footing. Their experience along with those of certain activists in the north eventuated in the Constitution of the United States. It must be remembered that the Constitution was designed by men who were for the most part deists—that is, having no particular church—and some of whom were frankly agnostic. This is the document we have and this is the document we live by. Until someone can draw up a better document, I'm afraid we're stuck with it.''

The faces had turned glassy.

''Turning aside from the purely legal aspects of the problem,'' said Maria sweetly, implacably, ''and speaking purely as a professional educator, I would like to say that I am not at all happy with the idea of exposing small innocent children to a patently homoerotic icon with deep implications of sadomasochism. This is the image that the Christian religion presents. I have heard numerous complaints about the art of the Renaissance, but we must remember that most of that art was religious in spirit. I think that all of you can be grateful that our images were not handed down from the Romans. The Romans, who were devoted to the idea of crucifixion, and crucified countless thousands of their subjects, would not have been so discreet in rendering the event. We know now from various medical studies that death by crucifixion is not that much different from death by hanging—there is a constriction of the muscles controlling respiration. In other words one dying of crucifixion is ultimately strangled. Now all of us know that hanging a male person results in certain priapic manifestations. If the Romans had painted the Crucifixion, you may be sure that they would not have painted in the carefully adjusted loincloth, so that the rendering of our Savior would have been . . ."

But Danford was already on his feet. He glared down the table, and I saw in his face the megavoltage that controlled an empire. When he spoke the tones must have been those of thunder. He said, "Young woman, I demand that you leave this house immediately!"

There was a shy satisfied smile on Maria's face as she stood up. "Thank you," she said.

I too got slowly to my feet. I looked down at the group of Christian thinkers. By their expression I was by no means sure that they had known what Maria was talking about. Perhaps Danford really had saved them. I said to Danford, "Maria didn't have her own car when she came here. She can't walk home. I'll drive her home. I really don't have anything more to say anyway."

After I had followed Maria out of the room and into the great hall I said to her, "Before we leave I've got to check with Johnson to see if the mail arrived. I'm expecting a letter. I'll meet you at my car, the blue Nova over at the side." She nodded and fled.

I tracked down Johnson in his hideaway off the kitchen and asked him about the mail. He walked with me out to the foyer, and there on a silver salver was a letter with the reassuring New York postmark on the corner. I thanked him, put the letter in my pocket and headed out the doorway to my car. Maria was already seated in it. When I got in she turned her face away from me. She had been crying.

13

I didn't try to talk to her as we drove toward the center of town. I can't really converse when I am driving because I can't turn my attention from the road to read lips. I said to Maria only, "Let's go have a cup of coffee and then I'll take you over to get your car fixed. Okay?" Because I didn't know the town I drove through it and headed for the Motor Lodge where I knew there was a coffee shop.

We got ourselves planted in a booth and adjusted with a cup of coffee and a cigarette. I looked at Maria and smiled—I admit it was a rather sad smile. I said, "You seem to have sawed off both ends of your limb."

Maria's face was very somber. She said, "I didn't want to get screwed on my back out on a country road, but I didn't want to get screwed sitting at a conference table, either."

I said, "You seem to have an easily accessible self-destruct button."

Maria said, "The only reason I stay in this god-damned place is because of Milly. That doesn't mean I have to take a lot of crap from jellybeans like Dana or from half-wits like Barlow."

"Doesn't it?" I asked her.

Her lips got very tightly compressed. "I know what you're thinking," she challenged me.

"Do you?" I asked her. "What I'm thinking is that you have a very serious temptation to get in with the right crowd and make a little money and a career, but that your conscience jumps up like a fiery dragon and turns the old flame thrower on just about anybody who can help you."

The tight line of her lips softened a little at the edges. "Except Milly," she said.

"What about me?"

"No," she said. "You too, I guess. I trust you. God knows why."

"Okay," I said. "Let's take things step by step. First of all we've got to get your wheels back under you. What's wrong with your car?"

"Dead battery, I guess."

"Have you got jump wires?"

"I don't think so."

"We'll buy a set on the way over, and from now on keep them in your trunk. We'll jump start your car, you take it over to a mechanic—you know a mechanic?" she nodded, "and get it fixed. Then you meet me back here at five o'clock this evening and I take you to dinner at the Dome Club."

"The Dome Club. Really? Why do you want to go there?"

"As far as I know they're the only outfit in town serving a steak that isn't chicken-fried."

"Are you a gambler?" The dark brown eyes became suddenly intense.

"No. I don't gamble. But I do eat. You think there's something wrong with eating?"

The smile softened a little further. "No," she said.

"For a while there I thought you were going to say yes."

We carried through the program. We found a Western Auto store and bought the jump cables. She directed me to where her little car was parked and we got the thing started. I threw the new cables into her trunk. She drove away.

I drove back to the middle of town and hunted down the little bar near the bus station. I put my car in a park-and-lock garage, however, because the shoebox with its vital contents was still locked in the trunk and I didn't want some juvenile delinquent heisting it. The barroom was still doing a pretty fair lunchtime business, but I managed to find a stool near the big front window where there was enough light for me to read the letter.

Dear Joe:

I couldn't make any sense out of Computrix over the phone so I went down there to talk to them. They are a kind of agency or computer store that puts together whole systems of computers.

I showed the man the packing slip you sent me and he took a long time looking at it. He said it looked to him like some kind of inventory control system. I asked him if he could check back on the registration number on the slip and tell me who bought it. This took a while, but finally he came up with the name of a company, the BDC Corporation. I asked what had been paid for the equipment and that turned out to be $17,365.82—which is a lot of money. So I asked him if he could locate the canceled check or bill of sale and tell me who signed it and all. I think he was getting pretty sore by then but I kind of gave him the idea that I was investigating a tax dodge. So he dug out the bill of sale, and the whole thing had been paid for right on the button. I mean there hadn't been any time plan or anything you usually have with a price that big.

The bill of sale was signed by, you guessed it, Charles D. Welland. But the check wasn't drawn on his regular bank. The notation said that it was drawn on the Bluestone Central Bank. That took me about as far as I could go with the Computrix outfit. The man there was very, very nice.

I went back to the office and called up Welland's home. I hate this part of things. I talked to Mrs. Welland and said that there had been a complaint about the computer equipment and what would be a convenient time for us to come out and fix it. She said she didn't know anything about any computer equipment and there cer-

tainly wasn't anything like that at their house. I apologized for bothering her, and I must say I hate doing things like that. I wish we didn't have to do it.

I thought that maybe Welland had installed a computer at the office, so I called up the sales manager and he said no, the only thing any salesman had there was a calculator. So where is all this expensive equipment?

The dress is beautiful. Thank you. Thank you. I am having Sunday brunch with David at the Jockey Club. Have you ever been there? David is very sweet and has beautiful manners. Everybody is very nice to him.

When will you be back here? I'm dying to talk to you.

Love,
Edna

I put the letter back in my pocket and sipped my bourbon and soda. Where indeed was all that expensive equipment? I thought I had a very good idea of where it was. Since it was Saturday, however, there was no point in my nipping over to Bluestone. All that would have to wait until Monday when the bank was open. What remained for me to do between now and five o'clock was to go back to the mansion and see if I couldn't repair some of the damage. The thought of that confrontation made me long for another drink, but I decided against it, left a tip on the bar, and departed.

Driving back to the mansion I had to skirt the courthouse commons, where I saw something that made me pull over and park my car. Honey Lewis, the white-haired boy, had collected a crowd around him again. He towered over it, but then I saw that he was standing abjectly isolated. His huge head was bowed and his hands were manacled in front of him. I imagine that the handcuffs must have been extended to their last notch. Next to him stood Sheriff McCleod, not a large man anyway, who looked almost like a midget reaching up to seize the big man's biceps. Nevertheless, Honey Lewis in his rags through which sun-bronzed muscles rippled and flashed followed McCleod meekly to the sheriff's car and got in the back seat. The expression on McCleod's face was utterly calm and peaceable. The expression on Honey Lewis's face had been unreadable. McCleod's car pulled away slowly and the crowd dispersed in little groups, some shaking their heads and muttering to one another.

When I got back to the mansion Johnson met me at the door and said, "Mr. Danford would like to see you as soon as possible. He's in the library." When I had crossed the big floor I found that the library door had been left ajar. I knocked on it, nonetheless, somewhat timidly I think, and Danford himself pulled the door all the way back to let me in. I was surprised to see two other people in the room. One of them I recognized—Ken Parnell, the manager of Pendragon. The other fellow was a complete stranger and looked as out of place as a tin cup in a collection of Ming vases. There was an angry band of red across his forehead from the sweatband of the Caterpillar cap he had just removed. Below that his long nondescript face with its washed-out no-color eyes bracketed by a set of jug ears showed signs of a fright that was mixed with sly defiance. He was not one of the drivers I had seen at Dooley's, but he was unmistakably a driver.

Danford gestured vaguely toward the man and told me, "Mr. Binney, this is Bobby McGowan, the truck driver who nearly ran you over." He looked sternly then toward the driver and said, "Bobby, this is Mr. Joseph Binney, the man you almost killed with your carelessness." The driver shifted uneasily and his fist squeezed the Caterpillar cap. It did not escape me that I was Mr. Binney and he was Bobby.

Danford said to me, "I asked our manager, Ken Parnell," Parnell nodded soberly toward me, "to check out what drivers of ours had been on the road at that hour, and finally it was narrowed down to this

McGowan fellow. He claims that he had no idea that he had brushed you so close. However, I think he owes you an apology, and furthermore, he has been suspended for two weeks without pay for careless driving. You may, of course," Danford added, "press legal charges if you wish." He waited while I shook my head in a quick negative. "Now, Bobby," he said to the driver, "I think you ought to apologize to Mr. Binney."

He had both hands on the cap now and was twisting it in front of him. He said, "I really am sorry I brushed you like that, Mr. Binney. If I'd of knowed you was hurt like that you can bet I would have stopped and helped you out some. I just swung a little wide in the road—cheatin' a little, you know—and I guess I never did think you was in any trouble. Like I said, I'm terrible sorry."

"Apology accepted," I answered quickly. I stared into the no-color eyes recognizing that I had just made an enemy for life. I filed the name McGowan away in my personal file of deadly dangers. I kept my face absolutely impassive. His face, however, had lost a good deal of its fright, and the rigor of his lips relaxed into something that verged on a sneer. The washed-out eyes sent their message across—I'll get you yet, you son-of-a-bitch.

Both Danford and Parnell relaxed too with the acceptance of the apology. They both heaved short sighs at the successful conclusion of a distasteful business. "You may go now, Bobby," Parnell said to the driver. Danford had already turned away to go back to his desk. The door to the library had been left open. I watched McGowan depart across the great hall. He looked neither right nor left, although there is a great deal to look at. Midway across the hall he untwisted his cap and jammed it on his head. He seemed to feel that he had enough distance between himself and the library to stand upright. He shook his shoulders, reorganized himself and stomped into the foyer, where, I suppose, Johnson let him out.

When I turned to look back into the room Danford
was already seated at his desk and was saying to Parnell, "I'm sorry to have interrupted your weekend,
Ken, but this had to be settled." Because my attention
had been focused on the driver I hadn't really taken in
Parnell. He was indeed dressed for the golf course
with red plaid golfing slacks and a light blue cashmere
sweater over his sports shirt. His back was turned to
me as he answered Danford, but I'm sure he was making the proper reassuring noises. But when he turned
to leave his back was to Danford and his face had a
look of irritated contempt on it. He fastened his eyes
on me for a moment and the expression developed into
one of outraged hatred. I was startled. It takes a special kind of mind behind a special kind of face to frame
that look. I filed it away and sighed. I had made yet
one more enemy.

When Parnell had gone—and there was none of
McGowan's tentativeness as he strode across the hall—
I stepped up to Danford's desk and said, "I want to
thank you for everything you've done, Mr. Danford.
I didn't mean to make so much of a fuss about a little
driving infraction."

"Perfectly all right," said Danford looking up at
me. "We had to get to the bottom of it, and I'm glad
it was nothing more serious. I'm sure that young man
will be a little more careful in the future."

I said, "About that meeting this morning, did you
reach any resolutions?"

He folded his small pale hands on the big desk and
pursed his lips. "Not really," he said. "They were
all too terribly upset after Miss Thorndyke's outburst.
Although," and his blue eyes lightened a bit, "I'm
not at all sure they knew what she was driving at."
He paused and asked, "What on earth got into that
young woman?"

I smiled, I hope apologetically. "I think she felt that
she was under attack and simply struck back first. I
think she might have taken offense on my part, for

which I'm truly sorry. I certainly hope that it isn't going to injure her career.''

Danford sat back and considered it. "I shouldn't think so," he allowed. "Apparently Milly values her quite a bit. And," he nodded, "I must admit that Reverend Barlow can be fairly blunt at times.''

I thought that the word *blunt* was about the kindest description that could be put to Reverend Barlow, but I let it pass. "Speaking of preachers," I said, "I noticed that the white-haired boy managed to get himself arrested while I was on my way back here.''

"The white-haired boy?" Danford was completely at sea.

"That's what Milly—Miss Rutledge—calls him. Honey Lewis, the big blond preacher in the park.''

"Oh, yes." Danford sat up suddenly, oddly alert. "Sim Lewis's boy. You say Milly calls him the white-haired boy, does she?''

I nodded. "Yes. She assured me that they'd never arrest him, but I guess she was wrong for once. He must have been burning somebody's ears off.''

Again Danford had that odd alertness in his eyes. "Yes," he agreed. "Yes. I understand that he's quite—terribly—charismatic." Then he smiled. "I'm quite sure that Sim Lewis will take care of whatever the trouble is. He looks out after the boy in his own way, you know, from a distance. And Sim Lewis," this was accompanied by a wintry smile, "has his own resources, which can be considerable.''

It seemed to close the conversation. I said awkwardly, "Now that we've got the accident cleared up there's really no reason for me to bother you any further. I'll get my stuff together and move back to the Motor Lodge.''

"Oh, really?" said Danford, surprised. "There's no rush for you to do that, is there? After all, we have the telephone installed here for you and you're certainly welcome to stay as long as you like.''

I thought about it. Ordinarily I would have bolted the hell out of there, but news of the bank account in

Bluestone meant to me that the case would be wound up in a day or two. There was also the matter of those pale circles of hatred in Bobby McGowan's eyes backed up further with the outrage in Parnell's big well-fed face. Something suggested to me that I would be less likely to have an unforeseen misfortune if I were sheltered under Danford's roof. I made up my mind and said, "I'm sure I'll be finished up here in just a few more days. So, since you extend the invitation, I'll be happy to stay on for a day or two. It's very kind of you." I prepared to leave. "I'm dining out this evening," I told him, "and may be a little late getting back."

"Perfectly all right," said Danford. "Johnson will let you in."

I turned to go, but caught the inquiring expression on his face and stopped. "You're quite sure, are you, that that's what Milly calls Sim's lad, Honey—the white-haired boy?"

"Yes," I reaffirmed it. "Although she mentioned it only in passing."

"Strange," muttered Danford, staring up and out beyond my shoulder. "How very, very strange."

14

I was settled in the bar of the Motor Lodge long before Maria got there, but I limited myself to one bourbon and soda, which I sipped very, very slowly. I was startled by her appearance when she came in. She had gotten herself up almost exactly as she had looked on the date with Martingale. The dress, the pumps, the clutch purse, and the special care to make-up were all the same. I was flattered and pleased although I recognized that she had done this more for her own morale than my benefit.

She ordered white wine again and was content to see the bartender place the miserable product of his jug in front of her. I allowed myself another drink. When preliminary compliments were over I said to her, "Maria, before I forget, there's one piece of business I'd like to get settled. Somehow I've really got to see Milly before Monday morning. On Monday I've got to report to Carlson on why the book hasn't sold or if there is any hope of its being sold, and I've got to give him the reasons why. Is there some way I can see Milly tomorrow?"

Maria took her time before answering. She said with a look of reluctance, "Well, Milly finishes up work around seven in the evening at the school building. If you were to show up there no earlier than seven I guess you could talk to her for a while. Don't come any earlier, though. I mean she gets really enraged if she's disturbed. I'll call her tomorrow and tell her to expect you."

I nodded, satisfied. I didn't like deceiving Maria about my mission, but that is part of the racket, and if you can't compartmentalize yourself you can't be a PI. As Edna had observed in her letter, there are certain aspects to this business that are less than fragrant. I also wondered briefly if Milly still believed that I was a book salesman. If she hadn't divined the truth herself, it was very likely that her old friend McCleod had filled her in.

When we pulled up the curved driveway to the Dome's marquee there was a car ahead of us. My jaw dropped and a smile wreathed my face as I looked at it. It was totally anachronistic, a 1947-48 black Pontiac with the emblematic torpedo back setting off the deep flanges of the rear fenders. It was not so much the age of the car that excited me as the condition. Under the lights of the marquee, which were turned on even at this early hour, the black finish of the car was dazzling, and the reflected spotlights burst like diamonds. The chrome of the bumper glittered and the whitewall tires shone as if they had never left the showroom floor. The driver's door opened and I was astonished to see Jackson Dashwood get out and walk around to open the rear door. The Pontiac, beautiful as it was, was a far cry from the capacious limousines of Dashwood's that I had ridden in. There was something in that mahogany face of his as the lights of the marquee caught it that made my breath jump a little. There was something in that face—something—but I couldn't locate what it was that surprised me. I put it away with the other mysteries that lie crowded at the back of my head.

The doorman had made no move to open the door of the car, which surprised me too. He waited for Dashwood to open it and stood back while the occupant got out on to the ground. The occupant, once he got clear of the door, turned out to be the old fellow who had the very good table and the solicitous service I'd noticed last time I was at the Dome. He was wearing an old but good dark blue suit and a white shirt, but the top button of the shirt was opened and he was tieless. He also wore a rather broad brimmed black hat that at its rakish angle shielded most of his face from me. I noticed now that he was a big man—six feet, even at his age, and heavy set to the point of being fat. Once he was solidly on his pins he didn't seem to require any more help. He turned to say something to Dashwood, who nodded and returned to the museum piece. And then with the doorman leading the way, the old man went into the Dome as Dashwood drove off.

When I handed my blue Nova over to the doorman I felt that I was offering him a kiddie-car.

I got a much better table this time, a pretty girl always being the useful ticket for this privilege. As we were getting settled I noticed that the old fellow had been given the same big table he'd had last time. That, apparently, was *his* table. A drink appeared before him, but he seemed in no hurry to drink it. He relaxed, sat back in his chair and surveyed the room.

When our drinks had been served I said to Maria,

"I hope you don't mind, but when I went back to the mansion I sort of felt out Danford on the reaction to what you had said at the meeting." Maria smiled ruefully and took a sip of her drink. "I got the impression," I continued, "that whatever damage was done to your career wasn't terribly serious. I mean, he was sore, all right, but I couldn't see him plotting or pulling strings or anything like that." Her smile straightened out as her dark eyes absorbed the message. "I mean," I finished lamely, "I don't mean to intrude in something that isn't really my business, but I thought it was the least I could do."

"Thank you," said Maria. She smiled again, this time a real smile.

I smiled back and took a sip of my drink. "The fact is," I admitted, "I've gotten interested in your career. I'm trying to figure out what you intend to do, what your goals are, you know?"

She smiled again, but there was a touch of the sardonic in it. "You mean what's a nice girl like me doing in a place like this?"

"Sort of." I suppose I might have looked as puzzled as I felt. "It's just hard for me to see where you're heading. Even if you go into Milly's job when she retires, is that what you're really aiming for? I mean, I can see why Milly did it, in spite of her gifts. This is her home, her community. Times were different, too, when she took the job. I can see her doing it out of a sort of local patriotism, and maybe for economic reasons. But her situation was very different from yours. There's plenty of opportunities for a well-educated young woman today and salaries four times the size of Milly's."

She stared into her white wine. "What you're asking me basically, I guess, is why I'm not a Yuppie."

"Jesus Christ," I responded earnestly, "I hate that word. It's a dog's bad name. Why shouldn't a kid try to make money? Are they trained for anything else? But you," I added warmly, "I don't think you're in any danger of being a Yuppie. But you are in danger,"

I put up my hand, "of becoming a square peg in a round hole. I mean, you must have plans beyond this place, don't you?"

"It's all pretty vague," she said, troubled. "Right now I'm so absorbed in watching Milly work that I can't see very far beyond her. What I hope eventually to do, I suppose, is to take what I'm learning here and apply it somewhere, somehow."

"Do history you mean?"

She laughed. "Do history,"she mocked me. "Yes, I suppose you could call it that. Yes. I guess what I have in mind is to take what Milly has taught me and cut out a patch of territory and do history."

"What's missing here," I said earnestly, "is any hint of domesticity. It used to be that young women were looking for Mr. Right."

"Speaking of history," said Maria, "that is very ancient history."

"No marriage? No babies any more?"

She pursed her lips and looked very soberly at me. "Do you know," she said, "that of all the young women I know who did graduate work not one single one of them has had a baby? A few of them got married, and then they got divorced. A lot of them were living with somebody until it broke up. But none of them I know of has had a baby."

"Should they? Should you?"

"Well," she said defensively, "I guess somebody should have babies besides teen-age dropouts."

"It's a tremendous sacrifice though, isn't it?"

"For the woman it is."

This took me aback. I thought about the neighborhood I had been raised in. Where I came from a baby was very often thought to be a serious misfortune for the family—another mouth to feed for the husband and another step toward the grave for his wife. There's an awful lot of blarney about the warm-hearted blue-collar clans, but let me tell you too there was a bitterness that was unbelievable as people watched their fortunes sink with every new mouth to feed. It's a little part of history that isn't too popular to recall these days.

Maria was looking somewhat downcast and I said to her, "For Christ's sake I didn't bring you here to depress you. Let's order."

She insisted on having the sole meuniere, although I touted the steak very highly, keeping to myself the observation that her bones could stand a little more flesh on them. I had ordered another drink and she had another white wine while we waited to be served. When the steak arrived it was everything I had hoped for and I was crunching happily into it as Maria picked at her sole when I recognized someone walking up to the old gentleman's big round table. It was Sheriff McCleod. He wasn't wearing his uniform. He was dressed in a loud blue sports jacket and tan slacks. The broad collar of his sports shirt lay on the lapels of the jacket. His hair was slicked down. He looked much diminished. The old gentleman greeted him with a smile and waved the sheriff to a chair next to him. A drink was brought to McCleod without his having to order it—he was well known here. The two of them together at the big table quickly had their heads together for a serious but apparently friendly discussion. Because of the angle of their heads, I couldn't begin to read what either of them was saying.

I looked at Maria. "I give up," I announced. "Who the hell is that old guy over there talking to Sheriff McCleod?"

She looked startled, then she said, "I keep forgetting you're really a stranger here. That's Sim Lewis. Everybody knows him."

"Honey Lewis's father?"

"That's right."

"Is he some kind of politician here?"

"Not officially. Sim Lewis was the biggest bootlegger in this half of the state before he retired."

"Oh, ho," I said. "How things start falling into place! Did you know that Honey Lewis was arrested today?"

"No," said Maria. "That's very surprising. I don't think he's ever been arrested before. What on earth happened?"

"I have no idea," I answered. "All I saw was this big guy put in the sheriff's car. McCleod made the pinch himself."

He couldn't possibly have heard his name mentioned, but as if by some kind of telepathy McCleod looked up and noticed us. He waved, and then Sim Lewis took a long look at us. I could read his lips saying to McCleod, "Who is that fellow?" What McCleod answered I was unable to see, but I hadn't the slightest doubt that Sim Lewis was getting the straight story and, as far as my cover in that quarter was concerned it was gone.

I returned to my steak but within a few moments a waiter appeared with two more drinks and said, "With Mr. Lewis's compliments." I nodded my acknowledgment toward the round table and Lewis nodded back. Now I was absolutely certain that Lewis knew exactly who I was and exactly why I was there. I polished off my steak and baked potato and watched Maria reluctantly consume the last of her sole. Neither of us wanted dessert. As our coffee was being served Sim Lewis got to his feet, not without some difficulty, and headed for a leather, padded door marked OFFICE.

"Does Sim Lewis own a piece of this joint?" I asked Maria.

"I have no idea," she answered. But then she looked at me and understood the question. "That's not really the door to any real office," she said. "That leads to the gaming rooms."

I asked her if she would like to gamble. She said no and I was relieved. If you know what you're doing in gambling it's not much different from brokering in the grain pit, and people get paid for that. You get paid nothing for gambling. She got up from the table and went off to make repairs.

I was waiting for the check when Sheriff McCleod came up to the table and at my invitation sat down next to me. "Well, Sheriff," I said to him. "I got a chance to see you in action today down by the courthouse. Very impressive, handling a big fellow like that."

He gave me a long look, wondering if I was putting him on. "Honey ain't never been no trouble," he said.

"What was the occasion?" I asked him. "Was he making a disturbance?"

"According to some he was," said the sheriff. "I was just sort of heading him off to cool him down."

"Was there a formal complaint?"

"Yes there was," he answered. "Inciting a riot."

"Hell," I said. "My understanding is that that's what he's been doing all along."

"Well, nobody ever lodged a formal complaint before."

"Oh, then it wasn't you?"

He gave me a look of disgust. "Course not," he said. "It was Reverend Barlow, and I had to act on it. Barlow was coming back from some meeting or other with that van full of women and they stopped to listen to Honey for a while and then they put in a complaint. There wasn't anything I could do."

"Anything specific in the complaint?"

"They said he was urging the people to blow up the courthouse and all the buildings around it—temples of corruption he called them—and to set fire to the town and blow up the churches and all like that and to leave their homes and follow him into the hills. Far as I can make out it wasn't too different from what he's been saying all along."

"What's going to happen?"

"Nothing." He waved his hand. "We reduced the charges to disturbing the peace. I'll let him out in the morning. No different from getting drunk." He nodded toward the padded door. "That's what I come over to tell Sim about. No need for him to worry."

"Sim Lewis," I said, "seemed to be interested in who I was. You tell him?"

"Yes." McCleod looked at me directly and honestly. "I did."

"Mr. Lewis," I said, nodding toward the empty table, "seems to be something of a fixture here. Does he own it or part of it?"

"Naw," said McCleod. "It's like you say. He's a fixture here. Likes to come here and eat and drink and pick up a hand now and then."

"I got a kick out of the car he arrived in," I said, "that old Pontiac. Is that a special car that Dashwood keeps?"

"That's Sim's car," said McCleod smiling. "Dashwood keeps it up for him and drives him around when he's not on something else. Sim and Dashwood go back a long way." He stared briefly into the past and smiled again. "Yes, sir," he said. "A long, long way."

"Did Sim Lewis put up bail for his son?"

"Wasn't no call for bail," said McCleod. "Honey ain't going to be arraigned or anything. I just put him off in a corner cell by himself and told Art to keep an eye on him. Honey ain't never been in a jail cell before and I don't want him acting up. Once I turn him loose in the morning that'll be the end of it."

Maria came back to the table and stood by uncertainly. McCleod got up and greeted her and then bade us farewell. I watched him nod to a few well-dressed solid citizens on his way out. The waiter returned with my credit card and I signed us out.

When we got in the car I asked Maria, "Anyplace you'd like to go tonight? A drink? Entertainment?"

She smiled and said, "No, thank you, Joe. It was a lovely dinner and exactly what I needed just to unwind. Actually, I'm pretty tired and I've got a lot of typing to do tomorrow. So I guess what I'd really like is just to go home."

"Okay, kid. I understand."

I drove her back to her car in the Motor Lodge parking lot. "One more thing," I said. "My liquor supply is running low and I'm going to be stuck in that castle all day tomorrow. Do you know where there's a nearby liquor store?''

She thought for a moment. "You pass the Capthorne on your way back to the mansion, don't you?" I nodded. "There's a liquor store off the lobby, right across from the hotel bar."

I thanked her, and then there was that awkward moment of saying good night that appears when relationships have not been truly established. I wanted to make her feel feminine and desirable, but certainly did not want to lean on her. I took her hand. "Thanks for an evening with a beautiful girl," I told her. "You've established my reputation at the Dome as a first-class player."

She laughed. I bent down and kissed her on the cheek. "Be careful driving home," I said. "I'd like to do this again quite soon."

"I'll be careful," said Maria. "Thank you again and good night."

At the Capthorne liquor store I got another bottle of Old Fitzgerald and went into the big old-fashioned oak bar for a drink. I longed to stay there and close the place up, but I didn't want Johnson padding down in his nightclothes to let me in. Reluctantly, I left and drove out to the hill. Johnson was still wearing his white coat when he let me in. I saw his eyes flash down to the easily identifiable paper bag I was carrying under my arm. But not a word said he nor did he crack a smile. I went upstairs, fixed a nightcap, read for a while and went to bed.

15

Dead as the town was at five minutes to seven on a Sunday evening, I was grateful merely for the open space, the vistas, the shrubbery and the weathered statues on the courthouse lawn. Aside from my appearance at breakfast in the mansion I had stayed in my room dividing my time among belts of Old Fitzgerald, *The Mismeasure of Man,* and a lengthy letter to Edna in which I attempted to explain what the hell I was doing here—a difficult task since I was by no means sure I had a ready answer.

After grace had been offered at breakfast Mr. Danford had asked me my plans for the day and I had told him I had letters to write and things to read. I left out the Old Fitzgerald. I also left out my planned visit to Milly's office that evening, since I didn't think it wise to remind him again of her extracurricular activities.

He seemed satisfied with the schedule I gave him. He and his wife were dressed for church. I got the idea that after church they were off to visit somewhere for the rest of the day. That pleased me more than I was willing to indicate, although it meant that my Sunday dinner would consist of another tuna fish sandwich. (This time I ate it standing up in the pantry.)

I had put my car in the park-and-lock garage and crossed over to the square. The coolness of the evening was beginning to creep across the grass of the commons as I strolled to the back door of the old building. When I tried the door, however, it was locked, and I cursed a good round curse. There was no bell. I stomped around the building to the big front doors and there I found a bell. As much as I hated to disturb Milly and make her walk all the way to the front I really did have to see her and I had no choice. I rang the bell and waited. Time stretched interminably. The doors were massive, the big front windows shuttered for the weekend with heavy boards to discourage vandals. To kill the time I tried to visualize her crossing the big assembly space. No matter, it took forever. Finally one of the big doors cracked open and it was Milly. "Come in," she smiled wearily. "I've been expecting you. I'm sorry about the back door, but Jack McCleod insisted that I keep the place locked while I'm in here alone."

When we got to her office door, however, she surprised me by saying, "I hope you can excuse me for a little while. Maria delivered some manuscript a bit late and I have to go over it before I close up for the day." She looked at me apologetically. "Either you can go out and come back in about a half hour or you can look at *The New York Sunday Times* I brought along."

I opted for the *Times*. There was absolutely nothing to do outside except stare back at the statues. Milly handed me the disheveled pile of newsprint and indicated a chair in the anteroom of her office. She also provided me with an ashtray. Then she went into her office and closed the door.

I began the long journey through the acre of newsprint that had used up so many of my Sundays back home. I had worked my way through the news, the editorials and columns, the sports section, and was just beginning the lead article in the magazine when the door to Milly's office swung open. It was ten minutes to eight.

"I can't detain you any longer," she said, smiling at me. "It just isn't fair. I've got a lot more cross checking to do that's going to keep me here for a while, so why don't you come in and let me see what I can do for you."

"I really won't take up much of your time," I said gratefully. "If I could have used the phone to call you this would have taken only a few minutes." I followed her into the office and sat across from her at her desk.

"What I really have to know," I said to Milly, "is Charlie Welland's understanding of where he stood. You told me that he should have known the book wasn't going to be bought here. But salesmen are optimists—otherwise they wouldn't be salesmen. Was Charlie Welland absolutely certain that the book wouldn't be used by your district?"

"I sat here with Welland," said Milly, "and explained to him exactly why the book couldn't be used by us. They had cut back so far that there wasn't really anything left in the book at all. There was no reason for him to think we were ever going to buy the book."

"All right," I said. "Now let me ask you something else. Dana Martingale signs off on the books you have chosen, right?" She nodded. "Is there a chance that Welland tried to make an end run around you? That he went to see Dana Martingale and got a commitment from him?"

"Dana would never go against the wishes of the board on a textbook," said Milly. "It would be too awkward for him. Furthermore, the textbooks are not the main source of his business."

"Not even if he was offered a—I don't want to put your back up now—" I warned her, "not even if Martingale were offered a consideration?"

Milly laughed and the flesh on her shoulders shook. "Small potatoes," said Milly. "Dana will get a consideration on every single contract that goes out of here. Why on earth do you think he or anyone else bought the job? But the rakeoff from textbooks—when you compare it with fuel, food, construction, all the million things he has to sign off, is relatively slight. It doesn't really matter what textbook we choose. Dana will get paid one way or another."

"Okay," I said. "But tell me this. Did you ever notice that Welland and Martingale spent an unusual amount of time together, considering what you've told me?"

"Maria seemed to think so," said Milly reflectively. "She'd seen them together a number of places— the bar at the Motor Lodge for one. Yes, she seemed to think it was unusual, and she mentioned it to me."

I beamed at Milly. "Believe it or not," I said, "that's really all I came here to find out. I'm sorry I had to disturb you like this but I'm supposed to turn in a report tomorrow morning." She nodded and smiled, obviously eager to get back to work. I stood up.

"I suppose you heard," I said, preparing to leave, "that Honey Lewis got himself arrested yesterday."

"Yes, I heard," said Milly sadly shaking her head. "I wonder what on earth got into Jack McCleod."

"Reverend Barlow got into Jack McCleod. So Honey Lewis had to spend the night in the jug. As far as I know, they let him out this morning, none the worse for wear."

"I wonder about that," said Milly thoughtfully. She lighted a Tareyton and squinted at me. "As far as I know, the poor thing has never been incarcerated. People like Jack don't realize what all the clanking and banging and manacling and all the paralegal paraphernalia, the stone walls, the stink, the ugliness, the open toilets, all that—they don't realize what effect it can have on certain people, particularly people who are already disturbed. What I sincerely hope is that they haven't turned Honey into a savage. There's no predicting these things."

"I saw McCleod at the Dome last night," I offered. "And he assured me that Honey was being treated very well."

Milly sighed. "The best treatment in the world in a place like the county jail doesn't amount to much," she said. "Well, we'll see what happens." Then she stared at me with real urgency. "You'll have to excuse me now," she said. "But I really do have to get back to work. I have to be back in this office at eight tomorrow morning."

"I'm on my way," I said rapidly. "And thanks for everything."

"Be sure to close the door when you leave," said Milly. "It will lock itself."

I did close the front door carefully and then tried it to make sure it had locked. I looked at my watch. It was just past eight at the moment. I went down the broad stone steps and was halfway down the path that snakes through the commons when I felt the ground shudder. The shock wave hit me. I wheeled on the pathway to see the entire school board building trembling. The facade had remained intact but the back end, where Milly's office was, collapsed very slowly into the ground. A ball of flame burst out of the roof at the back and a cloud of black smoke began a fiery ascent to the sky. I rushed to the front door hoping that the blast had ruptured the lock, but the door maniacally held fast. I ran around the side of the building to the back, but the entire back end of the building was a wall of flame.

The searing heat of the flames drove me back from the rear of the building. I ran around to the side again, where I had seen the walls buckle in the hope I might be able to find an entrance where I could get in to snatch at Milly. It was a foolish, hysterical hope. Smoke and flames were already spurting from the gaps that had opened. I continued to race around from one point to another and finally around to the front again, but even the front was aflame now and smoke had begun to pour through the heavy shutters that protected the windows.

A revolving beam of red light told me the fire department had arrived—the main station was within eyesight of the courthouse square. I ran down toward the truck that was just pulling up and shouted, ''At the back. At the back. There's a woman trapped inside at the back.'' The fireman threw a startled glance at me and began to run toward the rear of the building. I ran with him. All that was visible there was a roaring conflagration. It was impossible even to get near it, let alone enter it. The truck had pulled around into the parking lot and the men were laying hose. A hose tower went up from the truck as the other trucks came along to take up strategic positions. When the water was turned on the hose tower began to direct its powerful stream down into the center of the building. Other hoses came to life to wet the sides and to play directly through the collapsed back wall. A separate truck played water on the roof of the adjacent courthouse to protect it from the sparks and flying embers. Firemen raced past me in their rubber coats and helmets and finally they pushed me completely out of the way. There was nothing I could do but stand back beyond

the barrier they had formed and watch the terrible
burning.

I saw the sheriff's car pull up, its spotlight glaring
in the dusk and the rooflight revolving. I ran toward it
and just as McCleod was getting out I grabbed him by
the arm crying, "Jack—Jack—Milly, Miss Rutledge is
in there!" he gave me a wild look full of astonishment
and dismay, straightened up as if to rush at the building, and then seeing it for what it was slumped back
against his car. He began to curse, commencing with
"goddamned son-of-a-bitch" and continued on in an
unbroken stream of curses as he ripped the hat from
his head and flung it on the ground. Finally he subsided and picked up his hat and put it on his head. He
stared at me until his eyes cleared of the misery and
were able to contain a thought. He leaned toward me
then, his face full of rage and menace, saying, "How
do you know she's in there?"

"I was talking to her in her office just before it happened," I nodded toward the flaming hulk that had
turned the gray walls of the courthouse red.

Now McCleod seized me by the arm. "You come
with me." His hand closed on my biceps like a vise.
"Anything you got to say I want a witness to hear."
He marched me over to a highly polished red car that
had CHIEF painted in gold letters on the side. The chief,
a big florid man in full regalia and with a tall white
helmet, was barking out orders as men scurried past
him. Not lessening the grip on my arm McCleod took
me up to him. "Chief," he said, "this man says Miss
Milly, Miss Rutledge, was trapped in there." The
chief stared at me and his eyes widened with rage. I
thought he was going to strike me down. His right arm
jumped. He restrained himself and his face went icy.
He said to McCleod, "How does he know she was in
there?"

I answered for myself, and the chief got an odd expression on his face when he heard my voice. I said,
"I was talking to Milly Rutledge in her office in there
only a few minutes before the building went up."

"And you didn't try to get her out?" the chief asked me, his face still frozen, still rigid.

"I couldn't get back in through the front doors, they were locked. By the time I got around to the back it was too late."

"Too late? That fast?" asked the chief. "Just in the time it takes to run to the back of that building?"

"You don't understand," I said to him. My voice must have sounded strangled. I was beginning to shake with the delayed shock of realizing what had happened. I looked at McCleod's face. "Neither one of you understands," I said. "That wasn't just a fire. It was an explosion. It blew up not more than a minute after I left the building." I began to tremble violently.

The chief said to McCleod, "You'll have to get somebody else to help hear his statement. I got work to do."

We went back to the sheriff's car, and in fact I was glad to have him holding on to my arm for the sheer support that he lent me. I felt terribly weak, empty, and sick. He sat me in the passenger's seat in the front and called over a deputy to sit in the back.

I told McCleod exactly what had happened from the time I had left the mansion that evening. When I had finished he said to me, "One thing. Now I know Miss Milly smoked cigarettes. Do you think it could have been a gas explosion? A leaky gas pipe? An accumulation in the building?"

"Not possible," I answered. "I sat in the anteroom to her office for over forty-five minutes reading the newspaper and smoking cigarettes. If there had been any kind of gas leak I would have smelled it. If it had started after I left it still wouldn't have accumulated enough to go up like that."

The sheriff was looking beyond my shoulder as he spoke. He was speaking to some demon in the air. "I was happy to see him go this morning," said Sheriff McCleod. "Preaching all night long in that cell we gave him. Roaring out like some durned animal in a zoo. Keeping everybody awake. But we dassn't touch him to keep him quiet. Oh, no. Not Sim's boy. We dassn't touch him. So we put up with it all night long and happy to put him out.

"This time he ain't going to get no nice cell, and if he opens that crazy mouth of his I'll smash his teeth out." He glared into my eyes. "Get out of the car and go home and write me up a statement. Bring it down to the office in the morning, you hear?"

I stammered—"What—what makes you so sure it was Honey?"

"It came over the radio," McCleod said impatiently. "Somebody called in and said they saw Honey running away from the back end of the building just before it went up."

"Would that have been Reverend Barlow?"

"Deputy doesn't know who the hell it was. Never left a name."

I began to climb out of the car. "Get in the front, Art," the sheriff said to the deputy in the back seat. "We're going to go up and get that white-haired son-of-a-bitch and drag him down here and rub his nose in this shit that he's made."

16

When I turned in my statement at the sheriff's office early the next morning my shock had been replaced by sheer rage. The statement said essentially what I had told McCleod and his deputy in the sheriff's car. There was a different deputy at the desk to receive it.

I asked him if they had brought in Honey Lewis. He said yes, they had. "It warn't no trouble," he told me. "He's got this durned stone shack up there in the hills. It ain't much more than a cave—just stones put up and a piece of corrugated iron for a roof. He was asleep up there in that shack and we drug him out.

"We took him right on down to the square to show him what he'd done, you know," he continued with a little prompting from me. "The whole place was all lit up with spotlights from all the trucks and Honey just fell apart. I mean he just stared at it wild like and then he fell on his knees and he commenced to pray real loud and crazy like he always does. And we had to drag him into the van—he wouldn't stand up or nothing. We had to drag him in like one of them durn protesters. And we threw him in the back cell," he nodded toward the lock-up, "and he's been praying there ever since."

I got back in my car and headed for the Mine Five road. Having Honey locked up might have made the sheriff's outfit happy but it didn't satisfy me. I was by no means sure that Milly had been the only target, or even the primary target. I wanted a good look at the little town of Bluestone. I had finally unwrapped my shoebox. The heft of the thirty-eight was very comforting nestled in my side. Edna had found a pair of handcuffs in the drawer, too, and she had sent them along as a gesture of optimism.

I kept an eye on my rear-view mirror as I made the trip up over the hill past the wreck of Welland's car and then down toward the big strip mine. As I rounded the edge of the huge pit I could see the great land-crawling machines that ripped the guts out of the earth. They were the size of steamships—monstrosities. There was nothing in them that corresponded to anything human.

The Mine Five road led into, indeed turned into, the main drag of Bluestone. The beginning of the little town was announced by a row of forlorn frame houses which I presumed were the original company-owned miners' homes. They were still all painted the same color, a deep yellow with brown trim. Only a few of them had been recently repainted. On most of them the paint had cracked and peeled in numerous places. The tiny patches of lawn in front were mostly dirt and were littered with broken toys, abandoned washing machines, and all the other detritus that seems to ooze from the broken-down homes of the poor. The houses themselves seemed to draw themselves up and stare at me as I slackened speed and rolled down the street.

The business section of the town consisted of little more than a gas station, a general store, an auto supply store, a lunch room and, yes, a bank, which was my first target for the day. The bank was the only truly solid looking structure in the town. It was the classic small American bank building of gray granite erected with a nostalgic eye cast back on the era of Greek revival. I was too early for the bank so I repaired to the lunch room and ordered a cup of coffee. The only other customers were two work-hardened men in ancient washed out sports shirts who were probably not as old as they looked. One of them had a line of blue along his lips and coughed a good deal as he spoke to the other. I'd brought along a local morning paper and I read through it carefully as I sipped my coffee and waited for the bank to open.

There wasn't much trouble in finding the manager of the Bluestone Central Bank. I think the entire staff consisted of no more than three or four people. The manager was a portly, ruddy-cheeked fellow with iron gray hair and gold-rimmed glasses. He wore a summerweight blue suit, white shirt, and gray tie with small red horses on it. He invited me to sit across from him and asked me what he could do for me this morning.

"I'm going to make a sizable delivery to the BDC company," I told him. "But before I do all that I want to make sure that the check will clear. Now the payment is going to be over fifteen thousand dollars, so you can see that I don't want to deliver all this stuff and then have to go and take it all back. So I just want to know if BDC is in a position to cover the check."

"Do you have the check with you?" he asked me.

"No. I wouldn't carry anything like that around with me." I smiled at him. "We received the check some time ago but promised not to cash it until the equip-

ment was delivered. That was all right with us because
it takes a while to get all the equipment together—
compatible stuff, you know—and into a working system. The check was signed by Charles Welland, and
I just want to make sure it will clear before we complete the transaction. Funnier things have happened.''
I smiled at him again.

"Wait here," said the manager. The sign on his
desk said he was Henry J. Matthews. He went back
behind the counter where a lone teller was arranging
his tray. I was the only customer in the bank, and
indeed, I was not a customer.

When Matthews came back he sat down again and
told me, "I don't see that you'll have any trouble
clearing that check, Mr. . . . Mr. . . .''

"Walters. Ben Walters."

"Mr. Walters, you say the check was signed by
Charles Welland?" I nodded. Matthews looked grave.
"Mr. Welland is deceased, you know."

"Yes," I said. "I was aware of that."

"So naturally," said Matthews, "you'll have to
have the check countersigned."

"Whose signature?"

He looked surprised. "Why, Martingale, of
course," he said. "Dana Martingale. You get the
check countersigned and I'm sure you won't have any
trouble. The balance is quite adequate."

I rose from my chair smiling and shook his hand.
"I want to thank you very much," I said. "We'll ship
the stuff right away."

"Any time I can help," said Matthews. "Any
time."

"Incidentally," I paused, "as long as I'm down here
I might as well get the address straight for the delivery. Where is the building located?"

"You tell your driver to just head straight down
Mine Five Road till he gets to the Socony station. He'll
be able to see the building from there set back and off
to the right. It's a concrete block building, and to tell
the truth I don't know where they put all the equip-

ment they've had delivered there. The building ain't much bigger than a mechanic's garage, and in fact, that's just what it was some time ago. They've fixed it up some now, of course."

"Thank you again," I said.

"Any time," said Matthews. "Any time."

The building was set back more than two hundred yards from the Socony station. A narrow dirt road ran past the station and into the field up to the building and around the back, where it ended. Beyond the road in back the wild field was fragrant with millions of weeds and blooms whose names I did not know. I parked my car behind the building and went around to the front door. The door was locked. The building was deserted but I hammered anyway on the thick steel door of the front. The only indication that this was a business of any kind was a small black and white sign over the door that read BDC, INC. I hammered again and waited. I went around to the back, then, and looked at the windows. They were steel frame windows of the crank-out variety set in the concrete blocks. They had been blacked out. I inspected them very carefully for the burglar alarm lash-up but, astonishingly, there was no burglar alarm. Martingale, I realized, being on his own turf, was terribly sure of himself. I searched around in the weeds and found the discarded gear of a transmission. I smashed a small pane near the center of the window, reached in and freed the lock. I laboriously cranked the thing open and crawled inside.

The opened window let in just enough sunlight for me to hunt around for the light switch. After a bit, violet-colored light flooded the room from the overhead tubes. The center of the room was pretty much bare, but ranged against the walls was a series of desks and benches with computer equipment on them. There were none of the refrigerator-sized computers that line the walls of big institutions but there was an awful lot of equipment here with numerous keyboards, CRT screens and other components whose cabinets were connected by thick bundles of wire. A filing cabinet stood near one of the larger setups and I went over to it to see what I could see. The drawers held nothing but envelopes enclosing disks, disks which I presumed held the secrets of the Welland-Martingale enterprise.

I am of that generation that has never had occasion to operate a computer. Outside of general theory—digital versus analog, logic systems, truth tables, binary numbers, etcetera, I have no practical knowledge of them whatsoever. "I must learn," I promised myself as I uttered a few choice vulgarisms to go along with my promise. It was ridiculous that I, a grown man, should stand here with a world of information closed to me. But then I remembered that an inseparable part of every computer sold is the *manual*. I could still read, goddamnit. The trick now was to find a manual in the building and match it to one of the systems. I sat down at a desk overladen with keyboard, modem, and what have you, all surrounding a rather large CRT screen, and began to go through the drawers of the desk. I was reaching into the top left-hand drawer of the desk when I saw a rectangle of light appear on the screen. The light didn't come from the screen itself. It was reflected light. Someone had opened the front door.

I kept up my search of the drawer without, I hope, a revealing hitch in my movements. I did not want to show awareness before I knew what the play was going to be. The figure of a man appeared in the rectangle of light, and as the figure moved closer, picking up the fluorescent light from overhead, I saw that in his right hand he carried a long blunt instrument. I continued to search blithely through the drawer, but I was counting in my head. Now he is one step closer. Now he is two steps closer. When the screen seemed to fill with darkness I rolled the office chair on its casters sharply to my left and watched the tire iron come down full force helplessly on the expensive equipment that had been in front of me. By that time I had my gun out, safely buttressed against my belly.

I looked at him from my chair. "Put the tire iron down, Bobby," I told him, "and stand easy."

He did not put down the tire iron, which was a truck tire iron, incidentally, of considerably length and thickness. He said, "So you're a burglar. I should have knowed it."

"No, Bobby," I said, "I'm not a burglar. I'm an investigator. And either you're going to put down that tire iron or I'm going or shoot you."

He said, "You don't scare me with that durned tin pea shooter you got there." He stood in place defiantly, still clutching the tire iron.

I shot him in the foot—the instep.

It took him a little time to realize that he had been hit. He'd heard the shot and smelled the cordite and saw the tendril curling from the barrel of the gun, but there was a beat or two before the shock of the bullet through his instep reached his brain. When it arrived the bar fell from his hand and he cried, "You shot me!" His foot came up in the air where he could grab and cradle it, and his no-color eyes bulged out in astonishment. Apparently he had never been shot before nor had ever expected to be. Being hurt was something that happened to other people.

"Put your bad foot back on the floor," I told him, "and get over against the wall, face first. Get your hands behind your back where I can cuff them because if you don't my next bullet is going to go right through your thick head."

He hobbled over to do as I had ordered. I put the cuffs on him and led him over to a chair, where I pushed him down. I put the gun in my belt and picked up the tire iron. I examined it, walking back and forth in the free space at the center of the room. I stopped finally and stared at him.

"My shoe's fillin' up with blood," he cried.

"Don't worry," I told him. "It'll all run out the hole in the bottom."

I continued to pace back and forth with the iron held up in front of me, admiring its shape and its heft. I wiggled it back and forth. I showed it to him. "You were going to split my skull open with this," I said wonderingly. "That makes twice you've tried to kill me. You know what? I don't *like* people who try to kill me."

I paced back and forth some more. When I stopped to stare at him again he cried, "I seen you from the station there, snoopin' around and breakin' in. A durned burglar robbing Mr. Martingale."

I ignored all this blather. I paced a little while longer and then I stopped and held the bar up in front of him. "You were going to smash down on me," I mused, "just like you were going to stretch me out on the road. There's not too much brains behind something like that. Not even the cute trick of hiding my car so I'd have to walk.

"But actually," I continued pacing back and forth, "a piece of iron like this can be used with care and diligence." I stopped and looked at him. "Have you ever seen anybody who's been professionally worked over with one of these?" I asked him.

He shrank back from the question. His attention was divided between the iron bar and his foot. His foot, evidently, had begun to throb.

"Now baseball bats," I continued conversationally, "are great favorites of the mob because, I guess, they like the sound that the bat makes. But I'm a deaf man. I don't get any enjoyment out of sound. Now one of these," I wiggled the iron at him again, "hardly makes any sound at all except the sound of bone that's crunching. But that's all right with me."

He tried to struggle to his feet. I put the end of the iron against his chin.

"I want to explain something to you," I said. "What this piece of iron will do in the hands of an educated fellow like myself will be to turn you suddenly into a very old man. You know what a very old man is like? A very old man is a man who hurts all the time. Every time he breathes he hurts. Every time he tries to talk he hurts. Every time he turns his head he hurts. He doesn't sleep much because every time he turns in bed he hurts. He has to have a cane to walk, and usually he's way bent over so he's always looking at the ground." I stopped midstride and looked at him. "That's what you're going to be like when you leave this building," I told him. "And your face isn't going to be anything much more than a long smear." I spun the tire iron up in the air almost to the ceiling and caught it when it returned. He watched it, mesmerized. "That's what one of these can do when it's used properly," I told him. "In fact, I'm going to mess you up pretty bad."

The shock of the gunshot wound had gotten to him. I think it was more that than the fear itself which caused him to tremble. But he did tremble, and the trembling, I knew, would unman him further because no man like to tremble and most of all no man likes to be seen trembling. Nonetheless, his chin was trembling when he asked me, "Just what do you want, mister?"

"Not much," I replied. "An couple of questions. Number one: You ran Charlie Welland—the new Ford Victoria—you ran him off the road with your truck, right?"

He looked everywhere in the room except at me. I waved the iron enticingly. His head sank down on his chest and he mumbled something.

"You'll have to look at me when you talk," I told him. "I'm deaf. I have to see you talk."

He raised his head and mumbled, "Yes."

"Martingale told you to do it?"

"Yes."

"Okay. Next question. Martingale told you to run me down in the road?"

The white face was a curious mixture of defiance and acquiescence. "He said you were a durn snooper sniffing around after Charles Welland. He said you had to go.

"And you are a snooper," he challenged me righteously. "A durned burglar is what you are."

"Yes, yes," I answered pleasantly. "That gives you the right to kill me at your leisure. But on the other hand, I might just kill you.

"Now the last thing of all," I moved up and held the bar over his head. I was not certain what the iron would do if the answer was wrong. "Did you blow up the school building? Did Martingale tell you to do that too?" I must have looked murderous. He pulled back with fear and horror on his face.

"No—no. I never. He never!" He must have been shouting. His mouth was very wide open—like a gasping fish. His eyes were wide, staring, imploring. "I never, we never had nothing to do with that there blowing up. I never knew who done it!"

I believed him.

I retreated away from the chair and twirled the bar around my fingers like your young and toothsome ordinarily provocative drum majorette.

When I returned to him I said, "I'll tell you what we're going to do, Bobby. You're going to give me the emergency number to call that Martingale gave you and we're going to put in an emergency call to Mr. Martingale. You're going to tell him that this place has been broken into and that stuff is strewn all over the floor. You are going to urge him to get out here right away. Now," I paused, "you're going to do this all nice and correctly because I'm going to be watching you. I'm going to be watching every movement of your lips and eyes, and if I see the faintest flicker of insincerity in either your eyes or your lips I'm going to split your stupid face open with this tire iron, is that clear to you?"

"Yessir," said Bobby McGowan.

He gave me the number and I wrote it down on a piece of paper. I rolled his chair over to the telephone, where I punched out the number and held the phone up to his face. I squatted down in front of him, the phone in my left hand, the iron bar in my right. I stared with deep sincerity into his eyes while he made the call. I was pretty certain that he had convinced Mr.

Martingale at the other end of the line. He certainly convinced me. When he signaled that he was finished I put the phone back in the cradle. "What did Martingale say?" I asked him.

"He said he'd be right over, but I shouldn't leave or nothing."

"Very good," I answered. "You're not leaving of course."

I jerked one of the wires out of a computer and tied Bobby to the office chair. Then I rolled the chair out of the way. I scratched a little opening in the black paint on the front window, lit a cigarette and sat down to wait.

Martingale must have gone like hell over that mountain road. The red Porsche arrived in front in half the time it had taken me to drive over.

17

He came racing up to the front door and very nearly crushed me standing behind it as he flung it open. When he was truly inside, glaring wildly around, I kicked him squarely in the small of the back, which sent him halfway across the room and flat on his face on the concrete floor. I stepped on his neck and put the end of the gun right up to his eyeball. "Blink and you're dead," I told him.

I had already set up the wire in my hand with a running bowline. I very quickly tied his hands behind him and lashed them to his ankles. His nose was bleeding copiously and his nice new suit was a mess. I patted him down and found a Beretta nine-mm automatic. A pretty gun. I put it in my pocket and held on to my revolver. I've never really trusted automatics.

I went over and rolled Bobby away from his position

facing the wall. I went back to my chair near the peep-hole, sat down, lit another cigarette and stared at Martingale. Finally I smiled at him. "I suppose you're wondering why I invited you here," I said to him.

He was trying to shake the blood away from his nose and mouth. He'd have been better off letting it clot. When his face was clear enough he began hurling a stream of outraged curses and imprecations at me, none of which need delay us here. I let him run out his string until he had very nearly exhausted himself.

"Well, Mr. Martingale," I said, unheeding, "the reason I invited you here is that you were quite correct in assuming that I was a snoop. I am a private investigator hired by Carlson House to find out where in the hell a hundred and fifty thousand dollars worth of books disappeared to. To tell you the truth, I didn't expect to get results quite this fast. You appear to be a victim of your own self-confidence. You might swing a lot of weight down here on your own turf, but you've gotten yourself into interstate commerce, which is quite another thing. It's a big, big world out there.

"The reason I messed you people up," I continued, "is that you tried to kill me in a very mean, nasty way, just as you killed poor old Charlie Welland. When people are violent with me I tend to get violent right back. This all could have been settled quite peaceably—most of my cases are—but you really shouldn't run around trying to kill people, particularly not a pair of amateurs like you."

The bleeding had subsided. His bloodstained face stared up at me and the brown eyes were blazing with hatred. He began to struggle against the wire.

I picked up the tire iron and began to walk around with it. The struggling stopped and he regarded me warily. "You mustn't hold any of this against Bobby, here," I gestured toward the man in the chair. "He did the best he could with this tire iron. But he missed. Tough luck. I shot him in the foot. He didn't have much choice but to trap you.

"Now," I resumed conversationally, "I had to

threaten Bobby with this iron to get a straight story out of him.'' I smiled at Martingale and waved the iron at him. He stiffened. ''But I'm not going to have to threaten you.'' He relaxed somewhat but continued to watch me nervously. I think there's something about my voice that makes people nervous.

''What you've got here,'' I waved the iron at all the computerized junk along the walls, ''is obviously an inventory distribution control system, just like the nice sign says over your door—BLUESTONE DISTRIBUTION CONTROL INCORPORATED. The big trouble is that you, your company, doesn't have any inventory to distribute or control. As I see it, you were distributing other people's inventories without them knowing anything about it.

''The way I see it,'' I continued, ''is that when Charlie realized that he wasn't going to be able to peddle those textbooks down here to Milly—'' and there was a sudden flash of rage in me at the recollection of Milly that made both of them shrink back. I calmed myself and went on, ''he came crying to you about it. Well, you couldn't very well cross up Miss Rutledge on the one and only territory she really controlled. But you did get a bright idea. You could sell the books to another district that was a little less discriminating. And then you got an even brighter idea. Why should anybody really know anything about it? A computerized inventory control system means that all you have to do is tap into the line, order the books, and after they're delivered, tap into the line again and erase the whole transaction, right?

''Now sure as hell there's a hard copy made of the transaction back at the home office. But all you have to do then is get your confederate, the same guy that gave you the access code, to pull the copy out of the file when he gets back home and destroy it.

''Of course this meant capitalization to buy the equipment to pull the scam. And so you set up a company, you and Charlie. What's to worry? Nobody's going to fuck around with you down here, and as far

as Charlie was concerned, this place was the other side
of the moon. Nobody in New York really believes that
places like this exist. They're very provincial up there
in New York.

"So Charlie got the code entry. You bought the junk
and pulled the scam. But obviously you couldn't stop
there." I waved the iron at him. "You," I said, "have
a million business contacts. Charlie wanders all over
the region, meeting people and talking with them about
business. It's pretty obvious that you wouldn't have
invested in all this crap," I nodded toward the walls,
"for just one job. Opportunities are limitless, and so
you set up shop.

"Now as for Charlie," I pursed my lips and thought.
"I don't know why you killed him, and to tell you the
truth, I don't much care. Either he got greedy or you
got greedy; he got scared or you got scared. In either
event you told musclehead here," I nodded toward
Bobby, "to get into his great big truck and run him
off the road. It must have been a very frightening, very
terrible way to die, not that I know of many good
ones. But with Charlie out of the way and the case
written down as an accident you had complete control
of the outfit. You could tap in and out of computer
controlled warehouses almost at will. It turns out that
those famous access codes aren't all that hard to come
by.

"So here we are," I summarized. "I haven't got a
shred of proof that you killed Charlie, nor even that
you tried to kill me. Sheriff McCleod sure as hell
doesn't believe a word of it. As to the computer scam,
Sheriff McCleod couldn't care less. In the first place,
I don't think he'd know any more what to do with the
disks you've got in there than I do. My guess is that
McCleod would write the whole thing off. Your game
might be queered as far as computers are concerned
for a while, but basically, you'd get off without a
scratch, as usual. If anybody had to fall, it would be
Bobby, here, who appears to be a natural born chump.

"The trouble with this lovely scenario," I smiled at

him, "is that you were stealing across state lines. Now the Federal Bureau of Investigation is crazy about cases like this because they go right into the good old statistics. The statistics go right into making up the budget for next year—and budget is everything. So they're going to love you.

"They will know exactly what to do with the disks you've got in there. The FBI has been using computers since day one. They know everything about computers there is to know. And nowadays they've hired a lot of accountants, too, so they don't spend all their time chasing kids across state lines in hot cars. They'll work out all the information they need, right down to the size of the fillings in your back teeth."

Bobby McGowan struggled in his chair. "You're going to call the feebies?"

"You're too fast for me, kid," I told him. "You got the idea right off the bat. Furthermore, you're going to help me call the feebies."

He retreated in his chair with a look of disgust on his face.

"What's going to happen," I said, "is that you're going to help me put in a call to my home office. A lady is going to answer, and when she answers you're going to say, 'Joe Binney wants to speak to you. Hold on please.' Then you're going to nod to me to signify that I can begin talking. Now, after I've finished talking, federal agents are going to show up here within one hour or else I'm going to start working you people over with this bar—starting with you." I pointed at Bobby. "And I'm going to continue working you over until the feebies arrive. I don't have to justify anything. All I have to tell them is that it looked like you two were getting loose and ready to attack me.

"And don't think I'm bullshitting you either," I told them. "I'd love to give both of you a taste of this. So be sure you get the phone call right the first time."

I punched out my number in New York and held the phone up to Bobby's face. Martingale watched us from the floor. It was the system that had trapped him and he knew it. I saw a light go on in Bobby's sallow face signifying that someone had answered. I watched his lips say, ''Joe Binney wants to talk to you. Hold on.'' He nodded to me and I took the phone.

''Edna? Listen. This is an emergency call. I'm not at the mansion. Write this down. I'm in the building of the BDC corporation in Bluestone on Mine Five Road out behind the Socony station. Got that? I'm holding two dangerous felons at bay here, and I'm not at all sure how long I can hold them. These two guys are involved in interstate theft by computer and also murder and attempted murder. Make sure you've got that straight because it's important—the interstate business I mean. I want you to call the Federal Bureau of Investigation office in Caunotaucarius and tell them to get here in one hell of a hurry.

''Okay. Now for your own consumption. It's really not all that dangerous. I've got these two clowns tied up pretty good and they're not going anywhere that I can see. They killed Charlie Welland and they're the ones that tried to kill me. But I want the Feds racing up here with all sirens going and all steamed up, you understand? I don't want to sit around here all day with this garbage. The Feds will be sore when they find out it's not really an emergency, but there's nobody they can take it out on except these two, and that suits me right down to the ground.

''It looks like the case is all wrapped up, kid. Unless I have to hang around for a day or two to be a witness, I ought to be home by tomorrow night.

''Don't worry about me. I'm okay. Make the call now, and I'll call you on the Code-Com from the mansion when I get back.'' I put the phone back in the cradle.

It did take them almost an hour to get there. I was sitting in the chair near the door smoking cigarettes and glancing at my watch and then to the tire iron. I suppose that Bobby's foot was hurting pretty badly. He might have let out a moan now and then. He had a very mournful hound dog look to him. Martingale kept flopping around on the floor like a landed trout trying to loosen his bonds, although what he thought he was going to do when he got free was not something I could figure out. He was the kind of person who has to keep up a display even to himself. I'm sure he was shouting at me. I didn't bother to read him. Finally, out of sheer boredom I watched his mouth. He was shouting, "He was a thief. Charlie Welland was a thief. He never paid all that much money for those computers. He faked those bills and he raked off money from the top. From me! From his partner! After I set it up and all!"

I suppose there is no outrage in the world like that of a thief from whom something has been stolen.

They didn't come in like gangbusters at all. They strolled through the door with no more haste than two middle-aged men going to a lodge meeting. They were old-timers, both of them, who had apparently been put out to pasture in the boonies. They were very old-fashioned—they both wore white shirts and dark ties. Their attitude was paternal. In the older one, whose named turned out to be Burton, it was almost grandfatherly. The other one was slightly younger, although his hair, too, was turning gray, and his name was Jim Dunn.

When they came in I put my hands up shoulder high to show that I was harmless and introduced myself. I explained that it had been my secretary in New York who had put through the call. I then drew their attention to the two captives. The one on the floor was apparently yelling, and Dunn told him sharply to shut up. I pointed to the filing cabinet and the computer equipment and related the information essentially as I had laid it out for Martingale. I suggested that they hold this pair of beauties for murder and attempted murder—I was willing to sign the complaint—while they had their experts go through the files. They took it all pretty calmly, although they were definitely interested in the computer aspect, that being a hot item these days.

I said to them, "You don't have to bring my name into in at all if you don't want to. All my job amounts to is to make a report to Mr. Carlson to show what happened to the shipment. For all of me you can say your suspicions were aroused and you busted in here. You're welcome to it."

"No go," said Burton with a sad smile. "The phone call from New York is recorded. We'll have to play it as it lays, but that's okay with me. We don't often get a haul this tricky down here."

When they were taking him out Martingale was yelling, "My car! My car! What about my car?"

"I guess we'll have to confiscate that, sonny," Dunn told him with a smile.

I promised them I'd be down at the office in the morning to swear out a complaint, and I also pointed out that Bobby McGowan's foot was in need of attention. They carried out some of the file drawers with them and put them in the trunk of their car. Then they put a SCENE OF THE CRIME sticker on the door and told me they'd send somebody down for the rest of the evidence. A phone call produced a couple of local cops to stand in front of the door and guard the evidence.

When I climbed into my car I realized that I was exhausted. The big adrenaline rush had come and gone, leaving my body and my mind like a lonely beach from which the tide had receded. There were odd thoughts and odd emotions left behind sticking up out of the sand.

I got back to the mansion with the idea that I could put in a quick call to Edna and then go directly to my room. However, Johnson stopped me in the foyer and handed me a note. It said in his handwriting, "Mr. Simon Lewis telephoned to say that he wants very much to see you—urgent—tomorrow at two P.M. at the Capthorne Hotel."

It took me a while to make up my mind. Then I called Edna and related the happy events of the day. I thanked her profusely for quick and marvelous work. Then I added, reluctantly, that an unforeseen appointment had come up and that I would probably be down here for another day.

18

The old-fashioned saloon that served as the bar for the Capthorne Hotel invited me in from the hotel lobby. I was half an hour early for my meeting with Sim Lewis, but I could think of no better place to spend the time. I had the place pretty much to myself except for a couple of old-timers who were having a beer at a table in the corner. They regarded me with judicious care as I came in but decided that I was harmless and returned to their review of days gone by. I planted myself at the bar and ordered the usual.

To tell the truth, I was tired—at one-thirty in the afternoon! The statement I had made to the Feds that morning had not been brief. Burton and Dunn had more or less dismissed my first offering, which had not taken much more than two pages of handwriting, and had begun questioning me to get the story the way they wanted it. By the time we were finished it took up eight typewritten pages, which I signed.

Burton and Dunn were friendly enough but the guy they had flown down from New York was not. He was a computer expert, and they had for his benefit loaded all the equipment from the BDC building into a room at the back of their office. The guy from New York was outraged that I had jerked the wires out of these expensive machines to use merely as tie-ups. "What was I supposed to use?" I asked him plaintively, "shoelaces?" His real beef, I suspect, was that I didn't show the proper respect for the new technology. He appeared to be bitching and cursing as he removed the cabinets from the machine to refit the wires. He had already served his purpose, however, Burton told me.

Using one of the machines I had left untouched, he had mated a compatible disk and had turned up information that Mr. Martingale was hard put to explain. The disk had revealed the access code to one of the giant building supply companies and an inventory of one of their warehouses. A call from the Feds to the warehouse manager turned up the news that they too had suffered mysterious losses of their products. That alone, Burton told me, was enough to hold Martingale for a while. The attempted murder charge would stall the idea of immediate bail. They wanted Martingale around where they could find him easily, said Burton.

My confrontation with the Feds was at least straightforward, unlike the one I had had earlier with Mr. Danford. Because he and his wife had been invited out I had missed them at the dinner table. When I had come down in the morning, however, Danford was already at the breakfast table preparing himself for the day's business. He greeted me with a nod and commented, "You seem to have had quite an adventure yesterday." He paused and smiled encouragingly at me.

I didn't know how much Johnson had told Danford, or really how much Johnson actually knew. It seemed pretty clear that he had stood by listening to my one-sided conversation with Edna when I'd returned from Bluestone. It no longer made much sense to hold anything back from Danford.

I said, "First, I'd like to apologize for accepting your hospitality under false pretenses. It wasn't really part of my plan, but once Mr. Carlson set it up this way there didn't seem to be much I could do."

He accepted the apology with a grave little smile. He said, "I am not unfamiliar with private investigation agencies."

"Mr. Carlson sent me down here to find out if his salesman, Charlie Welland, had been stealing from him. It turned out that he had. He and Dana Martingale set up a computerized operation to steal from computerized inventories. I guess Welland was a computer buff or hacker as they call them. He gave Martingale the know-how while Martingale supplied the capital. Of course Martingale had many opportunities for theft. They'd tap into the company's line, order the stuff delivered, and then erase the order. That meant the material missing would have been quite legitimately delivered somewhere but there would be no record of it. It was a slick operation, but just a bit too slick for Mr. Martingale. I found out that once you punch through the facade what you've really got there is a little hoodlum.''

Mr. Danford asked me, ''Do you suppose that young Dana was actually stealing from the school board itself?''

I looked at Danford and considered him very carefully. He was not a stupid man but he had just asked a very stupid question. I wondered if he was toying with me. I decided to answer seriously. ''I don't think that Martingale would be *that* dumb,'' I said. ''It would all be too easily traceable. There really wasn't any need for him to steal directly. Everybody who was doing business with the school board had to pay Martingale up front merely for the privilege. It's the way an awful lot of business is done in this world and I think a lot of businessmen consider it to be more or less a legitimate expense. The semantics of the thing are in whether you are paying a premium or a bribe. After the sale was made, of course, there then had to be a kickback to Martingale. On the face of it would look as if the company was losing money on the deal. But that isn't the way it works. Either the company would have to adjust the price to cover the kickback, or if that got questioned, short on the product.''

''The product?'' asked Danford.

''Certainly. If we're talking about fuel, let's say a few tons here and few tons there are short to each school over the school year. If it's food for the school lunches you ship in hamburger with a high fat content and water the milk until the butterfat content drops to zero. What the hell do the kids know? Who'd listen to a kid if he did complain? If it's construction material the concrete gets mixed with a little more sand than is called for. When cracks develop in the building there's an inquiry, sure, but nothing ever comes of it. If it's roof repair the asphalt is laid on like so much onion-skin. So the roof leaks. Who's going to complain? Does the principal want to be a troublemaker? There are no real complaints and the patchwork continues. So Martingale didn't have to steal from the budget as long as he could go on stealing from school children. They're a very easy mark.''

Danford was looking very grim and disapproving, but just the bald recital of what goes on had heated me up a little and I plunged on. "We were all sitting around here talking about the mortality of school children, how to improve it and all. I think one of the first things to improve it would be to stop stealing from them.''

"You have a very cynical attitude, Mr. Binney.''

"I'd say I'm merely being realistic,'' I countered. "Government and politics has always been a den of thieves. It works on the prebendary principle. The salary is ridiculously low, but the job itself is a license to steal. It's always been that way and probably always will be. Although,'' I added grimly, "it doesn't show up all that much in high school civics textbooks.''

He was definitely scowling now. He liked what I had been saying so little that he changed the subject. "And what are your plans now?'' he asked me, his eyebrows raised in patrician politeness. His expression communicated really that no matter what my plans were he did not approve.

"I was hoping that I'd be going back to New York this evening,'' I said. "But something else has come up and I'm curious to find out what it is.''

"Something else?'' The eyebrows maintained their altitude.

"Yes. Johnson took a call here from Mr. Lewis, Sim Lewis, who wants to see me about something this afternoon.''

A shadow of definite disapproval, even anger, dropped across his face. I think the key word must have been *Johnson*. Johnson had neglected to keep him informed. Mr. Danford did not like surprises. He let his features soften before saying, "I wonder what on earth Sim Lewis wants with you?"

"I haven't got the slightest idea. Could it have anything to do with Martingale do you think? Or Bobby McGowan?"

Danford's mouth turned down in a very definite negative as he slowly shook his head. "I can't believe Sim Lewis knows young Dana at all, and I don't believe he'd have any interest in someone like Bobby McGowan unless they were related, and I'm positive that they're not. No—no," his eyes searched one way and another as if to poke into some cubbyhole of his mind. "I can't believe it has anything to do with the Martingale affair." I was a little surprised at the depth of his interest. Danford was more than surprised. He was concerned. I excused myself from the table and left him pondering.

The wall telephone behind the bar had apparently rung. The bartender went over to answer it. After he'd hung up he came over to me and asked, "Is your name Joe Binney?" And when I'd agreed, he said, "Mr. Lewis would like to see you now."

"How'd he know I was in the bar?"

The bartender said, "Sim knows where everything is." He smiled. "The bellhop will take you up there."

The bellhop turned out to be a wizened little guy who might have been hatched on the day the cornerstone was laid for the Capthorne, which was surely before World War I. The hotel was one of those buildings that are seen from the highway jutting up above the low structures of a minor league town. In the big cities almost all these old hotels have been torn down, but in the smaller towns they hang in there as a relic of former glory. The elevator had not been modified since the day it was installed, and it trembled with the effort of lifting us to the tenth floor, the top floor of the building. When we arrived he propped the gate open and I followed him down a short corridor to the end where he knocked on a door that had no number to it. Sim Lewis opened the door. I already had the dollar in my hand to tip the bellhop, who took it with an expressionless nod and retreated to his cage.

Lewis said, "Come in, Mr. Binney. Come in." He was wearing dark pants, an old white shirt that was open at the collar. His feet were shod in carpet slippers. He was neat, clean, and well shaven—his white hair gleamed—but his pale blue eyes had a tired and sober look to them. "Sit down, sit down," he said. "Over here where it's comfortable." He went over to one of the big mohair covered easy chairs and swung it around so that it faced its mate. Watching him do it, I saw the remnants of a powerful athletic man who still retained some of the main strength of his big shoulders and chest. Fat had covered them well but the muscles were still there. He had set up the makings for drinks in the kitchenette alcove. There was a decanter of whiskey paler than I was accustomed to and a pitcher of icewater. He did not ask me if I wanted a drink. He simply poured two fingers of whiskey into the bottom of a tumbler, looked at me and asked, "Water?" I nodded. He put in what he considered a judicious amount and handed it to me. Then he went back and fixed one for himself.

While he was presiding over drinks in the kitchenette I took in the room. I could have called it spartan except that the furniture as old as it was—and I figured it must have been out of style for more than sixty years—was well-padded and comfortable. The mohair had worn away at certain strategic areas and the base of the fabric shone through the gravy colored plush. The wallpaper had been nondescript when it was hung, but the years of coal smoke from the outside and cigarette smoke from the inside had laid across it a kind of varnish that obscured the pattern. I guessed that the other door to this room led to Lewis's bedroom, and in there, I would have been willing to bet, was a big double metal bed (metal discourages bedbugs), a waterfall chiffonier and matching dresser. The big corner windows in the room looked over the city, which seemed to drowse in the afternoon heat. Two of the windows were open to the air and the breeze up here was sufficient to keep the room cool and comfortable.

Lewis sat down across from me and raised his glass. "Your health, Mr. Binney," he said. I raised my glass and smiled and took a sip. It was superb. It was possibly the best bourbon I had ever tasted in my life or ever will for that matter. I suppose my eyes bulged a little. "This stuff is marvelous," I said. The pure pleasure had reduced me to an almost childlike wonder. "Really marvelous."

Lewis smiled, in fact, he chuckled. It seemed I had passed a very serious test. "Private stock," he said. "I've never sold a drop of it. This is front porch whiskey." We both took another delightful sip. Sim Lewis sank back in his chair and sighed. He looked at me then with some concentration. "Mr. Binney," he said, "when I was talking to Jack McCleod the other night over at the Dome he told me that you are a private detective. Is that right?"

"That's right," I agreed reluctantly, "although I don't think it was Jack McCleod's place to tell you so."

He waved this aside. "Jack and I have very few secrets from one another," he said. "And you can be pretty sure your secret's safe with me."

"It isn't much of a secret anymore," I grimaced. "I was about to pack up and go back to New York before I got your message."

"Well, you did show up and I'm grateful for that." He raised his glass again and we both took a sip of the astonishing balm. He said, "You figure everybody knows about it since you got mixed up with that young Martingale, is that it?"

"That's what it looks like."

"Damned young fool," Lewis said. "Anybody could have seen he was headed for trouble." He shook his head. "We've always had trash around here of course," he said with a sort of apologetic gesture, "but after the big companies moved in we got a different kind—trash with money." I smiled. "How'd you get on to him so quick?"

"Well, of course," I began modestly, "everybody knew he was stealing, but as far as I could see that simply went with the job." Lewis nodded his assent. "All that mattered to me was whether he was stealing from my client. I'm not out to reform the world." Again there was the appreciative nod. "If he hadn't tried to have me killed the thing wouldn't have happened so fast, and," I looked at him seriously, "I wouldn't have been quite so vindictive."

"Yes," Lewis responded. "Jack told me about that. He said he thought it was just an accident."

"An accident would have suited Jack better," I said. "But I knew it couldn't have been an accident. There were very few people who knew I'd be up there. Jack was one of them, of course, but I know that young Martingale was looking over my shoulder when I was showing Jack's map to Maria. I figured it had to be him."

"Maria," said the old man, "that's the young lady was with you at the Dome?"

"Yes. Maria Thorndyke. She is—she was—Milly Rutledge's assistant."

At the mention of Milly Rutledge he sank back in the chair again. His heavy face sagged and his sad eyes stared at a point just above his knees. He took a very deep draught of his drink in a way we are taught not to drink bourbon. "Milly Rutledge," he said, looking up at me. "Yes. That's why I asked you to come over here. I want to talk to you about that. You were there, weren't you?"

"Yes. I had just left the building when it went up."

He shook his big head. "Terrible," he muttered. "Terrible." Then he said with more energy, "Finish up that drink and let me fix you another and then we'll talk some."

I hated to scoff down anything that fine so quickly, but I did his bidding as he drained his glass. He went back to the kitchenette and fixed us another set. He put them down on the end table next to me where they remained untouched as he began. He said, "Before we talk about anything serious I think you ought to know a little about me. That's only good business, you being a stranger here." I signaled my agreement. He continued, "I don't know what you've been told about me, if anything, but we ought to get the record straight. If you've been told anything at all it's that I'm a bootlegger—*was* a bootlegger," he emphasized with a gesture of his hand. He picked up his glass and took a sip.

"Bootlegging down here ain't quite what it was up in the big cities—Chicago, New York, those places. Up there it came in with the prohibition and died out when Roosevelt came in with the repeal. Down here it's always been a way of life, a part of life since the country got started. Down here folks don't take to having their whiskey taxed. It's a natural part of life and it's kind of like having your well water taxed or the air you breathe. It's a natural thing for a man to make his own whiskey, and some folks can't see any reason why they shouldn't branch out a little and sell some of it."

He reflected on what he had said and took another sip. "Now there's bootleggers and there's bootleggers," he said. "There's some folks with a little nocount still out in the woods that'll make stuff that would blind a mule. They sell it around—a pint here, a pint there—none of it amounts to much. Pretty much they're harmless, but sometimes they get careless or hurried and they poison people and blind them or even kill them.

"I can't pretend I didn't start out that way," said Lewis, looking into his past with a sad blue eye. "Times were hard and it was a chance to pick up some extra money. I wasn't just hardly married and with a baby on the way when I lost my job as a carpenter at the mine. I started making whiskey. It was only natural, and I was careful. I don't think a single person in the world has ever been hurt by whiskey that came from my hand. I never told my wife anything about it. She was a Griffiths, you know—terrible proud. So when she'd ask what I was doing I'd just shunt her off with, 'Oh, this and that. Anything to make a dollar.' And I'd tell her I expected to get my job back at the mine pretty soon, although I knew that was never going to happen. And to tell you the truth, I was already making more money with whiskey than I ever could at the mine. Even so, when I thought I was getting things under control the baby died. Wasn't much more than a year old, and Marjory took it hard, real hard." He took another reflective sip, and this time I joined him.

"She just kind of drew back into herself. It wasn't that she blamed me for anything. I mean it wasn't like that. She kept the house and fixed the meals and went to church and all that, but her heart wasn't in anything at all. You couldn't approach her—I mean, I couldn't approach her. We weren't really like man and wife." He seemed to shrink from the delicacy of this subject and lapsed into a brief silence.

"Well, it went on like that for a long, long time—nearly up to ten years. I was mighty busy with branching out. It never occurred to me that I could do anything else, now that I was doing so well. Folks got to trust my whiskey and mostly they bought what I had to offer. I didn't see myself as much different from any other businessman. And of course the life—the life itself, running here and there, socializing, you know, being a good time Charlie, picking up bar bills here and there, helping folks out when they were in trouble—and an awful lot of them were in trouble—putting in a word here and there when somebody's youngster got on the wrong side of things, buying groceries for the family when some fella got sent to the pen. It ain't much different from being a politician, I suppose, though I never saw myself as quite that crooked. I was making money and I was spending money. Marjory never wanted for anything. And I was buying property on the side, too, a little here, a little there. She never knew much about all that. She never really knew very much about me, what I was doing and all. We were strangers in that house. It was a damned tragedy. I loved her. I never stopped loving her, even though I had other women. I'm only human after all. But Marjory, she was a godawful beautiful woman." He took another sip. His eyes now, I noticed, were becoming tragic.

"Well, Mr. Binney," he resumed, "we'd been living almost ten years like that when I did something I very rarely do—I got drunk." He paused to let me realize the seriousness of this. "My business just took a sudden jump where I saw that I'd be getting three or four times the amount of money I was already making, which was considerable. So I had a high old time with my friends and I come home in the middle of the night a roaring and a singing—I was happy. And I wasn't quite ready to go to bed just yet and I set a bottle of whiskey on the table in the kitchen there and was just sitting there drinking and singing old songs to myself just plain out of happiness. And Marjory come down then in her nightclothes to ask me what on earth was going on here. And I was so happy and full of everything that I bust out, 'By God, Marjory, I think we're going to be millionaires,' and I thought this would make her happy, her being a Griffiths and all. And I reached over and took her by the wrist to pull her down and talk to her." His face went slack.

"But do you know when I took hold of her like that it was like a bolt of lightning went right through me. She was such a beautiful woman—she had the most beautiful form—when I took hold of her like that I couldn't let go. May God strike me dead if that ain't the truth. I couldn't let go of her. And she never forgave me. She hadn't had nothing against me before that, but for that she never forgave me. Not even after the boy was born—the white-haired boy she loved so much. It would look like if you gave a woman something she loved as much as Marjory loved Honey, she'd forgive you, wouldn't she? But no. She never forgave me. She was a Griffiths.''

"The Griffiths,'' I asked, wondering. "Were they a very old family around here? A rich family?''

He stared at me, his dimming blue eyes returning from long years past. "Of course,'' he said, "you wouldn't know, you being a stranger and all. The Griffiths, old man Gareth Griffiths was a founder of the Pendragon mines, along with old Ephraim Danford.''

19

The need to explain all this seemed to agitate him. He rose from his chair and walked around the room in his gimpy way holding his drink alongside him. It was evident that he was talking to me because he was gesturing, but I couldn't see his face. I said sharply, "Mr. Lewis, I have to see your face when you talk. I can't hear anything at all and I have to read your lips to understand you.''

He was immediately contrite. He swung around, his face troubled, and he said, "I most surely do apologize, Mr. Binney. That was mighty careless of me and it won't happen again.'' He remained standing there facing me as he prepared to re-enter the past. "Well, Mr. Binney,'' he said, "Marjory was the only Griffiths left when I married her. Her pa had run off, that was David Griffiths Junior, the grandson of old Gareth Griffiths—everybody just called him Junior—he run off when Marjory was only a little girl. Couldn't have been more than ten years old. He deeded his interest over to the Danfords and just disappeared. It was pretty much of a mystery. His wife, Julia Griffiths, she'd died when the little girl was only six or seven. So

Marjory was left all alone in the world, as they say, and she was left without one single cent. I mean her who had been practically an heiress. Nobody knew what to do about her.''

"The Danfords," I suggested, "didn't they take her in?''

"No sir!" said the old man emphatically. "They did not. What the Danfords did was pay old Mother Henry out on the other side of town to let Marjory live with her in an old house that wasn't much more than a damned shack. She stayed there with that crazy old woman all the time she went to high school without hardly a decent dress or coat to keep her warm in the winter. And she went on that way until she graduated from high school and got herself a job in the dry goods department at the Sears and Roebuck. She moved out of there then and into a little room at Ma Kettle's rooming house, and the old woman froze to death in her shack that winter.

"Well," he said with a big sigh, "I saw her there at the Sears and Roebuck and I courted her and I won her." He took a sip of his drink as if aiding the warmth of the memory. "And the rest purely happened the way I told you."

He paused for a while to let his feelings subside, and then he came back to sit in the chair. "We were going to be millionaires," he repeated, and a slow, sad, ironic smile pulled down the corners of his lips. "What I didn't know, of course, was that all those chances I saw to spread out the business were just chances for the other side to come in and get me. And they got me. It wasn't six months after that night when they come right down to the house and arrested me. Marjory, of course, was in the family way by then. She was well along. Well, they arrested me and I went down and put up the bail and it all started up about the trial and all. But that was the first time that Marjory knew anything about what I'd been doing—where the money come from. She thought I'd been dabbling in real estate. Dabbling—that was her word for it.''

He gripped the arms of the chair. "The trial took a whole year. Of course we delayed as much as we could, and then they had a whole lot of evidence all taking lots of time to present. I was out on bail all the time, so I was there to see Marjory through her family time, although she wouldn't speak to me, and I was there when Honey was born. I was there when he was a little baby. A cuter little fella you never saw in your life." He looked at me directly, his eyes suddenly empty. "Honey's over forty years old now," he said. "It kind of takes you.

"I drew five years in the Federal pen," said Lewis. "Dash drew three years counting off his time for good behavior."

"Dash," I said. "That's Jackson Dashwood?"

"Sure enough," said Lewis, smiling. "He was my driver. He could go ninety miles an hour over a country road blindfolded. Nobody could touch him. He knew every rock and gulley in this half of the state. There wasn't ever anybody like Dash. Well, Dash took it like a man, and I promised I'd make it up to him when he came out. And I did. And," Lewis laughed suddenly, "he's been making it up to me for making it up to him ever since." The laughter expanded until his belly shook. Then he became serious again. "That was a very bad time for Marjory," he said with a soft look on his face.

"I don't mean she wanted for anything. I was able to sell off a little no-account property that kept her pretty much the way she'd been. But it was hard for her to live with being nothing more than a bootlegger's wife, and him in jail. You see," he leaned forward and stared at me earnestly, "it was terrible for her when her pa run off like that, and now she felt that kind of it was happening all over again, although I surely never left her bad off the way her pa did. But," he added, sinking back into the chair, "that didn't really matter to Marjory. She acted like I'd just up and left her after deceiving her, the way her pa did.

"The five years in Atlanta wasn't easy," said Lewis.

"And I suppose it was even harder for Dash. When I come out I helped him set up the livery business because I didn't want him falling for any second offense. That would have been too much." He paused and sipped his drink, thinking of what he was about to say. "Atlanta wasn't easy," he repeated, "but the real hard part was coming home to Marjory and the boy. The boy was just turning six, about to start first grade he was. But the fact is the Federal pen had been friendlier to me than that house was.

"Oh, I mean she never said I couldn't stay there. I mean I had to stay someplace to get my bearings and get started up again. But it was very cold there. She wouldn't talk to me, wouldn't answer me nothing at all. And the boy was scared out of his wits of me. He acted like I was that Frankenstein monster, you know. I bought him every kind of a toy there was, even toys that most boys would give their eye teeth for, but he wouldn't never touch them or have anything to do with me. I must admit," he said—and it was incredible the amount of pain that suffused the old blue eyes—"that hurt. That hurt an awful lot. Yessir." He finished his drink and gestured for me to do the same. I think he went to the kitchenette mostly to hide his emotion.

After he served the next set—and I was hoping that this would be the last because in spite of the silken smoothness of the bourbon it was very powerful stuff—he sat in the chair again and looked at me. "Well," he said, "it turned out that Marjory had got herself a bad tumor swelling up inside her while I was in the pen. It come about, finally, that it was cancer. And it killed her. Little Honey was just about past seven then. So I buried Marjory.

"The boy was something terrible to see after Marjory died. He was a pure lost soul, he surely was. I got in a good old woman to take care of him, Mrs. Clayton. She was a widow and her sons had grown up and gone to Detroit to work in the factories. She did a great deal for Honey. She knew what boys are like, and it was like she was making him into a real boy.

He got to the place where he could speak to me, and if I gave him something he could play with it. I gave him a good first baseman's mitt one time, and he played with it. I saw him do it, although he couldn't see me standing back there. I never let him see me watching him.

"Well, Mr. Binney, it got to the place where he'd actually ride in the car with me when I was going about tending to my business. Now, business was expanding right back to where it had been when I went to the Federal pen. I was about to put in a very big operation in the old Mine Five."

"Mine Five?" I asked, startled. "You mean like the Mine Five road?"

"Yessir. That old mine was abandoned and I bought it up. It was abandoned because it wasn't safe for mining any more—there was a seepage. It wasn't nothing that couldn't be took out with sump pumps, but they didn't think the mine would take any more blasting or drilling. They were afraid the whole thing would flood. So I bought it off them. It wasn't very much I paid for it, but it was just exactly what I wanted.

"If you're starting a big operation," he said, settling back again, "what you want is an old mine, because the smell of the mash—you know, that's what gives away all the no-count stills—the smell of the mash gets spread out in the mine and it just kind of drifts away. Now the mine wasn't safe for mining no more, but it was surely safe for making whiskey because there ain't any blasting or drilling going on and there ain't too many men working down there to get out if anything should happen. It was just perfect for what I wanted starting up.

"Well, I had the equipment brought in—in big semis they were—and parked around the old Mine Five. I wanted to go out and check out the equipment before we went to all the trouble of putting it in, which would have been considerable. I asked Honey if he wanted to go for a drive with me and he said 'Sure,' God bless him.

"So we drove out there and right away I started checking out the equipment, which wasn't easy because, you know, there were big boilers that I paid an awful lot of money for, and piping and—well, you know, I mean it was like I was starting up a whole damned factory right off the bat. Honey went wandering off to talk with the fellas that was there and to look around, as a boy surely would.

"Well," said Lewis, sipping a small amount from his drink, "I got most of the stuff checked out, but it was getting along evening and I didn't want any bright lights going on around there and attracting too much attention, although most of the folks surely knew what I was doing. I commenced to leave and I went looking around for Honey to take him back with me, but he wasn't nowhere to be found.

"We just looked all over the place and I was getting pretty worried, although there wasn't nothing around there that could hurt a boy. It never at all occurred to me that the boy might have gone off into the mine, the old Mine Five. It's only an old slope mine, you know, there ain't any shaft or anything, and it had been worked out pretty much. But after we looked all over the place we did go down by the mine, and sure enough there's coming up out of the pitch black down on the slope this big battery operated lamp we had. The boy had taken it down into the mine, you see.

"Now, sir, when he came out I was just so damned glad to see him safe I grabbed him and hugged him, and then I held him back to look at him, and all of us fellas we just roared a laughing. He was as black as the ace of spades from head to foot with just his blond white hair sticking up and the whites of his eyes showing out. It looked so darned funny that none of us right away saw that there was anything the matter with the boy. I mean his eyes would have looked big in that coal black face anyway you can think of. But when I got him down by the car I could see that he was shaking and trembling, and I asked him, 'What's the mat-

ter, boy. You got scared down there?' I was more
joshing him than anything else.

"But then he said something that scared *me*." Lewis
leaned forward and pointed to his chest. "The boy
says to me, 'Where's my Ma? The Ragged Stranger
wants her.' And I grabbed him by the arm and shook
him, and I said, 'What do you mean, boy?' I didn't
know what to say to him about his ma. And then he
commenced to yell and cry and he was hammering up
against my leg while I was holding him there and he
was yelling, 'Where's my Ma? Where's my Ma?' And
I purely didn't know what had come over the boy or
what I could do with him. He was like a wild animal.

"And then while I was holding him there and the
other folks were gathering around, we all heard, like
a big cannon had gone off way deep in the mine, and
the mine was like a trumpet, you know, that carried
the noise outside. And we all knew that there had been
a big explosion down there. We all jumped a foot, and
then we rushed over to the entrance and listened. None
of us dassn't go down into it, you know. But we stood
there and listened. And I said, 'Well, there she goes,
boys.' Because you could hear the water rushing in
from way back at the end of the galleries.

"I'd picked up the boy in my arms when I rushed
over there, but I hadn't been looking at him. Now
when I looked at him I saw the boy had fainted. At
first I had a terrible fright. I thought he'd gone and
died on me. But he was breathing and his heart was
beating. So I put him in the car and took him right
straight to Doctor Gullison's house. Old Gullison
brought him around and Mrs. Gullison cleaned him up
some, and Gullison said we shouldn't do nothing but
take him right on home and put him to bed and keep
him there for a few days. He said he'd drop by.

"But when Gullison come by the next day the boy
had a terrible fever. He was what you call delirious,
and he kept yelling and yammering about the Ragged
Stranger and how he wanted his ma. It was heartbreak-

ing, it surely was. And then we were afraid we were going to lose him.''

Lewis got up and felt his gimpy knees. He walked around the room to restore his circulation. He stretched and turned around to face me. ''And we damned near did lose him. Nobody knew what brought on the fever. It was just a fever, but it was serious. Old Mrs. Clayton stayed by his bed on a cot. After we cleaned him up we took his clothes and burned them, 'cause we didn't know what kind of germs he might have had. But we took the stuff out of his pockets—you know a boy's pockets—and piled them on the table next to him where he could see them. You know the things in a boy's pockets are sacred. They mean everything in the world to that boy and you dassn't touch them. He had the knife I gave him, four blades and a bone handle; he had fishing line and fishhooks and a bobbin; he had some marbles—shooters, I remember what they was like when I had them myself when I was a kid—and some other stuff and a big old oilskin tobacco pouch with some kind of a paper in it. We never looked to see what it was because I told Mrs. Clayton that ain't none of our business there what a boy has got in his pockets. I figured the paper in there might have been something personal, or a secret society he made up with the other boys.

''Now old Gullison came by again, and he looked at the boy and talked to him and listened to what the boy had to say, and he took me into the other room and shut the door. He says to me, 'I don't want you to get mad now, Sim, but I'm going to tell you what I think. I think that boy there has been interfered with. This Ragged Stranger he's talking about—it must have been some kind of a tramp or bum, and I think he interfered with the boy, maybe down in that coal mine there.'

''God forgive me, I was going to strike him. I pulled back my arm and I was going to smash him. He just looked at me. So's I said to him, 'Well if the son-of-a-bitch was in that coal mine he's a dead man now because it's blowed up and flooded.' ''

Lewis stared back into the past, willing the man to be dead. I said to him, "This was the first mention, is that right?—the first mention of the Ragged Stranger your son has been preaching about all these years?"

He drew his eyes back to confront the present. He heaved an enormous sigh. "Yes," he answered. "That's when he first began to talk about the Ragged Stranger. And the fact is there *had* been a ragged stranger hanging around the Bluestone, skulking out in the woods like a damned Indian. It was in the newspaper there. He'd been stealing chickens and raiding the vegetable gardens and scaring the hell out of the ladies there. That's what the newspaper called him— the Ragged Stranger."

Lewis shrugged with a slow roll of his big shoulders. "Whatever happened," he said, "it changed the boy back to what he'd been before. He wouldn't hardly look at me. He wouldn't really talk none with Mrs. Clayton. Nobody could reach him. In school he sat there like a dummy, although he'd been noticed as bright before. He went to church and the Bible school. He went to church every chance he got and he studied the Bible. That's just about all he studied. They set him back in school when he kept failing his grades and pretty soon wasn't only the biggest boy in his class he was durned near the biggest boy in the whole school. But he had his Bible. He was already reading it. It was the only thing he cared about. Then too, he spent a lot of time going out to Marjory's grave, out there on the hill. And folks told me he'd stand there talking to her in the grave. O' course," he gestured reasonably, "that ain't so different. There's plenty of folks talk to the grave out there in the cemetery."

The old man remained standing, transfixed, staring past me, his eyes unfocused. "He was playing truant from school then. He hardly ever went, and sometimes the only way he'd go was if I took him there like a damned convict. Finally, they just let him go. There wasn't nothing nobody could do with him. He'd come home for supper, but that was just about all we ever saw of him. Mrs. Clayton died when Honey was about fifteen, so it was just him and me alone in the house, and he wasn't hardly ever there. To tell the truth, I wasn't hardly ever there myself. You know, when the old Mine Five flooded I just got myself another old abandoned mine and set up the equipment. I kept to my business and prospered. By the time Honey was eighteen he wasn't home at all. He'd gone off to the woods up there in the hills and he was living by himself in a damned shack he'd built up there—not much more than a stone hut with a tin corrugated roof. I'd seen tramps and hobos make huts like that in the depression. Nobody bothered Honey. He wasn't hurting anybody. He wasn't stealing anything or scaring anybody, and he didn't come down into the town very much.

"But when he was a little over twenty years old he took to preaching. I guess he'd studied his Bible to where he could recite practically the whole thing—as they say, he could cite chapter and verse. And he'd come down and stand by the courthouse, and one time I stayed there in the back of the crowd and listened, and it was just reciting the Bible mostly, although every now and again he threw in something about the Ragged Stranger. Whatever it was that old bastard done to that boy it turned his mind.

"And that's what he's been doing for more than twenty years now, livin' up there like John the Baptist and preachin' down on the courthouse lawn. But he's never harmed a single soul. Never. There ain't an ounce of harm in that boy—that man."

He came over to my chair and looked down at me grimly. "And that's why I called you up here, Mr. Binney. And I surely thank you as much as any human being can be thanked for coming here to listen to all this which ain't rightly your concern. I want you to help me out, and I'll tell you why."

I put up my hands to protest. This whole thing with

its local law, its local politics, its local craziness was so far beyond my competence that it seemed impossible. But Lewis plunged on.

"Before you say *no,* just listen to me a little bit more. When I say there ain't no harm in the boy, I know what I'm talking about. I didn't run my business all my life without coming across some fellers who had plenty of harm in them. I know something about harm. You know where harm begins with a boy? It starts when he's running around with the other fellas and suddenly it's let's do this and let's do that—like it's an initiation. It's taking dares and doing dares to show that you're a man. There ain't hardly another boy in the world who ain't done that. It's just part of becoming a man. The trouble with a lot of them is that they never stop trying to prove that they're a man—like they got to prove it every day of their lives.

"Well, Honey never had none of that. After the Ragged Stranger he never had no friends or pals, no gang to show him no wickedness. He read his Bible all by himself and that was that. There ain't a grain of violence nor a wicked bone in his body. There ain't any way in the world that he's going to blow up a building."

I pitied the old man from the bottom of my heart. He was telling the oldest story in the world—"My Johnny never did this—My Johnny never did that—My Johnny is the sweetest boy—" about some serial murderer who's been haunting a city.

Lewis saw the expression on my face and said, "I know what you're thinking. But I don't care. I'll make it worth your while to find out who blew up that there building and Miss Rutledge, God bless her, along with it. If it turns out to be Honey, all right. So be it. If you can prove me wrong, you go ahead and prove it. I'll pay you just the same. But I want Honey to have a fair chance for his life. It suits Jack McCleod right down to the ground to have Honey locked up like that. I mean the boy was always *talking* about blowing up this and blowing up that and burning this and that, but in twenty years he never did a lick of harm. But now Jack only had to put his hand out and there was his conviction, am I right? He didn't have to spend any time looking around. It was mighty convenient for Jack, and for the rest of the town, too.

"You tell me what your rates are and I'll pay 'em while you go down there and poke around and find out what happened. I owe Honey that much, to see he don't get railroaded. If you're worried about payment, you don't have to worry none. I've put by a good bit of money. I own this here hotel we're sitting in, for instance, and I own quite a bit of property here and there. What are your rates, Mister?"

I told him—my new rates—the rates Edna had so cavalierly dismissed when she was talking to Carlson. I also told him that since I was out of town there would be expenses. His eyebrows climbed.

"That's pretty steep," he admitted.

"Well," I said, mounting the old defense, "living in New York is pretty steep. I have an office to keep up, a secretary to pay—and there's no way I could get along without her—so it does run into money. Probably more money that you'd want to pay."

"I never said I wouldn't pay it," he protested. "I'll give you a retainer right now if you'll take it on."

I felt helpless. I took it on. Maybe it was just in the hope of getting some more of that whiskey.

20

But as soon as I'd agreed to take the job I tried to back away. I said to him, "Mr. Lewis . . ."

"Call me Sim."

"All right. Sim, let's try to be realistic about this. I'm a foreigner in these parts with no connections really whatsoever. A lot of mysteries here are going to remain mysteries forever to me. But you do have a link with people who can do you a lot more good than I can and would probably do it for nothing.''

"Who do you mean?" He paused, still standing with his glass half raised.

"Well, I've seen you twice now at the Dome. Don't get offended if I tell you I can see the Dome has *organization* written all over it. And it's obvious that you're treated with a great deal of respect there." He nodded a satisfied agreement. "Now," I continued, "if you've got a connection with these people, can I suggest that they might do a hell of a lot more for you than I can? I don't want to sound like a cheap magazine, but it's a fact that the mob goes everywhere. They've got hot and cold running lawyers—they've got *connections*. They can probably get more information in five minutes of phone calls than I can get in a week of hauling my ass around.''

He eased himself back into the big chair and looked at me and smiled. He said, "You got it right as far as the mob is concerned. They do treat me right, just like they promised to do, and they ain't a bad bunch of fellas a'tall. I sold my liquor business to them years ago, the whole shebang along with all the good will I built up over the years, and they kept me on as a kind of consultant, you know, to advise them here and there.''

"You sold it to them? Just like that? No persuasion?"

He stared at me questioningly for quite a while before he answered. The he smiled again. He tapped his knees. "I see what you're gettin' at," he said. "You noticed my knees and the trouble I got with them. The boys didn't have nothing to do with that. I had to make a delivery one time myself. It was an emergency and, as I said, I wouldn't let Dash drive that way for me any more. Well, some damned fool deputy who didn't know a damned thing about it got on to it and he started to chase me down. I was driving the Pontiac, which anybody in the county could have recognized . . .''

"The same Pontiac Dash drives you in now?"

"That's right." He smiled, and I returned another smile of pure admiration.

"So I says to myself," he continued, " 'Here's where we have some fun.' I could have just stopped my car and told him to get himself lost if I'd wanted to, but I wanted some fun. So I was going lickety split over one of the back roads and I hit a washout I didn't know was there. Dash would have known. And I cracked the hell out of my knees.

"Charlie Silvero sent me flowers while I was in the hospital, which was mighty nice of him, and he come in to see me. Well, he made me a very nice offer. Couldn't have been fairer or more generous. I was gettin' old, and truth was I was feeling pretty low in my mind laid up like that in there. So I accepted, and they lived up to every word of it. I got no cause to complain about Charlie Silvero and the boys.

"But as far as this here is concerned—no, that won't do, and I'll tell you why. The boys would operate pretty much just the way Jack McCleod is doing right now. They'd just go out and collar somebody to take the fall. They'd rig it up if they had to—frame some fella, like they say, and that would be that. But that ain't what I want. I know that Honey never did nothing like that, but I sure as hell want to know who *did* do it. I don't want nothing trumped up. So I want a complete outsider—a foreigner, like you say, who ain't got any personal stake in the thing."

He got up and went to the kitchenette to make a final brace of drinks. When he came back he said, "Speakin' of the Dome, I'd like to take you to dinner there in a little while providin' you ain't busy this evening."

"On one condition," I said—and suddenly I got a cold blue stare from him that suggested that Sim didn't necessarily like conditions being laid down—"and that is that we invite Maria Thorndyke to come along with us."

"Miss Thorndyke?" He wasn't troubled, just puzzled.

"Two reasons," I said. "First of all, she must be feeling like hell. She was very close, almost like a daughter to Milly Rutledge. The second thing is I'm going to need somebody to help me. My own secretary is up in New York, and I don't want her down here because she holds down the office up there. If we can get Maria Thorndyke aboard it would be a big help to me."

He got up and went over to the phone on the other side of the room, where he made a few calls. When he came back he said, "Miss Thorndyke was just where I thought she'd be—over at the courthouse, now that the school building's gone. She'll meet us at the Dome. We'll go over in a cab, and I'm having Dash pick her up at her lodgings—the old Kettle place, although it ain't called that any more."

When Maria was ushered to our table at the Dome she looked terrible. She hadn't gussied herself up as she had on previous appearances there. She was wearing a plain dark dress, no jewelry of any kind, and her eyes were deep, sunken, and ringed with darkness. Her make-up was perfunctory. After she was seated she put a pack of cigarettes next to her setting, and throughout the evening she smoked incessantly. She drank, too, not white wine this time but scotch and soda.

She was offended at first to learn that I was a private investigator—no one likes being lied to—and she was further offended that I had lied to Milly. As the evening progressed, however, with many more scotches consumed in a blue cloud of cigarette smoke around her head, she became reconciled to my deception because it had, after all, put Mr. Martingale in the clink.

When the talk came around at last, however guardedly, to the exploded building and the death of Milly Rutledge she seemed visibly to shrink inside herself. She listened to us discussing it and then she tapped me on the arm to draw my attention. She said to me,

"You're going to look for ways to get Honey off?" There was more than dismay in her eyes; there was hatred.

I said, "Sim doesn't believe that Honey did it, and he seems to have pretty good reasons behind it, although none of them would count in a courtroom. Sim has hired me to find out who actually did it. If it was Honey, then that's that. But Sim wants proof that it was Honey."

Sim leaned forward over the table. He said, "Miss Thorndyke, there ain't nothing being rigged up here. But I don't want my boy being lynched, either legally or illegally. There's a lot of powerful feeling here."

Maria had the makings of a sneer on her face. She said, "I wouldn't worry too much about that. He'll cop an insanity plea."

Sim sat back in his chair and stared at her. It was a measure of his self-control that he answered her calmly, almost placidly. I began to see what had made him a success in the bootleg business. He said to her, "Miss Thorndyke, you're a young woman, and a very nice one at that. I don't think you remember the executions that used to go on around here, or the lynchings for that matter. In the thirties they both ran pretty high. But the folks around here never did have much against executions, and what's more they don't hold much with the insanity plea. This ain't New York. Now even if they did hold with insanity there's no way in the world they're going to let Honey plead insanity because he was always preaching the word of God. If Honey was to say he blew up that building because God told him to, why folks would just figure he was lying about it. They'd think that he'd done it just for the fun of the thing and he was lying his head off because folks around here would never believe that God told anybody to do any such thing. If Honey is guilty he'll be executed. And to tell you the truth, I'd just as soon see him dead as spend the rest of his life in the state nut house."

Maria looked abashed but defiant. She asked, "Is

that what Honey has been telling Jack McCleod—that God told him to blow up—to kill Milly?''

Sim told her, ''Honey ain't said a blessed word to Jack that Jack can make any sense out of. Honey just goes on the way he always has, a prayin' and a prayin', which is mostly just a recitin' of the Bible with a lot of stuff about the Ragged Stranger throwed in for good measure. Now Jack knows damned well that Honey ain't doing this for any kind of a coverup. But it fits Jack's case to pretend that he is. And if you twist Honey's words around enough you can probably make some kind of a half-baked confession out of it.''

I said, ''We're going to have to talk to Honey.''

Sim shrugged and held his hands up helplessly. ''There's nobody can talk to him,'' said Sim. ''There's nobody can get any sense out of him.''

I said to both of them, ''Up in New York, where they take insanity very seriously—and not without reason—I saw them bring in a guy who was threatening to blow up the UN building. I just happened to be there when the detectives were booking him. Now listen: this guy was going to blow up the UN because he saw it as an international plot to destroy civilization. All right. There's probably more than a million people in this country who believe the same damned thing—the UN, the Trilateral Commission, secret agencies, secret societies, all part of the general paranoia. But get this: when they asked him how he knew about all this he told them, and he was as calm as calm could be, that he had special information handed down through his family. And who was his family? Why—and this all came out very calmly now—it was the family of the Green Hornet. I'm not kidding you. He was the son of the Green Hornet. And he had a big mythology made up about his family—the Green Hornet's father, which is to say his grandfather, Kato the faithful servant, and on and on. This is the Green Hornet of the comic books and the old radio programs he was talking about. This man was living in a world he'd constructed out of comic books.

"Okay. The detectives in New York are very good with this kind of thing because there's an awful lot of it around. They deal with nut cases each and every day. They were dead serious with the guy. They kept him cool, and they called in a shrink to take him off for some treatment.

"Now I followed this guy's progress. I was interested. What happened is that the shrink gave him some kind of powerful antipsychotic drug—injections, I think, and the treatment went on for a few days. Finally, the detectives told me, they were allowed to talk to this guy again. They said he was sitting there saying that he knew he really wasn't the son of the Green Hornet and he didn't really want to blow up any buildings any more. So he turned out to be pretty much like anybody else who had been troubled and was working his way out of it.

"What I'm getting at is this. So far as I know, Honey has never had any psychiatric treatment, has he?"

Sim looked troubled. He said, "You don't know how often I asked myself if I done right by that boy. I thought about it a hundred times. It wasn't a question of money. But I knew the minute I called in a doctor for him, why they'd lock him up somewheres. And that never seemed right to me. You know, they can get a fella committed awful fast down here, and of course there's been an awful lot of just plain lyin' to get a man put away so's folks could get hold of his money. I've seen it a number of times. So I didn't rightly trust anybody to look after Honey. I mean Honey never *hurt* anybody or anything." He brought his hand down in a soft blow on the table top. "And if a man wants to live in a stone hut up in the woods and read his Bible and come down for a little preachin' now and then, does that mean you got to lock him up?"

"But he might have been helped," interjected Maria.

"Helped to do what?" asked Sim. "He never was

starving. If he was cold up there it never seemed to
bother him. He fixed himself an old oil drum stove up
there with a tin chimney coming out of the roof . . .''
he sighed. ''What really happened,'' said Sim, ''was
that the boy just kept drifting and drifting away. And
by the time I thought maybe we should do something
he was unreachable.''

I looked at the old man. ''He's got to be reached
now, Sim.''

He nodded soberly. ''Yes,'' he agreed. ''Somebody's got to talk sense to him somehow.''

I said to Maria, ''The State University here. Does
it have a medical school?'' She nodded, startled.
''Does it have a school of psychiatry?''

''Yes.''

''Could you call up there and arrange to have someone see Honey?''

''I know somebody there,'' said Maria. Her face
was an odd battleground of conflicting sentiments. She
was beginning to realize that she had been dragged
into a role of which she had wanted no part. She continued reluctantly, ''Jack Briggs—that is Doctor John
Briggs. He came down to see Milly about the high
school records of one of his patients once. And I went
out to dinner with him—one time.''

''Call him now,'' said Sim. He gestured for a waiter.

''Oh, I couldn't possibly.'' She colored. ''I mean,
it's already too late. I'm sure the hospital is closed . . .''

''Hospitals don't close,'' I said.

''Try the hospital,'' said Sim. The waiter had
brought over the phone and was fitting in the jack. ''If
he ain't there call him at home.''

As if at gunpoint, Maria got the number of the hospital through Information. When she dialed that (the
old-fashioned phones hadn't been changed) she was
given the number of the department of psychiatry.
When she dialed that she was given the number of Dr.
Briggs's office. When he answered she was totally unprepared. Because the mouthpiece of the phone cov-

ered her lips and chin I hadn't the least idea of what
she was saying.

What her eyes suggested was that she was embar-
rassed to be calling him at all. Yet the response must
have been reasonably enthusiastic because I could see
the facial outlines of a smile and then a slight blush.
Apparently she then launched into the burden of the
task we had given her. There were lengthy periods
during which she merely listened, her face breaking
into a frown. Sim watched her unblinkingly. She took
the phone from her lips, finally, and covering the
mouthpiece, told him, "Doctor Briggs doesn't believe
there is anything he could do at this point."

Sim said, "Give me that phone, please." He reached
across the table and took the phone from Maria. I
hadn't the least idea what he was saying because, unlike Maria's, his eyes never wavered in their expression of cold intent. I certainly got the impression that
he was speaking forcefully. Then his eyes softened
somewhat, and he began to nod agreement. Finally,
he lowered the phone sufficiently for me to see him
say, "Thank you, Doctor Briggs. I'll see you there
tomorrow."

I remarked to Sim, "That seemed to be a nice piece
of arm twisting. What's going to happen?"

"Briggs is coming down to the County Jail tomorrow to take a look at Honey. He says maybe he can
get him moved to the hospital, but he claims he won't
try to talk to anybody in a jail cell. He says it wouldn't
be proper."

"And how did you get him to agree to that?"

"I've sold a good bit of whiskey up at the statehouse and the governor's mansion in my time. It ain't
as if those people never heard of me. That is a state
university Briggs works for and I don't think he wants
any calls from the statehouse about what's going on
down there."

Maria's face was masklike. She seemed to be struggling between contempt and admiration. She said, "So
that's the way it's done, is it? If you hadn't sold whis-

key to the Governor nobody would pay any attention to your son.''

''I guess that's right,'' said Sim somewhat helplessly. Nonetheless, I could tell that he was pleased.

I said to Maria, ''How come Briggs turned you down with your dulcet tones and all?''

''He said he didn't want to get mixed up with either the law or religion.''

''I think he's in the wrong racket then,'' I opined. ''I'd think that just curiosity would bring him down.''

''What about your curiosity?'' asked Maria. ''Are you going to be there?''

''I don't think so. I think the fewer people around there the better, although Sim here will probably have to sign some papers. Besides, now that I'm working for Sim I'm going to have to hunt up a new place to live.''

''My goodness,'' said Sim, startled. ''Didn't I mention that to you? I got a suite of rooms just like mine right down on the next floor empty for you. You just move your trunk in there and it won't cost you a cent, nor your meals either.''

''Well, that's awfully nice. I . . .''

''It'd only go on some expense account of yours anyway,'' said Sim. ''This saves us all a lot of paperwork foolishness.''

Secretly I was very pleased to be moving to the old Capthorne. I have a hidden passion for old hotels. I guess that I feel some of the history that has washed through them has left a flood mark somewhere on the walls that can with time and patient contemplation be discerned. Somehow the history just doesn't stick to plastic. I smiled my appreciation and then said to Maria, ''No kidding. Was that all Briggs had to say about Honey's case?''

''Well,'' Maria began with an ashy look at Sim, ''he said that if praying out loud in public and preaching in the park were signs of mental instability he'd have to lock up half the state.''

I laughed. I said, ''You mentioned Samuel Johnson

at that meeting we had at the mansion. But I remember reading that when they came in to tell Johnson that his friend Christopher Smart, the poet, had gone crazy and was on his knees in the middle of the street praying to God and urging everyone around him to get down on their knees and pray with him, all Johnson really had to say was, *'I'd as lief pray with Kit Smart as anybody else.'* ''

21

Departing the Pendragon mansion the following morning was not as simple as I'd envisioned. While I was greeting Danford at my last appearance at the starvation table for breakfast, I was startled to see that Ken Parnell had already joined him. They were, it seemed, engaged in a power breakfast. My customary place had been reserved for me, but it put me directly opposite Ken Parnell. He greeted me with a curt nod. He was dressed for business and his mind it seemed was sullenly fixed on business. I was an interloper.

After I'd knocked off my soggy egg and toast and was sipping my coffee, I told Mr. Danford with all the graciousness I could muster: ''Mr. Danford, I want to thank you for everything you've done for me here. It has been a great experience to spend time in a house like this and I want you to know I'll always be grateful. But I'll be leaving today. I've already got my things packed up.''

Danford smiled his shy sweet smile. He said, ''I won't pretend that I'm surprised. Are you taking the plane or the train back to New York?''

''Well,'' I began a little uncomfortably, ''I'm not going directly back to New York.'' Although this caused only the mild raising of the eyebrows from Danford, it occasioned a long level stare from Parnell.

I explained, "I'm going to be staying at the Capthorne for a while."

"The Capthorne?" asked Danford, bewildered. Parnell's expression implied that I had just signed up for a cruise on a hell ship.

"Yes," I answered. "When I had that meeting with Sim Lewis yesterday he asked me to look into the explosion at the school building. You know, they arrested his son, Honey Lewis."

Parnell bent forward. He said, "What on earth does Sim Lewis expect you to do about it?" I got the feeling that Parnell's language here, like mine, was unnaturally restrained.

"Of course Sim doesn't think that Honey did it," I told them. "He's got a feeling that Honey might be railroaded. He wants me to look around."

"Look around for what?" It was more a challenge than a question from Parnell.

"Who knows?" I shrugged. "They can't even get a straight story out of Honey yet. Nobody's had a sensible word out of him. He might have an alibi kicking around somewhere."

Parnell was looking at me as if I might be a candidate for the nut house myself. His lips tightened as if he was about to burst out with something, but his restraint took over and all that he uttered was, "I doubt that."

"It can't hurt to try."

"It can't hurt Honey or Sim," said Parnell with the makings of a managerial sneer on his face, "but getting mixed up in this could certainly hurt you, if you have any thought for your career, that is."

I am always a bit leery when the talk turns to careers. I asked him cautiously, "How do you mean?"

"Sim Lewis," said Parnell, who had now mixed outrage with the sneer, "is one of the most notorious men in the state. The Capthorne is well known for what it is."

"Which is?"

Danford leaned forward, smiling. "I believe it has been called a den of iniquity," he said.

There didn't seem to be any graceful way out of all this. I said, "I'm sure you'll appreciate that I'm a businessman as well as a private investigator. I really don't care any more where my money comes from, within reason, than you care where your coal is burned."

This was not well received. Parnell seemed very much on the attack. "That's a false analogy," he said. "I happen to know that your license to practice depends on the good will of the authorities."

"My license to practice down here doesn't apply at all," I told him, trying desperately not to get into the antagonistic game. "I will be acting as a consultant to Sim. That's all there is."

I was surprised to see Danford become fatherly. He leaned toward me from the head of the table. "Joe," he said, "you really must listen. You can't imagine what a vipers' nest you're stepping into at the Capthorne. I know that Sim Lewis is a very charming, very persuasive man. He's very intelligent, but he can also be very deadly. He has made alliances with absolutely the worse elements of our society down here. It's not unfair to say that he himself is one of the worst elements. I don't suppose that your license gives you the right to join the underworld. You reputation could suffer very badly."

I said, "So far as I know, Sim Lewis has retired from bootlegging. If he has undesirable companions, that's his lookout, not mine. All he's done is ask me to look into the case of Honey, and as far as I know Honey has no criminal connections. Or am I wrong about that?"

Danford shook his head. "Of course not. But really, Joe, you must look at things clearly. Honey Lewis has been in need of care from the time he was a boy. Everyone down here has known that sooner or later there would be some terrible tragedy. He has lived like a wild man for something like twenty years. And where

was Sim Lewis during all this time? Out selling bootleg whiskey to ruin the lives of perfectly innocent
young men and the poor women who married them.
Now, suddenly the tragedy has struck—a most terrible
tragedy—and as far as I can see all that Sim Lewis
wants to do is get somebody to prove that it didn't
happen. He should have worried about this twenty
years ago. But as usual he's going to rush in and try
to patch things up just helter skelter without caring
who gets destroyed along the way—and professionally, you may be one of those who gets destroyed.''

I was charged with a hundred counter arguments.
But just as suddenly I saw the uselessness of employ-
ing them. I said, ''I'm very grateful for your advice
Mr. Danford. And again I want to thank you for your
hospitality. But I've agreed to see what I can do for
Honey, for the next few days at least, and I don't want
to back out of my agreement.'' I stood up from the
table.

''At least,'' said Danford, ''keep me advised. I
wouldn't lift a finger to help Sim Lewis, but if you
should happen to get into an embarrassing position, be
sure to let me know and I'll see what I can do to
help.''

Parnell had stood up too when I did. Danford said,
''Ken, I have to pick up a few things before I go along
with you. If you'll excuse me for a few moments I'll
meet you down in the foyer.''

Parnell and I walked down the broad stairway not
attempting to converse. When we reached the foyer I
saw that Johnson had already brought my bag down.
Parnell and I stood there while Johnson took my bag
out to the car. Parnell said to me, ''You really got in
tight with the old man, didn't you.''

''What's that supposed to mean?''

''It means that Elliot's a lot smarter than I thought
he was.''

''Elliot?''

Parnell smiled one of those bitter smiles that always
end up looking stupid or vicious or both. He said,

"We're old hands here with private investigators, Mr. Binney. We understand them right down to the holes in their rotten socks."

"How wonderful for you."

His face flushed. "I would have thought as a matter of taste that Elliot would have hired somebody better than you."

"Maybe he did," I suggested. But Johnson had arrived.

I drove away unable to resist glimpses of the towers, peaks, and flashing windows of the facade in my rear-view mirror as the mansion retreated behind me. What was it the picture lacked? Pennants and banners, I decided, and perhaps a herald with a long trumpet standing at one of the crenellations.

My route from the mansion to the Capthorne took me past the courthouse square. The ruined school building raised the empty brick shell of its walls. I parked the car and walked over to the line of wooden barriers that surrounded the building. They had been placed well back from the walls to keep the crowd away from the possibility of collapsing bricks. The walls would have to be knocked down into the rubble.

I went around to the back. That wall had already collapsed and I could see into the disrupted cavity of the building that now had dropped down into the basement. Sheriff McCleod and a man I recognized as the fire chief had clambered out of the rubble and were headed back to the barricades. I crossed over to intercept them and asked the usual stupid question, "Find anything?"

The chief was staring at me, trying to place me from the time he'd first seen me during all the excitement. McCleod regarded me warily. "Been trying to figure out how Honey did it," he seemed to grumble.

"Anything interesting?"

It was my voice that identified me to the chief. He said, "You were here when it happened, right?" I nodded. "You just heard one explosion?"

"I don't really hear anything," I told him. "But I

felt only one explosion, yes. Just the one big shock and then the fire jumped up.''

The chief nodded. McCleod looked unhappy. ''The way we figure,'' said the chief, ''it looks like he set it up under the hot water heater.''

''The building wasn't heated by boiler?''

''Naw. An old-fashioned forced air furnace. Hot water was separate.''

''The hot water heater, I take it, was operated by gas?''

''That's right. Wasn't too big for a building this size, but there wasn't much requirement for it.''

''Anything left from the tank?''

''C'mon over here,'' said the chief. I followed him to his red and gold car and McCleod trailed unhappily along. It was obvious to me that he wanted to stop all this in its tracks but couldn't overrule the chief. ''We found the controls to the tank,'' said the chief, opening the back door to the sedan. There on the back seat lay the twisted thermostatic control of the hot water heater. ''Found it blown right into the wall on the other side,'' said the chief.

I said to the chief, ''I don't want to touch the thing, of course, but could you bring it out into the daylight where I could look at it for a minute?''

''Why sure,'' said the chief, and suddenly a cold chill descended on me. From the accommodating look in his eye I suddenly realized that all this unexpected courtesy was a trap he was carefully laying. I could not blame him, and in fact I admired the technique. But, of course, the chief had seen plenty of firebugs and bomb nuts who couldn't resist coming back to look at their handiwork. And the fact remained that I had been the last living person in that building.

He took the mechanism out of the car and laid it on the deck of the trunk. However, he was not looking at the thermostat. He was looking at me. I, on the other hand, was looking very carefully at the dial. I said, ''That's a pretty low setting for hot water in a building like this. Could anybody have turned it since you found it?''

''No,'' said the chief. ''It was just me and Jack here. That's the way it was. Of course,'' he added, ''the janitor would have turned it way down before he left for the weekend. That's just regulations.''

''Then it's unlikely that the thermostat would turn the tank on over the weekend.''

''Not unless somebody used quite a bit of hot water. There's a thermal blanket on the tank to conserve energy and all, you know. Just a little hand washing wouldn't have turned it on.''

''Well,'' I ventured, ''if I were doing this,'' and Jack McCleod gave me a look of absolute scorn, ''there's two things I'd be looking for. One is a partly opened hot water tap, most probably in a basement sink, and the other is a floor plan of the basement to see how much room there was around the hot water heater.''

''You care to explain that?''

''If you set the fuse in on the burner of the tank you could use a hot water tap as a rough kind of timer. Figure out how long it would take for enough hot water to run out to turn on the thermostat. Once the burner goes on it lights the fuse, and away we go.

''The second thing is that the amount of space under or around the tank might dictate what kind of explosive was used. It was a hell of an explosion. It would have taken quite a bit of dynamite, and dynamite uses up quite a bit of space. If space was at a premium it could have been C 4 or C 7.''

''Or the fuse could just damned well have been longer!'' McCleod interrupted angrily, ''leading to any damned place around there in the basement he wanted.''

''I don't think so,'' I protested mildly. ''I think whoever did it wanted a fire, a good fire, a hot shooting fire. And the place to get that is near a gas jet, and the gas jet was in the water heater. So I think it was probably jammed right in under the hot water heater.''

The chief had a silky expression on his face. "You seem to know quite a bit about this here stuff," he said.

"I was in underwater demolition when I was a kid in the Navy," I told him. "That's how I lost my ears. I'm a private investigator now, or didn't Sheriff McCleod here tell you?" Sheriff McCleod was looking daggers.

"You're a private investigator? A licensed investigator?"

"That's right."

"Shit." The chief stared at McCleod, who turned away.

The chief swept the controls off the deck of the car, tossed them on the front passenger seat, climbed in and drove away. McCleod with pursed lips watched him go. Then McCleod turned to me. He glared at me. He said, "I hear you're working for Sim Lewis now."

"As a consultant," I said. "It won't involve my license at all."

"I'll decide whether it involves your license," promised Jack McCleod. "Any monkey business and you'll find yourself charged with obstructing justice."

"I certainly don't want to obstruct justice," I said innocently. I watched him glare again and then I asked, "Who told you I was working for Sim?"

"It just kind of leaked out down at the facility this morning."

"The facility?"

He stamped impatiently. "The jail. Sim come down there this morning with that doctor he's got now, a Doctor Briggs. And they had us take Honey up to the state hospital."

My eyes opened appreciatively. "Wow," I said. "That's fast work."

This seemed to enrage him. "If Sim thinks he's going to cop a damned insanity plea he can damn well think again," said Sheriff McCleod.

"You looking for blood, Sheriff?"

"I'm looking for justice." His face was inflamed.

"I hope we find it," I answered tiredly. I took my leave of him and felt his eyes on my back as I walked away.

I lugged my bag over to the registration desk at the Capthorne, left it with the bellhop and went back to find a place to park my car. There were no parking provisions at the Capthorne. When I got back the bag was gone and the clerk, who seemed to be as old as the bellhop although taller and fleshier, told me it had been taken up to my rooms. I asked him to call Sim Lewis and tell him I was here and that I would like to see him. He made the call and told me to go right on up.

I was surprised to see Maria there when Sim opened the door. She was sitting in one of the big old-fashioned easy chairs and looked like little more than a doll discarded by a careless child. She was dressed in dark slacks and a bulky turtleneck sweater. It made her face look small and pasty. There was very little enthusiasm in her greeting. She was terribly out of her element.

Sim, however, was very enthusiastic. After I had declined a drink he seated me and told me, "Well, it all worked out. That doctor showed up at eight o'clock and he had all the right papers with him. Jack was mad as hell, but there wasn't nothing he could do about it. We got Honey up there to the hospital and we got him a private room to stay in."

"What kind of papers did you sign?" I asked him.

"Just for evaluation they said it was. I mean it wasn't nothing that was going to put Honey away like a commitment or anything. They're just going to evaluate him."

"And how are they going to do that?"

"Well, like you said, they're going to give him this here drug. I thought there for a while this doctor was talking about Hadacol—it sounded something like that—but no. It's a different thing they got now."

"Hadacol," I said laughing, "was a tonic consisting of twenty-five percent alcohol."

"That's right," said Sim, beaming. "I remember the advertising. They said they had a man paralyzed from the neck down and after six weeks of Hadacol this fella went out and shot eighteen holes of golf."

"Great stuff," I admitted.

"*Haldol,*" said Maria. "Jack said he was going to give Honey Haldol by injection."

"I wish him luck," I said. "I wouldn't want to be the one to hold Honey down while they stick the needles to him."

"Oh, that all went all right," Sim assured me. "I was there while they did it. The doctor said Honey had veins like a garden hose. There wasn't no trouble. Honey just relaxed sort of."

"Like Saint Sebastian relaxed," said Maria.

"How long before we can talk to him?" I asked.

"Oh, 'bout two or three days," began Sim cheerfully, but Maria interrupted.

"We aren't going to talk to him at all according to Jack. Jack has set up a program to go with some study or other. He's going to tape everything and then we get to look at the tapes. But we don't get to interview Honey as long as he's up at the state hospital in this program."

"I've got to talk to Briggs then," I said sharply. "There are some important questions he's got to put to Honey."

"You aren't going to talk to Dr. Briggs," Maria answered dully. "Jack doesn't care if he's guilty or innocent. Jack has got Honey enrolled in a study. Jack is going to evaluate Honey. He'll let us see the tapes, but nobody interferes until the tapes are completed. Honey isn't the important thing here. The study is the important thing. Nobody is allowed to interfere with the study."

"All right." I gave up. "Two or three days? I guess we can hold still for that."

22

But standing still for the next few days was very difficult indeed. I kept leaning on Maria to call Briggs at the hospital to inquire about Honey's progress and the only answers she came back with were, "satisfactory."

Satisfactory to Briggs perhaps but not to me. I was filled with apprehension, with the fear that Honey would blurt out something that could damn him irrevocably. If he had been crying out for the destruction of the city for twenty years why should he stop now? And why shouldn't that be accepted as a motive? I knew that whatever showed on tape could not be used as evidence against him, not only because of confidentiality but because he would be talking under the influence of a powerful drug. But also I did not doubt that he could be induced to say the same things down at the police station.

I had also swung over to Sim's conviction that Honey was innocent, although I had nothing serious to back me up. I reasoned that if the explosion had been set up the way the chief described it, then it was very likely that a man who had lived for more than twenty years in little more than a cave and had restricted his reading to the Bible should have been able to set it up. I held a lot in reserve, however. No one, no one at all, really knew what Honey was doing up there in the hills.

I went to see the chief again and talked over my notion about the cracked hot water tap. "It's possible," he agreed. "Even just a dripping will lose you an awful lot of gallons a day." The hot water tank itself, he told me, was of an industrial size with the new-fangled electronic ignition instead of the gas-wasting steady pilot flame. "There wasn't any chance of a pilot light touching off a fuse," he said. We worked it out that a slightly cracked tap, dripping only by drop—drop—drop could have given the explosive up to a twenty-four-hour lead, the cold water flowing in drop by drop as the hot water dripped away until the critical temperature was reached.

As to the more sophisticated explosives, the chief told me, they would have been unnecessary. "There's been flooding in that basement," he said, "and the heater was set up off the floor to keep any water away from the burner. There was plenty of room under there for all the dynamite you could want." He was more convinced than ever that the charge had been set directly under the tank. The tank had been driven like an artillery shell right straight up through the wooden floor. When the thin copper gas connections ruptured (as the heavy galvanized lines leading in might not have) the pressurized spurt of gas flame set the fire.

"On the other hand," said the chief, "somebody could have kicked a hole in the basement window, chucked in the dynamite that rolled under the tank and just run like hell."

I sat in my suite, which was as Sim had promised, a carbon copy of his, and pondered these matters. I emptied a quart carton of milk down the drain and set the empty container under a tap in the kitchenette. I tried to crack the tap so that it would merely drip, drip, drip, but I found that this was almost impossible. The slightest cracking of the tap produced a tiny flow of water that was considerably more than a drip. As I timed it the carton took five minutes to fill up. That would be twenty minutes for a gallon. And how many gallons would be necessary to trip the thermostat in an industrial size water tank that had been set at near body temperature? That was something I would have to work on. Farfetched it might be, but it might be made into an important part of Honey's defense.

While I was playing games with my milk carton calculations, my eye kept straying back to Edna's letter,

which I had laid out on the table. I had wired Edna
the change of address to the Capthorne and the news
that I would be remaining here for a few days more
on another case. It could not have been welcome news
to Edna.

Dear Joe:
   *Please for God's sake get back here to New
York, will you? I have to talk to you—to somebody. I don't know where I'm at.*
   *David is absolutely overwhelming. I don't
know what to do with him. I don't know what to
do with myself.*
   *You remember how worried I was about get-
ting a nice dress? David has opened a charge
account for me at Bendel's and told me to get
whatever I need. David gave me a diamond clip
and matching earrings. And now—it just arrived—in a big box—a ranch mink coat. Full
length. Let out. Joe. My God.*
   *The one thing he hasn't bought me is a ring.
Would he give me all these things if he didn't
mean to marry me? Would anyone? But he has
never said anything about marriage.*
   *And if he did, what would I say? I don't know.
I really don't know.*
   *Oh, Joe. I have to talk to you. Please come
back.*

                                    Love,
                                       Edna

Edna was in need of the restraining parental hand.
David Carlson was in need of a swift kick in the ass.
I regretted now, more than ever, not having brought
Edna with me. I was alarmed not only by her situation
but by my own. Although I enjoyed the atmosphere of
the old hotel, I was pretty much a prisoner. The Code-
Com telephone had not been moved to the hotel, and
for that matter it would have been susceptible only to

messages from Edna. Of course I cannot hear a knock
on the door, and unlike my own apartment no lights
had been installed for a buzzer. To keep myself sane
I had set up a happy hour appointment in the hotel bar
(which, to my knowledge, had never initiated this
commercial maneuver. Instead, no matter what hour,
the bartender bought you every fourth drink). Maria
had agreed to meet me there every evening, although
she was not happy with the ambience. On the second
night she was unable to make it but phoned Sim, who
then came down and joined me for a ponderous drink
and retold the news that things at the hospital with
Honey were "satisfactory." On the third night, however, Maria met me again and had happy news. Briggs
had called her to say that at last he had something to
show us. We were to meet Briggs at the state hospital
at nine o'clock the next morning.

The state hospital looked as forbidding as any insane
asylum should. The dark brick bore three-quarters of
a century's worth of soot and grime. The open air bal-
conies were heavily screened with stout galvanized
fencing, and the exercise area on the roof was a cage
set atop the building. The grounds were well tended
and shaded by massive oaks. A few patients in bath-
robes who apparently had grounds privileges wandered
serenely if pointlessly among them. I pulled the blue
Nova—with Maria next to me and Sim in the back—
over to the designated parking area and the three of us
trooped up to the fearsome doors.

Jack Briggs met us on the third floor, where he had
directed us to go, and took us down the hall to a projection room. He was a soft looking sandy-haired fellow of about thirty-five in a light tan summer suit. I
suppose the aviator glasses he wore were meant to give
him some dash, but they failed to live up to the promise.

The projection room was comfortably furnished.
"Of course we don't really project things any more,"
Dr. Briggs explained to us. "It's all done with tape
now." The comfortable chairs (these chairs were

meant for doctors, not for patients) were drawn in a slight semicircle so that we could see one another as well as the expensive twenty-five-inch monitor screen. When the three of us were seated, Dr. Briggs addressed us:

"Mr. Lewis is responding to therapy, albeit slowly," said Dr. Briggs. "As you know, he has an extreme religious mania, which overlays a host of problems, none of which can be accurately identified at this time. The purpose of the medication is to calm him sufficiently to communicate on an at least nominally rational plane. So far we have not really succeeded in that, although we expect improvement as the medication continues.

"Yesterday afternoon, however, we had a manifestation so striking that I thought I had better call it to your attention. Although the medication is not primarily a hypnogogic, the results we obtained yesterday resemble the hypnotic state very closely. As you know, Mr. Lewis's communications are almost entirely couched in biblical terminology, most of which appears to be direct quotes and a great deal of which is from the Book of Revelations. The biblical references, however, are continuously interspersed with references to the Ragged Stranger, and the significance of this image is obscure. We have repeatedly asked him to explain the meaning of the Ragged Stranger but we did not get any coherent response until yesterday afternoon. It appears that the medication has had an unusual and striking effect on Mr. Lewis, so that, finally, he seemed almost to re-live—that is to experience again his encounter with someone he calls the Ragged Stranger."

It was pretty obvious that Dr. Briggs had found a little gold mine here, and was already writing the paper he would present at some future meeting. I looked at Maria and Sim. Maria had drawn back into her chair with distaste. But Sim was transfixed. He clutched the arms of his chair and his face was rigid with anxiety and dread.

When Briggs inserted the cassette in the tape machine he discovered that he would have to rewind it. And so we were treated to the experience of watching time run backward on the monitor. Images of Honey Lewis in a series of wild gesticulations flashed across the screen, abrupt and meaningless. Doctors and nurses appeared and disappeared in no rational sequence. What clove through and remained in the mind were the closeups of Honey's face, burned and rubbed by the sun and wind, wild and uncomprehending, staring with its burning blue eyes. By means of the monitor, we were closer to Honey's face than anyone had been since he was a child.

Briggs stopped the machine and began the earlier sequences in fast forward. Here we saw Briggs in a white coat attempting to deal with Honey, who was seated on an examination table, his feet resting easily on the floor. Briggs appeared as something less than heroic in these shots. He had placed himself between Honey and the door to the room, and had his hand firmly behind him ready to grasp the knob and bolt. Honey appeared to be roaring. At last Briggs came to the sequence he wanted us to see and he stopped the machine to freeze the image of Honey sitting in an ordinary chair, apparently calm, and Briggs sitting with his back to the camera across from him.

Briggs said to us, "The startling thing you will notice in this session we're about to view is that when Mr. Lewis recounts his meeting with the Ragged Stranger he is in a state very closely resembling a hypnotic trance in which one undergoes the experience all over again. What is striking is that when Mr. Lewis does this he actually assumes both roles—himself as a small boy and the Ragged Stranger, whoever that might have been. You will see that Mr. Lewis's features change with the assumption of each role and that his voice changes markedly from that of a small boy to that of a full-grown man, but a man quite different from Mr. Lewis. The voice and diction of the small boy have the usual regional accent we expect to hear in this locality. But the diction and accent of the man is quite different—not at all this regional accent. It is the voice and diction quite literally of a stranger.''

"For God's sake," exploded Sim. "Show us the picture, will you?''

I said rather desperately to Maria, "I'm not going to be able to know what questions the doctor is asking because his back is turned to the camera.''

Dr. Briggs interjected, "That won't cause you any trouble. All I said to Mr. Lewis was, 'How did you meet the Ragged Stranger? What happened?' '' He pushed the *play* button.

Even with his back to the camera I could see that Briggs was asking Honey the question as the tape unreeled. The effect on Honey was astounding. His face very nearly collapsed and assumed the soft wondering lines of a child. The corners of his mouth turned down and his eyes began to stare into a distance. He held his hands up in front of him as if he were grasping the handle of an object and supporting it with his other hand from the underside. I saw Sim give a short violent jerk of his head to signify understanding and I shot a look of inquiry at him. "The lantern," said Sim. "He's holding the lantern.''

Honey remained seated in the chair but his feet moved in tiny shuffles as one walks in a dream. Suddenly the shuffling stopped and his body became rigid. His eyes flew wide open with fright and astonishment. He raised the phantom light in his hands and said, "Who are you, mister?''

There was a brief pause while Honey stared up at his ghost, and then suddenly he leaped to his feet—Briggs pushed his chair far back away from the patient—and extended his arms straight out from the shoulders on either side of him. He raised himself on tiptoe and looked down on the phantom of the little boy who was himself. The expression on his face was one of intense sorrow, pain, and desperation.

"I am the Ragged Stranger," he said.

"Who, mister? Who?''

Again the face changed, although the rigid, almost impossible posture was maintained. "The Ragged Stranger you people have been reading about. I've seen your newspaper—out of a garbage heap. I've seen it. I am the Ragged Stranger." The eyes changed then and quickened with interest, even hope. The man said, "And whose little boy are you?"

"I'm Honey Lewis, Sim Lewis's boy," the child's face said.

The Ragged Stranger's face turned wild. His whole body, without changing the strange position, began to tremble spasmodically. "Sim Lewis!" he cried. "You're Marjory's boy! God has sent you! God has sent you here for my deliverance."

The man's eyes then changed focus to turn intently downward, the concentration nearly maniacal. "Do you see that thing in my pants, boy? That long yellow thing sticking out? Take it out, boy. Take it out."

Sim Lewis sank back in his chair. I saw him groan.

"Take it out, boy. Take it out and hold it. That's right!" said the manic desperate face.

"Now you listen to me, boy. You take that right straight to your mother and tell her what you saw down here. You understand? God has sent you here for a purpose, for my deliverance. You take that right straight to your mother, Marjory, and tell her what you saw. Don't you dare tell anyone else in the world. You understand me, boy? Don't you dare tell anybody else in the world what you saw down here. Just your mother, Marjory. Just tell her and her alone. God bless you. God bless you, boy. God has sent you."

The big face tormented by wind and sun shattered into tears. Sobbing, he now seemed to hang from the points of his hands stretched out into the air. "God has sent you," he cried, sobbing. "Run, boy, run. Run home to your mother and give her that and tell her I'm here. God has delivered me. He has delivered us all into his hand."

The huge man fell back into his chair and his feet began to scurry in the dreamlike run of his childhood.

His hands held up the lantern as he ran. Suddenly he began to cry out, "Ma—Ma—Where's my Ma. Where's my Ma." His big fists beat against the air. "Where's my Ma, damn you. Where's my Ma?" Sim was pushed back in his chair in utter agony. The tears rolled down his face.

Honey's face changed again suddenly to a look of astonishment. He was listening to something unheard by us. Then he cried, "No!—No!—Oh no! The Ragged Stranger!" His feet scurried in some direction and then he fainted and fell from the chair.

Sim had staggered up, forcing his bad knees to hold him, as if to catch the fallen giant when he fell. Dr. Briggs came over and touched him gently on the shoulder, but Sim jumped back as if he had been burned with a red hot poker. He pointed at the screen and cried, "That Ragged Stranger! I'd know that voice, that way of talkin' anywhere in the world. That was Marjory's way of talkin', that sing-song voice. I'd know it anyplace. That Ragged Stranger, whoever he was, he was a Griffiths!"

"Whoever he was," I said, "the man was crucified."

23

"We're going to have to see what's down there," I said to Maria.

"I hate this place," she said vacantly, staring unhappily around her at the saloon. "Can't we go someplace else?"

I had been haunted by the Ragged Stranger all day long. Riley continued to haunt me to—*Raggedy Man—Raggedy Man*. Maria and I were sitting at the bar of the Capthorne saloon, having met at the appointed happy hour. Sim Lewis was upstairs in his rooms at the top of the building. Dashwood was with him. They wanted to be alone together. Sim had made it clear that he did not want any other company, so I left him alone throughout the day.

"I don't know," I said to Maria. "I don't want to go to the Dome, and I sure as hell don't want to go back to that motel. Where do you want to go?"

She was wearing her lime green slacks again and a rose colored blouse over which she wore one of the feminine mock sports jackets I had seen so often in New York but never down here. A lime green bandeau matching her slacks held back her dark hair. Her make-up was not excessive, but it had been applied with care.

"Why don't we just go up to your room?" she said. "We can talk there, can't we?"

The old bellhop took us up in the elevator standing rigidly facing the front with that special air that identifies the illicit. It wasn't illicit any more, of course, to take a young woman up to a hotel room, but the old hotel shrugged such modern niceties aside. The fact that it was no longer illicit meant that the bellhop made less money. His attitude was merely one of long years' habit.

When we got inside I took out my fresh bottle of Old Fitzgerald and told her regretfully, "I don't have any scotch or white wine, but I can send out for some if you'd like."

"No," she said. "It doesn't matter."

There was ice in the refrigerator in the kitchenette, so I fixed us both drinks with ice and tap water. I was about to set them down near the sofa when Maria said, "Why don't we sit at the table over by the window? That way we can look out at the city." I put the drinks, bottle and ice bucket on the table. We sat down on opposite sides.

"You can't go down there," said Maria as if we had never moved from the bar, as if nothing else had been said. "It's full of water."

"I don't know whether I told you this or not," I

answered, "but when I was a kid in the Navy that was my job, going underwater. But usually it was to blow things up, not look for things."

"What would you expect to find down there," she asked. She seemed to dismiss my mention of the Navy as some sort of adolescent japery. Her expression was still vacant, as it had been in the bar. Apparently what was troubling her would not be solved by a simple change of decor.

"The Ragged Stranger," I said.

"What good would that do?" Her dark eyes were bitter, but her face was full of tension. Her lips were pressed together like those of a person trying not to scream. She picked her glass up off the table and took a sip that became a gulp. It made her cough, but she cleared her throat quickly and turned to stare out at the city.

"I get the feeling," I told her, "that you're asking, 'What good would anything do?' and the answer to that is not a hell of a lot. No matter what we do we can't reverse the run of the tape and make the building fly back together again with Milly back at her desk sawing away at the book—"

"Don't," said Maria. "Don't." She put up her hand to shut me off and took another, more careful sip of her drink.

"All right," I said. "But there is probably a little bit of good it could do. Supposing that was all a fantasy of Honey's. Suppose there wasn't any ragged stranger. It would mean that his nuttiness was truly congenital, or at least organic. It would mean that there is no perceptible logic to him, no method in his madness, which also means he might very well have blown up the school building. If I do find something down there, however, it would mean that we had found— what should we call it?—the root of his sorrow."

"You don't just jump in there in your swimming trunks," said Maria. She looked angry, even contemptuous. "It's very deep."

"Yes," I agreed. "I'll need equipment, and that's

something I've been wondering about all day—where to get it."

"God," said Maria, "it's hot in here. Why didn't they ever air-condition this place?" She got up from her chair and took off the jacket and laid it across the back of the couch. When she returned to the table she took a Lucky from my pack and lighted it. Before sitting down she took a reckless swig from her drink, and when she sat, finally, she sat straight and tense in her chair with her young breasts pushing against the rose colored fabric.

"I don't know any place you could get diving equipment down here," she said. "I certainly haven't seen any stores that carry it."

"I realize that," I answered. "But I'm pretty sure the fire department must have some—the police department or the sheriff." She looked at me with a kind of angry puzzlement. "But you're right," I gave her the hint of a smile. "The minute we bring any of those people into it they could simply forbid us the whole excursion, put up a guard around the place, and that would be that. So I don't think we can apply to them. Yet," I mused, "I can't figure out where would be the nearest place to buy the stuff."

"Cleveland," said Maria. "I know there's a store there that sells scuba equipment."

"You know that for a fact? You've seen it? Bought it?"

"Well," she faltered. "I'm pretty sure . . ."

I dismissed this with a wave of my hand. "Cleveland must be about a twelve-hour round trip drive from here," I said. "I sure as hell wouldn't do it unless I was certain. Could you call up the store do you think?"

"It's too late for that," said Maria glancing at her watch. Indeed it was getting late as a look out the window showed me. The evening sun was gilding the dome of the courthouse and shadows, black and purple, were filling the jagged holes in the rubble of the old school building.

"Is there anyone else you could call up there?" I persisted. "Anyone who would know?"

She did not like being pushed this way. She thought she had ended the discussion. Finally she said, "Yes, there is. There's an instructor in archeology at Case, Tim Crawford, who does underwater archeology in the Caribbean. I suppose I could call him and ask."

"Please," I said. "Please do it."

It seemed to take forever. First she had to call an acquaintance who knew Tim Crawford's number. When she reached that number Tim Crawford was not at home, but she inquired if there was a number where she could reach him. There was. She dialed that number and it was a century before they located the man and brought him to the phone.

I don't know how much of the story she gave away. I didn't watch her talk. But she did talk for quite a while and at last she put down the phone to say, "yes," to me. "You can go there. You can get absolutely anything you need. Tim buys his stuff there. A lot of it is special. He says you don't have to worry about finding what you want. They've got it all."

She seemed furious now. She stood up from the table and knocked back the rest of her drink. When she set the glass down she stared at me and the stare turned into a glare. She said, "You're really going down there to find whatever horrible thing is down there?"

"Yes," I said. "I am."

She came over to my side of the table and leaned down to kiss me on the mouth. It was a hard, grinding kiss, and she clutched the back of my neck as if she were drowning. She sat in my lap, then, jarring the table, and put her arms around me. Her breasts pushed up against my chest and the pressure sent the perfume from them in a cloud around my face. I could feel her jaw working and knew she was speaking, but of course, her face was hidden from me and I have no idea what she said. No matter. Whatever she was saying, it was wrong.

I took her by the shoulders and lifted her up. Then

I took her arms from around me and held her at a distance. Her face was wild, defiant. "You don't really want to do this, Maria," I said. Her arms struggled to get free so that she could strike me. I held on and moved her back to her chair on the other side of the table. I sat her down in it. "Sit still," I said, "and listen to me.

"You want to do all this because you think it will explode the world and when all the pieces have gone up in the air and come down again everything will be different. It won't be. It will still be the same only you will just feel that much lousier. Get drunk if you want to. I'll take care of you. You're a very beautiful woman, and under different circumstances things might happen. But not like this. Not just for shock therapy."

Maria said, "Make me a drink." Her face was dead white. She was trembling. I fixed the drink and gave it to her. She downed nearly a quart of it. She said, "First I wouldn't let anybody have it. Now I can't give it away."

I guess my smile was rather sad. "When a lady just gives it away," I said, "it has to be accepted under very special circumstances."

Maria said, "What am I going to do?" She began to cry.

"First thing of all," I advised her, "work a little on your drink. Contrary to the W.C.T.U., alcohol has done a lot of good in this world."

I finished my drink and fixed another and sat down across from her. She said, "I have nobody now. Not anybody."

I said, "That isn't really true. You think because Milly's gone now she left nothing behind her? Did all your memories of Milly go up in smoke?"

Maria stared at her drink and pursed her lips.

"Of course you've still got somebody," I told her. "Milly is part of you now. She's in your blood and your brain. She's part of your brain—living in your brain. Doesn't that count for something?"

Maria looked like a sullen preadolescent child. After

a lengthy pause she said to me, "When we were talking to those nitwits at the mansion you said that if you study physics you get into metaphysics. I don't know what you mean by that."

"Nothing mystical," I said. "If you follow physics in either direction, microphysics, macrophysics, you get to the inexplicable, the unpredictable. That's all that metaphysics is."

"Metaphysics," she said. She had been sipping steadily at her drink. It was nearly gone. "Do you think Milly might come back as a ghost? Wouldn't that be metaphysics too?"

"I'm sure she'd be a very sensible ghost," I told Maria. "I can't see her jumping out of a grandfather clock and shouting *Boo!*"

This brought the shadow of a smile to Maria's lips. She said, "That's just exactly the kind of thing Milly would enjoy doing very much."

It made me laugh. I could feel the rumble in my throat and I suppose the ring of it hung in the air.

The shadow vanished from Maria's lips. She said, "This morning up at the hospital I was terrified. I'd always seen Honey from a distance. I never was up close to him like that before. I'd never seen the real madness in his eyes. He really does believe everything he's saying, doesn't he?"

"I guess so," I answered, "but the important part now is whether it is true."

"Would he have gone through that whole episode, fainting and everything if it wasn't true?"

"Sure," I said. "There's no telling what he saw down there in the mine. It could have been anything. His imagination could have taken over. It could all have been a fantasy, a dream. That's why I have to go down there and see what's what."

"You're really going to do that."

"Yes," I answered. "And that's why we've got to go upstairs now and make sure that Sim Lewis agrees. If he says no, it's all off."

"I'm not going to get into the elevator with that awful little man again."

"No," I said. "We'll go up the fire stairs in the back. It's only one flight up."

There was a lengthy wait after I knocked on the door to Sim Lewis's suite. Finally it was opened by Jack Dashwood, who stood blocking the doorway and frowning at me and Maria. He began saying, "Mr. Lewis doesn't want to be disturbed—" but I interrupted him with, "We really have to talk to him. It's important. It won't take long." Sim must have called out something then because Dashwood half turned to the back of the room and then stepped aside to let us in.

Sim Lewis was sitting at the table near the window, just as Maria and I had been, and like us he had a bottle on the table in front of him. However, there was only one glass and the bottle was a decanter of very pale whiskey. He had apparently done that very rare thing for him; he had gotten drunk. His eyes were ruined, unfocused. He too had been staring out at the courthouse dome and the shattered remains of the school building. Sim looked up at me and said, "Sit down and have a drink." The expression on his face implied that this was not an invitation but an order. I sat down across from him and Maria curled up in one of the big easy chairs. I fixed myself a drink from the decanter and the cut glass pitcher on the table.

"What was it you wanted to see me about?" asked Sim. His lips were not easy to read. The flesh on his heavy face had gone slack. For the first time, his cheeks looked like wattles.

"I want to get your agreement to something I think should be done," I told him.

"And what is that?" He swayed in his chair as he tried to focus on me.

"I think I ought to go down into Mine Five and look around."

"Nobody can go down there. All flooded. All sealed up. It's closed forever."

"I can go down there with scuba equipment."

"What would you be looking for?"

"To see if there really was a man down there, of if it was all in Honey's head."

"You could do that?"

"Yes."

"You'd get lost down there. It's pitch black underwater. An old coal mine ain't nothing but galleries and rooms, you know."

"Rooms?"

"Where they work the coal face. Work out one room then go make another. Two galleries down there. Must be ten rooms on each side of each one of 'em."

"I know what I'm doing," I told him. "Believe me, I won't get lost."

Sim poured another drink of whiskey into his glass. No ice, no water. He sipped at it and looked at me with somewhat better control of his eyes. "You're thinking Honey just made up all that he said there on the tape? He just made that up out of his head?"

"He could have," I answered. "It could have been a hallucination. He came down with a fever right after, didn't he? He might have been getting sick right then. I think we ought to find out for his sake. For your sake too."

Sim stared at me. He said, "You're talking about scuba. That some kind of diving equipment?"

"That's right."

"You got it with you?" The strangeness of the idea straightened him up in his chair.

"No. But I know where I can get it."

"Where's that?"

"Cleveland."

"Cleveland!" The old watery eyes opened wide. "Why, man, that's hell and gone from here."

"We figure it's about a twelve-hour round trip drive from here."

"I know how far it is," he said irascibly. "Cleveland!" He shook his head.

"Maria dug up a store for me there that's bound to

have everything I need. I figure I can leave tonight, drive up there and be there when they open in the morning, drive back and make the dive tomorrow night. The sooner the better.''

"This stuff you're going to buy, it'll cost money, won't it?'' He reached for his back pocket.

"I'll put in on the credit card and we'll talk about expenses later,'' I told him. "I'm going to need a good underwater lantern along with everything else.''

Sim sank back in his chair and sipped his whiskey thoughtfully. He looked at me again with as much penetration as he could muster. "You figure you're going to drive twelve hours and have a few hours more to buy the stuff, say fifteen hours all told, and then you're going right on to dive down there?''

"Yes,'' I said. "The sooner the better. Also I think we should go to the mine at night. I don't think we ought to draw a crowd.''

"Dash,'' Sim called toward the kitchenette. "Come on over here and sit down, will you?'' Dashwood sat down between us facing the window. He and Sim began an urgent conversation with their heads together. Finally, they agreed on something. Sim said to me, "Ain't no way at all I'm going to let you make a twelve-hour drive and then go on ahead with all that. Dash, here, will drive you up and back. You can get your sleep in the back of the car. There's plenty of room to stretch out. I don't want you killin' yourself on my account.''

We agreed that I would leave the door to my rooms unlocked. "Ain't nobody going to fool around with you up here,'' Sim assured me. Dash would come in and awaken me when it was time to leave.

I accompanied Maria down in the elevator while she endured the studied aloofness of the bellhop. When we were standing outside the old hotel I offered to drive her home. "No,'' she said. "It isn't far. It's a nice night. I think I'll walk.''

She raised herself up to kiss me—on the cheek this

time, and very softly. I watched her until she disappeared around the corner down the block.

24

I was sound asleep when Dash came to get me in the early hours. I barely broke consciousness when he walked me to the elevator, where the night clerk waited to take us down. I had collapsed on my bed fully clad except for my shoes, and the brief trip outside to the limousine was made as if in a light and not unpleasant dream. I sank into the upholstery and returned to sleep as I felt only the barest breaking of inertia when the big car pulled away from the curb.

The second time Dash woke me it was bright daylight and I hadn't the least idea where I was. I sat up, rubbed my eyes, while Dash sat across on the jump seat grinning at me. "We're here," he said. "This is the place." I peered out the window to look at the front of a very large sporting goods emporium. Staring back at me through the glass doors he was just unlocking was a store clerk who did not hide his curiosity at the sight of a huge black limousine parked in front. He was even more curious, if not alarmed, when he saw me get out of the car with Dash. I was tousled, unwashed, unshaven and red-eyed. When we got through the door I suppose he could smell the powerful memory of last night's whiskey.

"I'd like to see your scuba department," I told him. "A fella named Tim Crawford recommended you." The name meant nothing to him, but when I repeated it to the salesman in the scuba department he brightened right up. I had written down a list of everything I would need and the salesman and I went over it together before we began looking at the equipment. We took it on, piece by articulate piece, and I inspected every item very carefully before setting it aside for purchase. It would not do for me to discover a defect when I was at the bottom of the mine. I tested the regulator with the tanks—making sure that they were fully charged—and that the airhoses had no leaks, nor the tubing. When it came to picking out the proper underwater light the salesman touted a top-of-the-line very powerful beam. I took his word for it. I did, however, make sure the batteries were included, and as we installed them I carefully inspected the gasketing for pinholes and dead spots, and the bolts with their wing nuts for jammed or broken threads. I did not propose to have the light short out on me. For a lifeline I picked out a light nylon cord of bright phosphorescent yellow about the size of ninethread. I bought twenty-five hundred feet of it, nearly half a mile. I did not think that Honey Lewis had gone any farther than that as a small boy carrying a heavy lantern. In fact, I could not see myself going much farther than that in the depths of the mine. If I couldn't find anything within that range, I would call it quits.

It wasn't until I had handed over the credit card to pay for all this gear that I broke into a chuckle and then began to laugh. Dash looked at me inquiringly. "My client," I said, "David Carlson, is going to have a shit hemmorhage when he sees the bill for this."

The salesman helped Dash and me carry all the gear down into the waiting limousine and store it in the trunk. Dash and I tootled off for the coffee and cakes before starting the long trip back. I picked up the local newspapers and a couple of magazines. At first I wanted to sit up front with Dash on the drive back, but he insisted that I ride in the tonneau. "You'll have plenty to do tonight," he said. "You get your rest now." And I did, letting the blunted perceptions of the news magazines lull me back to sleep as the big car rocked along.

When we arrived at Caunotaucarius, Dash drove the 9limousine straight to his garage, where the other big car, the one with the telephone, rested in the shadows.

"Won't be too much call for that now," he told me. Together we unloaded the gear from the trunk and stowed it in the back of a 1954 Dodge pickup that had been perfectly restored. There was a fitted tarpaulin for the bed, and we rolled that over the gear and tied it down. Dash put in a phone call to Sim then to tell him we had arrived in good order. Sim told him he'd meet us at the Dome for dinner. I objected to this idea because I looked like the wrath of Christ and stank like a stew bum. Dash showed me a clean lavatory in the back of the garage and lent me a razor. I would have to forgo the formality of a necktie. It was getting on toward six in the afternoon by the time we left the garage with the truck and headed for the Dome.

Sim had Maria with him at his table. I was brought up short by the way she was dressed. She had put on an old pair of blue jeans and a workshirt covered by a windbreaker. Her mouth now was very sullen. When we'd sat down I refused the offer of a drink and ordered a steak—a large one. Then I said to Maria, "I hope you weren't thinking of going along with us."

"Why not," she snapped, furious.

"I been trying to tell her," Sim interjected, "this ain't any trip for a lady." His expression implied that this had not been accepted gracefully.

"Oh, sure," said Maria. "It's all right for the lady to locate the psychiatrist, and it's all right for the lady to locate the equipment, and it's all right for the lady to do damned near anything except to be in on the—the—"

"The kill?" I supplied it for her. Her lips clamped together in a hard straight line. "Maria," I said, "first thing of all, we're going over there in a little pickup truck, and there wouldn't really be room for you in the cab. Secondly, I have no idea what I'll be bringing topside up out of there and something tells me it may not be anything you'd want to see—or that I'd want to see for that matter, except that I have to do it. Finally, since I'm the one who's going down, I have the final say, if only for my own safety, and my experience tells me that the fewer people we have to account for the safer I'm going to be. This may be very selfish of me, but you'd be surprised how selfish you can get when things like this are concerned.

"Now look," I tried to placate her. "Once we get there this whole thing isn't going to take more than an hour. I promise you we'll call you from Bluestone as soon as we can get to a phone. All right? After we've finished dinner—Did you come over by cab?" I asked Sim.

"Maria drove me over," he answered. He was sheepish about it.

"Okay. When we leave here, Maria, why don't you drive back to the hotel?" I dug in my pants pocket. "Here's the key to my room. Wait there. As soon as we're finished we'll call you and then we'll come back and tell you all about it. All right?"

In no way was it all right with Maria. But short of pulling a gun on us I couldn't see any way she was going to come along. She accepted it finally, and her fury turned to despondency.

The light was beginning to fail by the time we left the Dome. Maria climbed into her little car and made her unhappy way toward the hotel. Dash, Sim and I clambered into the pickup, Dash driving, of course, with Sim in the passenger's set and myself balanced uneasily in the middle. Dash took the little truck over the riddles of Mine Five road without the briefest jerk or pause in our locomotion. The man drove the way water flows; it was uncanny. We rolled through Bluestone, in which only a few lights were burning along the business section and arrived at last at a field that extended for as far as I could see. This was the end of the Mine Five road. Dash picked out a barely discernible path through the high weeds and followed it over a hillock until the headlights picked up the dim reflection of a large corrugated metal shed. Sim nudged me to get my attention. He nodded forward. "That's it," he said. "The old pit head."

Dash left the headlights on as he pulled up directly

to the door of the shed. The door had a huge stenciled sign on it: DANGER! KEEP OUT! It was locked with a big hasp and padlock. Dash reached under his seat and took out a tire iron. The key to the lock had long since been lost. He drove the iron between the hasp and the door and twisted off the whole assembly. Sim and I got out of the truck and waited until Dash had swung it around to back up to the door. Then he turned off the headlights. Sim carried a big battery-operated lantern with him, and when we stepped inside he flashed it on. It lighted up pretty much the entire shed. Some of the crude remnants of early mining were still there—a huge circular washing station where the miners could make their perfunctory ablutions after the shift was done. There were lockers rusted into ruins and wooden benches that had been rotting away in the darkness.

I took Sim's lantern and shone it down the slope that led into the mine, down which the working men had entered the darkness with the carbide lights clamped to their foreheads. The beam followed the slope of coal black ground and then it bounced off the water that had sought its level only about ten feet down the slope. The slope with its steel tracks for the coal cars did not extend too far across the shed. It seemed to be about the width of two driveways. To the left of that there was simply the pit that had been dug away and mined. Even though it was nearly midsummer, the dampness was penetrating. There was an ugly acidic taste to the air.

Sim held the lantern while Dash and I unloaded the gear from the truck. When we got it all inside we closed the door tightly to minimize any hint of light escaping. One brief flash of the lantern passing Dash's face showed me how tired he was. It revealed much more of his age, too, which I now realized was considerably more than I had thought.

Before getting into my suit I laid out the lifeline. There were five coils in all of five hundred feet each. I took the bitter end of each coil and bent it on to the leading end of the next coil. That gave me an unbroken line of twenty-five hundred feet to be paid out. The

bitter end of the last coil I made fast to the base of the
big circular washing station. I instructed Dash and Sim
on how to pay out the line as I went down and how to
gently retrieve the slack and coil it as I moved about
down there. Under other circumstances I would have
had them fake the line out, but I was afraid that in the
constricted lantern light they might trip over it and foul
it.

I took off my clothes, feeling the chill, and donned
the suit. I tested the regulator again, both before and
after I put on my mask. Then I began to walk clumsily
down the slope in my flippers until I was submerged. I
switched on the big light, and holding it in front of me
began to swim down.

I kept the light focused on the old steel tracks underneath me. They gave off the only reflecting surface.
Elsewhere the light, as powerful as it was, simply died
and was absorbed into the blackness of the coal face.
At last the long slope bent itself into the flat level of
the gallery. I shone the light straight ahead into the long
corridor of the gallery, where the trucks full of coal had
been pulled along the rails. The beam pursued the
straight course of the gallery but died before it reflected
anything. I moved the lantern from side to side and
could see the soft edges of the pillars humped in the
darkness. Each of these pillars formed a wall to one of
the rooms, supported the roof overhead, and provided
access to the coal face where the men had swung their
picks. I paused and shone my light directly to the left.
There it picked up the entry to the other gallery which,
like this one, would be broken by a series of pillars and
rooms. I reasoned that the boy coming down with his
lantern in this abandoned and spooky place would have
hewed to the right instinctively, as I was doing, and
would have followed this gallery before wandering off
to the left. Unlike me, the boy would have had a source
of light coming down from the pithead at the top of the
slope. True, he could have got himself lost, but as long
as he had stuck to this gallery and the rooms to his right

there was little chance that he would have been disoriented.

I shone my light back to the lifeline to make sure it hadn't fouled on anything and was satisfied to see the long wavering line of phosphor yellow behind me. I kicked off then and headed for the first room, turning into it on my right. I went along slowly, gently, looking at the coal face on either side where men had hacked out the heavy lumps that had kept this country alive for more than a hundred years. Spaced along the black wall were large wooden posts, which had not rotted because they had remained underwater all this time. Above them bolt-fastened plates held up the roof of the mine to keep it from crashing down on the men. Putting those posts in place I realized was what Sim Lewis had been doing as a youth when he spoke of himself as being a "carpenter." I swam on to the end of the room meeting there the great seam of coal that had been the main sustenance of the mine. There was nothing in this room—not on either side of it. I crouched at the end and shone my light back toward the gallery and up at the ceiling supported by the plates. For the first time in my life I realized what utter heroism had gone into the simple maintenance of everything we had done for a hundred years. The railroads, the steel mills, the factories, the public buildings, the individual homes of the entire country, the illuminating gas, the thousands of products, all, all had come from the labor of men who had crouched down in places like this under deadly threat of their lives. I looked at the supported ceiling again and shuddered. To have one cave in and trap you in the horror of an enclosure like this! To be buried in your sweat-stained clothes, your helpless pick gripped in your hand! Or to stand in a place like this, facing the coal seam, and see your workmate drop suddenly, inexplicably—fire damp—and drop down too, unable to move, to escape, your last thoughts being *Fire damp! Fire damp!* To spend your working life in this black enclosure to come up at last and find that you could not breath sufficiently to continue work, and to end up set-

tled on a rocker on your front porch with your lips turning blue. No. Not with all the glittering machinery of
every government printing office could they roll out sufficient dollars to pay me for working in a place like
this.

I seized the lifeline in one hand, holding the lantern
in the other, and kicked my way slowly from the end
of the room. I was relieved to see that the slack was
being taken up slowly, carefully.

I came out into the gallery, checked my line again,
and swam in to the next room down the line. There was
nothing there except the crushing claustrophobia at the
end. I came out again and repeated the process, making
sure that my line was clear. When I came out of that
room, however, I paused and thought about whether I
would have time to examine each of these spaces, including those rooms lying off the second gallery to the
left. I was not crazy about the idea of having to look
for somewhere that I could recharge the tanks. I shot
the beam of my light once more down the length of the
gallery.

At first I denied what I had seen—a tiny flash of
white. The eyes play tricks and never more than when
there is this odd unnatural mixture of oxygen and nitro-
gen flowing in the bloodstream tricking the nerves. I
looked away from it, staring into the darkness, and
breathed as slowly and regularly as I could from the
pressurized mouthpiece. Then I looked back, swinging
my light to the original point. It was there, a tiny flash
of white in the deep, deep dark. I brought the beam
back slowly and counted off the corners of three more
pillars. The flash of white had been three rooms down
from here. It could, of course, be an artifact. It could
be anything. I pondered whether I should go directly to
it or work my way down systematically room by room.
This was not an idle question. I did not want to go down
there and then forget where I had left off. I had nothing
to mark my departure from the corner where I was resting now. But time—time—I had to think about time. I
had only just so much of this manufactured air in the

tanks on my back, and I decided that I could count the pillars on my way down to the flash of white and then count back when I returned if, as I expected, this turned out to be nothing—a bit of rag, a white stone stuck in the coal. I trained my beam on it and swam slowly, carefully down the gallery.

The speck of white as I approached it assumed the shape of the phalanges of a spidery, white, skeletal hand. I focused the beam on the hand. When I swam up to it I saw that the wrist had been bound to a rock bolt with wire. The wire had rusted away so that it was merely the form of the coil that had been wound around the man's wrist. When I pushed it with my finger it fell away into flakes that floated down in the water. The hand, however, remained where it was, resting on the long shaft of the bolt. I moved the beam across the bare skull, sagging with its downward despairing look. The beam traced the long line of the bones of the arm to the other bolt. I moved over and flicked away the other coil of wire. Nothing stirred except the slow fall of the flakes through the water. He remained there hanging on the bolts—the Ragged Stranger.

If he had been ragged when he was strung up across these bolts he was more ragged now. Only tatters of the black coat, vest and trousers clung to the skeleton. If he had worn a shirt, the acid tinct of the water had eaten it away, as it had his flesh. The acid, over the years, had picked him clean. The poor man's feet were only barely resting on the floor of the mine. Around them was a tiny pyramid made of the material that had drifted down from his body in this still and lifeless water. I reached down to sift the little pile and the loose matter burst away in a tiny cloud. I picked up everything that had a form to it—coins, keys, and a small bar that looked like a tie clip with a little chain. I put them in my retaining belt. As I straighted up I noticed that something was hanging in the space between his ribs. It was apparently a watch fob that had fallen inwards as the shirt and vest had rotted away. I slipped this too into my belt. Then I began to search the floor around the suspended skeleton—out into the gallery and then deep into the room. I brushed away each pile pf subsidence with the edge of my hand very carefully, watched the small cloud disappear and then laid my hand very gently over the spot. It was slow and painstaking work but it revealed nothing else. All that I could come back with was the metal that had dropped through his pockets as the fabric had dissolved through the passing years.

Gentleness was what was wanted now. I did not want to shake loose and lose anything that might be clinging to the few tatters of his clothes. I put my forefingers under the bones of his armpits and lifted him off the bolts. To my dismay the long bony arms did not float down through the water to his sides. They remained outstretched—the shoulder joints had calcified. The legs, too, with the long bones of the foot pointing downwards, remained close together, unmoving. All the man's joints had fused. He had become a statue.

I thought about towing him back up. I would ordinarily have simply seized one of the bony hands and swum away, but now I wanted to keep him exactly as he was for the benefit of the medical examiner. I couldn't think of a convenient place to seize the skeleton without disturbing the position I had found him in. He remained upright, leaning against the wall of the pillar with his unsupported arms outstretched.

There was no other answer for it that I could see. I tipped him over and inserted my fingers into the eyesockets of his tilted head and began very slowly to make my way back through the gallery. I gave the lifeline two quick jerks to signify to the men above that I had finished.

25

I had dumped the little hoard I'd collected at the skeleton's feet into a saucepan from the kitchenette and filled the pan with water. Maria, Dash and Sim stood behind me at the sink looking on. I made sure that the strainer was securely fixed in the drain before I turned on the tap to rinse and rub each individual piece.

We hadn't told Sheriff McCleod and his deputies anything at all about these pieces when they had come racing down after Dash's phone call. We had agreed that Sim could straighten this out with the law after we had identified the stuff (and after I had returned safely to New York). Sheriff McCleod had been purple with rage at the sight of the skeleton stretched out in the spooky light of the pit head. He had more or less threatened to arrest everyone in sight.

"What are you going to arrest me for?" Sim asked him sensibly enough.

"For—for trespassing!"

"Trespassing on my own property? I've owned this place for years and years. You know that, Jack."

"For unauthorized search . . ."

"I need authorization to look into my own mine?"

"For endangering—endangering . . ." He saw the futility of it. "Ah, shit," said Jack McCleod.

Dash had been careful to explain the odd disposition of the skeleton when he had called the sheriff, so that they had brought along a rescue squad ambulance with sufficient room to lay out the skeleton in the back. None of us was sure of what forensic value this would be to the medical examiner, but on the other hand none of us wanted to be the first to crack those arms at the shoulders. The skull, too, remained at its downward tilt, frozen into a sad eternal gaze of emptiness.

McCleod had demanded the full story there and then and we gave him a fairly honest version of events. "After all," Sim told him guilelessly, "if there was a corpse down there at the bottom of my mine I sure didn't want somebody else finding it and blaming me."

McCleod regarded this with a long steady look at Sim. "We'll see about that," he said. He insisted then that all three of us show up at his office at eight the following morning to make our statements and sign them. We gave him every assurance.

Now I began to rub away the silted accretions from the metal disks. All of them were, as I had suspected, coins that had dropped down through the victim's pockets. None was dated later than 1948—and that one was a penny. One coin was a half dollar, one a quarter, five nickels, a dime, and six more pennies. I washed them all carefully and set them aside on the drainboard. If there had been a wallet, it either had been stolen or had dissolved along with his shoes, his belt and his flesh. I took up the key ring next. There was no tag on it. When I had cleaned them off the keys revealed were an old-fashioned door key of the kind that used to be called a skeleton key, a key for a Yale lock, and a small key that had obviously been made for a cheap padlock. None of them invited any kind of useful speculation.

I was extremely cautious with the watch fob I had found between his ribs and with the little clasp that had lain nearby. I poured out the dirty water in the pan and refilled it to soak the fob with its solidified chain and the clasp with its smaller chain. I began to work at the watch fob (where had the watch gone? I wondered) very delicately with my fingers and let the tap water run over it until a surface of unmistakable gold was revealed. Bits of material began to break away and as I rubbed it gently between my fingers two letters began to take shape. Each letter occupied a square inch of heavy gold. When the letters were completely cleaned and gleaming dully under the yellow light of the ceiling fixture they shone out as GD, with the stave of the D hanging through the crook of the G. Maria clapped her hand over her mouth. I looked up at Sim.

"That was the old Griffiths-Danford trademark, when they first formed the company," said Sim. "Wasn't till years later they called it Pendragon." His eyes were remote.

Maria said, "That's what the GD meant on the manuscript, then. That's what Milly was talking about."

I set the gold fob aside on the drainboard and picked the clasp up out of the pan. I soaked it again in clean water and then began to run away at it. The little chain broke away from the clasp. I set it aside and rubbed away at the clasp itself. This was not gold. It was electroplated silver, some of which had worn away to show the brassy metal underneath. Some lettering engraved in script became visible. It was faint, too faint, impossible to read in the light of the kitchenette. We took it into the sitting room and switched on the lamp near the table. As we stared and stared and rubbed and rubbed holding it this way and that Dash's face became more and more masklike. He touched my shoulder. "Let me see that for a minute," he said. He held it up near the bulb of the lamp, tilting it back and forth, and then dropped it on the table as if it had burned him. "Look at it," he said to Sim. "Just look at it. You know what it says, don't you?" Sim stared at him. "Tilt it this way," he said to me, "and look at it."

I tilted the clasp and the markings began to join and make sense. They said:

JOHNSON C. DASHWOOD
FOR PERFECT ATTENDANCE
19- -

The final numbers on the date were indecipherable.

"My brother," said Dash. "My brother. From Bible school." He was trembling.

"Ah, Dash," said Sim, his heavy face creased in sorrow. Sim stretched out a hand to the tall mahogany-colored man and took him by the arm. "Sit down here,

Dash,'' said Sim. ''Sit down.'' He led Dash—as if Dash were suddenly blinded—over to one of the easy chairs. He said to me sharply then, ''Fix Dash a drink.'' I went back to the kitchenette for my bottle.

When I came back with the drink Sim was seated in the other easy chair across from Dash. Dash had his hands over his face. I nudged him and handed him the drink. He took it and looked up at me. Then he took a sip. ''First one in thirty years,'' he said. His eyes had the expression of staring down a long, long corridor. Indeed, both he and Sim appeared to be momentarily spellbound. Both of them were staring into some unnamable area of time, and both of them looked much, much older. I asked Sim if he would like a drink too, but he shook his head against it slowly as if the question had been whispered to him out of the trees.

Dash took another swallow and looked up at Sim. ''What do you think?'' he asked him. ''Johnny was really down there when they strung up this man like that? Johnny did that?''

''Johnny,'' I interrupted. ''This is Johnson? Over at the mansion?''

''Yes, Johnny.'' Dash looked up at me, his eyes wondering. ''Changed his name, Johnny did, after I went to the pen. Didn't want to be—'' he paused, *''associated,* yeah, that's what he said, associated with trash like me. Told me about how our mother would have grieved. Our mother—up in heaven, you know, she was very religious—our mother up in heaven, he told me how she must grieve to see me going to the pen. Yeah, she was looking down on me, says Johnny. I was standing there in handcuffs. Hell, I was standing there in chains. Yeah, Johnny says, she's up in heaven looking down and grieving. It kind of took me, you know? I thought the whole point of going to heaven was that after that, I mean after you got in, you didn't have to give a shit for anything any more. But Johnny laid it down on me all right. A heavy burden. A heavy burden to carry.

"Yeah, well, that c, that c in the middle of his name, that stands for Charles. So he changed his name to Charles Johnson. Johnson was his christening name and he took that and made it his last name. He didn't want the name Dashwood any more. Like he was ashamed of it, you know? That hurt. That hurt plenty. I wonder what Momma thought about that."

Dash looked around the room, wondering. He said, "I never spoke to Johnny after that, after I came out of the pen. He never spoke to me." He took a long sip of the drink and then set the glass down carefully between his feet.

I said, "I think what we'd better do now is all of us sit down here and try to see what really happened. Maria?"—she had been standing off to one side, looking like a small scared ghost—"sit over here, baby. Can I fix you something?" She shook her head against the idea and moved slowly, uncertainly to a chair at the table. There was the quick flash of a look that suggested that she didn't much like being called baby. I went into the kitchenette and fixed myself a very mild bourbon and water. I was very tired.

I said, "So far the accounting of events we've had is what Honey told the shrink while Honey was under heavy medication. I thought at the time it could have been a fantasy. There wasn't any backup. All right. Now we've found a skeleton down there who was strung up pretty much the way Honey looked when he was speaking in the skeleton's voice—that is, I'm told it was another voice. When you heard that voice," I nodded toward Sim, "you recognized it as a Griffiths. The obvious conclusion is that it was a Griffiths down there and that he was alive when Honey saw him. But that is only the obvious conclusion. It could have been a skeleton that Honey saw down there, or it could have been a dead man who had not yet become a skeleton, and Honey could have fantasized the conversation. The Griffiths voice that you recognized could merely have been a projection of his mother's voice—her way of talking. I'm offering all this just to keep us on the straight and narrow.

"Any cop will tell you," I said, "that the obvious conclusion is usually the right one. But he'll also tell you that all the others have got to be considered if you don't want to get blown away in court. One thing that supports the obvious is the coin dated 1948 I found at the skeleton's feet. If these coins came from his pocket we have a stop time that says no earlier than 1948, which corresponds roughly with the time Honey went down in the mine. On the other hand we can't prove that the coins came from the victim's pocket. We found a tie clasp that belonged, presumably, to somebody else, although the clasp was found a little distance from the man's feet." Dash looked up and stared at me. He finished his drink and went into the kitchenette for another.

"The watch fob I found was hanging between the man's ribs, so I think we can safely assume it really belonged to him. It is the early trademark of the Griffiths-Danford Coal Company, later replaced by the name Pendragon. The obvious assumption is that this man was indeed a Griffiths, very possibly David Griffiths Junior, Marjory's father, Honey's grandfather. Everything that Honey said at the hospital points to that. The person speaking through Honey's brain knew who Honey was, who Sim Lewis was, and who Marjory was. But we also have to consider that it might merely have been a man who knew David Junior intimately, had got hold of the watch and chain and was here to steal his inheritance. That is always a possibility to keep in mind.

"The one thing that stumps me is Honey's saying, 'I am the Ragged Stranger.' How would this man know that he was the Ragged Stranger? Why would he call himself the Ragged Stranger?"

Maria sat forward. She said, "I can explain that. We know that the man told Honey he'd gotten a newspaper off the garbage heap. It was the newspaper that first called him that, not Honey. If he was truly David

Griffiths he didn't want to give Honey his name for fear Honey would blurt it out and the wrong people would come back to get him. He was much safer as just 'The Ragged Stranger.' " Her eyes widened suddenly. "Yes," she said. "Milly had me bring over back issues of the Bluestone *Courier*. And one place in the manuscript she'd made the marginal note—'Was RS DG?' I never knew what any of those damned notes meant."

"The next question," I said, "is why didn't the poor bastard get the kid to turn him loose?"

Sim said, "You're forgettin' that was only a little boy there. There wasn't no way he could reach up that high. There wasn't nothing there he could stand on to reach it. The man thought he was doin' the sensible thing just tellin' the boy to run off and find Marjory."

"All right," I said. "Let's restructure this. Sim and Dash were standing around the pit head checking supplies from the trucks. Honey wandered off and went down in the mine. He walked down the long gallery with his lantern and he came across this crucified man. 'Who are you?' says Honey. 'I am the Ragged Stranger,' says the man. Honey identifies himself in a way that the man recognizes. Then, if Honey is to be believed, the man tells Honey to take something from his pants—something sticking out—would it have been in his belt?—and take it to Marjory, his mother.

"There are two things here. Although the man was desperate, he did not want Honey to tell anyone else. This means, at least to me, that the man thought there was a conspiracy so great that he didn't dare trust anyone except his daughter. That is eminently possible, considering the situation he was in. The second thing is what was it Honey was supposed to take and where did he take it?

"You told me," I said to Sim, "that after you heard the explosion and heard the water gushing into the mine Honey fainted. You brought him home where he lapsed into a fever and was delirious. This means that he still had whatever it was the man gave him on his

person when you brought him home. You told me, **Sim, that** you had undressed him and put all his things **on the table** beside the bed. What the Ragged Stranger gave him, or told him to take, rather, should have wound up on the table there. What was it?''

Sim half started out of his chair. ''It had to be that damned tobacco pouch,'' he said. ''It was bigger than a tobacco pouch but it was oilskin and it had a piece of paper in it. And I told you I wouldn't pry on the boy, especially when he was sick like that. I just let things lay, but I never saw that tobacco pouch again. I never thought about it again. It just disappeared.''

''Okay,'' I said. ''The man told him to take it to his ma, to Marjory. But his mother was dead. The man didn't know that Marjory was dead, but he did know that she had been married to Sim Lewis. There had been some kind of communication somewhere.

''We're going to have to go with the obvious,'' I told them. ''And if that doesn't work out we'll have to look at the alternatives.'' I asked Sim, ''Do you have any idea where Honey might have kept that pouch?'' Sim shook his head. ''Well,'' I reasoned, ''there's only one logical place to look now and I'll go up there tomorrow.''

I turned to Maria then. ''Do you know the janitor of the Education Building?'' I asked her.

''Mike Polonski.''

''How long has he been there?''

''Since they built the damned place as far as I know.''

''Polonski's all right,'' Sim objected. ''There ain't any harm in that man.''

''I've got to see him,'' I said. ''Maria, I want you to call him up. Call him up right now . . .''

''It's late. He'd be in bed.''

''I don't care about that. Call him up right now and tell him we have to see him in my rooms here at the hotel at seven o'clock tomorrow morning. I want to see him before we go to the sheriff's because right after we leave the sheriff's I'm heading out to find that pouch.''

Sim had started out of his chair again, and Dash looked up at him. ''You can't go up there with your knees the way they are,'' said Dash. ''I'll go along with Mr. Binney here.''

That night was a restless night for me. The old bed in its metal framework sagged beneath me as I tossed and turned. Vivid dreams awoke me finally, although the image of them began to flee the moment I was awake. I lay in the darkness and tried to recapture what had been going through my sleeping brain. The impression was that of a thick jungle in which a clearing would appear with enormous rooms of well-appointed furniture. Jagged bits of colored light would shoot across the rooms and then the jungle would enclose the rooms and wild beasts would pad and stare out of the tangled underbrush and behind the beasts there formed in the denseness of the undergrowth thick heavy letters carved of wood. I strained to discern what these letters were and what they meant. They emerged finally as in an optical illusion—DG.

I sat up straight in bed and turned on the lamp to find a cigarette. Were those letters truly worked into the woodwork of the huge old house? More to the point: how on earth had a family like the Danfords come to build a house like that? Everything about them echoed the thin cry of *Puritan*. Even given the madness of the age of robber barons a house that the Danfords had built would have been more chaste, restrained, at least more classical. But the old mansion was a hodgepodge of dreamlike towers and crenellations from the magical age of fairylands, of legend, myth, and antiquity. And the huge figure of Galahad who brooded over the grand staircase, what on earth had a figure like that to do with the Danfords and their pursemouthed way of life? It was—it was *Celtic*. The word sprang out at me.

I extinguished my cigarette, turned out the lamp and went back to sleep, firm in the resolution that old

Ephraim Danford had never built the house in which his grandson was living out his arid years.

26

Dash favored the pickup truck again the next morning. We drove out past the motor lodge and then swung around a small country road that ran along the foothills behind it. It was not a very long trip for the truck, but I realized that Honey Lewis must have hiked six or seven miles each way whenever he came into town to preach. Dash parked the truck, and I followed him for about a hundred yards along the base of the hill before he stopped. He pointed up a steep slope that was marked only by the vaguest of paths. "Up there," he said. "It crooks off into a kind of a ledge and he built himself that shelter up under the ledge."

"How long ago was that?"

"Oh, must be about twenty-five years now he's been living up there."

"And you always knew where it was?"

"Sure. Sim used to keep an eye on him, you know. He'd send somebody up here with a basket of food every now and then while Honey was down there preaching. He'd never let anybody come up bothering him while Honey was here, though. To tell the truth, nobody much wanted to come around when they knew Honey was here."

"Anybody ever go inside the place?"

"Sim wouldn't allow that. He said the man had to be let alone."

We began to climb up the pathway made slippery by the slick grass that had just barely been parted with Honey's comings and goings. When we reached the first leveling of the hillside we were both winded. The previous day had been a long and active one. Both of us were tired. Neither of us, I think, had had a particularly good night's sleep. We sat on the level grass and stared out at the field below us from which the fragrance of onrushing midsummer rose. The motor lodge was visible but much diminished in this perspective. The city stretched out beyond it dozing in the midmorning sun. The Capthorne hotel was visible and the dome of the courthouse glinted. We decided to have a cigarette before continuing.

Dash asked me. "What do you think is going to happen to him?"

I asked thoughtlessly, "Who?"

His eyes flashed with impatience and irritation. He said, "Johnny." He took a deep bitter drag on his cigarette.

I said, "I think you're jumping the gun. Nothing has been proved. It's all circumstantial. Maybe nothing *will* be proved."

Dash said, "You're a stranger in these parts. Proof ain't all that important. Oh, there'll be a trial and all. That's the way it is nowadays. Used to be they'd just take him out and string him up."

"Things have changed," I said.

"Yeah," he answered. He did not seem to derive any particular satisfaction from it.

We smoked silently for a few moments, staring out at the city. Both of us were thinking about the early interview that morning with Mike Polonski.

Polonski looked to be about sixty years old and he was enough of an old-timer that the Capthorne still contained for him an aura reminiscent of power and money. He had bathed, shaved, and dressed carefully for the occasion. He was wearing sharply pressed slacks, a skimpy sports coat of a greenish tweed, and a Hawaiian sport shirt with the broad collar spread out over the lapels of his jacket. His face was blisteringly pink under the close and careful shave and his white hair gleamed when he took off the dark colored straw fedora with the feather in the band. His brown shoes had a newish look to them.

Sim, Dash, and I did as much as we could to put
him at his ease, but he was not to be unbent. He refused the offer of coffee, which I had just brewed. He
refused a cigarette. He picked the stiffest chair he could
find—an occasional chair that might have doubled in
an execution chamber—and sat there with his hat on
his knee.

"Mr. Polonski," I began, and he jumped at the
sound of my voice, "we're looking into the case of
the explosion and fire at the Board of Education building." Polonski sat rigidly, staring a blue eyed stare
directly back at me. I can't help my stare, of course,
because I have to read lips, but it does disconcert some
people and Polonski was one of those.

"I never had nothing to do with that," said Polonski.

"Of course not," I responded quickly. I noted that
Sim and Dash had also made comforting and conso-
latory gestures. "But the fact remains that someone
did and we really have to find out who it was."

"They already know who it was," said Polonski.
He was careful not to look at Sim. He kept his eyes
riveted on me.

"Well," I said, "they think they know who it was,
but of course nobody's sure until there's a trial. Now,
it so happens that there are a number of problems with
this case and we'd like to solve some of them and we
think you can help us with that." Polonski's round
face tensed. He sat rigid, unmoving.

"The problem we're having," I went on conversationally, "is that while they've picked Honey Lewis
as a suspect because he'd been preaching about blowing up buildings and burning down the city for twenty
years, this doesn't look like the kind of thing Honey
would do. Do you see what I mean?"

"No."

"Whoever did the job," I said, "did this very quietly, very secretly, so that when it happened he
wouldn't be anywhere near it. He sneaked in sometime
during the weekend while you were away and while

the building was empty except for Milly Rutledge, during the days of Saturday and Sunday. He set up an explosive charge and then he sneaked away again. Somehow that doesn't sound like the kind of thing Honey would do. Don't you agree?''

His face managed to look both blank and wary. He said, "I wouldn't know nothing about that."

I said, "Let's look at what had to happen. Everybody has agreed that there had to be a big charge of dynamite placed under the water heater. Now when you left on Friday night you had to go and turn down the thermostat. Is that right?'' He nodded a grudging assent. "And I take it that when you turned down the thermostat at the bottom of the tank you didn't notice any large sticks of dynamite with a fuse running out of them or any other large suspicious looking packages under the heater, now did you?''

"No," he agreed. "I never saw nothing like that."

"Well, what that means, Mr. Polonski," I told him, "is that sometime between the hour you left the building on Friday night and the hour in which the building blew up on Sunday somebody sneaked into the basement and laid a charge of dynamite and then sneaked away without being seen, or at least noticed.

"Now," I continued, "we have no way of knowing whether he smashed through one of the basement windows in the back because all that evidence has been destroyed. However, on Sunday I first approached the building from the back, and I certainly didn't notice anything like that. My feeling is that whoever got in to lay that charge had an easy entry. So," I paused, "I have to ask you—did you unlock a basement window for any purpose last week and did you forget to lock it up again?''

"No," he said, "I never."

"Did you check to make certain they were locked when you left on Friday night?''

He stirred impatiently, his first show of animation. "Why would I do a thing like that?'' he asked me. "Them windows ain't been unlocked in twenty years.''

"Would it be very difficult to unlock them? I mean from the inside?"

"I don't see why. It's just barrel bolts holding them in."

"Well, then," I said. "It seems to me as if whoever laid the charge down there had to get into the basement first and unlock the windows from the inside so he could come back later. Did you happen to see Honey Lewis fooling around down there at any time?"

" 'Course not," Polonski snapped. "Honey Lewis wouldn't come into no building like that."

"Then I guess you see what I'm getting at, don't you? That's why we think it was somebody else besides Honey who laid the charge."

Doubt, now, was entering the bright blue eyes. The round face became a bit pinker. I said, "You spend most of your time in the basement area, don't you, Mr. Polonski?" He nodded soberly. "Do you have any set schedule when people would know you were not there so that they could come down and fool around?"

He shook his head wonderingly. "No," he said. "I come up and unlock the doors in the morning and I go back to lock 'em up at night, but outside of that there ain't any way anybody would know I wouldn't be down there. No."

"Do you remember seeing anybody down there last week, anybody that works in the building, anybody at all?"

His round eyes searched the ceiling. "No," he said finally. "There wasn't nobody like that." Suddenly a smile split his face, revealing a very large gap between his front teeth. He laughed; his belly shook with it. "Unless of course you mean—" he could hardly get it out—"Mr. Danford."

"Mr. Danford came down to say hello, did he?" I asked pleasantly. I *felt* Sim and Dash stiffen behind me.

" 'Course not." Polonski managed to look scandalized. " 'Course it wasn't Mr. Danford hisself. He wouldn't come down there. He sent his nig—'' there was a quick shocked glance toward Dash. "He sent that fella works up in the mansion. Johnson his name is."

"Well," I smiled. "That certainly was unusual, wasn't it? What did Mr. Johnson want to see you about?"

"Mr. Danford was going to make another one of them gifts to the city the newspaper is always writing about. He thought the old Education Building might need some sprucing up. And it sure does. Like it needs—" He paused then and his eyes widened. He gestured as if waving something away. " 'Course," he said, "it don't need nothing at all, now, does it?"

"So you showed Mr. Johnson around the basement?"

"Yep. There's things in the foundation need looking after, where the water leaks in, you know. Things like that."

"Did you show him the water tank?"

"Yep. He was interested in that because it was a gift from Mr. Danford, you know. I explained how it worked and all. Never had no trouble with it."

"Was Mr. Johnson down there any time by himself that you remember?"

The blue eyes rolled back toward the interior of Polonski's skull. "Might have been," he said. "I remember I had to go up and check all the windows to make sure they were shut before closing up. He might have been."

I was saying, "You've been a very great help to us, Mr. Polonski," when I saw the big bulk of Sim moving past me. I saw him press something into Polonski's hand, lean over him in the chair and talk very earnestly to him. Polonski paid very sharp attention. "Yessir, Mr. Lewis," he said. "You don't have to worry about a single doggone thing."

Dash and I flipped away the butts of our cigarettes and hoisted ourselves up for the second leg of the climb. This was a steeper, rockier path, and led through pine trees that had driven their roots through the stony soil. An ancient carpet of pine needles and cones spread outward from the path and the air was filled with the beautiful and mysterious scent of woodland. The pathway curved to the right and then looped its way to the left to bring us up to the level outcropping that protected the shelter.

The shelter itself surprised me. It was bigger and more sophisticated than I had expected. From the earlier description I'd had of Honey living like a wild animal I'd envisioned something that was little more than a cave. But this structure, as rude as it was, stood about eight feet high. I judged it to be about twelve feet long and nine feet wide. It was built of stone, as I had been told, but it was not the helter-skelter sort of lean-to I'd expected. The stone had obviously been selected from the profusion that lay scattered on the mountainside and had been lugged individually by hand down to the site. The big stones, boulders, really, at the foundation demonstrated the strength of the man who had brought them along the sloping face of the hill. From foundation on up the stones had been carefully selected for size and shape and fitted to one another to minimize the gaps in the wall. There was no mortar. Such spaces as existed between the stones were plugged with moss and sod that had been hammered in. All in all, the walls looked pretty tight. The doorway faced toward the town, which was to the south, but in both side walls provision had been made for windows. These seemed to be parts of old metal framed factory windows with small panes that Honey had hacked down to size and inserted in the stone walls. The door was massive. It was made of dunnage roughly nailed together with crosspieces and secured against the wind with batten board. The door handle was a simple leather loop. A metal stovepipe with a conical cap jutted up from the corrugated metal roof.

Dash and I stood stock still in front of the dwelling, staring at it and catching our breath after the steep climb. I don't believe that either of us wanted actually

to enter the place. It was the enclosure of a terrible
privacy although there was no lock of any kind on the
huge rough door. The defiant eruption of the rude
shanty on the hillside exclaimed not so much that it
was a habitation as that it was a mixture of fortress,
shrine and tomb. A man had shut himself up in here
for more than twenty years, emerging only to cry out
the word of God to the populace below. I think that
both Dash and I were a little frightened of it.

We had been spooked earlier this morning down at
the sheriff's office. Dash, Sim, and I had made out our
statements, duly recorded and typed by a stenogra-
pher, and then we had signed them. McCleod's gaze
had been stony. The whole thing had been put through
as if McCleod and his deputies had never seen any of
us before in his life. But lying on McCleod's desk
were eight by ten glossies of the skeleton. They had
been taken first in the shed of the pit head under the
glaring lights of the photographer's kit. And then others had been taken after the poor ragged remnants were
moved to the state hospital for examination. Dr. Butler, the M.E., had hastened down to meet the ambulance there, and he had called in a pathologist for
consultation. Together they had quickly discovered
that the man whose skeleton this was had undergone a
terrible beating at one time in his life—not when he
was strung up on the bolts, but much, much earlier.
The awful wounds had healed, but they had healed
haphazardly. Nearly all of his ribs had been stove in.
His left arm had been broken just above the elbow.
His right hand and his left ankle had been fractured in
several places. But most astoundingly, his skull had
been fractured. There was a depressed fracture on the
right side of the occiput, as from the blow of a ham-
mer. His left jawbone and cheekbone had been shattered and there was a hairline fracture of the orbital
bone surrounding his left eye. Closeup photographs of
all these sites had been taken, showing the relics of an
almost unbelievable savagery. Incredibly, the man had

lived, lived long enough for his bones to heal so that he could encounter his fate at the mine.

Now Dash and I looked at each other. I shrugged, stepped up to the rough door and pulled on the leather loop. The door gave grudgingly on the big iron hinges. Looking into the depths of the room we saw that the windows did not really give much light, and both of us blinked at adjusting our vision. Dominating the interior was an oil drum stove. The drum had been laid horizontally on rock supports and the stove door had been chiseled out of the end of the drum. The stove pipe had been fitted in the farther end of it and went up through the roof. It was crude but effective, I thought, and would certainly supply ample heat for a space this size. Oddly, there was no provision for cooking on the stove. I surmised that if Honey did any cooking at all, he must have done it on a campfire outside the hut. To our right near the door Honey had placed a large square table made of the same kind of dunnage that furnished the door. A candle on a cracked saucer provided the light. I took out a match and lit the candle.

The soft glow of the candle lit up the room, and we looked to our left where Honey had constructed a bed. It consisted of a rough framework of boards laid on the flat stone floor. The framework enclosed an arrangement of pine boughs laid lengthwise and covered with an army blanket. Another blanket was folded at the end of the bed. It looked more like an iron maiden to me than a bed, but apparently it was all that Honey required. The only manufactured piece of furniture in the room that I could see was a kitchen chair that looked as if Honey had dragged it up from the town dump. An ax and a few tools were stacked neatly against the wall at the foot of the bed. Dash and I peered at the other end of the room beyond the stove. There was only empty space back there. The back wall had an army blanket hung up against it, presumably to ward off the draft.

I said to Dash, "There's something missing here."
Dash looked up inquiringly. "His Bible," I said.

We both began to move slowly, reluctantly back toward the dimmer end of the room. We saw that the blanket was not fastened to the wall itself but hung on a rod like a drapery rod supported on the side walls. I lifted the blanket at the bottom and slung it up over the rod. Both Dash and I stepped back quickly from what we saw. I don't know if he gasped, but I know I did.

An effigy had been fastened to the wall. It was about three feet high and made of straw. It was clad in the dark tattered clothes of a child—dark jacket and dark pants. The yellow straw stuck out from the extended arms of the jacket and the ragged cuffs of the trousers. The head was an onion shaped globe of yellow straw with blue eyes filched from a doll and stuck into the upper part. Two black dots served for nostrils. The mouth was a line of red flannel. A bit of white woolly material had been thumbtacked to the crown. Its outstretched arms rested on two bolts that had been driven into the stone wall. A small circle of wire fastened each wrist to its bolt. The onion shaped head was tilted downward gazing at what seemed to be an altar below it on the floor. There lay the Bible, a big one, on a polished board. The Bible was closed.

I squatted down on the floor in front of the effigy and began to riffle through the Bible. It had been his mother's. Her name was on the flyleaf, *Marjory Griffiths*, written in a neat Spencerian hand. The ink had turned brown. I leafed quickly through it to see if any papers had been inserted. Then I held it by its boards, something I disliked doing, and shook it. Nothing fell out. I handed the Bible to Dash and ran my hand over the polished surface of the board. I rapped it with my knuckles and asked Dash, "That sound hollow to you?" The board was fitted tightly in the stone floor.

"Do it again," said Dash. I rapped again.

"Yes," he said. "That's hollow under there, like a coffin."

The board didn't offer any purchase for prying it up. I wasn't carrying a pocket knife, and neither, it turned out, was Dash. He went over to look in the little pile of tools near Honey's bed and came back with a bone-handled pocket knife. He handed it to me with a pitying smile. "This is the one his daddy gave him," said Dash.

I inserted a knife blade in the crack and slowly eased up the board. Below it was an uncovered tin box, and in the box was a yellowish looking packet. I lifted it out very carefully by the edges and took it over to the table where the candle burned. Mold and moisture had darkened the oilskin and spread patches of fungus that wandered across the flap. I used the knife blade to ease back the cover and gently to open the pocket of the pouch. There was a paper inside the pocket and I carefully teased it out onto the table. There were, in fact, two pieces of paper. One was a heavy document that had been folded into quarters. The other looked like a letter on cheap stationery that had been folded in half.

I managed to open out both pieces of paper without cracking them or flaking them off. Dash and I read both of them and looked at each other. "Been here all this time," said Dash, "and Honey never said anything?"

"I don't think he ever read them," I answered. "He was told, 'Don't show this to anybody but your mother.' And I think he believed—he was only a kid—that included himself. No. I don't think he ever read them."

"Somebody gonna read them now," said Dash.

We blew out the candle, shut the rough-hewn door, and took the papers back to the hotel.

27

I had asked Maria to call ahead so there would be no surprises when I parked my Nova in the porte cochère of the mansion. She had been instructed to tell them merely that I had something important to discuss. Although she had spoken to Johnson first, Mr. Danford had come to the phone and agreed to see me that evening.

Nonetheless, there was a surprise. It was Mr. Danford himself who opened the big door to the foyer. The powerful overhead coach light seemed to foreshorten him. His white hair gleamed, his pink cheeks glowed, and his pale blue eyes had an almost feverish expression of expectancy. Nonetheless, even for the small man that he was he seemed diminished further in the high arch of the doorway and the vast spaces that ranged out behind him. He was dressed as per custom in a gray sack suit buttoned up to the breastbone, white shirt and dark tie. He reached out to seize me by the arm, and again I felt that touch of electricity that radiates from sheer power. He pulled me inside, saying, "Do, do come in, Mr. Binney. You can't imagine how eagerly I've been waiting. I hear you've made a fascinating discovery."

While we headed across the great hall toward the library I glanced up again at the brooding Galahad who in reverse illumination from inside shed none of his grandeur upon the floor. I also reflected that Jack McCleod must have wasted no time at all in getting the news of our find in the old Mine Five back to Mr. Danford. In the library Danford seated himself behind the huge ornate desk and I seated myself directly in front of it.

Danford made a steeple of his hands on the desk and

smiled his sweet smile over the peak of it. He said, "Well, Mr. Binney, you seem to have complete success in all your undertakings. I must say I'm deeply impressed. As I told you some time ago I am not unfamiliar with detective agencies. We have had occasion to hire some of the oldest, most famous names in the business. But I can't remember anyone getting results quite so rapidly."

I scratched my cheek. "That's very kind of you, Mr. Danford," I said. "But I haven't been handling anything quite on the scale that you're used to."

He leaned forward, saying, "You must tell me exactly what you've done and what you've found."

I looked around the room before I spoke. The door was open but I could not see any shadow or hint of anyone behind it. I said to Danford, "I think the first thing I should tell you is that Johnson—that is Johnson Dashwood—is going to be a prime suspect in the murder of Mildred Rutledge."

The steeple collapsed and he laid his hands flat on the surface of the desk. His expression was both thunderstruck and crestfallen. "I can't believe that," he said. "Certainly not Johnson. What evidence do you have?"

"Remember," I warned him, "I said suspect. We have no hard evidence but we do have what appears to be very suspicious behavior. So far as we know, Johnson is the only person who gained access to the basement of the building and the only person with the opportunity to set up the explosion."

Danford began, "What earthly motive . . ."

I said, "That, of course, is what puzzles us. Johnson had some cock and bull story about coming down in the basement and looking around because you were thinking of setting up a fund for some rehabilitation work on the building. But it doesn't seem likely that if you were you would send somebody like Johnson to get the data. We know that you've made gifts of this kind before and we checked with the city engineer to see what your procedure was. Everytime before this you seem to have gone through completely official channels. We've been pretty much forced to dismiss Johnson's story out of hand. It seems that he was taking advantage of your reputation.''

Danford looked greatly saddened. He said, ''I wonder what on earth could have gotten into the fellow. His whole life has been one of absolutely exemplary behavior.''

I said, ''As a matter of fact he's quite religious, isn't he?''

''Oh, yes,'' agreed Danford. ''He is extremely regular in attending church. He is a deacon there, you know. And he teaches Bible class.''

I asked, ''Has he had anything to do with Reverend Barlow and that crew?''

''No, no.'' Danford shook his head. ''Johnson's church is quite different. Furthermore Reverend Barlow and his flock are not quite receptive to—to, uh, Negroes.''

''Well, the religious motive seems to be uppermost in everyone's mind,'' I mused. ''First they stuck Honey Lewis with it, although they can't really place him near there. And now there's Johnson . . .''

''Being a regular churchgoer does not make one a fanatic, Mr. Binney,'' Danford upbraided me gently.

''No,'' I agreed, ''although they do seem to be raising a lot of hell lately. On the other hand,'' I smiled, ''there's always the guy who threw the brick through the front window of the Bible Institute with a note attached—'Disgusted Subscriber.' ''

Danford regarded me with a wintry smile. Then his face changed back to sadness. He said, ''I cannot for the life of me see what Johnson could have had against Milly Rutledge, or the Board of Education, for that matter.''

I answered, ''It will need looking into of course. By the way, I didn't see him around when I came in. Do you know where he is?''

Danford waved a small white hand and smiled wanly. ''Off on some mysterious errand as usual,'' he said. "You know, he has pretty much carte blanche here. There's never been anyone I trusted more." He sighed. He looked up then. "I take it this was the important discovery you came to tell me about?" His face hardened.

"Oh, no," I answered sitting forward. "Oh, no. That was just something I thought you ought to know first."

He nodded warily. "Of course," he said. "Of course."

I said to him, "I guess you've already been told that we found a skeleton down in the old Mine Five."

He looked up, his blue eyes very bright. "Yes," he said. "Jack McCleod was very excited about it."

"Really," I smiled. "Did he have any comments about it?"

The laughter from Danford was a short sharp explosion. "Nothing that could be repeated in a Christian household," he said. "Jack doesn't like surprises. I suppose no sheriff does."

"I'm afraid he's in for a few more before this is all over," I told Danford. "I thought it would be wiser to hold a few things back."

"Really," said Danford, straightening up in his chair. "What sort of things?" All hint of merriment had departed.

"Things that I thought would be better to check out with you first," I said cautiously. "I didn't come down here to upset any applecarts. All that Sim hired me for was to make sure Honey Lewis wasn't railroaded."

Danford folded his hands on the surface of the huge desk. His face assumed the expression of a very good businessman—or poker player. "What sort of things are you talking about, Mr. Binney?" he said.

"Well, to begin with," I reached into my pocket. "I found this hanging on the ribs of the skeleton." I put the gold chain with its heavy insignia on the desk and pushed it across to Danford with my forefinger.

He looked at it with a sad smile before picking it up. "Goodness gracious," he said, "I haven't seen one of these in ages. I wonder where the fellow got it.''

"Don't you have one like it?" I asked him.

He waved in the general direction of the ceiling. "I suppose there's one lying around somewhere in the house," he said. "I wouldn't really know where." He let the chain hang in his fingers. The heavy GD insignia swung like the tick-tock of a pendulum beneath his hand.

"There was also this." I reached into my pocket again. "This was a little ways from the feet of the skeleton when I found it." I laid the tie clasp on the desk. He picked it up and stared at it.

"I can make nothing of this," he complained.

"The inscription is hard to read," I admitted. "But it says *Johnson C. Dashwood for perfect attendance,* 9nineteen something or other. The last two numbers are gone. But it would seem that Johnson had this from the time he was a boy."

"Good heavens," said Danford. "What can Johnson have been doing down in the old Mine Five?"

"There's always the possibility that he sneaked down there as a kid to play around and lost the clasp down there. It just seems odd that I'd find it near the skeleton's feet."

"It certainly does," agreed Danford. "Very odd indeed."

I let it rest there for a few moments. Danford was staring at the gold chain and the tie clasp on the desk in front of him. I watched him for a few seconds and then shifted my gaze to the woodwork. It was lighted only by the lamp on the desk, but behind the vines and the feral visages of the animals the initials GD fairly leapt out at me. I kept shifting my eyes back and forth to make sure it wasn't a trick of the mind, but every time I looked back I picked out the letters. Optical illusion.

When I looked at Danford again he was speaking. He was saying, "This is certainly a great shock to me,

Mr. Binney. I hope beyond hope that Johnson has an explanation for all this and I suspect that he does.''

''There's more,'' I said.

''More?''

''Some papers were found,'' I said.

''Papers involving Johnson?''

''Papers involving you,'' I said.

I reached into my breast pocket and took out the oilskin pouch. ''These came to light during the investigation,'' I said. ''I'm not sure I know what to make of them, but I thought you ought to see them first.'' I took the two pieces of paper from the pouch and laid them on the desk. I shoved the letter over toward Danford first. I watched him read what I had memorized:

David Griffiths—General Delivery—
Tempe Arizona
Deer Mister Griffiths
Your daughter Marjory is got herself engaged to
a young man who is purty wield, tho he has a
job. His name is Simon Lewis. I hope you can
send me something. I don't get anything from the
Danfords anny moor now that Marjory is by her-
self. Winter is comin and I feel the chill in my
old bones. It is the winter that takes us off now
ain't it. I hope this reaches you.
                              Your friend Myra Henry

''Myra Henry,'' said Danford with a sad twisted smile. ''What a good old soul she was. Mother Henry, she was known as. A character, a real character.''

''Still around is she?'' I asked him.

''Oh, good heavens no. She died a long time ago.''

''Of what?'' I asked him, interested.

''Old age, I suppose,'' said Danford. ''I really don't know. But, yes. She was a good old soul.''

I opened up the other piece of paper, much heavier and thicker, and showing the wear of the creases in it. I'd memorized that one too. I watched him read it. It said:

AGREEMENT

I, Elliot Danford, the undersigned, do hereby agree that all heirs of David Griffiths, Jr., also the undersigned, shall obtain and enjoy equal share from all income and profits of the Griffiths and Danford Coal Company Inc. now known as the Pendragon Coal Company, Inc.

Signed this day of April 15, 1930

Elliot Danford, Esq.
David Griffiths, Jr., Esq.

Witnessed by:
Walter Parnell, Esq. Attorney at Law

The signatures were strikingly different. The first was in a heavy, ornate scrawl, the second a spidery, trembling progress across the space, and the third a bold, self-assured hand.

Danford's eyes seemed to mist over as he read it. "My goodness, Mr. Binney," he said looking up at me. "You do bring back voices from the past. What you have unfolded here is a terrible tragedy."

"Walter Parnell, the witness," I said. "That's Ken Parnell's father? Grandfather?"

"His father," answered Danford. "Just starting out with us then. Only a few years older than myself."

"And Elliot Danford?"

"My father, of course. After whom my son is named."

"I see," I said. "I see."

But his attention had gone back to the letter. He touched it experimentally, and when he spoke he seemed to be talking to himself. "So he was writing to old Mother Henry was he? One would have thought she'd have let us know about it." He stared past my shoulder and then looked at the letter again. He said to me, "Tempe, Arizona. That could explain a great deal!"

"How so?"

"Well, as you know, Griffiths disappeared from sight some time ago. It was a great mystery . . ."

"No, sir," I said. "I didn't know that."

"Sim Lewis didn't tell you?"

"No, sir. Should he have?"

Danford stared at me. "You haven't shown these, er, documents to Sim Lewis?"

"No, sir. I thought I'd—uh—try to evaluate them first. Except for the mention in the letter, Mr. Lewis's name isn't on them."

Danford watched me thoughtfully. "I see," he said. "I see." He continued to stare almost fixedly. Finally he spoke. "That was very wise of you, Mr. Binney. These documents could cause a great deal of mischief. I am amazed that they should have lasted so long underwater. You found them near the skeleton?"

"The pouch was hanging from his belt," I lied.

"And you had the foresight to secrete all these objects?"

"It wasn't foresight. I had to put them in my waterproof belt in order to bring them up. In the excitement I forgot to mention them. It wasn't until later that I recognized they might be significant."

"Significant, yes," said Danford. "Sim Lewis made no inquiries?"

"What was to inquire? We were all very excited when I found the skeleton, the Ragged Stranger that Honey Lewis had been raving about all these years."

"The sight of the skeleton quite literally drove him out of his mind, did it?"

"I guess so. Anyway, the fact that there really was a Ragged Stranger will make his treatment a little different now."

"Ah," said Danford. "Yes. I see that."

"Mr. Danford," I prompted him, "you mentioned that Tempe, Arizona had some significance. Could you tell me what it is?"

"Why, yes." The question seemed to invigorate Danford. "I think it means that Griffiths believed he had tuberculosis—perhaps knew he had tuberculosis—and simply decamped.''

"Leaving his daughter stranded?"

"Stranded?" He raised his eyebrows. "How was she stranded? She was placed with old Mother Henry."

"With an equal share of the income and profits of Pendragon?"

Laughter broke out of Danford's face, resembling the breaking of a sheet of ice. "Profits?" he said. "My dear Mr. Binney. There were no profits. We were struggling for existence. Every single year showed a loss.''

I said, "I'm amazed you were able to keep up the mansion."

"We were corporate officers, don't forget," said Danford. "And as such we received salaries commensurate with our responsibilities."

"And bonuses?" I asked. "Were there bonuses?"

"Well, yes, of course," he began. And then he stopped. "Are you suggesting that this young woman was being cheated?"

"I have no way of knowing," I replied blandly.

"Look here," said Danford, "I have another document, one that you certainly ought to see before we—uh—evaluate the importance of this one. If you'll follow me I'll show it to you."

He rose from behind the desk, again astounding me with the domination of the room by such a physically small man. As he strode out of the room I followed him. He stopped to turn out the lights of the great hall so that the staircase was lighted only by a few dim rays from above. The moon had risen and the vague light of it changed the coloration patterns on the floor from the dreaming Galahad to a variation of monochromes—varying shades of gray only barely tinged with color. I stopped Danford at the broad foot of the staircase. I said to him, "It was the Griffiths who built this house, wasn't it?"

He turned and faced me. "Yes," he said. "My fam-

ily would never have been guilty of a monstrosity like
this.''

Satisfied, I followed him up the stairs and through
the dining room. He flicked the lights on as he passed
through and then shut them off as we left. We went
through the parlor and then through the billiard room,
each one lighted and darkened by turn. At last we arrived at the office adjoining the billiard room.

I was surprised to see Johnson sitting in a club chair
in the corner. I was even more surprised to see that he
had a Colt forty-five automatic pointed directly at me.

28

Danford had preceded me into the room, but now he
stepped quickly away from me to leave Johnson a clear
target. He said to me, ''I know you're a resourceful
man, Mr. Binney, but I implore you not to do anything
foolish. Please put up your hands and step, slowly and
carefully, over to the wall there.'' I looked at the gun.
Even a nick from a forty-five Colt can be fatal. Johnson looked at ease but determined. He was not wearing
his white coat. He was wearing an old blue suit, shirt
and tie. I had the impression he intended to travel.

I put my hands in the air and moved slowly sideways toward the wall. When I got there I was standing
next to a pipe running from the floor to the ceiling. It
was a steam pipe left over from the antediluvian
plumbing in the house. I began, ''You're being very
foolish—''

But Danford cut me off with, ''Please extend your
hands around the pipe.'' Johnson got up and walked
over so that he had a clear shot at me. The gun was
ancient but it looked very serviceable—and huge. I put
my hands around either side of the pipe. Danford
opened a side drawer of the desk and took out a pair

of antiquated handcuffs. Keeping clear of Johnson's line of fire he came over and fastened the handcuffs on my wrists. The big serrated tongues went through the locks and shut very securely. I was fastened to the steam pipe. Danford said, "There is no reason for you to be uncomfortable, Mr. Binney." He got behind an occasional chair and pushed it across the rug so that I could sit down. I sat. It was awkward but not terribly uncomfortable.

Danford smiled at me. He said, "Those handcuffs are real antiques. They're left over from the old Pinkerton days."

I said, "How interesting."

"We had private detectives before you were ever born, Mr. Binney," said Danford. "They were absolutely necessary. The coal industry has always been—what should I say?—a very physical industry. There's no getting around it. Violent. Dangerous. Very often, I might say, desperate."

I said to him, "This looks pretty desperate to me right now."

"Well, yes," he admitted. "It is. But only because you've made it so."

I said, "I'm trying hard to follow all the reverse English here, and I really hope that you people are putting a joke over on me so we can all laugh about it later. But I don't see where I'm causing you any real trouble. I brought you these documents exactly because I didn't want to cause trouble."

"An innocent lamb," said Danford. His blue eyes twinkled.

I said, "I can't help it about Johnson. Even if I hadn't talked to the janitor somebody would have. You couldn't hide that kind of thing. It was a stupid and shameful murder."

"It was never meant to be a murder." Danford's face snapped into seriousness.

"Well, what in the hell was it meant to be?"

"You have already looked deeply into our past, Mr. Binney," Danford answered, "so I might as well tell you. I was astounded to learn that Miss Rutledge was writing an unauthorized local history. I was appalled to learn that she was doing it independently. You have no idea the amount of damage that could be done with that kind of investigation. It is all very well to talk about academic freedom and so forth, but serious matters were involved here, serious matters that were beyond my control. When that young woman who was with you, Miss—'' he groped for the name—''Thorndyke,'' he triumphed, ''let slip that Milly was noting the old Griffiths-Danford logo and had mentioned the Ragged Stranger, I knew that it had to be stopped. I considered it very fortunate that she kept the whole thing in the Education Building. To me it meant that we could destroy it without endangering anyone. Milly's death was purely accidental. Johnson had calculated things very nicely, but Milly overstayed. It shouldn't have happened. I can't tell you how much both of us regret it.''

I said, ''What in the hell is so important about the old logo and the Ragged Stranger?''

Danford turned to say something to Johnson that I couldn't see. It was apparently a request for a chair. Johnson pushed over one of the club chairs and Danford sat in it across from me. He stared at me earnestly. He said, ''Mr. Binney, it is my duty as a Christian to tell you that you are not going to leave this house alive.'' He sat back and regarded me sympathetically. He said, ''I tell you this so that you can make your peace with God.'' Johnson too stared earnestly at me.

Danford said to me, ''You have asked two questions that deserve an answer and I will try to satisfy you. I can't imagine what you think of us here, but I assure you that we are not criminals. God moves in mysterious ways and occasionally we are required to do things which seem distasteful, even sinful, to answer correctly the commands of God.''

My throat was very dry. I managed to say, ''I've just got one thing to mention to you—the Bible school veteran and the upstanding Christian—Thou shalt not kill.''

Danford leaned back in his chair and smiled. He said, ''Easily the most ambiguous of all the commandments, don't you think? David killed Goliath. The community killed Jezebel. The Bible is full of killing, holy killing. If one were to take that literally there would be no wars, no executions, nothing. An earnest Christian cannot accept that literally.

''That does not mean we take it lightly,'' he added. ''But the ways of God must be fulfilled.'' He held up the gold chain and the GD fob swung back and forth. ''We simply cannot permit the reopening of old questions about Griffiths-Danford,'' he said. ''It would expose us to all sorts of inquiry that would result in the degradation and humiliation of good Christian endeavor.

''Very well,'' he settled himself back into the chair. ''As you noted just before we went up the stairs, this house was built by the Griffiths—old David Griffiths and his romantic ideas about William Morris and the Celtic revival. He had notions of community that were absolutely abhorrent to my family. But Griffiths had bought up the property with the coal. I will say he understood coal, if nothing else. And my family had no choice but to go along. Griffiths intended that both families should live together in this house. He was a romantic fool. Also, like many of his ilk, he was ungodly. He was a womanizer and a boozer. Disgusting.

''For all of his flaws, however, the old man did understand business—the coal business. His son, David Junior, was quite another matter.''

''Marjory's father,'' I clarified.

''Yes, Marjory's father. Now, when the old man died, my father, Elliot, acted on instructions from his father, Ephraim, and those instructions were to keep David Junior as far removed from the nuts and bolts of the business as possible. It was very evident, quite early on, that the young man was a weak-willed idiot who showed absolutely no promise in running a business as active and demanding as the coal business. We set him up in an office, but kept him on what we thought was a firm leash. He had little to do except blind alley jobs that had no particular point to them. We felt that he was sufficiently disengaged from the business so that he could do no harm. We were very, very wrong. It turned out that he completed these simpleminded little tasks we gave him in very short order, which left him with a good deal of time on his hands. With this spare time and energy at his disposal he managed to get into very bad company—indeed, he could have ruined Pendragon. We took the name Pendragon as a sop to the Griffiths. We certainly wanted to change it from Griffiths-Danford because we wanted to disassociate ourselves forever from the Griffiths name. We wanted the independence we thought we deserved."

"Just what kind of bad company did he get into?" I asked, intrigued in spite of my position. "Gamblers?"

"Far, far worse than that, Mr. Binney. Far worse than anything in the so-called underworld. David began associating with the very worst scum in the world—socialists!" The blue eyes darkened at the thought of it.

"We learned that he was not only seeing these people individually, but he was actually going to their meetings. What was worse, and in fact insupportable, was that he was beginning to agitate for a union in the Pendragon mines.

"This was not very long after the First World War, Mr. Binney, when radicals of every description were infecting the life blood of American business. Vigorous action was taken against them, of course—the Palmer raids for instance—but here we had a radical right in our midst, in our own house."

"I don't want to get shot for interrupting," I said, "but it was his house, too, wasn't it? Just as the business was his business too?"

Danford's face assumed a masklike solemnity. His

eyes penetrated mine. The question so disturbed him that he got up from his chair and walked around it so that he could lean his arms on the back of it as if on a lectern—or pulpit. "I don't believe you have seen the significance of what I have been saying, Mr. Binney," he reproached me icily. "The Danfords, as I have suggested to you before, belong to the very roots of the nation. We were not immigrants. We were not Welsh gypsies like the Griffiths. Our family, our reputation, our enterprises have on them the mark of God's will. It is no accident that we have prospered all these years and have been made the stewards of great wealth. It is God's will that this should be so. It is part of the infinite wisdom of God that our wealth, our righteousness, and our responsibility be made visible to the world. We are the visible saints. We are the elect of God. It will not do that His will should be tarnished or his visible saints held up to ridicule or opprobrium. Above all, it would not do that our pure and beautiful enterprise should be linked in any way to the Godless rabble of socialism. Our lives as the stewards of great wealth are given in the service of the Lord." The burden of this message made him tremble. He became conscious of it and stepped away from the chair. He stood next to it for a while, making sure that the import of the message had sunk into me. Then he came around and sat down again. He crossed his legs.

"It simply would not do," he repeated with a flattening gesture of his hand. "When my father confronted David with evidence of his activities David erupted into a lot of wild shouting and ridiculous accusations. It became clear to my father that David was serious—serious, mind you. There was nothing to be done with him."

"So you bought him out?"

Danford cocked his knee and clasped his hands over it. He looked at me with disapproval and disappointment. "That certainly would not have been a very good use of our stewardship, would it, Mr. Binney? To have given a creature like David the immense power that fifty percent of Pendragon would represent? Who knows what he would have done with it? Whatever he did, it would have been ungodly. We felt even that quite possibly he would have used the money to work against us. There was no question of giving David any money.''

I leaned forward, forgetting the steam pipe for an instant. ''But it was his!''

''It was God's! It is God's! We are merely the stewards of wealth. I cannot impress that on you strongly enough!

''If you cannot realize that,'' he said leaning back in the chair, ''then you cannot understand what it was we had to do.''

I asked with dread, ''What was it you had to do?''

''We had to convince David that he must leave,'' said Danford.

''That can't have been easy.''

''I don't believe you understand what coal mining was in those days,'' Danford told me. ''It was terribly, terribly violent. In fact someone, some mine operator told—I think it was Clare Booth Luce—that you could not operate a mine without machine guns. He wasn't far off the mark. You must realize what sort of person we were dealing with, Mr. Binney. Men who would go down in the darkness, in the wet, in the gas, with picks in their hands, into these tunnels of blindness and would spend the light of day hacking out black stones—sometimes crouching for the entire day, sometimes even lying on their sides in the wet and muck. Who would do such things unless he were absolutely desperate? And what is more dangerous than a man who is absolutely desperate? No. We had to be very, very careful, staunch, absolute. To give an inch was to give everything. Yes, there was violence, brutality even. It could not be helped.'' He sighed.

''Was there killing?'' I asked.

''Oh, yes, I am sad to say. It was done. It had to be done. It would be difficult for a person like you to understand.''

"I'm sure," I agreed.

"Killing, yes," said Danford. "David knew about it, of course, as well as we did. And so he was able to understand what he was told."

"And what was it that he was told?"

"David was told that he would have to go away. That's all. We were willing to give him a little money, we told him, to see him off, but we insisted that he must be severed from Pendragon forever."

I said cautiously, "He must have taken that rather hard."

"There was no help for it," said Danford. "He was told that if he did not sign over and leave he would be killed. He would not have been the first person killed to maintain proper control of the business."

I asked, "Did you mean to kill him anyway?"

"We assumed that it might be necessary. We got him to sign over the papers, and then he insisted on that silly agreement you discovered. We signed it because we didn't want him shouting the house down. There were always guests here, you know, and also we didn't believe it would go anywhere. And then after all the papers were signed, we had him taken away.

"You must understand," said Danford, "that we did not order him to be killed. We told the men to rough him up a little so that he would be reluctant to return. When they came back they told us that they had roughed him up so severely he was dead. They said that they had thrown the body into an empty gondola that was to be filled at the tipple. Everyone assumed that the body would be unrecognizable. Nonetheless, we kept track of that particular line of gondolas because if there was an outcry we wanted to be ready."

Danford pursed his lips. His expression became disappointed. "It turned out that the line of gondolas wasn't sent to the tipple after all," he said. "The empties were transferred out west with David in the bottom of one of them. It is apparent now that he survived. At that time, however, everyone assumed that he had died and had been discarded somewhere as just another railroad tramp. Dead men in freight cars were not an unusual phenomenon.

"You will notice," said Danford, "that I have been saying 'we' because our family has always been very close. Actually, it was my father who handled all of this extremely difficult and distasteful business. I was not to be personally involved until many years later.

"That occurred, as you will have recognized, with the advent of the Ragged Stranger. David had finally come back, penniless, a tramp, as we would have predicted. He had been skulking around Bluestone, getting up his nerve, I suppose, and finally sent us a telegram. We were to meet him at the old Mine Five. He was, as always, a fool.

"My father was dead then and I was in command. Johnson, here, had come into service with us. I asked Johnson to come along with me. We met David at the pit head. He was much altered. I hadn't really seen too much of him when I was a boy, but at that time he was not anything at all that I could recognize. We convinced him that standing in the pit head risked a chance of discovery and talked him into coming down into the mine with us. We went down into the abandoned mine—we had lanterns left over at the pit head—and there he told us that he had come back to reclaim his share of the company. It appears that he had been out of his head for a long, long time after the beating and his exposure in the gondola.

"Well, sir," said Danford, grasping the arms of the chair, "I can assure you that we had no intention of letting this semi-idiot come back into a position of power. We didn't really know what to do. We certainly couldn't let him run around loose. Johnson overpowered the man, he was only a weak, sick old man who had never been very vigorous to begin with, and we secured him in the mine there while I could decide what to do with him.

"We had no idea, of course, that Sim Lewis had plans for using the mine. However, when we saw the

trucks and equipment collecting around the pit head
we knew we would have to act quickly. I could not
see a way of getting David out of the mine without
risking discovery. Johnson solved the problem by going down there with dynamite, which was still available in the pit head. We knew, of course, where the
water was seeping in. Johnson laid a huge charge at
the fissure, far, far in the back of the mine. He came
out through an air shaft in the back—it's been covered
up for years now—and plunged the detonator. No one
could see him from the pit head of course. The dynamite went off and Johnson told me that he could hear
the water rushing in. That solved our problem, at least
until quite recently.

"So, you see, Mr. Binney," said Danford, "that
having invested so much—what shall I call it, culpa-
bility?—in this matter, we cannot permit you simply
to walk out of here and begin to stir up all this murk.
It would dishonor us and—what's the matter?"

Danford was responding to an expression of extreme
agony that was distorting my face.

"My back," I gasped. "Oh, my God. My back!
It's spasming. It's killing me. The muscles are tearing
me apart!"

Danford stared at me, his mouth open, rather fish-
like.

"Please," I begged him. "Please let me stand up.
My back. I strained it swimming in the mine. Please
let me stand up."

"Of course," said Danford. "By all means." He
waved at Johnson to relax with his gun.

I stood up and leaned my chest against the pipe,
gasping. I rolled my shoulders and arched my spine. I
pulled my hands in to clutch my abdomen and stretch
my back. When I straightened out I had a thirty-eight
in my hand, and it was pointed directly at Danford.

"Freeze, asshole," I said to him. "If Johnson
shoots me you die too, just by reflex. Tell Johnson to
put his gun down or you're a dead motherfucker."

Both of them had become instantly rigid as if a blast

of arctic air had solidified the room. Danford's face was a mixture of outrage and fear. "Mr. Binney!" he said as if I had instituted a terrible breach of manners, "this is . . . this is—"

But he never got a chance to finish it. Johnson had done the intelligent thing. He shot the gun out of my hands. His shot hit the cylinder of the revolver and smashed it into the wall. My hands were absolutely numb. I had no idea how much damage had been done to them. They hung uselessly from the cuffs around the pipe. I was shaking, exhausted. Danford looked at me with an expression of rage and hatred. He stepped back from the chair and raised his arm magisterially to point at me. He said to Johnson, "Kill him." Johnson raised the big automatic that was still sending wisps of smoke from the barrel.

Suddenly the gun swung away from me and toward the door. Johnson was flung backward and fell upon the floor. Danford's eyes seemed to start from his head. I turned to see Dash and Sim coming through the doorway. Dash's gun, a revolver, was smoking. He threw the gun from him and it skittered across the floor. Dash cried out, "Johnny. Johnny. Brother! Baby brother!" He threw himself down across the body.

29

"Gimp or no gimp, you looked pretty good in there," I said to Sim.

We were sitting in a little bar off the cavernous lobby of the Thornwood, Sim, Dash, Maria and I. Dash had driven us down in the limousine, the one without the telephone. They had come along to see me off. My train, the *James Whitcomb Riley*, was scheduled to carry me away at the ungodly hour of 2:41 in the morning. It was now past midnight. There was no one else in the tiny bar, and we had the place pretty much to ourselves. Sim was fairly jubilant; Maria was endlessly curious as to what had happened; Dash sat silent and unmoving, his face as immobile as carved mahogany. He had a drink in front of him and he was drinking it professionally. I had got the feeling this evening that Dash would continue to drink and that he would never stop.

My remark to Sim had been apropos of describing the situation to Maria. After Dash had thrown away his gun, I told her, Danford had jumped over to pick up the forty-five from Johnson's lifeless hand. Sim, however, on his ruined legs, had never broken stride. He had chased down Dash's gun across the floor, grabbed it and wheeled on Danford. The two white-haired men faced each other, each with a gun. I strained helplessly at my cuffs, although my hands were more or less useless. They had been numbed by the blast and I still carried the bruises on my fingers where the gun had been torn from my grip. In fact, they still tingled, the way one's hand will tingle after being badly chilled or frozen.

The two old men stared at one another. Sim said, "If you shoot me you die too. I ain't going to back away. I'm going to count to three and if you ain't put down your gun I'm going to pull this here trigger. That's all I got to say: *One.*" Danford's face clenched. Sim kept his eyes fastened on the forty-five. *"Two."* Danford began to tremble. I saw Sim take a deep, deep breath, preparing to shoot. Danford lowered his gun and it dropped to the floor. Thank God it didn't go off.

"I still don't know how the hell you got up there," I said to Sim.

"Followed the lights," he said. "Off and then on to the next room. Soon as we saw the lights changing like that we knew something was up."

"But how . . ."

I noticed that Dash was speaking. His jaw moved like that on a ventriloquist's dummy. There was no expression in his eyes or face. He was saying, "Johnny

and me played in that house a million times. Momma
used to go up there to do the laundry. They wouldn't
send it out. She had to do it right there in the house.
And Johnny and me played hide and seek and cops
and robbers and all kinds of crazy games in the house.
They didn't seem to mind. I mean we never made no
noise nor bust in on anybody. But I know every way
there is to get into that house, and there are a hundred
ways. And I know every room in that house and there
must be like to a hundred rooms. But it wasn't any
trouble finding you or listening outside the door.''

"Well," I said, "I thought I could trap him all by
myself. You know, that's what I get paid for. But I
won't say I'm not grateful.''

Dash said, still expressionless, "Momma didn't
want Johnny to go to work for them like that. Poor
Momma. I made her cry because I was wildassed—
begging your pardon, ma'am," he added with an expressionless nod toward Maria, "but she didn't want
for Johnny to turn out to be somebody's house nigger,
neither. She thought the sun rose and set on Johnny,
did Momma. There was always talk about how the
Danfords were going to send Johnny off to college
because he was so smart, you know? But that never
happened.''

We were all still for a moment thinking about the
special meaning of the word *never* now.

Maria spoke up then. She appeared to be speaking
timidly. She said, "What do you think will happen to
Mr. Danford now?''

I looked at her. I was very surprised. I said, "Why
nothing. What could happen?''

"You mean he just walks away from it all?''

"More or less," I said. "What's to stop him?''

"There's Sim, and Dash, and you as witnesses to
what he confessed.''

"Do you think that a judge and jury are going to
listen to Sim and Dash and me testifying against Gideon Danford? Do you think there'd even be an indict-
ment down here? Are you smoking funny cigarettes?''

"It's not fair," said Maria, "that a man should be able to walk away from that."

I put my hand on hers. I said, "Putting him in jail won't bring Milly back, Maria. There's no use your looking for vengeance. It's beyond vengeance."

"It's not just Milly," she answered, withdrawing her hand. "I can't get that poor man out of my mind. To be there in the dark, the blackness, tied up, helpless. To hear the explosion and then to hear the water rushing in. To feel it lapping up around your shoes, your legs . . ."

"Stop it," I said to her.

"To have come all the way back, to have gone through everything and then to end up like that . . ."

"Yes," I agreed. "I keep trying to figure out what really happened. You know, Danford was giving me a song and dance about David Junior thinking he had TB and slipping off to Arizona—it would have made a nice out for Danford. But I guess what really happened is that somebody discovered the poor bastard in the bottom of the gondola and, miracle of miracles, they actually got him to a hospital. He had a fractured skull, among other things, and he may have been loony for years. And then, in a flash of lucidity, he must have written to Mother Henry. But why Mother Henry? He couldn't have known that the girl, Marjory, was living with her. At least I can't see how he would have known."

"Mother Henry," said Maria, "was one of the little bunch of socialists that used to have those meetings David Griffiths went to. I remember her name on one of Milly's notes. I guess the Danfords didn't know about that."

"So he must have written her," I mused, "swearing her to secrecy—I suppose that Pendragon had a very long arm—and the guy had every right to be in mortal fear of his life. And she wrote him that one letter. And then, as I reconstruct it, he must have gone off his rocker again or he must have been trying to scrape up the money to get back east and put together the courage for a confrontation. And it sure as hell would have taken a lot of courage.''

"You," Maria said to Sim. "How can you let Danford just walk away from it all after what he did to your wife—cheating her out of everything—and by extension to your son, to Honey?''

"Well, he ain't exactly going to walk away," Sim corrected her. "He may not think that agreement is worth a hell of a lot, but I disagree with him there, I surely do. It happens I know some pretty good lawyers myself, having had the need of them now and then. I'd be surprised if we can't make that paper stick—or at least some of it. It seems to me Honey's going to need every cent we can lay our hands on.''

"That reminds me," I interjected. "How is Honey now? I mean after that fainting fit and everything, did he come out of it? Is he all right?''

"I called Jack yesterday," answered Maria. "He said that Honey is responding, although, of course, he's got a bumpy road ahead of him. But Jack thinks the prognosis is good.''

"Prognosis?" asked Sim.

"His future," Maria replied quickly. "The future of his illness, actually, but all in all his future. They don't think there's anything organically wrong with Honey. They think it's mostly a matter of getting him out of his religious mania.''

"Being religious doesn't mean you're a maniac," objected Sim.

"To the exclusion of everything else it does," said Maria.

"Is that really true?" I asked her. "Were they all crazy, the saints? Simply madmen? Hearing voices, talking with God, seeing visions, torturing themselves, letting themselves be tortured, does it just mean they were nuts?''

"Jack would think so," said Maria. "Tell the truth, I think so too.''

"Is that all it amounts to, human nuttiness?''

"Human beings like to kill each other," said Maria. "Religion is a good excuse."

The opinion seemed to leave her empty. She looked around the table and said, "I wonder what I'm going to do now."

"Why surely, miss," Sim hurried in, "they're going to need you down at the school board more than ever. You're about the only one who can put the whole thing back together again."

"I wouldn't be any good at that," said Maria. "I'm not Milly. Really, I'm not anything like Milly. I could never balance things out the way she did."

I said to her, "Why don't you become a historian?"

She smiled a grim little smile. "A historian of what?" she asked.

"Schoolteaching," I replied. "I don't know of a good book about actual schoolteaching in America, I mean the real guts of it. Who they were, what they did, why they did it, what they were told to do, why they did what they were told and who told them. If there's a book like that I sure as hell haven't heard of it."

"You're being ridiculous," said Maria sternly. "Where would I start?"

"I thought you told me once that Milly taught you something. Where did Milly start? Where does anybody start? Why is everybody so goddamned helpless these days?"

I must have spoken more roughly than I meant to. A general silence fell around the table. Sim looked at the big turnip watch he carried and said to me, "If you're gonna catch that train it looks like we ought to be on our way." He got up on his bad legs and went over to give the bartender some bills. The bartender appeared happy to see us leave.

The big limousine glistened under the yellow light of the lamp on the high pole of the platform. We huddled together not for warmth but from the sheer loneliness of the place. Maria said to me, "You're going

back to New York now, to another life, and I'll never
see you again. Is that right?''

I pondered the idea of giving her a bit of the old
soft shoe but rejected it. ''That's pretty much right,''
I said. I thought of the letter I had from Edna in my
coat pocket: *Joe, Dear Joe, For God's sake get back
here quick. I need you. I need you.*

When the long silver train glided up to the platform
and the conductor descended, Dash swung my bag up
on the car. I shook his hand and then I embraced him.
''Thank you Dash,'' I said. ''Thank you for saving
my life.'' He looked at me but his face did not change.
I had the feeling that his face was never going to
change.

I shook hands with Sim. Sim said, ''We'll ship that
rubber suit of yours up on the UPS. Ain't any more
call for it down here.''

I answered, ''Thank you, Sim. Thanks for everything.''

I kissed Maria on the cheek. I said to her, ''Do
whatever Milly trained you to do. You don't have to
do it here, but do it somewhere. It could save your
life.'' She held on to my hand. I turned myself loose
at last and climbed up on the train.

The club car, of course, had long since stopped
serving, but the lights were still on so that I could sit
and smoke and read. I also had two pint bottles of
Sim's special whiskey, so that I was able to fix myself
an amiable drink while I settled down with my *Mismeasure of Man*. As I sipped away at the miraculous
bourbon I came at last to the final page. It bore the
statement of a woman who had been condemned as an
imbecile—completely unjustly—and had been steril-
ized in an operation that she had not understood. She
had spent much of her subsequent life with her husband trying to conceive a child. When she discovered
what had happened she said, ''I broke down and cried.
My husband and me desperately wanted children. We
were crazy about them. I never knew what they'd done
to me.''

I sipped my bourbon and stared into the obsidian reflection of the train window. This was science, not religion, that had severed the cord of life for this woman. It had all been done on the best scientific principles. It seemed that you could take science, religion, philosophy or law, and somewhere in them you could find a motive for supporting that vicious, predatory fearfulness and hatefulness coiled in a feral spring at the base of our brains, far, far below the failing light of reason, which lies waiting to strike out at the innocent.

30

If it weren't for the honey gold hair that cascades from the crown of her head I would not have recognized Edna so quickly. Nobody had been stupid enough to touch *that*.

But as for the rest of her—well. I had seen the flash of gold at her top, and the little white line of jaw jutting out beneath it as her face turned away to search for me in the crowd of Penn Station. She had missed me getting off the train and was searching, panic stricken this way and that. I came up behind her, dropping the bag at my feet, and said, "Edna!"

She wheeled, almost fell because of her new shoes, and threw her arms around me. Because I could not see her face buried in my shoulder I did not know what she was saying, of course, but I could feel the vibration of her voice as the words tumbled out.

I detached her from my shoulders and held her at arm's length. The crowd eddied around us, the men swiveling their necks to stare. Edna was something to stare at all right, but it wasn't the same Edna I'd left when I boarded the train for Thornwood.

It was a different face I looked at from my arm's

length. They had done a great deal with her. Her
cheeks were high and hollow. Her eyes, those beautiful green eyes, were so surrounded with artifice that
they warred with the make-up. Her mouth had a new
delineation. Her eyebrows were no longer of the kind
that could wrinkle into the puzzlement that I adored.

The clothes, too, stumped me. The word *money*
jumped from every invisible seam. Although it was
summer she was wearing a light coat, not really much
different from the duster that Milly wore down at
Caunotaucarius, except that this duster had drama and
vivacity to it and a price tag that exceeded the limits
of my imagination. The rest of her clothes, too, cried
money. They were not the kind of cute assertive clothes
that Diane Keaton wears in movies; they were *official*
clothes. They went with the mind-zinging cloud of
perfume that had billowed up when she pressed herself
against me.

People continued to stare. We were an odd looking
outfit. I had not shaved and my suit was wrinkled from
the trouser cuffs to the neck of my jacket. I was bleary,
she was as stamped at the mint. I said to her, ''For
Christ's sake, Edna, let's go somewhere and get a
drink and something to eat. I'm starving.''

We tromped off, me lugging my bag that I had kept
in the luggage rack, and found a spot in the station
where we could both eat and drink. Edna here, too,
caused a sensation because most of the people here
were what could be charitably described as cruddy, as
indeed I was myself. Edna, now, did not belong to
this world. She appeared as a Martian. Necks craned
and people stared. I felt uncomfortable.

I was already devouring my corned beef on rye and
sloshing it down with bourbon when she said, ''You're
all right then. You didn't get hurt.''

I nodded an assent with my mouth full of sandwich.

''What do you think?'' said Edna. She raised her
arms to indicate the new splendor that had overtaken
her.

"You look very different," I said, trying to smile around my mouthful of corned beef and rye.

"Different? Is that all?"

The corned beef helped me to smother back the words that were boiling in my throat. I did not say, *You look like a high-priced whore.* As the corned beef filled my vitals with calories and the bourbon facilitated connections in my brain, I began to assemble what was evidently Edna's recent history. "You look great, kid," I told her. "Gorgeous."

Was there something in my voice, my expression? How could there be with my mouth full of sandwich and my cheeks bulging at mastication? But there was a rigidity behind the rigidity of the make-up. Distorted as they were by the eyebrows and shadow the green eyes managed to express doubt.

I saw what had happened. Carlson had given her access to his charge accounts. This required a phone call from him to the stores in question. They had had such calls before. They knew what Mr. Carlson liked his ladies to wear. Thus was Edna touted; thus was she accoutered. She seemed to be searching for something to say. Finally she contented herself with, "I'm glad to see you're all right." There was a pause. "Even if you do look like hell," she added.

I shrugged. "I was pretty much on my own down there," I said. "It was a mistake not taking you along."

"Wasn't there anybody at all to help you?" The eyes were suddenly sharp with more than curiosity.

"Well, yeah," I admitted uneasily. "There was this young woman, Maria Thorndyke, helped me out some."

"What was she like?" asked Edna, suddenly intense.

I finished off my sandwich and my drink and then ordered another drink to give myself time. The question was too difficult for a snap reply. I leaned back in the chair and thought about it. "Well, she was probably a couple years older than you," I began.

"Beautiful, was she?"

"In her way, I suppose," I answered. "She was small and dark."

"And smart? Was she smart?"

"Yes," I said. "She was very, very, very smart—in some ways. She had an advanced degree in history, although I don't see that it was helping her very much."

"But what was she *like?*" demanded Edna with a small thump on the table that shook her coffee cup.

I said at last, "She was a profoundly puzzled young woman who seemed to be having a lot of trouble finding her way."

"You were in love with her," Edna accused me.

"No, no," I protested. "I was not. Not that she wasn't lovable to—to somebody, somewhere. But she didn't seem to be able to connect up with that somebody." I looked off into space trying to summon up Maria. "She had only one commitment that I know of, to a wonderful old lady who was her mentor and her friend. But even then, before the lady was killed, she didn't seem to know really what she was, where she was going or what she was doing. She trusted everything and trusted nothing. She wanted to go ahead in the world, and defeated herself at every turn. She couldn't find a man she could be really comfortable with, although men pursued her. She doesn't really feel at home anywhere at all, although she was happy working for Milly, the old lady I mentioned. Now she doesn't know what's going to become of her. To tell you the truth, I can't guess what's going to become of her either. Somewhere she's going to have to make another commitment—to life, to the world as it is."

"You *were* in love with her," Edna challenged me.

"No," I said softly. "I liked her an awful lot, but I pitied her too. There was no real attraction, no magnetic pull."

"Ah," said Edna. "That's what you need, huh? Magnetic pull?"

"Sure," I answered. "Otherwise what in the hell

are you talking about? Either the person occupies your whole mind or the person doesn't. If the person doesn't, you're just kidding yourself."

Edna stood up. "Let's get out of here," she said. "I hate this place."

We didn't try to talk in the cab. It is difficult for me at best, and this was far from the best. Edna kept her face turned away for most of the ride.

Up at the office there was an attempt to get back to "business as usual." She had taken off her expensive duster as I stared at my grubby surroundings with a sinking acceptance of recognition. Edna, bless her, even made coffee, looking very incongruous in her fine new clothes. She brought in two cups and sat down across from my desk where I had majestically placed myself.

"Okay, kid," I said. "Spill it."

What she spilled first were tears. Apparently she had some new kind of tear-proof mascara that did not run. I suppose it's a special requirement of the times. She blotted her eyes and said, "I haven't heard from him in three days. It's like he disappeared from the face of the earth."

"A business trip?"

She shook her head. "No. I know he's in town. But whenever I call he's in conference, or I'm told he'll get back to me, which he never does. Or he's gone for the day."

She looked up at me with her lips tightly pressed together. "It's over," she said. "I know it's over. I feel it. I don't have to be told. What happened? What did I do wrong?"

"My God," I said. "You're blaming yourself?"

"I must have done something," insisted Edna. "After all this . . ."

"After all this what?" I asked rudely. "So he takes you out, buys you a few things . . ."

"A few things!"

"To him it was a few things."

She had begun to cry again and I let her alone. Another rag of poetry sailed through my head, not by an American this time but by an Irishman who was writing about Leda and the Swan:

> *Did she put on his knowledge with his power*
> *Before the indifferent beak could let her drop?*

I said sternly to her, "You must love him very, very much."

The bald harsh statement seemed to catch her in the midst of a sob. She looked up at me suddenly and her dimmed eyes widened. She was perfectly still for perhaps as much as a minute. Then she said, "No. No I don't."

"Then why are you crying?"

The corners of her mouth turned down. She said, "I feel, I feel so cheap, so used."

"There didn't seem to be anything going on here that looked cheap to me," I said. "Not in financial terms, anyway."

"I didn't know if I would marry him or not," said Edna. "But I expected him to ask me. I mean, after all this rush, all this stuff, shouldn't he have asked me?"

"I don't know the protocol in these things any more," I replied. "I don't even know if there is a protocol any more. I don't think anybody today knows where the hell he's at." She looked even more despondent.

"I know one thing though," I told her. Her head jerked up. "If you send him all the stuff back then you've acquitted yourself with honor and you have no reason to feel cheap or even used. You enjoyed yourself at all those high-priced classy joints, didn't you?" She nodded. "Send him his junk back then and forget it," I advised her.

"These?" she indicated the clothes she was wearing.

"I didn't say you had to strip yourself naked," I growled irritably. "That stuff can't be returned anyway. Forget it. But the other stuff you mentioned in the letter. Yeah, that stuff should be returned.''

She had been afraid to keep the coat or the jewels in her apartment. They were indeed in the office, along with the boxes they arrived in. Slowly and with infinite care she repacked them in their tissue paper, the great fur, whose price I did not even try to estimate although I've had to do exactly that on some cases of mine, the diamond clip and matching earrings, and various other trinkets of heavy gold and precious stones. They all fitted into the box the fur had come in. Before she put on the cover, however, I said, ''Wait a minute.'' I took out the Carlson credit card and cut it in half with the office scissors. I put the halves in an envelope and laid it on top.

As we were tying up the box, I began to laugh. Edna demanded, ''What are you laughing at?''

''I was just thinking about Carlson's friend Elliot Danford up there in his fancy designer office,'' I said. ''I wonder how he's going to like having Honey Lewis for a partner.''

JACK LIVINGSTON was an ex-merchant seaman who worked as a medical editor and lived in upstate New York. His first two Joe Binney mysteries were nominated as the best private eye novels of the year by the Private Eye Writers of America, and *Die Again, Macready* was nominated for the British Crime Writers Association's prestigious annual award for the best mystery.